Evan heard his name called

and did open his eyes a few times before he could actually make any sense out of what he was seeing.

"Come on. You can do it. Come on, Evan. Open your eyes. Keep 'em open. Can you hear me? Evan?"

It sounded to Evan like his own voice, calling to him. It was disorienting, especially coming out of a prolonged, drug-fueled unconsciousness. Nothing seemed quite real. Staring straight ahead of him at a face he knew well, Alek's face, Evan felt his left hand taken by someone else, someone who wasn't Brennan. Jimmy was there, too, Evan realized, and standing a few feet away.

Why is Jimmy here? Is it happening again? Did I try to kill myself again? Why does everyone look so upset?

No. The bar.

I got jumped at the bar.

Also recommended...

You may also enjoy these other Forbidden Fiction works:

Don't... by Jack L. Pyke
"Don't... open me." Three simple words that tease Jack, taking him places from his dark past. For Jack, BDSM is a way to resist his worst impulses. Yet, the stranger calling himself The Unknown seeks to use that to seduce him. As Jack slips further down into the abyss, two men hold the power to save him. Will it be Gray, the Master who knows Jack's every secret? Or Jan, the first man to give Jack a reason to hope? With deadly ghosts coming out to play, Jack may lose everything, even his life. (M/M)
http://forbiddenfiction.com/story/JP2-1.000134

Learning from the Master by Lynn Kelling
Most things in life come easily to eighteen-year-old Jenner Parrish, who's on track to inherit the family business, and is popular, well-liked and good looking. He has everything he could want, except when it comes to love and sex. Closeted, lonely and desperate, he acquires an invitation to an event at a nearby private gay club, Manse. Feeling out of his element and for the first time quite shy, Jenner is unable to play the wallflower when he captures the attention of the suave, seductive owner of Manse, David Davenport. David is used to getting what he wants, and what he wants is gorgeous young Jenner, who begins to realize every fantasy and wild desire could be his for the taking, if only he dares to ask and obediently serve. (M/M)
http://forbiddenfiction.com/story/LK1-1.000196

Dual Affairs

Twin Ties: Book 2

Lynn Kelling

ForbiddenFiction
www.forbiddenfiction.com

an imprint of

Fantastic Fiction Publishing
www.fantasticfictionpublishing.com

DUAL AFFAIRS
A Forbidden Fiction book

Fantastic Fiction Publishing
Hayward, California

© Lynn Kelling, 2014

CREDITS
Editor: Rylan Hunter, D.M. Atkins
Cover Design: Siolnatine
Cover photo: Migfoto at Dreamstime
Production Editor: Erika L Firanc
Proofreading: JhP323 and Kaye O'Malley

SKU: LK1-000168-02 FFP
ISBN: 978-1-62234-247-1

Published in the United States of America

DISCLAIMER

This book is a work of fiction which contains explicit erotic content; it is intended for mature readers. Do not read this if it's not legal for you.

All the characters, locations and events herein are fictional. While elements of existing locations or historical characters or events may be used fictitiously, any resemblance to actual people, places or events is coincidental.

This story is not intended to be used as an instruction manual. It may contain descriptions of erotic acts that are immoral, illegal, or unsafe. Do not take the events in this story as proof of the plausibility or safety of any particular practice.

For Rose, with respect and love. Never say never.

Contents

Chapter 1
Good Gone Wrong

In a seedy bar in the rough part of town, eighteen-year-old mechanic Evan Savage nursed his beer and kept to himself. The place was packed with dangerous-looking clientele openly carrying their preferred means of self-defense, hiding their intentions more carefully than their weapons, under beards and biker gear. There were few women and even fewer young men, so the slim, pretty-faced teenager dressed in nothing but well-worn jeans and a blue t-shirt stood out like a shout in a quiet room.

Evan tolerated his prettiness with reluctance. He bore it as more disfigurement than blessing since it had always drawn mostly the wrong kinds of attention—flirtatious gestures from equally pretty girls he wasn't attracted to, or ugly boys wanting to beat the good looks out of him. In that particular bar, his age and appearance were the two things most likely to get him in trouble, so he stayed silent and tucked away in darkened corners.

Evan was only at the bar because his boyfriend, Alek Popović—older than him by seven years—had to work late at his unsavory job there. In order to be close to Alek, and also have some time to himself, Evan offered to hang out until Alek had finished his shift. The plan was to drive back to Alek's house afterward and crash there for the night. If they were patient, they'd get to have a few hours alone together after a long day. As an added bonus, Evan and Alek's identical twins, Brennan and Luka respectively, would benefit from some alone time of their own.

Though Evan and Alek had only met because of a random hookup in the bar's bathroom a few months earlier, against all odds, their relationship had developed depth and meaning for both of them. Now, they were committed to each other. Evan had finally gotten to experience what it was like to tell someone, who wasn't family he loved them and have the sentiment returned in kind.

He loved Alek. Alek loved him, too.

But, it was complicated. In fact, to say it was complicated would have been an understatement. Ever since Evan and Alek began seeing each other, they'd rarely been together without other people around.

Logistics were part of it. Alek lived with his brother, Luka, and two other male friends—Presley Owens and Carter Raed. Evan lived with his brother, Brennan Holt. No matter where they were, someone else was usually there, too. That left them with the options of seeking solitude out in the fields beyond Evan's home, at local make-out spots, or coping with company.

If that was all, it would have been challenging, but manageable and normal. Evan's situation with Alek, however, was far from normal. Months ago, the lines cleanly dividing the two couples began to blur. It was no longer simply Evan and Alek, Brennan and Luka, two distinct pairings—distorted mirrors of each other. It was the four of them, together, in almost every sense. Evan had been intimate with Brennan in ways he had a tough time facing in the light of day. But, since Alek and Luka had had an equally intimate relationship with each other for years, it was accepted and allowed as yet another form of deep-seated affection.

The ramifications of having a lover's closeness with his twin had only begun to settle upon Evan. As someone who had struggled with depression for years, Evan had been trying not to question the path he had begun to follow. He simply put one foot in front of the other blindly, hoping disaster didn't wait around the next bend, though certain at the core of his being it did.

Evan hadn't known Brennan existed until very recently. When their mother died, their father decided to finally tell the truth and introduce his sons to one another; young men who had been previously ignorant of the fact that they had an identical twin in another part of the country, raised by an estranged parent. For Evan, Brennan wasn't a sibling. He was a stranger who had suddenly entered his life, creating chaos.

They'd had sex in front of each other, they'd had sex *with* each other, and they'd grown to love each other in non-traditional ways.

More recently, Evan and Brennan found themselves crawling into bed together when sleep initially eluded them, quickly dozing off once they were cuddled up, before anything more could happen. They didn't kiss. There was, admittedly, more touching than was typical for brothers, when passing in the hall or in the kitchen getting something to eat, whether it was fingertips trailing over clothed skin or a quick embrace. They were happy with that much. A strange balance had been created by each of them giving up the most intimate part of themselves to the other, doing the unthinkable in defiance of their upbringing and the lies surrounding it.

Sexual intimacy had lent a sense of permanence and devotion. It had given them a peace long sought over the course of their whole lives. For Evan, Brennan wasn't *only* a brother. He was so much more than that. Needing Brennan, and being needed just as intensely by him, made Evan feel more complete than he ever had felt. The terrible emptiness which had plagued him, causing untold mental distress, provoking Evan to go so far as attempting suicide at the age of fourteen, was miraculously lifted.

However, the atypical closeness between the brothers was also the reason for Brennan's request for an evening alone with *his* boyfriend, Alek's twin, Luka. Brennan and Evan both were secretly worried they'd crave each other's presence and it would intrude on Luka and Alek's happiness. Evan knew Brennan had promised to put Luka first, so he allowed Brennan to try to do exactly that.

Evan played pool and sipped a single beer, lingering in quiet spaces apart from the press of restless, testosterone-fueled energy.

He watched the crowd and the clock. Alek was hidden away on kitchen duty and not even available as eye candy, working behind the closed kitchen doors instead. It was partially because of Evan's boredom that he noticed a man almost as young as himself scanning the room. Evan was careful to avoid the guy's searching gaze, knowing what the intent was from previous personal experience — he was looking for a hook-up. Evan had tried the very same thing himself, after all, not too long ago in that very place.

After a while, the guy appeared to have success with someone. He headed out a back door to the parking lot, followed closely by the man whose eye he caught, and Evan was happy for him.

Not seconds later, though, a few more men, huge and burly, followed the pair out.

Evan was instantly concerned. He spared a moment to consider telling Alek, but decided there wasn't time and ran out the back door after them. His plan was to check if anything was wrong and, then, if there *was* something wrong, to duck back inside for help.

It might have worked if one of the men wasn't watching the door.

As soon as Evan pushed the door open, he was grabbed by someone waiting outside.

A hand wrapped over his mouth, muffling his yell of alarm as he was pulled away from the building. There was shouting from farther away, on the other side of the parking lot, but Evan didn't manage to make any of it out. All he knew was, right in front of him, the young gay guy who Evan had been idly watching was getting the living hell beaten out of him by two of the men who had followed him outside.

It started with repeated punches to the guy's stomach until he doubled over. Then, his feet were kicked out from under him. He crumpled to the pavement where brutal kicks were delivered to his head, legs, back and torso.

Horrified, terrified, Evan fought the man holding him, bucking and kicking. He clawed at the hand on his mouth and screamed from behind the rough, sweaty palm.

Time slowed to a crawl. Everything started to happen in slow motion. The men cheered each other on, yelling, pumping their fists in the air, jumping around the body on the asphalt.

"Yeah!"

"Kick him harder!"

"Teach him a lesson!"

"I'm gonna knock his fuckin' teeth out!"

Evan bit down as hard as he could on the hand wrapping his mouth. He actually slipped free for one brief moment, darting back to the door he'd come through. His hand was on the handle when he felt a hard punch.

Sharp, exquisite pain flared in his gut.

Stumbling backward, Evan fell back onto his ass and looked down at himself as someone towered over him, his face in shadow.

A knife handle protruded from the side of Evan's stomach. He moved to pull it out with trembling fingers, but that was when the first, pointed kick to his face connected, and it all turned to darkness.

"Alek? Hey! Your boy is gone. He went running out the back door like he was freaked."

Alek stopped what he was doing and looked up at Jason. The six-foot-seven bartender who doubled as a bouncer had just been in the bathroom. He was leaning through the hinged kitchen door, half in, half out.

The words sank in, slowly. At the grill, the tongs dropped from Alek's hand, clattering to the dirty floor.

Alek ran to the exit, only stopping at the last minute to grab a shotgun from where it was tucked out of sight for emergencies.

He called back over his shoulder, "Hey! Come on! Jase?"

"Yeah," Jason said, jogging over.

When they got to the back door, pushed it open, and sprinted outside, they saw instantly they were too late. It was bedlam. Meryl, a fifty-something biker and a regular at the bar, had his sawed-off leveled at a gang of guys gathered by the building's rear entrance. With the yellowish glow from the streetlamp above casting weird shadows over the darkened lot, shapes were distorted, bleeding together.

Men started to scatter once they saw Alek and Jason, yelling, "Come on! Let's get out of here!"

"Oh, no you don't!" Meryl shouted. He whistled through his teeth to get the attention of the other bikers who were still gathered around the bikes parked on the other side of the building. When a few of them arrived at a sprint, they took off with Meryl after the gang.

That was when Alek finally saw what they'd been gathered around, only understanding right before sickening, mind-numbing horror obliterated all reason.

Stricken and shaking, he finally dropped his gaze, having been so reluctant to look down.

"*Evan!* No! No God, No!"

Alek didn't think, he just ran. He fell to the pavement, scraping his knees and shins. His fingers skittered through the air above Evan, afraid to touch him due to all of the blood masking his form. Alek barely, carefully, made contact, laying his hand on Evan's arm, too afraid to do more than that. Then, he saw the source of the bleeding, soaking Evan's blue shirt blackish-red, and pressed the heel of his hand against the wound.

"Call 911!"

"Already on it!" Jason yelled with a phone to his ear before he resumed giving their address to the person on the other end of the line.

Only a single sob escaped Alek before he pushed the terror down below his determination and anger. Holding Evan's hand gingerly, pressing on the gushing slice just below Evan's ribcage with the other, Alek tried not to overanalyze the injuries and focus.

"Help is coming, baby," he said, his voice sounding to him uneven and muffled by endless, internal screaming. *This can't be happening. It can't. Not to Evan. Not like this. It's wrong. There's been a mistake.* "Hold on, please hold on. I'm right here. It's Alek. I've got you. Help is coming."

Evan's face was a mess, his nose askew and clearly broken. His eyes were swelling shut, his white teeth stained red. Gagging on, then spitting up blood, it spilled over his chin as Evan groaned. It seemed like he'd almost regained consciousness, but Alek wasn't sure.

"...We have two males here, badly injured. One looks like he was beaten and is unconscious. There's not much blood on him except for some he spit up. He's breathing, though. The other has a stab wound to the stomach. There's a four inch blade lying next to him. His face is bloody and swollen and there may be more injuries. I don't know... Alek! They say three minutes, okay?! The ambulance is three minutes out! Is he breathing? He has a pulse, right?"

"Shit. Shit. Evan…. Oh god, *Evan*…." Alek saw the rise and fall of Evan's chest, and yelled back, "Yeah! He's breathing!"

"Good! Don't move him! Is he conscious? They want you to try to stem the bleeding by putting pressure—"

"*I know! DON'T YOU THINK I KNOW?!* No, he's not awake. He's not—*Fuck*!!"

Alek hissed through his teeth. The fear reached up from deep inside him, clawing at his mind with icy fingers, making it hard to think. For a brief moment, he fell back through time, through weeks of days, and remembered Evan confiding in him, whispering about attempting suicide, of dying for a handful of minutes before he was brought back to life thanks to the determination of a loved one.

Certainty settled on Alek, a terrible notion that Death was angry at being denied Evan and was trying to reclaim him. A thick trickle of blood leaked from the side of Evan's mouth. Alek leaned in to listen for breath sounds. He felt for a pulse, and it was there, but weak. Too weak.

"He's losing too much blood! Jase! What do I do?!" He pressed harder at the wound as Evan's blood flowed between his fingers. Alek prayed, "Don't leave me. Please don't go. Hang in there. Hang in there for Brennan. You can't die on me, okay? You can't. Evan, I love you so much… please hold on. *Please*."

Minutes later, Evan was surrounded by EMTs and being loaded onto a gurney. There was an oxygen mask covering his face and he was wearing a pulse monitor. Efforts were being made to keep him from losing more blood and Alek hovered, dazed, and unable to let Evan slip away from his sight.

With trembling, bloody fingers it took him three tries to get to Luka's name in his phone's contact list. He almost dropped the blood-slick phone when it started to ring.

"Maybe it's food poisoning," Luka suggested. He rubbed Brennan's back, both of them seated on the edge of the couch, but Brennan was doubled over, clutching his side, just under his ribcage.

Call Alek. Call him, instinct whispered to Luka.

He instantly banished the thought. There was no logical reason to call Alek. Not for a stomachache.

Call him anyway.

Again, Luka shrugged off the bizarre inclination.

The stomachache had come on suddenly. A few minutes earlier, Brennan had been feeling absolutely fine. He'd been laughing and in a great mood, excited they'd have the house to themselves for some uninterrupted quality time. Then, out of nowhere, something had come over him. His good mood died and he kept insisting something was wrong. Part of Luka was secretly disappointed this new development might put a damper on their evening, ruining a night he'd been looking forward to also, but if Brennan was sick, helping him feel better was the most important thing.

As Brennan groaned, growing quickly paler, he argued, "We ate the same things for dinner, though. And lunch." Unsure what to do—whether to raid the mostly barren medicine cabinet or offer to run to the drug store—Luka fleetingly marveled at how Brennan made him want to act with maturity and responsibility when all of his life Luka had been anything but. All he wanted was to stay by Brennan's side, doing whatever he could to bring the smile back to his face and help him feel better. Before, with Luka's previous love interests, he always mentally signed off whenever one of them felt unwell. It never felt like it was his problem to fix. Usually, he was only there for sex anyway, so if sex was off the table, he was out the door. It made him cringe to remember such awful behavior. If he could help it, he'd never go back to being that kind of person.

When Brennan shifted to lie back on the couch, Luka saw his ailing boyfriend's face more clearly. He was way too pale, his eyes losing focus, pain lacing his expression. Something was definitely wrong. Luka's whole body went tense as if readying for a fight and his thoughts whirled, searching for an idea, an answer.

What do I do?

Fuck, what do I do?

That's when Luka's cell phone started to ring.

"Look, it's not really a good time, Aleksy, something's—" Luka said tensely.

"Listen!" Alek snapped. "Evan's hurt. He was mugged. He was…."

Bile rose in Alek's throat as he got a better look at Evan's pallor once he was lifted into the ambulance and the overhead fluorescent lights shined down upon him.

Alek climbed in beside the EMTs, and stared dumbly at the broken form of his lover.

"*Alek!!* Alek, talk to me damn it!" Luka screamed, Alek's fear feeding his.

"He's been stabbed. And beaten. And he's," Alek said in a hollow voice, "I think he's dying."

There was a choked noise, then Luka gruffly asked, "He was stabbed in the stomach, right?"

"How did you—" Alek started to ask.

But Luka cut him off with, "—What hospital? Mercy Gen?"

"Yeah."

"Don't you let anything happen to him. You hear me, Aleksy?"

Alek's throat closed up. Hot tears squeezed from his eyes. More scared than he'd ever been in his life, he ended the call and leaned in closer to Evan, listening to the beeping of the monitors attached to him as the ambulance raced down the street.

Luka's faith that everything would be okay stemmed mainly from the pure, sheer miracle he was even able to get Brennan in one piece over to the hospital. He almost had to deck Brennan just to get him to relinquish the driver's seat of the truck and settle for hyperventilating and losing his fucking mind in the passenger seat instead. The sudden stomach ache was gone, like the terror created by what they'd heard Alek say about Evan chewed up the pain, digested it and used it as fuel to make itself stronger.

"He's gonna be fine! He's tougher than this! You know that. Have faith in him. Bren. Brennan! *Wait!*"

Luka hadn't even come to a stop and was still rolling up to the emergency entrance of the building when Brennan threw open the passenger-side door and darted from the vehicle, running as fast as he could into the hospital.

Luka pulled over to the curb, clicked on his hazards and bolted after Brennan.

Brennan hadn't said a word, not one word since the phone call. His reaction had been purely emotional and physical—his mouth a tight line, his skin nearly bloodless and gray, his blue eyes huge and scared. But he wasn't lacking for energy as he flew into the waiting area where Alek was standing. Alek caught and held on to him as Luka sprinted to join them.

"Hey. *Hey!*" Alek shouted, trying to get Brennan's attention. "Calm down. Listen. Listen! You wanna know what's going on, right? He's being prepped for surgery. They say he has a few broken ribs, a broken nose and other minor injuries. They're worried about internal damage, but, from the looks of it, the blade doesn't seem to have punctured any major internal organs; it's mainly blood loss and patching him back together. They think."

Huffing and puffing, Luka caught up, clutching his side and cursing. "Yeah, *now* you can run. Fuck."

Brennan set his jaw and stared angrily at Alek.

"I'm not letting you go," Alek warned. "We need to let the doctors help him now."

Somehow this only enraged Brennan more. He almost was able to surge free of Alek's grasp, but then from one of the side rooms, Evan was wheeled out into the hall. Evan's face was colored with blackish-purple bruises blooming across his cheekbones and he had two nasty black eyes. His face was swollen and misshapen, but, as Luka watched, he saw Brennan recognize his twin immediately.

"*Evan,*" Brennan sobbed weakly. Alek let him go.

Brennan raced to the gurney, remembering their mother, Maggie, on her own gurneys, in her own hospital emergency rooms. Once he'd found out what was going on with his phantom stomach pain, he quickly realized he couldn't feel Evan anymore. More and more every day, the connection between them had strengthened until Brennan had begun to rely on that sixth sense for comfort. Somehow, being abruptly unable to sense Evan's presence or his pain scared Brennan more than anything else. Evan was connected to tubes, just like their mother was near the end. The worst injury was temporarily hidden beneath a sheet, but Brennan knew the worst injuries were the ones you couldn't see.

"Sir, we need to take him to surgery," one of the nurses said.

"I know, just…." *I might never see him again. This might be the last time I ever see him alive. Oh God.* All of his blood rushed downward, leaving him lightheaded. His vision narrowed until all he could see was his brother. The moment seemed to magnify, making every word, every thought, every gesture seem that much more important. "Evan? Can you hear me?" *Please hear me.*

Brennan touched Evan's hand and searched his face. Evan's eyelids fluttered and Brennan couldn't tell if it was a response or not. "I'm right here," he told his brother. "I'll be waiting right here until you wake up. I love you. They'll fix this. It's gonna be okay."

His voice broke on the last word, feeling like it was maybe the worst lie he'd ever told. Then they were taking Evan away, rolling him steadily farther from Brennan and toward the bank of elevators.

Shivering, Brennan watched until they got to the bend in the hallway. There were strong arms looped around him, and it was a good thing, because as soon as he couldn't see Evan's gurney anymore, Brennan's legs gave out. Darkness spread across his vision, thickening like congealing blood.

From far away, muffled and fading fast, he heard, "Bren? Brennan! Hey! I need help! Someone help us! *Please!*" Strong arms lifted him up as awareness was ripped from him with cold finality.

Chapter 2
Aftermath

Luka liked being busy, and useful. This was especially true when shit had hit the fan; everyone around him was in crisis mode, and he anxiously craved some kind of helpful action. Sure, for a while there, the most useful thing it seemed he could do was to sign off and take off in order to simplify things for everyone. But when it came to Alek — and now Brennan or, it seemed, Evan — it was a whole other story. The same inclination toward being useful had also defined him when he and Alek were little and things had been bad at home. Because Alek had always felt more like a part of Luka than a separate, distinct entity, there had been no choice in the matter. If Alek hurt, Luka hurt. If the thing making Alek hurt was something Alek couldn't fix, then Luka fixed it. He would take what was needed, do what had to be done and not think about it much at all. It was survival. It was instinct. They were essentially on their own, just the two of them, and in their world, they set the rules.

Out of the pair of them, Alek was the thinker. He'd puzzle out how to get their collective asses out of whatever problem they were faced with. Luka, on the other hand, was the doer. He simply did whatever seemed to be the best thing to do at the time, whether that turned out to be a good decision or a bad one. At least he was active, useful, and this maintained his sanity. Typically, Alek was the one giving Luka the orders, telling him to take care of this or look into that. It was how they'd always worked. Most people didn't understand why or how the Popović twins were so close. But, when you started out as identical twins, with all of the innate connections that implied, and grew up in an atmosphere of emotional and physical isolation—without the love and affection of others to draw you away from your twin and out into the world where different kinds of meaningful connections could and should be made—before you knew it, anything was possible. Luka had no expectations of Alek, and vice versa. They simply were. They belonged to each other and there was no formality between them. They would always be there for one another, with one another, no matter what. It wasn't even a question anymore, but a given. Maybe they had grown up too fast and had held on too tightly to each other, but they couldn't change who they were.

But, for once, Alek wasn't the one giving Luka direction. Luka was completely on his own.

Alek was there somewhere, pacing the halls of Mercy General Hospital, focused on his phone and texting back and forth with Brennan, who, at the moment, was the only one permitted to be with Evan. Immediate family only, no visitors, according to the doctors and nurses in charge of Evan's care. Brennan had been at Evan's side since he was brought out of surgery. He was there when Evan was in the recovery area, and he was there now, in Evan's room on the fourth floor, just down the hall from where Luka had been sitting in the waiting room for the past uncertain amount of hours. Luka keenly felt Alek's emotional chaos, and, therefore, it was Luka's unspoken job to be the strong one, the functional and stable one, for a while. He had to carry them both until Alek was reassured Evan would be okay.

Luka was not entirely sure of where Alek was. He'd been moving from floor to floor, down to the cafeteria, up to maternity, wandering pretty much everywhere. When it got too hard to be on Evan's floor and not able to get closer to him, Alek sought other distractions.

Luka missed the comfort of Alek's presence as well as his advice. Since Evan had been attacked, solitude in the small, sterile waiting room had only brought Luka greater heartache—for Alek, for Brennan, and, most of all, for Evan. Luka couldn't quite accept what had happened and why the world would be so unfair. Evan was only trying to do the right thing.

There was a plastic bag filled with food and drinks by Luka's left leg. Whenever Alek did stop by the waiting room, he brought sustenance for Brennan and Luka. Not that they'd partaken of any of it. Each time Brennan was able to bring himself to leave Evan's side for a few moments, he came bursting into the waiting room without warning. Luka would jump to his feet, expecting there to be news or an emergency, but so far Brennan's visits had just been to report there was no change in Evan's condition. Evan was being kept under sedation for the time being, while they assessed his internal injuries, so they didn't expect him to be awake yet. As long as his blood pressure and heart rate didn't drop, they were able to hope he was beginning to heal.

Luka had been trying to hand off some of the food from the bag, or at least a soda, figuring Brennan could use the caffeine. But, Brennan never took any of it. After falling into Luka's arms for comfort, and fleeting reassurance, he'd leave again, rushing back to Evan. Luka wanted to go with him so desperately it hurt. The need to see Evan with his own eyes was something Luka couldn't explain, but only felt.

The only thing Brennan would talk about was Evan, and only to Luka, Alek, or the nurses. Nothing else existed for him. He couldn't bring himself to speak of what had happened to anyone outside their little circle, either. Explaining the details of their present horror was beyond him.

That was why Luka had appointed himself phone duty. There were people who needed to know what was going on and no one else to call them but him. Clutching the phone numbers scrawled in Brennan's looped, slanted handwriting, Luka tried to think of what to say to Evan and Brennan's father and sole living parent, Charlie Savage. Jimmy Bennett, Evan's best friend and pseudo-guardian also needed to be notified. He debated who to call first.

Luckily or unluckily for him, his phone rang before he could decide. Seeing the caller ID, Luka sighed and answered with a simple, "Yeah."

"Where the hell is Alek?" Carter blurted, sounding furious. "He was supposed to give me a ride to the city today, and he said he was gonna be here but he never even fuckin' came home last night and now he ain't even pickin' up the damn phone!"

"Oh. There's been an accident," Luka heard himself saying in a calm, emotionless voice, like he was floating above himself and wasn't connected at all. "We're both at the hospital. He must've forgotten, Carter. Sorry."

In the kitchen of their house across town, Carter went very pale. The suddenness of the fight draining out of him scared Presley, who was standing nearby, to the bone.

"What happened?" Presley asked, before Carter could say the words himself.

"What kind of accident?" Carter put Luka on speaker on his cell, then Presley could hear him, too.

"It's Evan. Some guy was jumped out back of Alek's bar. Evan went to break it up or help the guy, I guess. He was, um, stabbed? They beat on him until Meryl showed up with his sawed-off. Evan's out of surgery now, but he's sedated and hasn't regained consciousness yet. He hasn't been awake at all since last night, before it happened. He's got a lot of... head injuries. His nose is broken, three ribs are fractured and I think his teeth went through his lip. The oral surgeon said he's got some loose teeth. They're giving him blood transfusions. The blade almost opened his large intestine but didn't. Could've died of septic shock. He's lucky."

"Yeah, really lucky," Carter said vacantly. Presley watched Carter, knowing the look on his face and that he was already thinking about finding the guys that did this, and planning to get in touch with Meryl.

Carter asked, "And Alek?"

Luka admitted, "Alek's not too good right now. He won't even talk to *me* about it. He's around here, somewhere, waiting to see Evan. I don't think he's coming home until he does, even if it's days."

Luka wondered in a detached way why everything he said sounded like a question and why his voice was so soft and tranquil.

It felt, though, like if he spoke any more forcefully, it would break the ephemeral spell holding his fragile, shattered world together with only faint wisps of hope. If he let himself be upset, he might tumble into a dark place that'd be too hard to come back from.

It had never been this bad before. In all of their youthful recklessness, it was never this dire. Alek never had cause to wonder if Luka would live through the night. Maybe this would put him over the edge. Maybe Alek's unnaturally desperate need to safeguard those who loved him would be his downfall should Evan take a turn for the worse. To Luka, it was more than Evan — and by extension, Brennan — on the line. He could lose Alek, too. He could lose everything.

"And Brennan?"

"Brennan… is, uh… holding it together, I guess."

"What can we do? What happened to the assholes that did this?"

Luka tried to remember. "We heard Meryl and his buddies ran 'em down and brought 'em in to the station with some 'mysterious' injuries no one could explain. My guess is the bikers beat the piss out of those punks before dragging them to the authorities, but now the cops are questioning Meryl and all. I'll talk to you more later, okay? I need to call some people."

"Luka, man, how do we help you? Just name it."

"I don't know. Well, I think Evan's car and Alek's truck are still over there if you guys can get 'em back?"

"No problem. We're on it. If there's anything else, you let us know."

"Sure. Thanks."

"And Luka? Tell Brennan and Alek to hang in there, all right?"

"Yeah."

Luka hung up, cleared his throat and dialed the first number while he knew he was still able to talk.

It was picked up on the fifth ring, right before the panic about what to say on a voicemail message could strangle him senseless. "Oh thank god," he sighed as Charlie answered with a hello.

"Yes, Mr. Savage? My name is Luka Popović and I'm currently dating your son. Er, Brennan. I'm not sure if you were already contacted by the hospital or not, but I'm afraid I have some bad news. It's Evan."

The whole story tumbled from Luka's lips. He left out the nature of Evan's relationship with Alek, but included everything else. There wasn't a word or sound from the other end of the line the whole time he was talking and Luka worried they'd been cut off due to a bad connection, but plowed on anyway. Once he'd finished, with Charlie caught up to the present and everything Luka knew about Evan's condition, Luka paused. Then, he asked, "Sir? You still there?"

"I'm here. Just gimme a minute," the older man said in a strained, gruff, gravelly voice.

"Brennan would have called you himself, but he's fairly upset right now so he asked me to tell you instead. I'm sure he'll want to speak with you once things have settled down and he's feeling more like himself."

"Tell him I'm coming, will you? I'll see what I can do, the soonest I can get down there. What do you need? Insurance information? Medical history? Anything?"

"Yeah. Once I get the forms from Brennan, I'll call you back so you can help me fill them out. We do have the insurance thing covered, I think, and I'll keep you posted if there's any change. I'm sure Evan would be very happy to see you if you can be here."

"Th-thank you for the call, Luka," he said, sounding overwhelmed, with good reason. "Seems like Brennan is lucky to have you there for him right now. I'm grateful for it. Those damn kids. Gonna send me to an early grave with worry for 'em. Have Brennan call me."

"I will."

"And let me know if there's any change."

"I will."

Once the call was ended, Luka felt drained and thin, like there wasn't much left he had to give. Thinking of Brennan, though, and what he was dealing with, gave Luka the strength he needed to call the next number.

He put the phone to his ear and squeezed his eyes shut, rubbing over them.

"Hello?"

"Yeah, is this Jimmy?"

"It is. Who is this?"

"It's Luka Popović. Brennan's boyfriend. Brennan told me about your history with the family and all, so let me preface this by assuring you he's in stable condition right now, but Evan's been hurt. He was attacked outside a bar, and—"

Jimmy interrupted, cutting Luka off. "Where are you? What hospital? Mercy?"

"Yes, sir. Fourth floor. He's not allowed visitors yet, he just came out of surgery a few hours ago, and—"

"I'll be there in ten minutes," Jimmy said abruptly. The line went dead.

"Jesus Christ," Luka groaned, sinking down farther into his chair, leaning his head back against the wall. Wanting sleep and some sort of peace of mind, Luka knew it was still very far away.

On Alek's phone, a new text popped up with Evan's latest vitals printed out neatly for him, sent from Brennan.

Any change? he sent back.

The numbers looked good. Evan's blood pressure was up closer to normal levels again, his heart rate steady and temperature only slightly raised.

He groaned. Might be dreaming, Brennan replied.

Alek pulled up the camera-phone shot Brennan had sent him only after much prompting and pleading, an image of Evan asleep in his hospital bed. Alek had looked at it a couple hundred times already, touching the tiny screen like Evan could feel him there, watching over him, too. It was a horrible sight. Evan's nose was bandaged, his eyes and cheekbones bruised dark, swollen and discolored. His lips were also badly swollen and dry, particularly his lower lip which had six stitches in it from where his teeth punctured it. Wearing a hospital gown, Evan's hands laid at his sides on the bed, a puffy wad of bandage raising the sheet slightly at his middle where the wound was located.

Send me another picture, Alek typed.

No. Brennan answered.

Seething, drowning in jealousy of Brennan and how close he was able to be to Evan, how he could hold his hand and wait by his side… it drove Alek insane.

The phone rang. When he answered, Alek's tone was clipped and angry even though he saw it was only Luka calling. It was too easy to unload on his brother. He was an easy target because he knew Luka would always forgive Alek instantly, unasked. And Luka knew how upset Alek was, so he'd be expecting a sour mood. Even if Alek could pretend to be okay, it would have been a waste of effort with Luka anyway because Luka could *feel* Alek hurting — nothing as crude as words was required. But, no matter how riled Alek was, he couldn't take it out on Brennan. Luka was a safer target, and possibly the only one.

"What?"

"Can you come up here? We need the keys to Evan's car. Carter and Presley are gonna go and get it. Jimmy's here, too."

"Fine," he snapped, ending the call.

The waiting room on Evan's floor was quite full when Alek got there.

For whatever reason, it was usually when Alek was overextended or not really focused on what he was saying his twin connection with Luka became more apparent to everyone else. As soon as Alek was by Luka's side and had managed a tight-lipped nod of welcome to everyone, the twins began responding to questions in tandem, finishing each other's thoughts.

"They gave us Evan's things," Luka said.

"And I was going to take care of his car," Alek added.

"But it's not like there's a rush to get it out of the lot."

"I just didn't want to forget about it. He loves that car."

"So thank you for getting it."

"You have the address to Evan and Bren's?"

Carter raised an eyebrow, glancing at Presley. "Yeah. Luka hooked us up. How are you doin', man? Hangin' in there?"

Alek replied, "I just want to see him."

"They haven't allowed visitors yet," Luka said.

"But we're hoping that'll change today," Alek finished.

"The doctor said head injury patients can have a lot of swelling."

"And can be combative, so since Evan suffered multiple blows to the head...."

"For safety reasons, they medically induced a coma."

"Until the brain swelling comes down."

"So Evan's been given fentanyl for the pain and sedation." .

"And norcuron, a paralytic agent. Bren texts me all of the names, to keep track of everything." .

Luka dug in the bag of food and offered Alek a protein shake while Jimmy — sitting with paperwork laid out on his lap, attached to a clipboard — looked up at the twins with some amazement.

"Drink this. You look like shit," Luka said to his brother under his breath. "Or sit down for a minute. Close your eyes."

"I'm fine."

Luka unscrewed the cap and physically put the beverage in Alek's hand.

"Thank you," Alek sighed, drinking it down.

"We're gonna take off, but we'll come back after," Carter said.

"If you guys want anything specific for lunch or dinner, call us and we'll pick it up," Presley offered.

The pair left after brief, one-armed hugs for Luka and Alek, as well as muttered sentiments of support, encouragement and hope. Then it was only Alek, Luka and Jimmy.

Collecting himself, Alek stepped up to the thirty-something-year-old man who had been Evan's support system for so long, and extended a hand to him.

"I'm Alek. You must be Jimmy. I'm really glad you could be here for Evan."

His jaw set and expression stern, Jimmy nodded curtly and took Alek's hand, pumping it twice, and squeezing hard.

"I must admit," Jimmy said. "I did not get the best first impression of you, Alek, because of what I heard from Evan about your first couple of dates. But just the fact that you're here and clearly very concerned about Evan's well-being is slowly convincing me not to castrate you for having sex with him."

"…Oh," Alek managed, taken aback.

Sighing and running a hand over his face, Jimmy appeared to instantly regret what he'd said. "Look, I apologize for my anger. I know you're dealing with a lot and I, uh, tend to be very frank when stressed. Evan has always confided in me. You could say I've been his self-appointed counselor for the past number of years. So yes, I know who you are, and some of what's happened between you and Evan. He called me in tears some weeks ago with remorse over how quickly and how far things went with you, so I admit that has colored my perception of the whole thing. I feel it's only fair to be honest about that. I'd like to remind you of his age, and his vulnerability given the many things he's endured in his childhood and adolescence. Please attempt to show some responsibility in your, uh… *handling*… of him. I'm sorry. I just needed to say that upfront for my own peace of mind, even if it's a bad time to bring it up."

Flustered, upset, Jimmy stared in the direction of Evan's room and appeared to lose his train of thought. Then he apologized again and continued.

"I realize there are other priorities right now, other than my opinions about Evan's sex life. With Charlie away, it typically falls on me to manage Evan's care and I feel like I'm playing catch-up right now. Luka has kindly explained everything that has happened since last night and, I must say, I'm not surprised Evan did what he did, trying to stand up for that young man. That's who he is; Evan does whatever seems right without thinking it through and consequently putting himself in harm's way. He's always been reckless like that. I'm just sorry it turned out the way it did for Evan. But it sounds to me like Evan may have saved that person's life by sticking his neck out. Now, are there any new developments? The doctor hasn't been in to update Luka since six a.m. but I hear you've been in regular communication with Brennan?"

"Yeah. I have," Alek said, tightly, dealing with his own raging emotions but trying to be diplomatic. "No change. Evan's blood pressure has improved gradually over the course of the morning and they're just watching for any sign of infection or complication."

"Of course," Jimmy nodded.

Not too long after that, Alek decided the waiting room was once again too stifling to endure.

He excused himself to wander the halls again, thinking of his next course of action, of what all of this meant and what he'd have to do because of it.

Chapter 3
Shaken Up

Complete consciousness kept slipping from Evan's grasp. He clawed his way to awareness, hearing beeps and muted voices from all around him. Sometimes he felt someone…

Brennan. It's Brennan….

…holding his hand or touching his legs. It got his hopes up. He tried to hold on to that sensation, to let it keep him there, but then the pain came back and he let go, giving up. Tiredness and the drugs weighed him down, clouding everything out. He sank into the blackness of his mind, detaching from his battered body entirely.

It happened again and again until, finally, he had success. Perhaps that was because there were more voices.

Alek….

Or because Brennan was actually laying next to him, on Evan's good side—the one that didn't feel wrong, patched together and screaming.

Evan's bed was tilted, positioned slightly upright so he wasn't flat on his back, allowing him to bear the broken ribs more easily. But Brennan was there, curled up on his right, holding his hand and urging him to open his eyes. Evan heard his name called and did open his eyes a few times before he could actually make any sense out of what he was seeing.

"Come on. You can do it. Come on, Evan. Open your eyes. Keep 'em open. Can you hear me? Evan?"

It sounded to Evan like his own voice, calling to him. It was disorienting, especially coming out of a prolonged, drug-fueled unconsciousness. Nothing seemed quite real. Staring straight ahead of him at a face he knew well, Alek's face, Evan felt his left hand taken by someone else, someone who wasn't Brennan. Jimmy was there, too, Evan realized, and standing a few feet away.

Why is Jimmy here? Is it happening again? Did I try to kill myself again? Why does everyone look so upset?

No. The bar.

I got jumped at the bar.

It wasn't my fault. I didn't do it.

...Did I?

The white hot, blistering sensory noise of excruciating pain zapped away all thought as Evan tried to move. It flared outward from his ribs and gut, up his spine to the top of his skull, out through every single bone, every nerve in his body.

He cried out sharply in a hoarse, worn voice. Tears sprang from his swollen eyes, coursing down his bruised face. Whining back in his throat, he battled through it, wanting to be asleep again.

"Hey, take it easy, baby. You had surgery and you've got more than a couple fractures, so don't try to move right now. Do you know where you are?"

"A-Alek?"

His vision swimming, blurred with wetness, Evan blinked at the dark-haired, hazel-eyed, towering man standing at the foot of his bed, the one with the deeply concerned, piercing stare, drawn expression and bloodshot eyes.

"Right here."

The beckoning words came from Evan's left, his bad side and he tried to at least turn his head that way. It was very hard to see anything clearly and Evan didn't know why. There was warmth radiating on his right side where Brennan was pressed against him in places. Reassured by Brennan's closeness, Evan tightened his grasp within Brennan's encircling hand. Blinking his eyes clear, Evan finally saw Alek, understanding at last it was Luka at the foot of his bed.

"Why is it so hard to see? Did I forget my glasses?"

"You don't wear glasses anymore. Remember?" Brennan spoke the words softly by Evan's ear. Evan didn't entirely realize the words weren't spoken from inside his own head.

"I don't? Oh."

"The tissue all around your eyes is pretty inflamed right now," Alek told him, stooping down and sitting on a chair, which he moved more into Evan's line of sight. "There are also bandages over your nose. That's probably why it's hard to see. You have a concussion, too. Do you remember what happened?"

He glanced around the room, pausing when he saw Jimmy again, by the door. Jimmy glanced between Evan and Brennan, at their joined hands and physical closeness, but it didn't mean anything to Evan.

"They were gonna.... They were gonna hurt him. He was just looking for a hook-up, like I was, but they... they all went after him. Because he was gay. I couldn't... I couldn't let them do that. But I went outside, then.... Oh."

He was quiet for a minute, as it all sank in. They gave him time.

"You said I had surgery? Did it go okay?"

"Yeah." Alek smiled encouragingly, looking like he was trying his damnedest not to cry, which made Evan want to cry. "You did great. No complications. I guess you can feel your cracked ribs, huh?"

Evan nodded, carefully glancing down at himself, afraid to move his head too much, lest it make his headache worse. Brennan's fingers brushed lightly up and down his right arm. It felt good. It distracted from the pain that sliced through Evan every time he breathed.

"Guess they did a number on my face, huh? Do I sound weird to you, too?"

"You have a few stitches on the inside of your lower lip," Brennan told him. "It's still healing and kind of puffy. They reset the bridge of your nose, and that's probably swollen up."

"Fantastic. So when can I get out of here?"

"Soon," Alek promised. "But for now, just rest. We'll take care of everything and anything we need to. The doctors are going to make sure you get better fast. Okay?"

"Yeah," Evan sighed.

As Alek kissed the back of his hand, Evan's eyes slipped shut.

He was asleep again in seconds.

That night, Alek was permitted to stay with Evan. Looking somewhat pacified, he camped out in a chair by Evan's bedside when the others left to try to get some rest, lulling Evan to sleep by gently brushing his fingertips over Evan's arm. It was only because of how peaceful they looked together that Brennan was able to part with his brother.

Brennan was at Evan's side when he had talked with their father briefly over the phone. Not much was affected by the conversation. It was same old, same old — promises to come home soon, unsurprising concern for Evan's safety and health, all spoken over a crackling connection across long, long miles.

Brennan empathized with Evan's subsequent frustration. Brennan already had plenty of experience with Charlie's attempts to overcome distance and his noted absence from his children's lives with insubstantial words. It was clear, as much as Evan, with his young body in tatters, craved his father's reassuring presence, he was just as glad Charlie wasn't there, adding to the tension and stress. That realization just made the ache of regret stronger, knowing how Evan never got to experience the comforting, loving presence of their mother.

Angry, sad, scared, all Brennan wanted to do was safeguard his beloved twin, and do whatever needed to be done to make him healthy and whole again.

Exhausted, finally leaving the hospital after days without real sleep, Brennan drove back home with Luka. The plan was to get to his house, shed all clothes, crawl into bed dragging Luka in with him, and curl up with his pillow for many hours.

He didn't get that far, and fell asleep in the passenger seat of Luka's truck before they'd even left the hospital's parking garage. Brennan slept the whole way, and even stayed knocked out when Luka carried him into the house, to bed.

The world was bright and sunlit when Brennan did wake. Thankfully, no tears came that morning. Dry-eyed, Brennan stared at the shifting clouds through the window's sheer curtain; thinking of his mother, of Evan, and of the future.

He was aware of Luka lying behind him. Gentle, skittering movements of fingers over Brennan's body entranced him. They went along the side of his arm, just inside the cradle of his hips and down his thigh before dragging back up to do it all over again.

"You have to work today."

"I do," Luka agreed.

"I have to get back to the hospital. Maybe they'll release Evan soon. I can always drive him back home myself, when they do release him, but do you think Alek can be there to help me?"

"Yeah, shouldn't be a problem," Luka assured him.

"Good," Brennan exhaled, rolling onto his back. His chest rose and fell with quickened breath, and his eyes were half-closed with something other than sleepiness. Spreading his legs when Luka shifted to lie on top of him, Brennan almost smiled. "Can I ask a favor before you go?"

He raked his fingers back through Luka's long, dark hair, brushing it back from his face, tucking it over Luka's ears.

"You want me to drop you off?"

"Well, yeah, but...."

"But what?"

"But, I want you." He swallowed a soft moan when Luka rocked in a slow drag against him. Brennan's hips stuttered, rutting up into Luka, whose pelvis was pinning Brennan to the bed. Luka reached down and caressed Brennan's hipbone, peeking out from under his low-slung briefs. "You were amazing, you know. Staying there at the hospital with me that whole time, making those calls for us, handling everything I couldn't, and holding it all together when Alek and I were freaking out. I don't know what I'd do without you."

"You're welcome," Luka grinned softly, pressing a kiss to Brennan's lips. "So, is this my reward? I get to ravage you for being the dutiful boyfriend?"

"Fuck no," Brennan scoffed, his head thrown back as Luka slipped lower to suck a mark on Brennan's pulse point. Simultaneously pushing Brennan's underwear down in front and tugging him free, Luka squeezed slowly, firmly, repeatedly up his shaft. "I just really need you in me right now. Like, *right now.*"

I want to feel something else, besides fear.

I'm sick of it. I want to feel good, feel something tangible, vital, and alive before I have to go back there and face my nightmare — the wreckage of someone else I love so much.

Just because you love someone doesn't mean you won't lose them. I almost lost him, just like I lost Mom.

But this was worse, there was no warning. No build up. No slow burn, just a call in the night that Evan was dying.

Evan was dying.

Please, Luka. Give me that. Make it last. Make me feel before the numbness sinks bone-deep and nothing can touch me, ever again.

Some of this flickered in his scared, child-like, trusting gaze as he hid behind crude words. "You didn't bring a cock ring, did you? Cause that'd be awesome if you did."

"Filthy slut," Luka breathed, playing along, choosing passion over heartache.

For a brief heartbeat, Brennan slipped. His lips turned down at the edges and quivered. His eyebrows tilted and forehead creased as he beseeched with a glance. Holding his breath, holding Luka, Brennan squeezed his eyes shut against hot tears as Luka coaxed, "Hey, stay with me. Look at me. Don't think about it. You're fine. It's fine. He's safe."

"I hate it."

"I know. I know you do. I hate it, too."

Brennan exhaled heavily and pressed his face against Luka's neck, anchoring to him. Luka cupped a hand behind Brennan's head, kissed his temple. After a few more deep breaths, Brennan felt steadier.

"You don't have to prove anything. How about I help you relax and we can get out of here."

"I'm not proving anything," Brennan argued. He pulled back slightly to look into Luka's eyes. "I just need you. Please."

"Okay," Luka sighed. He brushed the backs of his knuckles through the hollow of Brennan's cheek, along his jaw. There was a strangely anguished expression on his face and Brennan couldn't quite place it. Then he saw the glassiness of Luka's eyes. He was about to cry.

"What? What is it?"

Luka tried to smile, glanced away, bit at his lip. It took him a moment to find his voice.

Without looking directly at Brennan, he confessed quietly, "You look like him when you're sad."

Tears slipped down the sides of Brennan's face as his expression crumpled, but Luka kissed his breath away before heartache could win out. Tangling his fingers in Luka's hair, Brennan moaned softly as Luka caressed greedily over his body. He was turned over, onto his stomach. Luka grabbed the lube and hurriedly got Brennan ready for him, stretching him out with slick fingers, breathing hot and heavy into Brennan's blond hair.

Luka settled atop him, pressing Brennan to the bed with a pillow fitted under his hips. When he started to try and enter him, Brennan wondered if Luka was thinking of him, or of Evan.

Crying out as he was breached, muffling the sound against the sheets, Brennan heard Luka moan his name, nudging farther. Held down by Luka's hands, pinned by his hips, Brennan relaxed into the stretch and stopped trying to be quiet. Luka sucked at a spot under Brennan's jaw and thrust even harder when Brennan's groans and gasps grew in strength and volume.

"Brennan… love you," he heard, breathless and wanting, by the shell of his ear.

He didn't have air enough in his lungs to respond. Luka drove into him and just kept moving, fucking and taking. Overheated, stuffed full, gasping and uncomfortably erect, Brennan's every sense was dulled by the ferocity of Luka's lovemaking.

He drew Brennan back and up onto his knees without pulling out, guided Brennan's hands to the rungs of the headboard, wrapping his fingers there. Then he caressed back along his arms, down his sides to his hips, holding them firmly as he tugged out almost all the way just to push back in with a smooth, long push that took Brennan apart.

Luka began to tug Brennan's dick in short, steady pulses and Brennan's head fell between his extended arms, his cries piercing the air. With long, slow movements in and out of his ass, and rapid pumping of his shaft, Luka sent Brennan's climax racing up on him fast. Teeth scraped the nape of his neck. Lips brushed the skin, and long hair tickled his jaw.

"Gonna make you come so hard, Evan'll feel it."

Brennan's eyes rolled deliriously as he imagined it—Luka reaching out to Evan through him. He fought against the need to push into Luka's restless hand. He shifted his knees wider as the easy, ceaseless slide of Luka's thick member made him yell. The thrusts got sharper, louder, quicker, and shallower.

Held by the hip and the cock, Brennan's orgasm hit him with force. He came over the sheet beneath him and Luka's fingers swiped and rubbed over the head, smearing the hot fluid, triggering Brennan again. Cursing, sweating, Brennan's every muscle slowly started to unclench as Luka squeezed two fingers into him alongside his cock. He heard Luka hiss and grunt, still pushing, chasing completion.

"*Luka*," Brennan pleaded.

"Wanna see if you could take me and Aleksy at the same time. You want that, Cupcake?"

"Fuck." Brennan clenched intentionally around the fingers and cock inside him. Luka moaned and snapped his hips, coming with a shiver, gasping against Brennan's neck.

The fingers pulled out. Brennan moaned, "Jesus." Luka slung an arm under him and moved him, changing their position again, bringing Brennan upright and settled on Luka's lap. Brennan was still full of him and dizzily drinking down gasps of air, his head lolling back to rest against Luka's shoulder.

"Good distraction," he grinned.

"Thanks," Luka smiled back, tenderly brushing the sweat-damp hair back from Brennan's forehead, kissing his cheek.

"I love you."

"Good. Me too."

He folded his arms over the ones encircling him. Exhaustion of a different sort made him suddenly sleepy.

"You can have the shower first if you want."

"Okay," Luka agreed. His hands stroked downward to rest atop Brennan's thighs, clamping down on them, keeping Brennan on his lap. Luka thrust up against him gently, his lips dragging over the shell of Brennan's ear.

"Gonna let me off?"

"Mm, maybe," Luka teased, still moving languidly within him. One hand released Brennan's thigh only to move up to twist his left nipple. Brennan's skin pebbled with fresh goosebumps. He shot Luka an accusatory smile over his right shoulder as Luka leaned back and let go, planting his hands behind him on the bed as he stared unabashedly at the sight of his cock sliding wetly out of Brennan's body. Licking his lips to hide a devilish grin, Luka raised his eyebrows briefly in reply.

Brennan lay down on his side with a contented sigh. Luka got up off the bed only to lean down and give Brennan a quick kiss. Pulling the covers up over him, Luka left Brennan there.

Not five minutes later, Luka found Brennan sleeping peacefully. He decided to let him have the extra rest and busied himself around the house in the meantime, doing dishes and cleaning up until it was time to leave for work. Eventually, he roused Brennan to get washed up and ready to go.

Golden eyelashes fluttered and blue eyes opened as Brennan slowly woke up, followed by a warm smile that lit up his face. He appeared to be rested, and more at ease than he had been. It seemed to be progress.

While Brennan was in the bathroom, Luka took out the trash and sorted through the stack of mail that had piled up by the front door. Days had passed since anyone had been home, so he looked for bills or anything urgent to either pay for himself or give to Brennan. Once finished, Luka discovered the bathroom once more open and empty, but Brennan was also not in his room. Luka went in search of him, quickly finding him in Evan's bedroom.

Standing by the bed, Brennan hugged Evan's pillow to his chest, staring blankly forward. The air of warm contentment about him had already faded away. Other than a small crease in his brow, Brennan's expression was vacant and weighted.

"What's up? You okay?"

"Maybe I shouldn't have hid the gun from him," Brennan murmured. "If he'd had it on him that night, maybe he could've stopped those sons of bitches before things got that bad. This could all be my fault."

"Or," Luka said, "they could have taken the gun from Evan and turned it on him instead. He could've gotten shot, and killed. I'm not a fan of guns, Bren. I think you did the right thing here. It's one thing to use it to hunt, but carrying it on you into bars is asking for trouble."

Luka watched this all slowly sink in. It appeared to displace some of the heavy responsibility loaded on Brennan's shoulders.

"What're you doing with his pillow?"

"I thought I'd bring it to him, if it'd make him more comfortable. Is there anything else you think he'd like? If I bought him a 'Get Well Soon' bear, is that completely lame? And clothes, I guess. He'll need clean clothes. I would bring him food, but he's on that liquid diet because of his teeth. He's not even off the IV yet, as far as I know. When he comes home, he can't sleep in here. He's going to need to be upright, with his ribs and all. The stuffed chair in the living room might be a good bed. He could watch TV."

"Bren," Luka said softly. "It'll be fine. You're doing great. The pillow's a great idea. And the bear isn't lame, it's adorable."

"Yeah?" he asked hopefully.

"Coming from you, yes."

Luka wound an arm around Brennan's shoulders and guided him from the room. He could see the corners of Brennan's mouth curling down again, the look in his eyes changing with fret, making him appear older than his years, and much more like his twin. It was haunting.

"I know how much you want him home," Luka said. "But once he's here, the bulk of the caretaking is going to fall to you. At least in the hospital they can keep an eye on his progress and handle anything that comes up."

"He'd be better off at home. Mom always preferred to be at home instead of those places. It's never quiet there. It's sterile and cold and it smells weird."

"Plus, if he's there it means he's really not okay, huh?" Luka offered. They'd made it out to the truck, Brennan with the pillow and a small bag filled with clothes, Luka, already dressed for his shift at the gym, and carrying bills to mail back.

"When can I see you again?" Brennan worried, "God, I'm gonna miss you."

"I'll call you on my break, see what's what."

"Okay."

Chapter 4
Initial Implications

Jimmy was at the hospital for morning visiting hours. Brennan glimpsed him through the waiting room door once he'd gotten to Evan's floor. When Brennan peeked into Evan's room, a nurse was changing Evan's bandages and tending to his wounds. He lingered by the door, waiting for her to finish and watching her work. He knew he could go to the waiting room instead, but that would mean facing Jimmy and having to talk. Brennan was still not really in the mood for that, but he couldn't avoid everyone for long. After only a minute's reprieve, Alek and Jimmy emerged into the hall.

Alek saw Brennan first and made a beeline over to him. He folded Brennan into a bear hug, pillow and all. It was nice. Brennan felt Alek gripping him tightly, kissing the top of his head and letting out a held breath. After the tension and jealousy between them since Evan had gotten hurt, the tenderness was received with more heartfelt appreciation than Brennan anticipated.

It hit him hard that he seemed to care fairly deeply for Alek, and in a way wholly different than the way he loved Luka. Brennan hugged him back and didn't want Alek to let him go.

"How is he?" Brennan managed. Alek's touch, so reminiscent of Luka, was strengthening in other ways. There was pure affection there, apart from sexual desires. Brennan thought about how both he and Alek were the ones who had to learn, quickly and too young, to be strong purely for the sake of others, and how they both probably still carried some resentment for the fact. It made Brennan feel safe with Alek in a way he didn't with Evan or Luka, because Alek understood what it was like. With Alek there was no need to sugar-coat anything for appearance's sake.

Alek braced a hand behind Brennan's head, stroking over his blond hair, breathing him in. There was fear for Evan in the touch. Brennan sensed it clearly, along with gratitude for being able, just for a moment, to hold someone so like Evan, a real part of him. Brennan felt the same thing with Alek concerning Luka. There was a piece of Luka's spirit there, inside him. However, it was how Alek's touch wasn't about Evan at all that really affected Brennan, provoking him to cling to Alek's shirt, inhaling the scent of him, savoring his warmth and strength.

But Jimmy was right there too, now, watching everything. Brennan was aware of how signs of intimacy between him and Alek might concern Jimmy. It gave Brennan pause, preventing what might otherwise have become more.

"He's a little better, but he's in more pain today," Alek lamented. "I just want to make it stop. It should be me, not him. I should've been paying more attention. Evan shouldn't have been the one to go out there. Hell, I shouldn't have let him come to the bar at all. Funny how, after being so afraid of him hurting himself, I'm the one who ends up hurting him."

Hearing Alek's self-flagellation, so like what Brennan felt when standing in Evan's room not an hour earlier, Brennan ached. Before he could say anything in reply, he saw someone else over Alek's shoulder. It was a woman with long, dark hair and cat-like eyes, staring right at them.

"Hey, you know her?"

Alek turned, "Oh. Katie. Yeah, hey. What're you —? Bren, I'll be right back, okay?"

"Sure," Brennan nodded, letting go, feeling colder and lesser without him there. Jimmy cleared his throat and moved closer to Brennan as Alek went to talk to the newcomer.

"How are you holding up?" Jimmy asked Brennan, looking him over. "It's good you went home to sleep. You've got to keep your strength up. Hospitals can be really draining."

Feeling self-conscious of the dark circles he knew were under his eyes, Brennan squeezed Evan's pillow and shrugged. "I'm okay," he muttered.

"You two have gotten closer, you and Evan."

Unsure how to respond to that, Brennan didn't even try, but held his ground and met Jimmy's gaze.

"I talked to Charlie a little while ago. He's having trouble getting time off," Jimmy admitted, regretfully. "He's very frustrated and angry about it, but there's nothing he can do. I'm sure he'll work it out somehow."

A selfish sort of relief flooded Brennan at the thought of not having to face his father for a little while longer. He instantly felt guilty about the reaction, for Evan's sake.

"That sucks. But I'm sure Evan understands."

"Yeah," Jimmy grumbled. "He understands all right."

Across the hall, about twenty-five feet away, Alek and Katie stood close together, talking quietly.

"The cops were here first thing this morning, going over everything with Evan, getting his statements," Alek told her. "Do you have any idea what the hell happened? I mean, they told us they have all of the guys in custody now, but they wouldn't give us any specifics. We've been going on rumor from what we've heard from Jason and other guys at the bar that night."

Katie shifted the purse strap slung over her shoulder a little higher and looked past Alek's shoulder at Brennan for a moment. "That's the brother?"

"Yeah."

"He's cute," she said, then brought her focus back to Alek. "Well, you didn't hear it from me, but Meryl and those guys ran 'em all down and kicked their asses. They were all brought in bloody and you know Meryl. He said the assholes fought 'em hard, trying to escape, that he was just doing his civic duty. Total bullshit. That was just their excuse to treat 'em like human punching bags. Guess the cops let Meryl and all of 'em go, no problem, just a wink and a nod. It's all pretty fucked up if you ask me. And what's this I hear about you quitting?"

"Yeah. I quit," Alek admitted. "I called in a couple hours ago and let 'em know. I'm done with that place. I want to be home nights for Evan and I don't want him ever to have to go back to that fucking bar or have to think about me going there every goddamn day."

"So what the hell are you gonna do for a job?"

"Get another one. A better one. Maybe actually use my degree for once."

"Wow. You're growin' up," she smiled. "That's great, Aleksy. Being in love suits you. We'll miss ya, though, big guy." She hugged him goodbye, saying, "Good luck. Don't be a stranger."

"Thanks, Katie."

A nurse let Brennan know he could go in to see his brother as Katie headed to the elevator. Brennan crept into the room, hanging back while fresh gauze was taped down over Evan's side.

Lying in bed, Evan seemed unaware of much going on around him at all, let alone that his brother was nearby. Brennan watched, unobserved, as Evan reacted to each touch of the nurse's fingertips like she was pressing barbed spikes into his torso. Evan winced, sucking air through his teeth, gripping the bed's sides.

Flinching as she got the last of the adhesive into place, Evan fought to bear it calmly. But, even when she was done, had left and he once more was covered with the dressing gown and sheet, the pain didn't seem to dull one bit. He didn't relax or open his eyes. Brennan could practically feel what his brother was going through. As much as he wanted to go to Evan and hold him, he hesitated. Maybe, Brennan thought, he should just leave Evan in peace so he didn't make things worse.

A few moments later, though, Brennan compromised with himself. He went to the bedside and tentatively took Evan's hand. On the bed, Evan slowly opened his eyes. At first he was foggy and didn't react at all.

Staring at their joined hands, Brennan waited patiently, trying not to compare the moment to the times he'd spent similarly attending to his cancer-stricken mother. Then, he heard, "Bren? Thank *god.*" Evan's voice cracked over the words. "It fucking hurts!"

Anxious to help, Brennan asked, "What can I do? I brought your pillow but it looks like it's not a good time to sit you up and get it under you."

"No, help me up. Fuck, I hate this. She laid me down to clean around the stitches after she took my temperature and blood pressure and whatever, and I need—I need to sit up."

"Okay." Brennan stood at Evan's side, setting the pillow on a chair so his hands were both free. "Take my hand, let me move you. You stay relaxed and breathe. Nice and slow, okay?"

"What's going on?" Alek asked from the doorway, coming quickly over to Evan.

"Help me get him up. I want to do it without him straining anything," Brennan said. "Get his other arm."

Evan clasped both of their hands and whimpered in anticipation. Jimmy was by the door, looking like he wanted to help but didn't know how.

They eased Evan upright, bracing his back and holding each of his hands in one of theirs.

Evan screamed once. He was pale and trembling as they got the bed's angle corrected. Soft, fluffy pillows were set behind him, including his own, the softest of them all. When it was done, he didn't open his eyes or let either of their hands go.

Brennan listened to Evan's broken, aching grunts, getting angrier and upset for him.

"We've got you, Ev. Just breathe. It'll get better. I promise. You're doing so well."

"When?" he asked. "When's it gonna get better?"

"You've got to give it time," Brennan told him.

Exhaustion dragged Evan into a restless sleep. Hours later, he woke up. Brennan and Alek were still there, watching over him. Alek was asleep in a chair by Evan's left side. Spying the object clutched in Brennan's hands, Evan peered curiously at it.

"What's...."

"Oh. This is for you," Brennan mumbled, embarrassed. His sudden shyness provoked Evan to smile.

Grateful to see even a fleeting moment of happiness in his brother, Brennan only somewhat reluctantly set a furry, white bear in his hand. Its belly was embroidered with 'Get Well Soon'. A cloth bandage was stitched to its head at a cockeyed angle. Evan's smile grew even wider.

"It was between that and flowers, so…. You don't have to keep it if you don't like it."

Tucking the bear under his arm on his good side, Evan said quietly, "I like it. C'mere."

Brennan leaned in. Reading the warm affection in Evan's eyes, he placed a soft kiss to the corner of Evan's bruised mouth and pushed his fingers through Evan's sleep-tousled hair, brushing it back. Flustered to be so close, to finally have an unobserved moment in which he had Evan awake and alert, Brennan's gaze skittered over the angry, ugly wounds, settling on none of them.

"Thanks," Evan whispered. "You get some rest last night?"

Brennan's lips curled in a playful grin. "Some. Luka actually *carried* me to bed from the truck instead of waking me up, if you can believe that. So mortifying."

"And? What happened?"

"Oh, I slept through until morning. *Then*, well…."

"Well? You know, I'm gonna have to live vicariously through you for a while, so spill. Gimme the details."

Glancing around to see if anyone was in earshot, Brennan glimpsed Jimmy out in the hallway, leaning against the far wall. After a moment, Jimmy turned and walked away. There was no one else, but Brennan lowered his voice to barely a whisper anyway and shifted closer to Evan as he spoke.

He described everything as vividly as he could while gently caressing Evan's skin. When he explained how he took Luka's cock and his fingers at the same time, and what Luka hinted could happen next—what he and Alek could both do to him—there was visible heat rising under Evan's previously pale skin, making it rosy and vibrant. It was a hopeful spark of vitality, not a side effect caused by injuries, the medication, or fever.

They sat quietly after that, holding hands.

"Do you think Jimmy suspects anything?" Brennan asked.

"Maybe, but I doubt it. Any more news from Dad? Jimmy mentioned something, but…."

"Not really. He's trying to get here to see you."

"Hmm."

"What? Is that good or bad?"

Evan had no response at first. Then, he admitted, "I honestly don't know. I don't know if it's worth it to see him for a few days just to have him go again, and to have to explain... *this*."

"Yeah," Brennan agreed. "Right now, the most important thing is for you to recover and rest. Everything else can wait. I don't want you doing anything that stresses you out or makes this harder on you than it has to be."

Brennan stroked through the junction of Evan's thumb and index finger. Evan gazed down at the touch and while he was thus distracted, Brennan examined Evan's fragile state. It was hard to see him there, clearly, under the bruises and physical torment. It was hard to get past the fear that no matter what he did to try to help, he was only going to cause Evan more pain.

He weaved their fingers together and placed a kiss to the back of Evan's hand. Monitors beeped. Medication and fluids dripped into tubes hooked up to Evan as he lay there, trapped in his broken body.

Chapter 5
Afraid to Touch

Two challenging, grueling months had passed. Evan lay on his back on the hardwood floor of his room, staring at the ceiling, wondering if his sleeping patterns were ever going to be the same again. If it wasn't the nightmares, it was phantom—or real—pain, yanking him roughly from blissful, peaceful forgetfulness.

He woke earlier than Brennan now. It started when he was still sleeping out in the living room on a chair. He would turn on the TV and try to doze off, but it never worked. The pain from his broken ribs, coupled with a healthy dose of good, old fashioned insomnia, was always too severe to allow it. Now that he was back in the comfort of his own bed, on a real mattress, it was the same damn thing. Not much sleep, lots of questions and nightmares buzzing around his head, and the near-constant noise of his discomfort.

But Evan had begun exercising instead of just lying there like a lump. Maybe that was because of Brennan too—guilt or inspiration. Evan would get out of bed and grab a set of weights from the rack in the corner, and do a few reps in an effort to improve his muscle tone and get his body into even better shape than it was in before the attack. It made him feel better to think he was gradually improving his ability to fight back, should anyone try to overpower him again.

After the free weights, he would do sit-ups and pushups. It was the sit-ups that killed him. Each one hurt him in places that shouldn't hurt. Nevertheless, he pushed past the sharp twinges, making himself do at least as many as he'd done the day before. He even went out on runs with Luka sometimes, while Brennan stayed behind to meditate.

That was where Evan had seen the most difference—how far he could go before becoming out of breath. Cigarette free for two months, one week and six days, he battled cravings all the time but persevered. Evan could run a mile before needing to stop for a break. Luka, the dutiful personal trainer he was, made sure Evan stopped when he should, leaving him with water and a phone before continuing on for another five miles himself, then doubling back to fetch Evan for the run home.

His physical successes lifted Evan's mood. It was a joy to take on the challenge and keep pushing for more. He *didn't* love the nearly unending pain and the cravings he still had, not only for nicotine but also for the painkillers that were prescribed to him after his surgery.

Not once had he slipped up, though. His will strengthened along with his body. If it did get to be too much, of all people it was usually Luka who Evan turned to—raging about how unfair it all was. Luka listened, and sympathized, but encouraged him to keep going anyway, like any good trainer should.

"Two hundred seventeen, two hundred eighteen, two hundred nineteen, two hundred twenty."

Evan collapsed and clasped a hand to his side, sucking in a sharp breath through his teeth when another twinge stabbed deeply into his chest, flaring out through his ribs.

"Fuck it," he huffed, curling up toward his legs yet again, feeling his abdominal muscles clench. He did twenty more before he had to stop for good, and sprawled out, catching his breath.

Struggling to his feet, he shuffled to the bathroom. He popped his head through the doorway to Brennan's room, and waved silently to Luka who was lying there, awake. Brennan was asleep, snoring lightly, and using Luka's chest as a pillow.

Luka tenderly ran his fingers through Brennan's hair, again and again, soothingly as he slept. Evan yearned for a similar kind of comfort which he knew Alek could bring, and Brennan as well.

With his body throbbing from the exercise, sweat dripping down his back and over the new, starkly defined muscles of his chest and stomach, Evan headed to the shower and told himself maybe, just maybe, today would be different. Today would be better. Today, his brother and his boyfriend would stop treating him like an invalid and would finally be willing to give Evan what he desperately craved.

Evan peeled out of his clothes and stood naked in front of the mirror. The water sprayed from the showerhead into the tub, slowly warming in temperature. He traced over the scar on his left side, just under his ribs. It was still dark and fresh, but fully healed over now. He was proud of it, but would be just as glad when it faded more. His nose looked almost the same as it always had, with only a new, slight bump on the bridge. Those were the only physical signs anything had ever happened to him. They seemed insignificant, fully surmountable.

So why, he wondered — not for the first time or the hundredth — wouldn't Brennan or Alek be with him?

Why wouldn't they let him press up close to their bodies in bed? Instead, if he tried to instigate more than an innocent embrace, he was met with a scolding look, grunt, or simple, sudden, noticeable tension before they shifted fractionally away.

Why did they both spurn every advance he made toward intimacy? Neither had laid hands on him for anything more than a too-careful hug or perhaps a caress of his cheek, arm, or leg.

It was maddening. It just served to remind him something was wrong with him, and made him feel guilty for being injured.

Of course, Evan *knew* why. He knew the answers to all of those questions. Alek and Brennan were so afraid of hurting him, it paralyzed them. They were terrified of accidentally knocking an arm against Evan's ribs or connecting with the wrong spot and provoking that dreaded sharp cry of pain that he only let out when he was by himself, working his muscles until they burned. Though his bruises faded and his broken bones were mostly mended, when Alek and Brennan looked at him, they didn't only see Evan as he was — healed and recovering. They saw him bloody and dying, weak and wounded.

The only action Evan had seen in months was his own hand, and only when he was sure he had privacy — either in the shower or when the others were busy. That was mainly because of the shame. They wanted him to wait until he'd been cleared by his doctors for normal activity — sexual or otherwise — but Evan *felt* ready. A couple of weeks before, Evan had pushed himself too hard with a run and wound up back in the emergency room, afraid he'd re-broken a rib.

He hadn't. He was fine, just sore and sprained but, ever since, Alek and Brennan had been overly cautious. They didn't approve of his exercising; since he could do that on his own, though, he did it anyway, without their consent. They had asked him to stop running, stop doing sit-ups and push-ups, and got frustrated with him when he ignored their pleas. Their fear for his health created space. His exercising against their wishes made the space larger. But then the old loneliness would set in. For his whole life, Evan was on his own in so many ways. He lived in a rural town, in a house in the middle of nowhere, without friends or much family. His job isolated him in a garage all day. His absentee father isolated him at home. He had no one but Jimmy — Evan's only friend, a man who was years older than him and, in some ways, more of a father figure than his actual father. After falling in love with Alek and bonding with Brennan, Evan had hoped his days of feeling so intensely alone were blessedly over.

But, they weren't.

Nothing was more infuriating for Evan than the guilt he saw in Alek and Brennan's eyes when they would turn him down yet again whenever he managed, somehow, to shed any semblance of pride and ask outright for them to be with him. Evan had asked so many times, as recently as the night before.

He tried Brennan first, before Alek got home, coming up to him in the kitchen. Evan reached out and touched Brennan, caressing his arm and leaning in for a kiss — just a kiss.

"Wait," Brennan said, sadly, after the briefest touch of his lips. He imagined Brennan's only thought was about the stitches that had been removed from Evan's lip weeks ago, or the remembered sounds of Evan's cries as his bones began to knit back together. He was seeing the past, not the present, and pulled away. It felt like being stabbed in the gut all over again. He wanted to scream at his brother for not trusting him, for not wanting him enough to try. It was because Brennan loved Evan so much that he'd become so hesitant to have sex. It should have been a consolation to know he was loved that much, but the return of the old, agonizing loneliness made it hard to care. Evan knew he was being impatient and maybe a little reckless. Before, it wouldn't have mattered.

Now, it did. Death had followed Evan home from the hospital. His brother sensed the specter waiting in the shadows, ready to pounce. Evan could see it in his eyes, a holdover from the trauma of failing to help Maggie beat her battle with cancer, knowing she was dying, just waiting for it to actually happen.

Give it time, they said. *It's going to take time. You need to heal. You know we love you.*

Funnily enough, Evan knew Luka was willing to provide Evan physical relief. He'd said so himself, in passing. It sounded like a joke at the time, but later Evan had caught Luka looking at his body when he was changing clothes. That was when Evan realized it wasn't a joke at all.

It didn't matter. There had been rules established since Evan was discharged from the hospital for the second time. The rules now governed their four lives and prohibited any intimacy between Evan and Luka whatsoever. Brennan had privately asked Luka to promise not to be with Evan for the very same reasons why Alek and Brennan had agreed between themselves not to be with Evan, for now. Evan felt it very likely Brennan also did it out of spite and a streak of possessiveness. But, it made no real difference one way or another *why* Brennan did it, because Alek had essentially required Evan to be celibate until it was certain his ribs had healed.

"I won't risk you hurting yourself. I can't bear to see you in any more pain," Alek often said.

Or, he'd tell Evan, "We can't. I'd never be able to forgive myself for hurting you."

Then there were the more straightforward commands of, "No," "Don't," and "Stop." They made Evan feel like a scolded dog, when all he'd been seeking was simple affection.

How is someone supposed to go from a life filled with an abundance of sex, to one utterly devoid of it? How am I supposed to not be hurt by them when they shut me out just when I need them the most?

It's because they love me so much, he told himself. *They got scared by the extent of my injuries and the level of my pain. Brennan can't handle the idea of me getting hurt again, or being the cause of it, and Alek is over-protective because he cares.*

It made sense, but it didn't change the way Evan felt. Once they realized Evan was fragile, breakable, and hurting, the safer choice became for them to stay away. But the longer they stayed away, the harder it would be for them to try to come back and take a chance. And the longer they stayed away, the more it felt like he wasn't a lover or a boyfriend at all, but only the old Evan from before Brennan entered his life—closed off from the world and desperately needing, with only himself to rely on. Over the past few months, so much had changed but at the same time, *nothing* had changed.

Evan's shower was a quick one. He scrubbed himself clean of sweat and ran the water through his clipped-short hair before shutting it off. Without another look in the mirror, he went to his room and got dressed. A new bureau now stood beside his old one, full of Alek's clothes since he had officially moved in. Its presence was, like Evan's new exercise regimen, one of the rare bright points in his life. It was needed, tangible proof Alek loved him.

Leaving by the back door, Evan went outside to savor his last day of freedom before having to return to the grind of work. His long sick leave from Mike's Garage was at an end.

This time tomorrow, he thought, *hopefully I'll be under a car or truck, getting my hands dirty—contributing, being useful.* It made his heart swell and put a spring in his step. Very much sick and tired of being coddled, Evan wanted to reclaim life and grab it by the balls, whether his newfound family liked it or not.

It had occurred to Evan, though he didn't like to think about it, it might not be his injuries that kept Brennan from wanting to be with him. Brennan might simply have decided after all what he and Evan had done—have sex—was *wrong*. Just the possibility of that being true hurt more than any broken bones ever could.

What if Brennan doesn't want me anymore? What if he's decided what we were doing was sick and me getting hurt was karmic punishment for committing incest?

Evan simply didn't know and he was too afraid to ask.

Digging his hands down into his pants pockets, he walked, cutting across the lawn, through the fields to the left of the house, toward the woods beyond and the path snaking through it. Wrenching his troubled thoughts away from Brennan, they turned to Alek instead.

Evan lost Alek in some ways that night, outside of the bar. Fallen to the asphalt, Evan stared up through a film of blood which obscured the one he loved for the very last time before unconsciousness yanked it all away. When Evan next awoke, the Alek he fell in love with was gone, and there was someone else there—someone who was Alek but was also not Alek at all—holding his hand and waiting ever so patiently for him to get better.

The new Alek didn't work at a bar; he worked downtown, on the tenth floor of an office building, with a job title so specifically technical Evan kept forgetting exactly what it was. This Alek wore suits every day and brought his lunch to the office in a washable bag which Evan rinsed for him every evening before bed. The purpose of the packed lunch was to save money for Alek's share of the rent he still paid to Presley and Carter even though he really didn't live there anymore. The money was for Evan too, to help cover bills while he was out of work. It was a very responsible and 'new Alek' type of thing to do.

New Alek didn't make sexual advances or indulge in overly passionate kisses that might lead to dangerous things which could theoretically hurt Evan. He didn't touch Evan's body like it was something that drove him wild with desire, like he used to; he touched it like there were shards of glass hidden under the skin.

They slept on their self-appointed sides of the bed each night, and if Evan shifted too close, new Alek shifted away, just in case. This Alek slicked his hair back with gel before he went out and acted like an adult at all times. He didn't make passes at Brennan or dare to dream of getting involved when Brennan and Luka were making love nearby. In fact, he tried to get Evan out of the house entirely, like Evan might get some uncouth ideas if he realized other people still indulged in things like sexual intercourse. This Alek also didn't partake in intimate kissing or touching with Luka, in order to spare Evan the sight of such things which might lead him to get ideas about being with Brennan before he was "officially" ready. Just like Evan, Luka hadn't felt his brother's touch in months either.

And finally, this Alek didn't allow discussion of the existence of the new Alek. He simply worked a nine-to-five job every single day and got home in time for a healthy family dinner around the table — a dinner at which Luka may or may not be present, depending on his work schedule, but Evan and Brennan always were — followed by light conversation in the living room and TV before retiring to bed.

He just doesn't want to be tempted, Evan thought as he walked, deeper and deeper into the shadowy wilderness, his bruised heart feeling like it was being squeezed dry. The part of him that was more mature than his eighteen years scolded his abundance of self-pity, but didn't know how to escape it or let logic triumph over lust.

His primary job used to be taking care of Luka, but now, since Luka doesn't need to be cared for like that anymore, he takes care of me instead. He made so many poor choices when he was my age, he just wants better than that for me. He thinks he can save me from myself if he tries hard enough. He doesn't want me seeing anything that would make me jealous and want to do things that would harm me physically or mentally. I get it. But it's becoming absolutely fucking ridiculous. I just want him to listen to me for a change and believe I'm okay now, that it won't kill me to give in a little bit and at least get a taste of what we used to have. Why can't we at least start to ease back into normalcy? What the hell do I have to do to show them I'm healed and not lying, letting a teenager's libido put my health in danger like he says it is?

Evan walked along the path through dense trees in order to reach a clearing on the other side. Golden, heavenly light filtered down into the small meadow from the treetops above, making the earth glow. Sometimes there were deer here, or rabbits, or groundhogs, but Evan's presence always quickly scared them away. He headed to the center of the grassy expanse and lay down, his body flattening the supple, dew-damp blades all around him. Staring up at the thin, drifting white clouds above in the wide blue sky, Evan tried to remember how wonderful his life used to be, for such a horribly brief time before fear began to rule them all.

He thought of that night in the bathroom of the bar, when he first met Alek, and learned firsthand of the power in him, the determination to claim and possess. It was easier to think of their second sexual encounter though, since it was in a place so similar to the one he was in, how they'd rolled around on the grass, getting dirty, getting off, and not caring about anything but exploring each other. He thought, too, of the night under the stars in the back of the truck, how Alek let Evan call the shots and do exactly what he wanted to do.

Evan's thumb popped the button of his fly, pushing the zipper down halfway. Slipping his hand inside his boxers to wrap around his shaft, he started to stroke himself hard. He thought of Alek — the *old* Alek.

He imagined Alek was out of his mind with desire; he just couldn't take it anymore and needed Evan in the most carnal ways. Alek scratched and clawed at Evan's body, leaving careless marks and bruises without being afraid Evan would hurt, Evan would die. Alek was only reckless and passionate, an animal. He turned Evan inside out with every possible filthy, forbidden touch of his fingers, his tongue, his sweat-slick, hard body and even harder cock.

Evan's hand pumped faster inside his pants as he dreamed of Alek — *his* Alek.

"There you are," Luka said breathlessly with Alek's voice, appearing out of nowhere and slowing rapidly from a full run. He stopped completely a few feet away with a hand braced on his hip, towering over Evan.

Ripped so abruptly from fantasy, Evan yanked his right hand from his pants as soon as he heard the first word from Luka's lips, cursing a muttered, "Fuck," and sitting up as fast as he could manage. He drew one knee to his chest to help hide his erection.

Resting an arm on the knee, Evan turned his head away from Luka, toward the far end of the clearing as he attempted to master his expression. He was blushing fiercely. His jeans hung open in the front. Swallowing his pride, Evan tried on an awkward grin.

"Luka. I didn't hear you coming. The hell are you doing out here? You checkin' up on me?"

"Something like that," he replied, licking his lips wet and taking slow steps closer, his gaze flicking noticeably to Evan's lap and exactly what Evan was failing to disguise. "I was out on a run. Bren texted me when he saw you were gone. He's worried about you."

"What else is new?" Evan muttered bitterly, adding more loudly. "How'd you find me?"

"You're kind of predictable. Hate to tell ya, but it is what it is. So," he cleared his throat, "what's up?"

Evan tiredly wiped a hand over his face, partially out of weariness, partly from shame, partly just wanting to block out the sight of Luka — immaculate, glistening, shirtless and dripping sweat like Evan's desire given life... and *lots* of muscles.

"Spare me the witty puns, please. You can go now."

"You're dismissing me?" Luka smirked, sinking to his knees in the tall grass just inches from Evan.

"I'm trying to. It doesn't seem to be working," he grumbled, shifting his knee slightly to better block Luka's line of sight. The move, however, sent a serrated, cutting pain corkscrewing into Evan's gut. Gritting his teeth to hold in a strangled shout, Evan forced himself to breathe through it. He blew air out between his lips and inhaled deeply through his nose.

"Hey, what's going on?" Luka asked, quite seriously.

Wanting a cigarette or drugs or simply to escape, Evan shook his head. "You know, I'd really appreciate it if *you* didn't treat me like a child or an invalid or like I'm gonna try to off myself again. I get plenty of that from everyone else."

"Is that how you think we see you?"

"Don't you?"

"No."

"Bullshit. That's bullshit! If you all had one ounce of confidence in me or respect for me, I wouldn't have to fucking sneak away to just to have some peace without some wannabe Daddy figure trying to tell me what's good for me!"

While yelling, Evan threw his arms open in a wild gesture. It pulled something in his bad side. His eyes instantly flooded with tears. His mouth fell open around a harsh gasp and for a second he couldn't breathe for the pain. Making a small, broken sound, he tried to blink his eyes clear. Tears slipped down his cheeks. Then Luka was on him, guiding Evan carefully down onto his back. He placed a hand on Evan's chest while the other cupped the side of Evan's face.

"Okay, you're okay," Luka said softly, calmly. Evan wasn't sure if it was for his sake or Luka's own because he could detect a chilly under-layer of fear behind the soothing tone, the kind he sensed in Alek quite often now. "Small breaths, come on. It'll pass. There ya go."

Pursing his lips against a soft whine, Evan closed his eyes as he did as Luka said. Gradually, too gradually, the ache became merely overwhelming instead of crippling. Silent tears continued to fall. When he was past it completely a minute later, Evan still couldn't look at Luka, who was still hovering over him, touching him.

At least he's touching me, Evan thought hopelessly, wondering why hope was so hard to hold on to. *At least I'm not alone.*

Chapter 6
Undone

"This is only gonna make it worse, isn't it? When they find out, they're still not gonna believe I'm getting better. They'll be more worried than ever and—"

"Evan...."

"It's been months, Luka. *Months*," Evan growled, his voice sounding choked with emotion. "Alek can barely look at me without being afraid and don't pretend you don't see it—how he is around me. And Brennan won't let me in. It's like I have some disease, like *I* have cancer now. So I got hurt! So what?! It happens! And I'm just so fucking *lonely*, you know? I just don't want to be the one that's fucked up anymore! I want to feel like they love me again. I *miss* them. I miss them *so much*."

Later, Luka wasn't sure what came over him or why he did it. It was like Evan was a new drug, his heartbreaking tears slipping in under Luka's defenses and logic, distorting them.

Dipping his head, angling it to the side, Luka sucked a hard kiss to Evan's mouth. It made Evan whimper beautifully. Parting his soft, luscious lips, Evan let Luka lick back past them into the warm, wet heat of him. That first taste had Luka irrevocably hooked. Framing Evan's sweet face in his hands, Luka held Evan down so he could be properly, thoroughly kissed, like he deserved to be kissed. Licking hungrily over Evan's tongue, sucking his lips, Luka plunged in deeply and took as much as he could get, taking everything until he was dizzy and pulsing with primal lust for *Evan*—alluring, magnificently flawed and held tightly beneath him.

Needing to get his hands on Evan, skin-to-skin, Luka reached down and guided Evan's erection free of his pants. Moaning Evan's name, Luka felt out the silk-sheathed, steely flesh now trapped within his grip, sliding smoothly against Luka's palm, through his fingers as he stroked. Evan gasped audibly, mouthing over Luka's lips, grabbing hold of Luka by the back of the neck, breathing hot and fast. Starkly blue eyes framed in long, golden eyelashes, surrounded by light freckles, closed over with heady relief.

Watching his hand move, staring fixedly down between their bodies, Luka ravaged Evan with his eyes as well as his fingers, tugging hard on Evan's cock one moment, rubbing feather-light over Evan's torso the next, over his washboard abs and up to the rosy, silken nub of his nipple. Needing to touch him absolutely everywhere, Luka tried to, lightly caressing every inch of flesh he could access by shoving clothing impatiently out of the way.

"Tell me to stop. Evan," Luka begged, "*Please* tell me to stop. Tell me it hurts."

Trembling, chasing each touch, reacting with evident greed for more, Evan thrust against Luka's hand desperately when it grazed teasingly over his shaft. Evan bit down on his bottom lip, surged up as he tried to rub against Luka's body, moaned softly in a way that was so sexy it shattered what was left of Luka's resolve not to hurt Brennan like this, by willfully ignoring his heartfelt promises to be faithful, to respect Brennan and Alek's wishes and leave Evan alone.

Luka sat back on his heels, taking hold of Evan's jeans and underwear. After pulling them down and off, he nudged Evan's legs apart with a knee. Leaning over him, they were face-to-face and his restless fingers now had even more places to explore. Luka palmed the right side of Evan's ass, tilting Evan's hips and squeezing lightly. Inhaling the heady, clean, freshly-showered scent of him, Luka licked with the tip of his tongue up the side of Evan's neck, tasting his skin and just *Evan*.

"Luka, kiss me," Evan begged, sounding hoarse, parting his thighs more in invitation, letting his knees fall open widely. "Be with me."

Luka moaned, surging in for an un-careful, bruising kiss. His busy hand kept exploring, tugging gently on the soft skin of Evan's balls, rubbing under and behind them, over the sensitive, smooth spot there. Just barely, Luka's fingertips skimmed over Evan's hole before quickly stroking back up to squeeze in a slow, tight stroke up from the root of Evan's cock to the tip. He rubbed over the crown when it wept pre-come, spreading the slick fluid around. Tracing Evan's shape, he triggered nerves that hadn't been stimulated in a long time, sensing Evan's intense pleasure, getting off on it. Evan quivered and tensed, almost thrusting against Luka's hand but holding back like he was afraid to give in to instinct. As Luka gazed down avidly, he watched as Evan forced himself to not move at all, putting himself utterly at Luka's mercy.

Nipping at the swell of Evan's bottom lip, then licking over it, Luka was breathing more roughly than if he had just sprinted ten miles, every inch of his already deeply tanned skin flushed pinker now, sweat-slick and overheated. He was hugely hard, but using every ounce of what little restraint he had left to keep from grinding frantically against all of Evan's bare skin and possibly re-injuring his ribs. Twisting up and down Evan's erection, over and over again, Luka milked a few more clear drops from his slit and growled, dragging a thumb through the fluid. Slinking down low, crouching between Evan's parted thighs, Luka touched the tip of Evan's dick to his tongue, licking hungrily over it in a wide stripe, then sucking it clean.

Closing his lips just behind the ridge, Luka tongued repeatedly over the smooth, salty, hot flesh. Evan cried out with pleasure instead of pain and tangled both hands in Luka's long hair, holding on to him, and pleading beautifully in small, choked grunts and gasps for more.

So, Luka gave him more. He sucked hard, taking Evan in. Evan's cock slid thick and hot over Luka's tongue and back into his throat until his lips were kissed around the root before slowly pulling back off. Evan fell, soaked in saliva, from Luka's lips. When Luka didn't continue and instead crawled back up Evan's body, Evan made a frantic, impassioned sound. He gripped Luka by the neck and shoulder, clawing at him in lieu of pleading with words.

Staring hard right into Evan's lust-drunk but unbearably bewildered eyes, Luka knew in his heart what he was going to do and, by doing it, he was betraying both Alek and Brennan.

"*Fuck*. Evan, God help me...."

It came out sounding apologetic, but also wildly animalistic. Luka tried to warn Evan he couldn't stop now; it was too late to say no.

Then, Evan gave him permission. "Okay," he said. "It's okay."

He turned his face into the touch when Luka brushed the backs of his fingers gently through the hollow of Evan's jaw. Luka nuzzled Evan's neck for a brief, tender moment, then straightened. He pushed two thick fingers through Evan's full lips which kissed instantly around them, then slid his fingers back along Evan's tongue. Evan sucked them, his tongue curling around them, licking between, over and around to get them as wet as he could. Luka worked them in and out, staring at the way Evan's lips pursed around the fingers, his eyes now closed.

Luka withdrew his fingers and reached down between Evan's legs, rubbing over Evan's puckered hole, stimulating the skin. A sweet, sharp exhale, a small frown, and moist, parted lips were Luka's reward as he savored the moment, letting Evan ready himself and try to relax.

Luka pushed two fingers through the ring of muscle. Evan grunted, grasping Luka as he spread the fingers, pulling Evan open, rotating and bending them to work his sphincter loose. Luka felt Evan shiver and shifted his legs, breathing more roughly. Sucking light kisses to Evan's trembling lower lip, Luka moaned Evan's name over and over again, like a prayer.

Luka tugged his fingers free. Looking nervous but ready, Evan didn't wait to be asked, and rolled, flipping over onto his hands and knees. He glanced back as Luka moved to kneel between his legs, pushing his exercise shorts down and out of the way. Spitting thickly into his palm, Luka used the saliva to wet his dark, heavy cock, cradled in a hand. A hard shiver raced down Evan's spine, pebbling his skin from head to toe.

Planting both hands on Evan's ass, Luka spread his cheeks and angled his own hips so his dick fit snugly at Evan's opening. The contact made Evan shudder and moan. He grabbed handfuls of the grass beneath him as Luka gripped Evan by the hips and pulled him back, effectively impaling him. Thrusting just hard enough to squeeze past Evan's rim, Luka breached him as Evan let out a breathy groan. When he met resistance, Luka withdrew slightly and spit on his hand. After smearing the fluid on himself, Luka tried again, thrusting inside a little harder, needing to make Evan take it all and have his cock fit completely inside.

Evan swallowed soft sounds Luka could barely make out, pushing back onto the flesh filling him up as Luka split him open. Luka curled forward to fit himself to Evan's back, pressing in the last few inches until they were fully joined. Breathing roughly against Evan's neck, feeling Evan's whole body thrumming under and around him, Luka moaned brokenly. Soft, delicate tissue perfectly gripped him, hugged around his thick, throbbing girth.

"Oh *God*, yeah... Evan... *Evan*. Wanted you. Feel so good. Wanted you like this for *so long. God*...."

Thrusting shallowly, Luka stayed mostly buried and pushed helplessly in, repeatedly, like somehow he could get deeper and take over Evan completely. Luka moaned and rode Evan slowly, wanting it to last. Reaching around under Evan's hips, Luka brought him off with only a few squeezing tugs. Luka breathed deeply to rein in his own orgasm as Evan fluttered around him in climax. Rippling squeezes and contractions of muscle barraged Luka as Evan quivered with a release that was much too long overdue.

Evan came, crying out roughly, arms unsteady as he held himself up. Luka pumped him with a hand until he softened and only pulsed dry. Once he was done, Luka used him, taking his time with deeper, longer strokes, pulling out of Evan completely once only to realign and plunge back in, popping through Evan's hole, and making Evan moan wantonly. Luka watched avidly as his length was swallowed up by Evan's pink pucker. Luka fucked him for long, long minutes, trying to make up for all of the times they'd been unable to be together, though Luka had watched so avidly, and imagined what it would be like, to feel and fuck Evan like he'd wanted to so badly. He held back his orgasm whenever it got close, taking a moment to wait for it to fade back again, then resuming once more.

With Luka moving easily within him, Evan sighed deliriously as Luka draped over him. Luka got as close as he possibly could, pressing open-mouthed kisses to the spot just below and behind Evan's ear. Luka shuddered hard, ready to release. His hips twitched and slapped against the curve of Evan's tight ass. Whimpering, Luka fit himself to Evan, rutting helplessly as he spilled a huge load of come deeply into Evan.

"*Motherfuck*. I should've pulled out. The hell was I thinking? Damn it," Luka panted as he came down. "I'm sorry."

"Don't sweat it," Evan rasped with a woozy chuckle.

"How are you? Are you okay?"

Evan nodded, smiling more when Luka wrapped an arm around him, palming his belly, kissing his ear. "I'm fine. I'm great, actually. That was... *mmm*."

Luka sighed, kissing the corner of Evan's mouth. Evan pressed back onto him and closed his eyes, a happy, sated expression lighting his face. "Yeah. It was," Luka agreed. "I guess we proved you're getting better, huh?"

Evan exhaled sharply, his smile vanishing as realization set in. In a small voice, he asked fearfully, "What did we do? What the hell did we just do?"

"Made love," Luka said softly, caressing down the side of Evan's waist, the tickling touch making him shiver.

Evan reached behind himself to hold Luka, pulling him closer.

Sounding guilt-stricken, he said, "They're gonna *hate me*."

"Don't. They're not gonna hate you," Luka hissed, burying his face in Evan, embracing him more tightly when he felt Evan's breath hitch with tears.

Once they were both somewhat clothed and standing in the middle of the flattened swath of grass around them, Evan first hesitated, then went to Luka, getting swallowed up in Luka's awaiting arms. Encircling Evan with his arms, Luka felt him clinging frightfully.

"It's gonna be fine, Ev," Luka hushed to him, not really believing it himself.

"How?" Evan groaned. "How is this gonna be fine?"

"...I don't know. But we'll figure it out. *I'll* figure it out. Let me worry about it."

Evan broke away from him, snapping, "No, not gonna happen. This concerns me, too. We *both* promised this wouldn't happen. You made Brennan promise to put you first, to be your boyfriend above all else and he did! He stayed away from me, just like you wanted. How am I supposed to go back there now and face him? For Christ's sake, we're both covered in each other's bodily fluids. And yours are kind of starting to drip down the inside of my thigh."

Rubbing a hand over his mouth, trying to come up with a plan, Luka was ripped from his thoughts by this, his gaze drifting right to Evan's thighs.

"Luka!"

"Sorry. Yeah. Okay. Okay, I know what we can do. We have to get cleaned up before we can do anything, and going to your place isn't really an option, so… okay." Luka pulled out his phone and started to type a message.

"What are you doing?"

"Sending Bren a text," Luka mumbled, clicking at the tiny keys. "'Need to run home. Be back later.' There. Done. Come on, we'll jump in my truck. It's parked around back of the house and Brennan's probably meditating anyway."

"Well, what if he's not? What if he's waiting for us? He'll take one look at us and know. He'll know we cheated on them and what the hell am I supposed to say to him?"

Luka sighed and kissed Evan's forehead. "Such a worrywart. It's just Brennan. If he's waiting, we'll address it somehow before we get cleaned up. No big deal."

The wide-eyed, scared expression didn't leave Evan's face, though, so Luka took him by the hand and started to lead him slowly back to the house.

Chapter 7
Illicit Activity

There was no sign of Brennan when Luka and Evan arrived, so they got into Luka's truck. Luka started it up and they were cruising down the road before anything else could happen. Minutes later, crossing a few towns, as the miles slipped away, the buildings began to crowd in closer and closer until the fields were gone and they were in the much more urban town of Michellsburg. Pulling up to Luka's home, they sat in the cab without moving to get out, both of them eyeing the vehicles in the driveway. Presley and Carter both appeared to be home and it was possible Jamie was there, too.

"Shit. Okay. Let's see." Luka rooted around in the space behind the seats "Ooh. Perfect." He pulled out a knit cap, handing it to Evan. "Wear this. Be Brennan."

"Be Brennan. That's your solution?"

"Yeah. It's just so we can get upstairs. They won't question it. They see me bring Bren home all the time. Sometimes he wears contact lenses."

"This is so fucked up," Evan groaned, but he put the hat on and went with Luka's plan because of the intensity of his need to shower. Overly focused on how Luka kept taking his hand like Evan was *his* now, Evan followed along beside the looming, enormous man who used to just be a complicated sort of friend and now had suddenly become a lover. Or, rather, *another* lover since Evan had two of those already. Trying not to fixate on exactly what sort of reaction Alek and Brennan would have when they found out what had happened, Evan and Luka walked through the front door, heading right for the staircase leading to the second floor.

Luck was not entirely with them as they passed the den. It was full of the three people they suspected to be at home. Evan plastered on what he hoped was a friendly, easy, Brennan-esque smile and waved.

"Hey Luka. Brennan. What's goin' on?"

"Not much," Luka called back, not slowing down, his thumb dragging distractedly over the skin on the underside of Evan's wrist, sending a wriggling tickle racing out over Evan's body. "How are you guys?"

"Not bad. You wanna join us? Cowboys are on," Carter offered as Luka and Evan began to ascend the steps.

"Maybe later. Thanks."

Evan's heart hammered in his chest. His breathing quickened. His legs felt sticky with Luka's come trickling down them. His ass throbbed in a not unpleasant way from the long, hard pounding Luka had so recently given it and a constant, dull ache spread throughout Evan's ribcage. It was probably time for another handful of ibuprofen, the only pain medication he was allowing himself, but he didn't have any on him. The one thing bothering him most, though, was how he was pretending to be his brother in order to avoid discovery of the fact — the *fact* — that Evan had just fucked the man his brother was in love with.

"I'm a bastard. I'm an evil, heartless, bastard," Evan said with marked awe as Luka pulled him into the bathroom and shut the door behind them.

"I'd argue maybe it's because your heart is so *big* you keep getting into trouble," Luka retorted, fitting himself flush to Evan's back. Pushing up the front of Evan's dirty shirt, Luka worked it off of him, taking Evan's arms with it so they were pulled momentarily over his head. Evan hissed at the stretch, wincing as the shirt fell away and his arms came back down. They overlapped Luka's which were already wrapping him from behind. Luka carefully touched the scar and watched Evan's reaction in the mirror.

"You're completely full of it, you know."

"Does it hurt?" Luka touched the wound, and the previously-fractured ribs.

"I think it's always gonna hurt. Doesn't mean I can't live my life anyway." Evan clenched his jaw as Luka tilted his hips, thrusting in a gentle drag against the seat of Evan's pants. Luka hooked a thumb in the waistband of Evan's jeans, inching them down on his hips. It made Evan tingle with want and lean back instinctively against Luka, seeking more. Luka exhaled sharply and reached inside, under Evan's come-soiled boxers, fondling him as he thickened.

"*Luka,*" Evan moaned.

"I still want you," he growled softly, tugging, groping. "Can't stop thinking about my come running down your thighs, how wet and stretched you must be. I could slide right into you. Wanna be in you again...."

"We shouldn't. We really —"

"It's not like we all haven't crossed the line with each other before. Like I didn't have to watch Alek suck Bren off, or watch Brennan put his hands all over you, screwing you when he should have been with me. I've helped you fuck him. You ordered Alek to fuck me. It's all tangled. It's just sex."

"No, this is different. This feels different," Evan argued in a small voice, staring at Luka in the mirror as the rest of his clothes were peeled from his body. The betrayal felt worse because of the emotions and sentiment behind it. They were both cheating with their hearts more so than their bodies. Evan felt Luka inside of him, a piece of him left behind to linger in his heart. The possessive fire behind Luka's eyes, reflected in the mirror, said maybe Evan had already been precious to Luka for quite a while, though now it'd been made permanent. Now, Luka wasn't ever going to let him go.

Both of Luka's hands slid down the sides of Evan's body, along the tapered line from his shoulders to his pelvis, hooking over his narrow hips and drawing them back. Evan knew what Luka wanted. He grasped the counter's edge and pushed out his ass, dropping his gaze, helplessly undulating when Luka leaned in to kiss his neck while fondling between Evan's legs. Fingertips rubbed through the sticky come leaking from Evan's hole. Luka growled and nipped at the side of Evan's jaw. Not wasting a second, he pulled his cock out, grabbed Evan by the waist and thrust, entering him, drawing a startled, wrenching cry.

It was easier the second time. There was less discomfort, even more pleasure. Letting out every ounce of want that had been bottled up inside both of them for months, Luka violated Evan, who was bent sharply at the waist, fitting into him like he belonged there; claiming Evan for his own. He began to suck a dark bruise under Evan's jaw once Evan's head fell to the side, exposing more of his neck. Evan pressed back onto Luka, inviting every rut, begging softly for more.

Luka's fingers found Evan's nipple, playing with it as they made love. Emotions flitting between angst-riddled and blissful, for Evan it felt like what Luka was doing to him was taking him apart on a fundamental level. He rocked gently back into each penetration. Reaching behind his shoulder, Evan tugged on Luka's hair, gasping and moaning as each stroke raked over his prostate.

Luka whispered things in a low, gravelly voice near Evan's ear as they moved together. Things like, "This isn't about them. It's about you, and me, and how fucking beautiful you are. If they can't give you what you need, I will. I'll give you everything. *Everything.*" He clasped Evan to him, grunting hard as he released, coating Evan's passage with another load of come, marking him again as Luka's.

It was all a blur of intoxicating touching, mind-blowing, blissful sensation, and burrowing, radiating ache. The words of protest sat on his tongue but Evan couldn't voice them. His need for exactly what Luka was giving him silenced him utterly. Evan's will and loyalty shattered at the way Luka took him. It was intense, sweet, slow and deep.

When Luka was spent, he sank to his knees at Evan's feet. Turning him around and swallowing down Evan's reddened cock, Luka gave him a lazy, thorough blowjob.

He drew it out, making it last as long as possible. Luka dragged his fingers through the semen leaking from Evan, stroking in, out, around and inside his tender rim. Rubbing his hole, then sheathing two fingers in Evan's ass, Luka explored every inch. It was possessive and unhurried. Luka sucked every last brain cell Evan had left out through the tip of his dick.

As soon as Evan was close, stiffening and preparing to unload, Luka pulled off. Three fingers were stuffed to the hilt inside Evan's hole, tapping his gland, triggering his prostate relentlessly as Luka milked him dry. Thick, pearly white seed spurted from Evan's slit. Some splattered onto Luka's face, over his mouth and chin. Luka hungrily licked away the thick drips that began to run down the underside of Evan's cock, sucking the head clean.

Evan knew, vaguely, he was crying out. He was probably being far too loud, but, as he trembled and climaxed hard enough to white out his vision, he just couldn't bring himself to care who heard.

However, he was quiet in the shower moments later, letting Luka wash him off. Standing there like he was in a trance, Evan didn't realize Luka could tell he was in real pain until they were drying off and Luka handed him some brand-name painkillers and a glass of water from the tap.

"Thanks," Evan murmured, swallowing them greedily down. He squeezed his eyes shut through a random, twisting twinge that eventually faded.

"I'm gonna go find you some clean clothes to wear. Take your time. Meet me in my room when you're ready," Luka told him tenderly. Evan nodded and stretched up on his toes, brushing his lips over Luka's as Luka held Evan's jaw. The tips of their tongues touched then tangled in a fervent kiss both of them moaned softly through.

Luka threw on a pair of shorts and went downstairs, remembering Brennan left some things to be washed, thinking there might be clothes for Evan in the laundry room. He was right, and Luka grabbed some pants and a shirt, racing back with them to the steps.

He ran into Presley at the landing.

"Oh, hey. Brennan asked to borrow this and I keep forgetting to give it to him," Presley started, holding up a CD. He stopped as Evan emerged from the bathroom. Though he and Luka were standing at the bottom of the steps and Evan was at the top and at the far end of the hall, Presley could see him clearly enough. He was wrapped in a towel at the waist, the scar on his mid-section perfectly visible, his short hair sticking up in tousled, dark spikes as he walked into Luka's room without noticing he was being watched.

"That's not Brennan." Presley turned to Luka, astonished, horrified. "Luka, what the hell is going on? Why is Evan—?"

"It just happened, okay? Let it go," Luka whispered, taking the disc out of Presley's hand.

"It just happened?!" Presley hissed back. "You didn't actually.... Holy shit, you did, didn't you? Are you out of your fucking mind, Popović?!"

Presley smacked him hard on the shoulder like he was trying not to punch him in the jaw instead. "You really can't keep it in your pants, can you? Even when you've got a really, really good thing going. I thought you *loved* him. I thought you guys were happy!"

"It's not like that." Luka frowned, dragging Presley farther from the steps so no one else overheard. "I'm still with Brennan. Nothing's wrong. It's just complicated."

"You bet your ass it is, now. Alek is gonna seriously fuck you up, man. Even more than usual, too. Evan's got an excuse. He's just a kid who's been through hell and he's probably confused by all the screwing around you all do. *You* know better, or you should. What made you do it? Was his ass just that tempting?"

With a hard look into his eyes, Luka glared defiantly back at his friend. "I don't expect you to understand."

"The fuck has gotten into you? Hell yes, I understand. You saw something you liked and so you took it. I know that shit very well, son. And now Brennan and Alek, and Evan most of all, are the ones who are gonna pay for it."

"No one else hears what he's going through. *I'm* the one he talks to. *Me.* Alek and Bren are dealing with it in their own ways but they're both too scared of losing Evan to actually listen to what *he* needs. They think shutting him out and handling him like he's gonna shatter at any given moment will protect him. But all that's really doing is making him think nobody gives a *fuck* about him, that he's on his own and can't confide in them. I'm not gonna stand for that! He deserves better and I'm not gonna stand by and let him beat on himself anymore for not being good enough when I can do something to help him be happy."

"You're fucking ignorant if you think this will make Evan happy."

Hurt, Luka backed away. He shook his head, dropping his gaze to the floor before turning and sprinting up the steps, leaving Presley standing there, watching him go.

Luka burst into the bedroom. Evan was standing there, biting nervously on a thumbnail. He smiled broadly when Luka appeared, and did in fact look incredibly happy, despite it all—for the moment, at least. Joy became colored with confusion when Luka gathered Evan to his bare chest, holding him close. Guilt for betraying Brennan, fear of what was going to happen next, and pure, newfound love for Evan all burned through Luka's heart. Evan's fingertips skittered over Luka's chest, brushing against him like butterfly wings.

He wanted to promise Evan so many things—that he could make it all better, that he could keep him safe, that no one was going to get hurt—but he just couldn't. He couldn't lie. Nothing seemed right except the feel of Evan in Luka's arms.

"I'm sorry," Luka professed, choking on the words. "I just couldn't stand to see you hurting anymore. It was killing me. I didn't mean to do anything to hurt Bren or Alek. I really didn't."

Evan made a soft sound and tilted his chin up, combing his fingers back through Luka's damp, tangled hair, opening for him like a flower as they fell into a kiss.

"We can do this," Luka resolved. "We'll tell them. We have to be honest. And no matter what—whatever happens—I will not abandon you, okay? *I won't give you up.* I need you."

"*Luka,*" Evan sighed. It shifted into a moan as Luka claimed Evan's mouth yet again, while lifting him up. He hooked his hands under Evan's legs, which wound readily around Luka's waist. Luka held him, worshiped him like a treasure, uniquely special all on his own, stealing his heart away.

Chapter 8
Splintered

Luka and Evan lingered beside Luka's truck in the driveway of Evan and Brennan's house, knowing Alek and Brennan were inside, as they had been asked to be. After ignoring numerous calls from both Alek and Brennan all day long, Luka had finally called them back an hour earlier, requesting they all meet because they needed to talk.

The autumn sunset lit the heavens with purples, pinks and burnt oranges, streaked with thin, insubstantial remnants of clouds. Luka held Evan's wind-chilled face in both of his warm hands, tracing with the pads of his fingertips the contours of his cheekbones, lips, and the delicate skin under his bright, beautiful eyes. They were ringed with faint dark circles brought by Evan's fits of weeping, his insomnia and the strain of his ill health. The gravel from the driveway crunched under their heels as they shifted in place. Crickets called to each other from the grass. Bats swooped through the gathering dusk. There was a brisk, biting coldness in the air, seeping under their skin, drawing them closer together in search of warmth.

"Don't say it," Evan said plaintively. His hands wrapped Luka's arms, grasping tightly like they were the only thing connecting him to sanity. Closing his eyes, Evan seemed to gradually relax thanks to Luka's delicate, explorative touches, but the furrow in his brow stubbornly remained. "Don't say it. You don't mean it. You don't. We just screwed around. It didn't mean anything. It doesn't have to mean anything."

"I'm in love with you. I think I've been falling in love with you since I met you; I just didn't realize it."

Evan's expression crumpled. His full lips drew back as he

sucked in a rough breath, burying his face in Luka's chest, holding his breath. His hands twisted in Luka's shirt. His parted lips dragged over the cotton fabric covering Luka's broad chest which Evan had spent most of the day lying against, as they covered each other with kisses and love bites.

"How am I supposed to do this? I can't do this to them."

"Do you love them any less? Hmm? Do you?"

"No. Of course not."

"Then it'll be okay."

"I want to believe you but it sounds like a lie. Because all I want right now is for you to take me the hell out of here and go far, far away where no one can find us and we can be together and nothing else matters. I don't want to hurt them like this."

"It's not a lie," Luka said gently, sweetly, tilting Evan's face up with a finger hooked under his chin, pleading with his eyes. "Running away won't help anything. You'll just feel more miserable about it and miss them. I'll handle it. Okay? If you don't want to say anything, you don't have to. Just being there and facing them will help. We've been over this. We know the plan. We just need to do it. Face it. Man up."

Evan nodded, gathering courage. "Okay."

Luka took two steps towards the building before Evan caught his hand and held him there for one more moment. Dropping his head when Luka looked back at him, Evan chewed on his lip and said in a choked, rough voice, "I do love you. *I love you.*"

Luka sighed, clutching Evan to him one last time.

Somehow they made it inside, going through the back door and the kitchen, into the living room. Alek and Brennan were there. They immediately seemed to spot the dark circles Evan knew were under his badly bloodshot eyes, the too-pale hue of his skin as fear made his blood drain away, and the undiluted misery in his expression. It visibly stirred panic in them, which was only intensified when Evan also couldn't meet their gazes. He stared right at the floor, hovering near Luka but careful not to actually touch him. With his arms wound tightly around himself, Evan sank onto the couch, bouncing a knee restlessly, curling forward and biting hard at the insides of his cheeks.

His expression grave, Luka nervously tucked his hair behind his ears and sat beside Evan, weaving his fingers together and resting his forearms on his knees. They didn't say a word—not even hello. Brennan was seated in the large, stuffed chair, his right leg curled back to his chest. Alek was standing and pacing back and forth, wearing a pair of carefully pressed trousers and an unbuttoned dress-shirt, with a white t-shirt underneath. His hair was combed slickly back but one tendril escaped, curling at the side of his chiseled face.

"What the hell is going on?" Alek demanded. "Evan, you know I don't like you leaving the house without telling us where you're going. You didn't answer your cell or check in with us at all today! Do you know how worried we were?!"

Since the attack, Alek's aversion to Evan being out by himself had increased exponentially. Evan knew some of this reaction was because the guy he went out behind the bar to protect had disappeared completely. One day the other victim had been recovering nicely in the hospital, the next he was gone, checked out, and nowhere to be found. The men who stabbed and beat Evan had been sent to county jail, awaiting trial, and were there still. But the possibility remained, for Alek at least, that the gang had friends who might seek out Evan for the trouble he'd caused. To Evan it seemed like a stretch, and paranoia. Alek wouldn't let it go, though. So, usually, they didn't talk about it. It only came up in vague reference in times like this one, where Alek's inability to reach Evan at a moment's notice caused him to jump to the most extreme conclusions, like there'd been a drive-by shooting while Evan was out for some fresh air.

Evan averted his eyes and stayed quiet, resenting Alek's patronizing tone. Alek continued, "Why were you two gone all day without an explanation, and why the formal meeting? Did something happen?"

Alek glanced between them. "Say something! You're really freaking us out."

"Yeah, something happened," Luka nodded tightly. "Evan and I were out... talking. He was upset about some things, and I was trying to help him. I wanted him to tell me what was wrong, and he did. He vented and seemed to feel better afterward.

"Then," Luka continued, tripping over the words. "Things happened. We, um. We had sex. I know we should have talked to you two first, and we feel incredibly bad about that, but—"

Alek cut him off with a slice of his hand through the air. Jaw clenched, eyes blazing, Alek seemed to be zeroing in on how destroyed Evan looked. Rather than thinking this was due to worry, Evan suspected Alek was wrongly assuming it was because of what Luka and Evan did together.

Alek was still and silent for one small moment before losing control and screaming at his brother, "*Did you hurt him?! DID YOU?!*"

Evan covered his face with both hands, whining in the back of his throat like he was just kicked in the chest. Luka circled Evan's back with an arm.

"No. I'd *never* hurt him," Luka said defensively. "It only happened because of how much I care about him, and *I* am not afraid to show him that! Maybe if you weren't keeping your distance so fucking much Evan wouldn't be feeling like you've abandoned him!"

"Abandoned him," Alek echoed. "I *abandoned* him?! Why do you think I work downtown every day? Why the *fuck* am I busting my ass to be a better man for him? Why do I stay here every damn night watching over him and taking care of him if I fucking ABANDONED HIM?!"

"Emotional abandonment, Alek," Luka clarified. "You stopped asking Evan what he wants. So *I* did. I asked. He's not going to break if you get too close, you know. He's healing—"

"He almost died! He fucking almost *died* and it's only been—"

Luka cut Alek off, continuing, "He's going back to work tomorrow! He's been going on runs and working out! He's doing great! I'm so proud of him and how far he's come. So why won't you be with him? Do you know how cruel that is?"

"That's bullshit. *I* do love him. His doctor ordered him to abstain from physical exertion until his next check-up. I'm not selfish enough to risk his health just to get off. His recovery is more important than my desire to fuck him, but clearly you don't feel the same way, huh? It isn't *my fault* you forced yourself on him. You were just horny and jealous and, as usual, couldn't keep it in your pants."

Alek seethed and Luka got to his feet, looking like he was ready to fight. Evan glanced up, panicked. Brennan was pale, his eyes directed up at the ceiling, blinking rapidly and looking like he was trying not to cry. "No. Luka, don't. *Don't.*"

Brennan cut in, his voice soft and hollow — hurt but not angry. "How many times?"

Luka looked to Brennan, the anger deflating from him all at once, leaving him only bruised and shamefaced. It seemed to occur to him, then, how every harsh accusation directed at Alek had also struck Brennan. "Bren...."

"More than once?"

Folding his arms over his chest, Luka hung his head. Brennan took a deep breath and nodded with resigned acceptance. Evan stared pleadingly, regretfully at his brother, wanting to ask for forgiveness. The thing that hurt the most was how Brennan was able to meet his gaze levelly, openly, wearing his heart on his sleeve.

"I'm *so sorry*," Evan told him. He began to stand. A searing pain sent him grabbing at his side, and swallowing a low, shuddering groan.

Instantly concerned, Alek stepped forward, focused only on Evan. He went to him, kneeling by his feet. Hanging his head, Evan got lost in the fog of ache, letting it distract from his emotional torment. He waited for the pain to pass, wishing Alek wasn't so sweetly holding his hand, but needing the reassuring contact nonetheless.

The pain didn't ease up or go away, but neither did the confrontation they were all in the middle of. Evan didn't have to see Luka's face to know Luka was wishing he was in Alek's place at Evan's side, but was holding himself back.

Brennan must have seen it too, because his next question for Luka was, "You love him. You're in love with him, aren't you? I can tell. All of that time you've been spending together alone lately...."

"It doesn't mean I love you any less," Luka said urgently. He moved toward Brennan but when Brennan held up a hand, Luka stopped dead in his tracks. "We're family now, right? The four of us? There were never clearly defined boundaries here. If we're going to have sex with each other, shouldn't we all love each other, too? Evan and I didn't do anything bad or terrible! *I love you*, Brennan. And *Alek*... after everything... you're *everything* to me." Luka clutched his heart, his face tensing with emotion. "Yes, I love Evan, too. Of course I love him."

"I didn't plan for this to happen. Neither of us did," said Evan speaking quietly through teeth gritted against a scream of agony that kept wanting to bubble up. "I just wanted to be alone but, Luka, he found me and... he *found* me. There's been this distance lately. I understand you just want to protect me. Both of you." He took a shaky inhale and his connection to the world seemed to thin, growing tenuous. The room tilted and shifted. His eyes rolled deliriously. He swayed backward and for a second he almost lost consciousness. Alek guided Evan to lean back against the cushion and shot Brennan a starkly worried look. "I-I really am sorry, Alek. Bren. We shouldn't have been sneaking around behind your backs. We should have been able to stop and talk to you first. That's the rule, right? That's how this is supposed to work."

Alek's gaze slid over to Luka, and turned mean. "*You*. You did this to him! He's in pain because of you and whatever the fuck you did to him, you son of a bitch!" Lashing out at the easiest target—the only target—Alek was up and on his feet in a heartbeat, slamming into Luka, knocking him back into the wall with a crash, his hand locked around Luka's throat, squeezing his windpipe.

"No! Don't," Evan cried. "*Please.*"

Standing from his seat, Brennan ran a hand back through his hair and blurted, "I can't. I can't be here. I can't deal with this shit right now. I just can't." Without another look back at Evan or any of them, Brennan left, grabbing a sweatshirt from a hook on the wall, going outside through the front door.

"Go ahead, Aleksy. Do it. Punish me," Luka rasped thinly with a rebellious, determined, headstrong gleam in his eye. Alek's wildness was perfectly contrasted by Luka's calm. His hand pulled on Alek's wrist. "Come on. Fuck me and choke me like you used to when we were their age. Teach me a lesson."

Sneering, Luka smiled at Alek as he released him. Luka coughed hoarsely and rubbed his throat, staring his twin down. He turned to Evan. "If you need me to come by and get you later, if you don't want to be here, call me. Okay? Please? I'll be checking on you either way."

Then he was gone, heading through the hall to the kitchen and leaving through the back door.

With his feet under him before he even knew he intended to stand, Evan blinked his eyes to clear them as the edges darkened, his vision narrowing. He stumbled when everything went black, his knees giving out. Alek caught him, holding him up.

Clutching to consciousness, Evan sagged in Alek's arms, letting out harsh, gut-deep sobs that wrung the air from his lungs and turned him inside out. For long minutes he poured out everything as Alek gathered him close, wrapping him in a strong yet careful hold. Evan clutched his aching side as sharp cries of anguish interwove between his guttural weeping. It went on and on until Evan had fallen quiet, his body limp, passed out from stress, shock, and the failings of his form.

Chapter 9
Up from Down

Evan woke periodically throughout the night from vivid nightmares in which he was either stranded in a barren wasteland with nothing but cracked earth and blistering sunlight in every direction, or there was a swarm of creatures around him, beating his flesh to a bloody pulp with their enormous, iron-like fists. Ripping himself out of these visions, gasping softly, he opened his eyes, peering into the gloom to find Alek, right there beside him in bed. Their hands rested side-by-side on the bed, barely grazing each other. Each time Evan woke, Alek already had his eyes opened and was watching him with concern—which only deepened when Evan couldn't bear to meet Alek's gaze after only a fleeting glimpse.

Once or twice, Alek asked if Evan needed more pain meds. Evan shook his head. Another time, Evan held his breath as tears sprung from his eyes. Alek tenderly caressed his cheeks to wipe them away. The kindness killed Evan and made it all so much worse. Exhausted, he slipped back into sleep time and time again, only to be tormented by the creations of his mind until dawn arrived.

Evan lay awake as Alek got dressed for work, saying nothing to him, but turning in gratefully to Alek's touch when Alek caressed his cheek. Alek asked if he should call out from work for the day and stay home with him, but Evan shook his head, burning with self-hatred and regret when Alek lovingly kissed his forehead in goodbye.

Hours passed. Sometimes there was a presence lingering in the hall or doorway and Evan could feel it was Brennan without having to look, but he attempted to block it out. There were three pillows wedged, by Alek, under Evan's back to prop him up in bed to relieve the discomfort in his ribs. He dozed off, or pretended to, in that position for a while before pushing the pillows away and curling up on his side instead, despite the pain it caused him, or maybe because of it.

Nothing mattered — not the things Evan was expected to do, like get out of bed and take a shower or eat breakfast; not how he felt or whether or not he'd managed to re-break his bones; not what he wanted, because the things he wanted were what led him further into misery, tormenting those he loved.

It didn't matter if Brennan was standing a few feet away, watching him, or why Brennan was there, when the last thing Evan would have expected Brennan to want to see was him. It didn't matter if the phone kept ringing with Brennan speaking in fervent, strained whispers to whoever was on the other end. It didn't even matter that it seemed like Alek and Brennan weren't angry with him. It didn't matter at all.

All that mattered was being very still and very quiet, doing nothing and affecting others as little as he possibly could. Tired of doing the wrong thing, of touching those who mattered to him most in negative ways, he wanted to escape, to get in his car and drive as fast as he could in any particular direction, just as long as it was away. But Luka was right; there was no running away from this. He couldn't do that just as he couldn't wander out to the road and step in front of a tractor trailer right as it went by. There was no painless, noble way out. He made his bed. Now he had to lie in it.

So, that was exactly what he did, and nothing else. It was better that way for everyone.

A floorboard creaked in the hall. Wood groaned as there was another step taken into Evan's bedroom. His back to the doorway, Evan willed Brennan to leave. He pretended to be sleeping.

"You were supposed to be at work by now. Mike called, wondering why you never showed. Evan?"

Leave me alone. Don't pretend everything's fine. Just go away. Please go away.

"I'd like to check out your ribs and take you for an x-ray if they're really bothering you."

I can't even tell him to get lost. He shouldn't want to have anything to do with me. He shouldn't care about my damn ribs.

I wish Luka was here.

I wish I had my damn gun.

I wish Jimmy never found me.

I wish they'd left me to rot in that field.

Small and hushed, right by the bedside, a low, familiar voice asked somewhat fearfully, "Evan?"

Brennan hesitated, lingered, then lay down behind Evan's turned back, spooning there. "Evan?"

Fingertips brushed gently back through the hair at Evan's temple and down to the nape of his neck. It was the only point of contact between them. Brennan stayed a breath away; heat radiated from him, reaching out toward Evan. Brennan hadn't touched Evan like that in weeks. It felt like an apology, like Brennan's attempt at making some amends for staying away for so long. The only problem was, most of Evan had receded too far into himself to care.

But then, Brennan started to speak, very softly and right from the heart. Between them, formless, was Evan's darkness and the possibility for ruin. Evan could sense how he had caused Brennan heartache. Sounding scared to the bone, Brennan tried to reach his brother.

"When I got really sad about Mom being sick, and afraid of losing her, she'd sing to me or just talk to me about whatever was on her mind — things she remembered from her childhood, the weather, our noisy neighbors, or a flower she saw growing in the garden. She'd hold me and just hearing her voice like that really made me feel better. It made me feel like she was really there with me, like I wasn't alone. Sometimes even now, I feel like if I'm really quiet and listen hard enough, I can still hear her voice telling me to stop moping around and live my damn life already. So I just...." The back of his bent index finger dragged lightly down the back of Evan's neck, right over the ridges of his spine, before pulling away. "I don't know. You mean more to me than anything. You're at least as important to me as she was and I'm not going to shut you out just because you hurt my feelings over a guy. Because that's just stupid. Especially when I can, like, *feel* how much pain you're in. I really can feel you, even when I'm trying not to. Maybe I've gotten too afraid again, for you. I was so scared for Mom for so long, then I had these reasons to be scared for you, and I couldn't fight it. I just *was*. And it didn't help you at all and I'm sorry for that."

Evan reached back for Brennan's arm. Finding it, he drew it around himself. Brennan, for a second, twitched away, afraid of making contact with Evan's ribs. But it only lasted a moment. He let Evan lead and gave in to the embrace, sighing as his hand flattened, palming Evan's chest. It settled both of them, made it all a little easier.

Brennan shifted forward, molding their bodies together completely for the first time in a long time, breaking some of the spell keeping them apart. Evan pulled Brennan's arm even tighter, even closer, but still couldn't bring himself to say a word.

After a while, Brennan said, "I make a mean macaroni and cheese if you want some. Interested? I mean, it's not like I'm doing you any favors. I was going to make up a batch anyway. And I'm fully capable of spoon-feeding it to you and taking blackmail pictures of the whole thing for later if you don't fucking say something already."

Evan was surprised into a small laugh. "Fine. You win."

"Ah, the sweet taste of victory."

Brennan shifted away, sitting up and got off of the bed. He crossed the room and paused before leaving. Taking the stuffed 'Get Well Soon' bear he had bought for Evan when he was in the hospital from atop the dresser where Evan had placed it, Brennan brought it to Evan and tucked it into his now-empty arms.

Evan shot Brennan a look of pure wonderment, but hugged the bear to his chest after Brennan walked away.

The steaming, incredible-smelling bowl of pasta was hand-delivered to Evan's bed. The brothers sat there, cross-legged and facing each other on the bed. Brennan smiled when Evan began to eat the food he'd prepared, with the teddy bear tucked protectively next to his side. Filling the quiet between them, Brennan told Evan about his latest progress in his search of good nursing programs in the area, as well as classes he could take online towards his certification.

"There's a school about forty minutes from here and I think that's my first choice. I could commute from here and it's a two-year program so I'd be done pretty quickly. Mercy General would be where I'd try to find a position. After spending a couple of days there, I kind of got the flavor of the place. Seems like something I'd really like. Maybe sometimes I could volunteer at the clinic downtown, too. The next semester doesn't begin until after the holidays, but registration already started, so I've gotta get my ass in gear. I, um... I'd probably need a car, if I was going to be doing all of that driving. Maybe you could help me with that?"

Evan glanced up when he felt Brennan's pointed stare. For the most part, Evan's eyes had been on his food, and it was one of the first times they had made eye contact. There was so much conveyed between them in that moment, but rather quickly, apologetic angst shifted to simple, unadulterated affection.

"Yeah. I can help."

"Thanks."

The tension was still there. Part of Evan wanted to throttle Brennan for being so nice to him when he should have been pissed off. Maybe Brennan thought Evan would feel better for voicing his feelings, but he didn't push. Each moment, every passing second, felt like a step in the right direction. Being with Brennan, with all of the truth laid out bare, no secrets, no reason to hide, felt like a small miracle. Brennan's company did fill the empty places for Evan, as hard as it was to believe and as easy as it was to forget when they did spend time apart. Slowly, too slowly, the darkness lifted. The dread dispersed. Everything that felt wrong began to feel right again. Hope sparked.

"Do you like it?"

"Sure. Beats the instant kind."

"Good. You going to work tomorrow?"

Evan shrugged.

"You should let Mike know what's going on before he fires you or something."

"He wouldn't fire me," Evan mumbled. "But I guess I can call him."

"Will you let me take a look at your side?"

Raising an eyebrow, Evan hesitated and gave Brennan a doubtful glance.

"Please."

"I'm fine."

"Maybe I don't believe you."

Evan stabbed a few noodles and popped them into his mouth. Picking through what was left in his bowl, his expression soured and, eventually, he said, "Will you get off my back about it if I agree to this?"

"Yeah."

Evan set the food aside and turned his face away from Brennan when he shifted closer.

"Sit up straight. Lift your shirt."

"Why?"

Brennan gave him an exasperated look. Evan rolled his eyes, tugging up his t-shirt on one side, just enough to bare the area by his healing ribs. When Brennan pushed the fabric up farther for a better look, his fingers feeling for tender spots, watching Evan's face for his reaction and signs of pain, a dark red, small, circular bruise was also revealed just underneath Evan's pectoral muscle. Brennan touched it gingerly with the fingertips of his left hand as his right continued to move over Evan's ribs.

"That's not—" Evan started, trying to pull his shirt back down.

"I know what it is. That's why you didn't want me to look, isn't it?"

Evan didn't respond.

"Does this hurt at all?"

Brennan pressed harder at Evan's side, and saw his jaw clench. "A little. It's not a big deal."

"Are you lying?"

"I don't know, Bren. Am I? You tell me if you know so much."

Brennan's hand fell away. Evan yanked down his shirt and folded his arms.

"Why can't you just be mad at me like a normal person? Don't you know it makes it worse when you do this? I betrayed you and you're making me lunch and worried about if I hurt myself while your boyfriend was fucking me and I *just can't take it*! Just *be mad*! Yell at me! Tell me off! Hit me! Something!"

"No," Brennan said softly, shaking his head. "I won't. Sorry."

"'Cause you're so much better than me, right? You've got it all figured out. That'd make sense, wouldn't it? Because I've got absolutely *nothing* figured out so, you know, it all balances."

"No, I know that's what you like to think, Evan, but that's not reality. I just refuse to hurt you anymore because you hurt yourself plenty. I'm not going to make it worse for you."

"Can't you just screw up once? Just *once*? And not be so fucking perfect all the time?"

"I'm not perfect, Evan! I'm really kind of flattered you see me like that, but I'm not. I wasn't perfect when I pushed us into having sex, when I snuck in here that night and took advantage of you when you were half asleep. I knew you'd let me do it, that it would be easy to get you to go along with it once we started going in that direction. When Luka told me his first was Alek, I wanted that, too, with you. I wanted you to be *my* first, and I didn't ask or talk to you about it like I should have. I just took it from you, and you know what? Luka almost broke up with me over it.

"I don't blame him, either. Maybe he should have. That morning, after our run, he was ready to break it off because he knew what I did, and *why* I did it. He saw through me. He saw how selfish my motives were, and now that I think about it, that was the first time I started to suspect he was seriously falling for you. He loved you even then. But I mean, *fuck*, Evan! Alek forced Luka into having sex with him, and at least Alek had the excuse of being high and being led into it by someone else. There is no excuse for what I did. No wonder Luka wanted to end it! I was reenacting with you the very thing that's haunted him for years, without really hearing what he was trying to warn me about. And the guilt I've been carrying around over that—for you *and* for Luka. I pretty much pushed you two together. *I* did it. That's why I'm not mad, okay?"

"You asked permission," Evan insisted, quickly getting upset. He was surprised by his tears and the way his chest tightened. "You asked and I said yes. You didn't *force* anything."

"No? How about when I held you down and kissed you when you *begged me* to let you go?"

"You do realize I could have stopped you if I really wanted to, right? You're strong, but not *that* strong. I was scared of being attracted to you, and what you would think of me when you found out how attracted to you I am, but it's not like I was afraid of what you would do to me. I was into it. I thought that was pretty clear with my boner poking you in the ass. The reason I let you lead those times is because I got off on it. How you held me down, how much you wanted me that night. It was hot. We're *not* Alek and Luka. We're different. You never forced yourself on me, Bren, I just let you top. I wanted you to top me like that. Kinda wish you *would* force yourself on me. I really miss you, but I thought you regretted the whole thing, us hooking up."

"No," Brennan sighed. "The only thing I regretted was the way I went about it. I guess I was just stuck in my own head for a while, plus I agreed with Alek it was better to let you recover and give you space instead of making your injuries worse. It was easier to not be with you at all than to be really close to you but not be able to have you. Now that I see how much it upset you, if I could go back in time, I wouldn't have done it. I wouldn't have stayed away. I miss you, too, but it's hard to accept you're okay already, especially when you don't seem okay. But if you say you're ready, I believe you."

"Trust me, I'm ready," Evan assured him. "Whatever you want when it comes to you and me, go for it. I like when you take control. Consider this my formal permission from now until eternity, okay?"

They each took a breath, savoring an understanding too long in coming.

"We should have talked about this earlier," Brennan said softly, with regret.

"Ya think?"

"I have no idea why I turn into such a toppy bastard around you, or how you bring that out of me," Brennan wondered. "It's so weird. You're the only person I've ever wanted to overpower like that. Every time I think about you, I want to get inside you."

"Good. 'Cause I want you to be there. I can't believe Luka almost broke up with you over me."

"He was pissed. Got all protective of you. I guess him and Alek have that whole 'possessive' thing in common. Maybe we were just misreading each other, too. Luka thought I was a careless jerk with you, and that never went completely away, so when he saw his chance to have you instead, he took it. Seems like he never forgave me completely."

"No, I don't agree with that. He's not replacing you. He loves you more than ever, it's just… complicated. Can you at least admit what he and I did yesterday upset you?"

"Yeah, it upset me. I'm kind of really angry, jealous, and turned on all at the same time."

"Thank you."

"You're welcome." Brennan said hesitantly, "You should talk to Jimmy. I think he's been giving you as much space as he can, just like me and Alek were, but he's still really worried. He calls me *every* day for updates on how you are, since you never take his calls."

"He's only worried because he suspects shit."

"Maybe. He still deserves to know you're okay. *Are* you okay?"

Evan laughed softly, tiredly. "I'm gettin' there."

Smiling gratefully, he held out an opened hand. Brennan laid his hand on top and smiled back when Evan held on tightly.

Luka answered the phone sounding startled and concerned. "Brennan? Is everything all right?"

"Yeah. Guess I'm the last person you were expecting to call, and how much does that suck?"

"Bren," Luka sighed, sounding heartbroken.

"No. I don't wanna get into it. I just wanted to tell you Evan wants to see you if you can stop by after work. He wouldn't call you himself to ask, because he thinks it'd hurt my feelings, so yeah. That's why I called. You should stop by."

"Brennan, I am *so* sorry for hurting you. I love you so much. Please give me a chance to—" Luka started.

Brennan cut him off sharply. "*Don't.*"

There was a deep sigh and a pause. When he next spoke, Luka's voice was audibly strained, like he was fighting not to sound like he was crying. Brennan hoped he was. "I guess it must be bad if you're calling. Should I try to get out early? Are you really worried about him?"

"Well, we did talk. He seems better. He had a scary look earlier. It's gone now, but he's still not himself. I was… yeah, okay, I was really worried this morning when he just blew off work and laid in bed for hours, but we're cool, me and Evan. I can tell he misses you, though."

"Uh, but… Alek… not like it can get any worse with him, but he might literally kill me if he finds me over there."

"He might, yeah. Guess you have to make the call as far as your priorities go. I made mine."

At that, Brennan hung up and muted the phone when it started ringing seconds later.

Chapter 10
Best Intentions

Luka was not someone easily dissuaded from making a stupid decision just because it might turn out badly. If he had enough incentive to try, he'd go for it. It had, mostly, not steered him wrong thus far. It was what got him and Alek together, sexually-speaking, and kept the spark between them burning for so long. If it had been purely Alek's call, they might have left off fucking each other years ago, chalking it up to an unusually bumpy journey through adolescence. Luka's deep-seated need for affection, much more than only a strictly-brotherly relationship and casual sex with other people could ever provide, drove him on.

It was also what got him Brennan, running after him after only a glance. Luka saw something in Brennan that he craved, so he latched onto it and asked Brennan out. On their date he defied everything his body and heart was screaming for — to give in to what Brennan wanted and fool around, no strings attached — and instead followed another nonsensical impulse by saying they should wait and get to know each other first. That was a good decision, because it was probably why Luka had been with Brennan for so long. It could've, would've been a one-night stand, but it wasn't. Luka was incredibly grateful for that and now he didn't intend to let Brennan go, even if he had to fight to keep him.

Of course, Luka's impulsiveness was what landed Luka and Evan in their current situation of having upset their boyfriends and brothers. Luka went for it with Evan because that was the kind of person he was — act first, following his heart, and deal with the consequences later. As bad as things seemed to be with Alek and Brennan, Luka had faith it would all turn out okay if he continued to go with his gut instinct. This was mostly because when Luka acted, he typically acted with good intentions.

Alek had some of this same quality too, but it was tempered by his slightly more substantial inherent wariness. The impulse to act foolishly was always there, and sometimes he did, when persuaded by intoxicants, whether chemical or human in nature. But the disposition of his other half, Luka, called for Alek to be more logical, more responsible, when Luka wasn't or couldn't. Always being together, leaning on each other to pick up the slack when one of them fell, got them through whatever tough times came their way. It had always been the way they'd survived and Luka couldn't imagine his life working any differently in the future.

When Luka got the call from Brennan, he saw a flicker of hope not only to be around Evan and help him in some way, but also to possibly get to work things out with Brennan. It didn't matter that Alek was angry with Luka. Temporary upset, no matter how severe, could never sever the bond connecting them. So, Luka did what was in his nature to do. He acted. He finished his shift restlessly, driving Presley crazy in the process, with one eye on the clock when both eyes should have been firmly fixed on the clients he was supposed to be training.

Luka muddled through. After a few near-miss accidents—including someone almost dropping a barbell on himself when Luka didn't spot him as well as he should have—he tried a little harder to pay attention to his job despite his impatience. He had called out sick the previous day to be with Evan and couldn't pull the same disappearing act two days in a row.

Finally, five o'clock rolled around. Luka ran to his truck after a lightning-fast shower and outfit change. He sped all the way to Brennan and Evan's and was surprised to find Evan sitting outside on the front stoop, though not as surprised as Evan was to see Luka.

Luka parked in front of the house rather than in the driveway for a quicker getaway if Alek came at him with murder in his eyes. Evan was on the phone, so Luka walked up to him without saying a word. Waiting for the call to end, pacing restlessly, Luka bit at his nails and fidgeted maddeningly until Evan was finished.

"Yeah. No, I haven't seen Jimmy recently. No. Yeah, okay, Dad. I will. Yeah, I promise. No, I know. Mm-hmm. Mm-hmm. Sure. Don't listen to Brennan, it's fine. Really. Nope. Well, can't you tell me what the surprise is now?"

Evan sighed and braced a hand against his temple. There was the briefest flash of heart-swelling relief in Evan's eyes before he turned away, covered it up, and shut Luka out to get through the conversation with his father.

"Fine. Yeah. Okay. Talk to ya later. Me too. Bye."

"Hang up, hang up, hang up," Luka murmured. He bounced slightly on the balls of his feet, squelching the instinct to tackle Evan to the grass, kissing him all the way down.

When Evan ended the call, Luka fell to his knees at Evan's feet and scooped him up into his arms. Evan exhaled thickly, then buried his face in the side of Luka's neck.

"God, it feels so good to hold you," Luka moaned. He breathed in the scent of Evan, filling his lungs, holding the back of Evan's head. "I missed you. I was really worried about you. Didn't sleep a minute last night, so I'm kinda pumped on, like, four thermoses-worth of coffee. How are you?"

Evan let out a shaky gasp, tangling a hand in Luka's hair.

"Ev, don't. Please don't cry," Luka sighed.

Pulling back mere inches, Evan, frowning heavily, caught Luka's lips in an urgent kiss. It broke down all the walls containing Luka's more base impulses and Luka surged into the contact, licking past Evan's lips, claiming his mouth. Their jaws worked as the kiss deepened. Evan gave Luka everything he had until they were both breathless.

"What are you doing here," Evan marveled.

"Bren called me."

"*What?*"

"He said I should come over, that you might want to see me."

"Hell yeah, I want to see you," Evan said, keeping hold of Luka, his blue-eyed gaze searching.

"Why, he didn't tell you?"

"No. Wow. I can't believe he did that. Can you stay? Please stay. Just for a while?"

"Yeah, of course I will." He held Evan's face in his hands, taking a moment to examine the state of him. "You look exhausted."

Evan shook his head, glancing around at the yard, back at the house with Brennan inside, at the car driving slowly past, at the evident lack of seating.

"Let's go sit around back," he suggested. "There are chairs and, um...."

"Less people watching? Sure. C'mon."

Once at the back of the house, they positioned two chairs together in a secluded spot and sat. Looking like he didn't know what to do or say, Evan scratched restlessly over the back of his hand and asked, "You want a drink? Beer? Water?"

"No thanks. I'm good. Talk to me. How are you doing today? Be straight with me. You look like you didn't sleep well. Is it the nightmares again?" Evan nodded, his eyes haunted and ringed with stubborn dark circles. "Which ones? The ones about the attack or the ones about being abandoned?"

"Both," he rasped, rubbing a hand over his brow. "Worse than ever."

"Maybe you should reconsider the sleeping pills they prescribed."

"No way," Evan insisted. "Too dangerous. It's not worth it."

"That was your dad on the phone, right? It's good you talked to him. What's up there?"

"Nothing, really. I've owed him a call for a few days now and he tried me again, so I picked up. Dad was asking me to talk to Jimmy more than I have been, and he was hinting he had some news but didn't want to say anything yet. When I said I'd flaked on work today, he was kind of upset, and said I'm not ready to go back. He said I should wait a few more weeks, spend more time with Jimmy or at the shelter, just to get out of the house. I don't know."

"Well, he's right that being at home isn't really helping you anymore. I heard you talked to Brennan?"

"Yeah. It was kind of annoying how nice he was being. I wish he was just mad at me. It'd be simpler. Maybe he is, underneath, and he's mature enough to not show it. But, he's like an angel. He just knows how to make everything okay again."

"Good. I'm glad you guys worked it out a little. It really seems to affect you two in a major way when you're fighting, and I hate to see either one of you miserable. How about Alek? You two talk?"

Evan shook his head, staring down at his lap. Luka took hold of Evan's hand, giving it a light squeeze.

"He wanted to, but I fall apart around him. It's weird. For so long I've been able to pretend things were okay, or at least be able to push it all down so I could get out of bed in the morning. Hell, I've been lying to Dad for years. I'm good at it. There's something about Alek, though. It's too hard to talk to him about a lot of stuff right now, but I can't hide anything either. It's like how I used to be with Jimmy, and it's not just that Alek knows so much. I mean, you all know so much about me, but Alek just…." Evan let out a heavy sigh. "It's different with him. *I'm* different with him."

"What happened last night after I left?"

Swallowing thickly, Evan paused, then said, "I kind of lost it and Alek…." He shook his head once, dismissing the memory. "When I woke up in bed, I had no idea how I'd gotten there until I saw him watching me sleep. He was so sweet, so worried. He's done so much for me. I've been so ungrateful and immature. Christ, I have to get out of here."

Raising his head, Evan stared off into the distance, his smaller hand fitted perfectly inside Luka's.

"What is it?"

Evan asked, "Will you come with me somewhere?"

"Sure. Where are we going?"

"To do what you said we should do last night. I'm gonna be a man. Go to see Jimmy. Talk to him. He's been my best friend for so long and I've just been hiding from him like a child. I can't avoid facing him anymore."

Chapter 11
Bad Boy

"Oh, you've gotta be fucking *kidding me,*" Alek groaned.

He parked in the driveway, got out of his truck, and headed for the house. The sight of his brother's truck out front boiled Alek's blood. He couldn't help but imagine Luka taking advantage of Evan once again, but tried to temper his anger until he had at least gotten changed and seen Evan for himself. A small, scared voice at the back of his mind whispered maybe something had happened. Maybe Luka was there because of an emergency. Why the hell else would he come with everything in such chaos? It quickened Alek's pace.

In the foyer, he dropped his keys on a table, calling, "Evan? Brennan? Everything okay?"

"Yeah," Brennan said, coming forward from the kitchen, drying his hands with a dishrag. He was wearing drawstring pants slung low on his hips, a long, white tank and his silver-framed glasses. He was an alluring, welcome sight, even more so since he was smiling and calm. There was no emergency, Alek could see right away. He sighed and loosened his tie, popping open the top button of his shirt's collar.

"How was your day at work?" Brennan asked.

Alek returned Brennan's smile with a sly one of his own. "Just fine, sweetheart. Same old, same old. Another day at the grind. I see you've been slaving over a hot stove, cookin' supper?" he asked, nodding toward the kitchen.

"Nah, no supper, just dessert," Brennan teased, planting his hands on his narrow hipbones, biting uncertainly at his lower lip at the sound of low voices from outside. He took Alek by the arm and led him back in the direction of his own bedroom, saying, "Can I talk to you for a second?"

"Sure."

They got to the bedroom. Alek slipped his hands into his pants pockets while Brennan shut the door, frowning down at a small spot on his shirt, scratching at it. Pulling the garment up and over his head, he tossed it into the laundry pile before turning back to face Alek.

"You know," Alek said. "I think I saw a stain on the leg of your pants. Maybe you should take those off, too."

Brennan narrowed his eyes and stepped up to Alek, right into his personal space.

Barely inches away, Brennan said quietly, "Look, last night sucked and honestly so did the entire morning, but I made an effort to get over myself. I actually made some progress with Evan today. We talked. It was good. So, I'd really appreciate it if you stayed the hell away from Luka right now until you both cool off so we can avoid any more drama."

"I'm the one that lives here. I think *he* should leave."

Brennan sighed, looking frustrated, probably because Alek was right. But Brennan argued, "He's with Evan. Helping. I asked him to come over. It wasn't his idea."

"How the hell do you know he's helping? Maybe he's giving Ev a reach-around and laughing at both of us right now."

"Alek," Brennan half-warned, half-begged, his voice a low, rough rasp. He grabbed Alek's tie, wrapping it around his fist, tugging firmly on it. "It's just Luka, and you of all people should know he's not that much of a jerk. Don't fuck this up. Stay in here with me for a little while. I'm sure once they realize you're home Luka will take off anyway so he doesn't get throttled."

"You're all about keeping the peace, huh?" Alek glanced down at Brennan's grip on his tie. Then he dragged the second knuckle of his index finger slowly down the center line of Brennan's lean, defined chest and abdomen, making the skin pebble with goosebumps. His small, dark nipples stiffened. "Sweet as sugar, twice as tempting. Saint Brennan."

"Yes. I'm trying. I'm—stop that," Brennan said hoarsely as Alek dragged the knuckle over Brennan's navel then hooked the finger in Brennan's waistband. Sliding the finger back and forth, side-to-side, Alek inched the pants down slightly on Brennan's hips. Brennan's breathing quickened and he twisted his hand more tightly in the tie.

"You first," Alek dared. "Tell me, *Brennan*, what could we possibly do in here to pass the time, all by ourselves? We'll have to be quiet. Wouldn't want to disturb them."

Alek scooted the waistband lower. Brennan's hipbones were fully exposed, as were a few golden curls of pubic hair and the top of his ass. He moved Brennan by taking hold of his bare hips and turning them so Brennan's back was to the wall. Rubbing a hand down over the firm, rounded muscle of Brennan's left butt cheek with his fingers dipping under the fabric, Alek squeezed a handful.

Brennan sighed, "Yeah, that would be really… bad…."

Brennan's eyes fluttered shut, his hips canted forward. The grip on his tie dragged Alek lower. He began grinding into the shorter, younger, slender teenager, feeling the hardening line of Brennan's cock pressed between them, sliding right alongside Alek's.

Like a skipping record, Brennan moaned, "Really… really… *really*…."

"…Bad?" Alek chuckled, fondling velvety-soft, smooth skin. "How does that make you feel, hmm? Thinking about them fucking, over and over and over again. Getting off on it so much they *just… couldn't… stop.*"

Yanking once, hard, on the tie, Brennan pulled Alek in by the neck, their lips barely touching. Brennan opened for him, breathed into Alek's mouth. After the softest exhale of wicked laughter, Alek sucked a kiss to Brennan's bottom lip. Alek pushed his hand further under the back of Brennan's waistband, palming his bare ass greedily, kneading it roughly.

Brennan released the tie and let Alek spin him to face the wall, pressing him against it. He yanked Brennan's pants down impatiently. With his left hand, he found Brennan's swelling erection, playing with it. The shaft slid through Alek's opened hand, his fingers curled loosely. While Brennan moved in shallow pushes against the palm cradling him, Alek spat onto his right hand. Reaching down, Alek rubbed the spit around Brennan's hole. Two fingers pushed through the tight ring of muscle as Brennan parted readily around them.

Brennan's mouth fell open around a gasp. He braced his hands against the wall and widened his stance. Grunting through the stretch, he turned his head to the side to find Alek's mouth right there. His full lips hovered by Alek's, his breath roughened while Alek watched every reaction.

Half-chuckling, half-growling, Alek was suddenly achingly hard. He spread his fingers apart, prying Brennan open more, dizzy with lust from the feel of him and the sound of his soft, pleading sounds. The side of Brennan's face was flush to the wall as Alek trapped him against it, fondling, exploring. Alek's mouth skimmed over the edge of Brennan's jaw. He thrust with his buried fingers deeper into the gripping heat of his ass, adding a third, tugging slowly on Brennan's cock.

"A-Alek. *Yeah*. More. Harder. *Harder*."

"You want it?"

"Yeah. Fuck me. Come on."

"But we shouldn't. It would be *bad*," he teased, intoxicated by Brennan, how hot he was for it, pushing back onto Alek's hand.

"Shut up and fuck me. Hurry up," he rasped. "Pull your cock out. Put it in me."

Alek freed his hands and said, "Get on the bed."

"*You* get on the bed." Brennan pivoted in Alek's embrace, planted both hands flat on Alek's chest and shoved him backward. Startled, Alek tipped, then fell. The top half of his body sprawled over the bottom of the bed, bouncing a little as he settled.

With a curse, Alek fumbled, somehow getting his pants opened while Brennan, naked, climbed onto him. Spitting again into his hand, Alek squeezed up his shaft twice, spreading saliva and pre-come. Then he aligned himself with Brennan's hole and tilted his hips. Brennan helped him out, steadying Alek's cock beneath him as he sank down onto it. Alek breached him while simultaneously covering Brennan's mouth, muffling his loud, jagged moan behind a palm.

Hissing through his teeth at the spectacular grip of Brennan's body on his cock, Alek worked his way steadily deeper, letting Brennan press down inch-by-inch onto him. Pure lust shivered Alek to the core, lighting up every nerve as some of Brennan's bravado melted away with a whimper while he writhed on the thick cock impaling him. Then, inexplicably, Brennan sucked a kiss to the palm Alek had sealed over his mouth to quiet him, and licked at it with the tip of his tongue.

Alek lost it. With both hands, he grabbed Brennan's hips, held him in place and began to fuck him hard, driving the breath from his lungs.

Brennan leaned forward. Planting his hands on Alek's chest, he started to circle his hips, riding Alek's cock, taking control. Brennan ripped Alek's button-down shirt open, tiny white buttons skittering everywhere over the wooden floor. He pushed up Alek's undershirt to expose his chest and played with Alek's dark, peaked nipples, pinching and twisting them.

Their movements built to a fast pace, their bodies slapping together. Alek moaned long and low and took firm hold of Brennan's cock, pumping it. He held on to Brennan's thigh, gripping it hard enough to leave bruises as his climax rocked him. Alek came, swallowing back a cry, twitching, pushing up frantically into Brennan's ass, holding Brennan down to make him take it. Seconds later, Brennan had released, hot and messy over Alek's fingers, splashing come over his own chest and Alek's torso.

They both gasped and slowly recovered, clinging to each other, dizzy and spent.

"So that happened," Brennan said weakly.

"Yeah. Gimme a sec. I wanna do it again. We still have a few more rounds left until we're even."

Brennan moaned.

"Plus," Alek added, "I've always fantasized about having you sit on my face while I eat out your ass, so let's do that next."

"Oh *hell* yes. You know, I'm much less upset at Evan and Luka now. Sex therapy works."

Alek laughed brightly, then groaned when Brennan flopped down onto his chest.

As Evan and Luka got closer to Jimmy's trailer, they stopped holding hands. Evan inched away from Luka's side, putting a more normal amount of personal space between them. Noticing this, Luka asked, "How do you want to play this? Am I just here for moral support? Keep my hands off and mouth shut?"

"I have no idea," Evan admitted. "Somehow I want to show him I'm okay without provoking too many questions about what's been going on. Jimmy talks to my dad all the time and I don't know exactly what's being discussed between them. But Jimmy is someone I've always been able to be brutally honest with, so it'd also be a big red flag if I didn't tell him anything. Plus, I don't know how much he already knows."

"So, you wanna feel him out, then?"

"Yeah. I guess just let me lead. If he doesn't know about us, it might be better for everyone right now to keep it that way. No offense."

"None taken. Presley was unusually pissed at me when he found out about you and me, so I fully understand wanting to avoid the topic."

They walked up to the trailer's door, which was propped open with soft music lilting from inside.

"Jimmy?" Evan called, shoving his hands into his pockets. "You home?"

"Yeah, that you, Evan?"

"Who else would it be? My identical twin?" Evan grinned as Jimmy appeared in the doorway.

"It's good to see you. Come in. Um… Alek?"

"Luka," Luka nodded with a supremely polite but somewhat strained smile.

"Of course. Sorry, I just haven't figured out how to tell you apart, yet. And I figured… well. Anyway, come on in."

Jimmy led them into the tiny living space, indicating for them to sit on the couch. He turned off the radio and pulled up a chair for himself across from them. "Thanks for stopping by, I've been wondering how you're doing. You look good. Healthy. Tired, maybe, but healthy."

"Yeah," Evan said, trying to sit still and not obsess over the amount of space between himself and Luka on the cushions. "You know, I have my good days and my bad days. Still eating soft foods for my damn teeth and being careful not to re-break anything."

"You look good, like you've been working out or something. That must mean you're feeling a little better. And are you still not taking the pain pills they prescribed?"

"Nah. I don't need 'em. Luka... he's kind of been my physical therapist lately. He's a personal trainer, so he's been helping me work out safely and get back in shape."

"Oh, good," Jimmy replied, watching the pair of them. "I was wondering why you were with Evan instead of your brother, but that explains it. So, you've been bonding?"

"You could say that," Luka answered, choosing his words carefully but playing it cool.

"Sometimes it's easier to hang out with Luka and talk to him about stuff. You know, like whatever's bothering me. He doesn't worry as much as Brennan does, and Alek... he's very protective of me. Which is good, but I don't want to worry him by complaining a lot, so then I talk to Luka instead. And he's a really good listener, too."

Luka shot Evan a smile and Evan broke into a helpless grin to see it, rubbing a hand over the back of his neck in a nervous gesture he instantly realized Jimmy noticed.

"So you two are friends."

"Yeah."

"Just friends? Don't get me wrong, I could be completely misreading the signals here, but you seem very close. I'm glad you've been able to open up to Luka, Evan, but I have to ask."

Evan couldn't look Jimmy in the eye. He'd never directly lied to the man, his best friend in the world for so long, the only reason he wasn't six feet under and nothing but worm food. There was also the sticking point that Jimmy had always been able to read Evan like a book, so much better than his own father, just because he'd been around Evan more often than Charlie had, though that was also the reason why Charlie so frequently used Jimmy as a source to gauge Evan's mental health.

The words lodged in Evan's throat. He couldn't get them out.

"I don't want to freak you out or anything, you just seem a little stressed and you know you can always talk to me, no matter what it is."

"No, we're not just friends," Evan muttered, half-swallowing the admission. Turning slightly toward Luka, he frowned and put a hand on Luka's knee to ease his own racing heartbeat and break the tension. Luka reacted without hesitation, wrapping an arm behind Evan's back.

"You broke up with Alek?"

"Not really. But Alek knows. Brennan does, too. We had a big fight. We're working it out."

"Thank you for being honest with me," Jimmy said softly. "It must be difficult if you're all at odds with each other."

"We're handling it. It's fine," Evan replied shortly.

"Good."

There was a long, awkward pause.

"Evan, you and Brennan… are you on speaking terms? If you need any help mediating things, or…. I'm just thinking of you two together in such a confined space, by yourselves, if there've been arguments."

"Bren and I are fine. We talked it out. He said he wasn't going to let it come between us, that family is more important. He knows how sorry I am," Evan murmured, staring at his feet.

"Is Alek still living with you?"

The question hit Evan like a slap. He sat up straighter and looked right at Jimmy. "How did you…."

"Oh, come on. His truck is in your driveway every night, including last night. I pass by your house every time I have to leave mine, you know."

Evan struggled with a response, knowing that a lack of response was answer enough. "Yeah. He is. He's been covering some of the bills and helping to take care of the property."

"Mm-hmm."

Another tense, drawn out pause was broken only when Jimmy looked right at Luka and asked politely, "Do you mind if I have a word alone with Evan for a minute?"

"Anything you have to say to me you can say in front of Luka. I tell him everything," Evan interjected defensively.

"Really? You tell *Luka* everything and you're obviously intimately involved with each other but *Alek* is your live-in boyfriend? You know what? Never mind. You don't want to use labels, I won't either." Jimmy sat forward, resting his elbows on his knees, locking onto Evan with a piercing stare. "Look, I know you've been avoiding me, and that's fine. You've been through a lot and you have more people surrounding you now than you've ever had before. I think it's great you've got a bigger support system, but as your friend, I'm also concerned about the secrecy and some of the things I've noticed. In your father's absence, and as the person who has known you longest, I feel it's my duty to watch out for you and to speak up about things no one else can or will."

Evan was tempted to drop his gaze, to look anywhere other than at Jimmy, but felt he'd only be implicating himself if he did.

Jimmy's tone was gentle enough, not accusatory, as he asked, "Is there anything going on between you and Brennan?"

"What do you mean?" The reply was instantaneous, instinctual. Evan willed himself not to flush with defensive anger or guilt, not to give in to Jimmy's leading inquiry and give anything away.

"Anything to be concerned about," Jimmy clarified.

"No."

"No?"

"No," Evan repeated, more firmly.

"Well. Guess that settles it."

"Good. I need to get back if there isn't anything else. It's kind of been a rough day."

Evan stood, pulling Luka up by the hand with him.

"You just got here," Jimmy griped, following as his guests headed quickly for the exit.

"Yeah, well." Evan took the steps quickly. Pausing in the dirt, he glanced back at Jimmy and added, "See you around. I appreciate the concern, but I'm cool. Really. Catch ya later."

With that he turned his back and walked away in the direction of home. Luka slipped a hand around Evan's back and, when they were out of Jimmy's earshot, groaned.

"Tell me about it," Evan commiserated. "At least Dad isn't around. That'd suck even more."

Chapter 12
Screwed

Back at the house, in Brennan's bedroom, Alek was splayed across the bed, his pants down around mid thigh. Brennan was straddling Alek's face. Alek's right hand was circled loosely around Brennan's shaft, stroking lightly while the index finger of his left hand was buried to the second knuckle in Brennan's hole, and pulling him open. Lips sealed around the spot and his tongue thrust inside as far as he could reach, Alek nuzzled into him, trying to somehow get deeper, growling and moaning. A never-ending stream of humming, gasping whimpers escaped from Brennan, trapped between Alek's mouth and fist, working him toward delirium. Bent sharply over, Brennan suckled the head of Alek's cock, his hand wrapped around the rest, pumping what he couldn't fit in his mouth. Every sound he made traveled up Alek's shaft, tickling his balls and sending him into a frenzy of need.

Brennan pulled off with a slurp. "Fucking harder, Alek! Come on!"

Alek chuckled and scraped his teeth over Brennan's slightly swollen rim.

Brennan gasped.

Extending his tongue and pointing it, Alek slipped it through Brennan's pucker and bobbed his head, moving it in and out until Brennan got more frustrated and just started rocking back rhythmically onto the tapered muscle.

"Yeah," he groaned. "Faster. Faster, damn it."

Alek grunted and directed a hard slap to the side of Brennan's ass. After a few more pumps of Brennan's hips, Alek pulled off of him and said, "You are a demanding little bitch. Where are my god-damned handcuffs when I need 'em? Should I tie your ass down and teach you a lesson in obedience?"

"I'd like to see you try."

"*I'd* like to see you use your pretty mouth for sucking my cock instead of giving me orders."

"You son of a…." Brennan grabbed Alek by the root and swallowed him down, humming as he relaxed his throat and fed Alek all the way back. At the same time, he rubbed over Alek's balls, back through the crease of his ass. With two saliva-coated fingers, Brennan pressed them through the clenched ring of Alek's asshole.

"Ahh! Fuck!" Alek's head fell back against the bed for a moment. He shuddered and the fingers pumped in and out of him while Brennan deep-throated him, the muscles of his throat hugging Alek's dick. Alek moaned his name, eyes rolling back. He tilted his hips, pushing into Brennan's mouth before Brennan began to pull back off, cheeks hollowed, and tongue wrapping him. Struggling to not get lost in how amazingly spectacular it felt, Alek fit the base of Brennan's sac in the junction of his thumb and index finger and opened his mouth wide. First, he just licked repeatedly over Brennan's balls, feeling Brennan moan thickly, but then he opened wide to fit them both in his mouth, cradling them on his tongue, and sucked.

Brennan whined and shivered. Alek kept stroking Brennan's dick too lightly, too slowly, but Brennan was like hot iron in his hand, very close to unloading. Keeping his hand loose, Alek rubbed over Brennan's crown, over the pulsing vein on the underside of his shaft. There was one jagged, wrenching whimper and Brennan shuddered violently, pushing helplessly against Alek's hand as hot semen spurted from his cock, splattering Alek's stomach and Brennan's chest and neck, all the way up to his chin. Alek stroked him gently through it, milking every drop, still sucking hard and humming around Brennan's testicles.

As soon as he was past the peak of his climax, Brennan resumed his attack. He sealed his lips just under the ridge of Alek's dick. The fingers lodged in Alek's hole twisted and bent. The knuckles pushed into Alek's passage to open him up. Pulling the fingers apart, he ex-tracted them only to jab back inside. His other hand worked Alek's shaft. Alek writhed and cried out, unloading into Brennan's mouth. Brennan sucked him down to the root one more time then pulled off.

"Fi... fingers..." Alek panted.

"What, these fingers?" Brennan smirked, grinding them against the delicate walls of Alek's anus.

"Mother*fucking*...." Grabbing Brennan by the balls, Alek tugged on them hard and squeezed.

Brennan gasped violently. "Aahh! Okay! Truce! Truce! Stop." He withdrew his fingers and planted his hands on the bed instead. "Let go of my balls!"

Alek rolled them in his palm and bit down on the thick muscle of Brennan's left butt cheek.

"*Alek*! Goddammit," he shouted.

Finally, Alek released him. Swinging a leg over him and off, Brennan rubbed the bite mark and the indents left behind by Alek's teeth, pouting something fierce. Alek watched him, neither of them moving for a long moment, but then Alek just couldn't take it anymore. He lunged up, tackling Brennan backward onto the bed again. Taking hold of his wrists and pinning them together over his chest, Alek wiped off the come smeared over Brennan's chin.

Brennan fought only for a second before going still and lying there, eyes locked to Alek as he diligently cleaned away the fluid.

"You are *completely* adorable," Alek smiled. Brennan just narrowed his eyes warily as Alek dragged a thumb over his bottom lip.

Both of them were flushed, breathing heavily, and the whole room reeked of sex.

"We should fuck more often. You're quite the little bunny in the sack. I like it."

"I should fuck *you* more often," Brennan countered. "Let's do *that* next."

"Yeah, right," Alek laughed, using his knees to keep Brennan's lower body in place even as Brennan tried to wriggle free.

The back screen door slammed and two sets of footsteps approached from down the hall.

"Oh *shit*," Brennan hissed.

Panicked, Alek jumped off of him, off of the bed too, struggling to get his genitals tucked away inside his pants, semen dribbling down his torso. Completely naked, Brennan was scanning the room for clothing. He picked up a pair of pants just as there was a knock on the door.

"Bren? Is Alek here? His car's—" It was Evan. He pushed open the door without waiting for a reply. Luka was right behind him and they both stood agape at the sight before them. "What?" He took a step backward, and collided with Luka, who was red-faced with fury in seconds. "Oh."

"Stay here," Luka growled, moving Evan aside and launching himself toward Alek. As Alek had no chance to brace himself, he was tackled down to the come-splattered sheets. Luka grabbed him by the throat and started to squeeze.

"*Stop it!*" Brennan cried while Alek made a horrible, strangled gurgle, trying to breathe and push Luka off. "Stop!"

"You *son of a bitch*." Luka let Alek's throat go but threw a sharp right hook that connected with Alek's jaw. "*How dare you touch him?!*" He drew back his arm for another punch. Brennan stopped him by grabbing it, yanking Luka off of Alek.

"I said *STOP!*"

Groaning and coughing, throat aching, Alek flexed his jaw, rubbing it as Luka seethed.

"What's wrong with you?!" Brennan yelled at Luka.

"What's wrong with *you*? What, you're fucking *Alek* now?"

"Yeah, and you're fucking Evan. Big deal! Who fucking cares? Stop *hurting each other*, for Christ's sake!"

"What is this?" Luka shouted at Alek. "Revenge? Or did you just want a taste?"

"Oh, believe me, I got a taste," Alek grinned maliciously. Luka started to come at him again but Brennan stopped him for a second time with a hand to his chest.

Brennan pulled on a pair of dirty jeans from the floor and entreated them, "Quit it! Just stop. Both of you. *Try* to act like the older ones, for once."

Evan was still hidden in shadows out in the hall with a hand covering his mouth and his head bowed. He said to them loudly and emotionlessly, without looking at any of them, "Can we talk about this? Like adults? Please? After, you know, some of us get cleaned up. And dressed. Luka, c'mon. Now."

Evan figured maybe it was the novel fact that he was the one with the most level head and taking charge for once, but they listened to him. Luka stormed out of the bedroom and Evan followed behind.

"Are you okay? Are you upset? Maybe you should sit down," Luka suggested distractedly, as if he suddenly remembered Evan's condition.

"Maybe *you* should sit down, because clearly you're more upset than me," Evan countered.

They waited a few minutes in tense silence in the living room before Brennan and Alek came out to join them.

Luka was pacing at the far end of the room. Evan was perched on the edge of the couch. When Brennan walked in, Evan rose to his feet, locking eyes with him while Alek hung back. Somehow the weight of knowing Jimmy was aware, at least on some level, of what was going on between the four of them, and he was in regular contact with Charlie, was much more worrisome than finding Alek and Brennan post-coitus. Brennan looked nervous and whispered Evan's name in question.

"I'm a terrible person," Brennan said to his brother. "You've already got so much to deal with and I just made it worse."

"We'll fix this, okay?" Alek added from over Brennan's shoulder. "You look pale. Maybe you should sit—"

"Enough," Evan said loudly, cutting him off. "Like I've said *many* times before, I am not a child, nor am I going to break if scary things happen. Knock it the fuck off with the coddling. Bren? C'mere."

Looking worried as ever, Brennan bit his lip, twisted his fingers and took two steps forward. Evan met him, opening his arms. They fell into a hug filled with relief. Evan needed the comfort of Brennan's love and Brennan just seemed glad Evan wasn't trying to strangle him, too.

"Jimmy knows," Evan murmured to him fearfully. "What the fuck do we do? What if he tells Dad?"

"Wait, what?" Brennan pulled away to look at Evan in the eye. "What do you mean, he knows?"

"I mean, he *knows*. About all of it. That I've been screwing both Alek and Luka. And he... he asked me about us. *Us*, Bren."

With wide eyes, Evan searched Brennan's face which clouded over fast.

"What?"

"Charlie's coming home," Brennan confessed quietly. "He asked me not to say anything to you. He was finally granted leave."

An icy shiver raced down Evan's back. Brennan stretched up to kiss Evan on the forehead. "Don't freak out. We can handle it."

"When?" Evan croaked.

"In a few days."

Alek stepped forward, his gaze fixed on Evan who was growing more forlorn. Mentally, he drew away from them just as he'd done so many times before. It was easy, a reflex. Disconnecting was better than facing truth.

But, of Evan's three lovers, it was only Alek to whom Evan was able to confess his darkest secrets, by torchlight and starlight in the back of an old truck. It was Alek who was there to keep him from getting lost in the terrible blackness of what could have been, and it was Alek who had shown passion, devotion, love, and selfless patience.

Evan looked up as Alek moved closer, approaching slowly while Brennan backed away. Fragile and strengthened all at once, a portrait in contradictions, Evan was as laid bare as he'd ever been; surrounded by the three men he loved so intensely.

"What can we do?" Alek asked gently. "How do we help with this? You want me to clear my stuff out? Would that be easier?"

Shaking his head back and forth in response, Evan closed his eyes. He pressed himself, suddenly, to Alek's chest, embracing him without warning. Evan sensed Alek's surprise in his stiffened posture and hesitation. If he'd expected another punch to the face or more yelling, he wasn't going to get it from Evan. Hugging Evan back extremely cautiously, Alek wound one arm to clasp behind Evan's head, and the other circled his lower back. Then, Alek exhaled a deep breath and finally seemed to relax.

"Please don't leave me?" Evan asked, without pride or shame. "I need you here. He's gonna know either way, and…. Look, I don't care about you and Bren getting off on each other, literally or metaphorically. It's like Luka said; we're a family. Each one of you is family to me now and I don't know how I'd get through this without you, Alek. But if you don't want to be here with me, then that's—"

The rest was cut off when Alek, frowning, tilted Evan's chin up and kissed him softly. Tasting minty toothpaste and feeling every ounce of Alek's love for him, Evan surrendered to it, moaning softly. He grabbed on to Alek's waist and gave him as much as he wanted to take.

Brennan and Luka stared at each other from across the room, wary and hurt. Both of them had their arms crossed over their chests, clinging to the last shred of hope. Luka saw Brennan's eyebrows tilt in a wordless, heartfelt plea and that was it. His gorgeous, sweet blond Cupcake slipped under his defenses and broke Luka down.

"Bren, c'mere you crazy little fucker."

Brennan smiled helplessly even as a sob choked him. Luka went to him, scooping him up into an all-encompassing embrace. While clutching to Luka, Brennan sighed and didn't let go. There was so much to say and so many complex issues lingering between them, threatening to rip them apart again. But Brennan said everything Luka needed to hear with the words, "I love you, Luka. I'm so sorry."

"I'm sorry too. I never wanted to hurt you. I love you," Luka replied. "God, I've missed you *so much* and it's only been a *day*."

"I know. Me too," Brennan groaned, grabbing Luka's face with both hands and kissing his lips. "Can we never fight again? Please?"

Wanting it to be true, Luka swore, "Deal."

Ten minutes later, Brennan and Luka were sitting side-by-side across from Evan and Alek, with the ottoman pulled up across from the couch. There was still one more hurdle before peace could reign again in the household. It was the elephant in the room and it was right next to Luka, scowling and exuding stubbornness. Brennan looked between Luka and Alek, demanding, "Apologize to each other."

Alek glared at Luka with eyes like daggers, at first it seemed doubtful it would happen, but Luka broke first, as usual. "Sorry."

Alek rolled his eyes, but was nudged by Evan. "Yeah, me too. Sorry."

"That was amazingly pathetic," Evan said.

"Now kiss and make up," Brennan instructed.

"Are you kidding?" Luka laughed. "You are kidding, right?"

"Does it look like I'm kidding, Popović? Go on, we're waiting," Brennan retorted, gesturing to Alek.

"I don't want to."

"How old are you?" Alek sighed.

"Old enough to kick your ass around the block."

"Stop it," Evan growled. "You two have to figure out how to share with each other, or else this isn't going to work. Just because you're scared or angry about something doesn't mean you get to beat the piss out of each other. Use your damn words like grown-ups."

"We understand you're not exactly used to this, you're only used to loving and sharing each other, not your partners, but this is it. Either you get over it, or we're done. You can't each have both of us if it makes you want to strangle each other. So fucking kiss and make up and make it believable or get the hell out," Brennan commanded.

"God *damn,* you're bossy," Luka gaped.

"You're telling me," Alek muttered. "I don't know how you put up with that crap. No wonder you spank his ass so often."

Brennan's mouth tightened, but he didn't respond. He only looked at them expectantly while Evan masked a smirk.

"I still don't want to," Luka said simply.

"Jesus H. Christ," Alek sighed. He got up from the ottoman and came right at Luka, pushing him back into the couch and bearing down on him. He twisted a hand in Luka's shirt, grabbed him by the jaw and claimed his mouth with a growl, biting Luka's bottom lip, provoking a small, sharp sound of complaint. Then Alek's tongue pushed into Luka's mouth when Luka opened with a gasp. They kissed angrily for a long moment.

Alek let him go and slumped back down onto his seat. "Happy?"

"Fucking toppy bastard."

"What, you think you can do better?"

"I do, actually."

"Okay. Bring it, smartass."

Luka saw Evan and Brennan glance at each other with amusement and wonder. Standing, Luka grabbed Alek, hoisted him to his feet and shoved him back roughly against the wall behind him. Using his considerable strength from regular work-outs, Luka easily pinned Alek's wrists to the wall on either side of his head and closed his mouth over Alek's pulse point, sucking hard. Drawing a knee up between Alek's thighs, Luka parted his brother's legs and, grinding the muscle of his thigh against Alek's balls, elicited a low, rolling moan.

The moan became a breathless chuckle. Luka followed the sound, trailing the tip of his tongue up the side of Alek's throat, scraping his teeth over the ridge of his brother's jaw, brushed his lips over heated skin. Eyes glinting, Alek dared Luka without saying a word. He was ready for it when Alek tried to break free of Luka's hold, trying to pry his wrists from the wall. Arms flexing, Luka renewed his grip and Alek didn't even budge.

The expression on Alek's face said to Luka clearly, *Evan is mine.*

Calm, unprovoked, but easily overpowering his slightly older brother, Luka responded in kind, lifting an eyebrow as he radiated the message, *Brennan is mine.*

"I could do this all day, you know," Luka warned, speaking softly, only for Alek.

"If you hurt him, I'll kill you." It was barely sound, but Luka heard. The laughter was gone, from Alek's gaze and the curl of his lips, leaving only what the bitter amusement tried to hide — wounded fear.

"Hurt who?" Luka retorted, adding with nothing as crude as words, *you're the one who hurts people, Aleksy.*

Stepping back, letting go, Luka gave the identical pair of innocent, beautiful, vulnerable young men behind him a glance over his shoulder, then said to his twin, "I love them. I don't need to fight you for them."

Alek took a moment to absorb this. He nodded. "Okay. Truce."

"Truce," Luka agreed.

Chapter 13
Your Baby No More

In the hall outside of Evan's room, Alek avidly watched Evan eat a banana while Evan pretended Alek wasn't watching him eat a banana. Brennan was changing the sheets on his bed and Luka was debating whether or not to stay the night, and with whom.

"So what, specifically, does Jimmy know?" Alek asked as Evan closed his lips in a wide circle around the column of fruit. His cheeks hollowed for the briefest second as he withdrew the banana and simultaneously took a bite.

Eyes twinkling, Evan repressed a triumphant grin at the rapt expression on Alek's face. After he swallowed, Evan answered, "That you live here now. That Luka and I are fuck buddies. That something troubling is going on with me and Bren. Yeah, I think that covers it."

"Do you think he just assumes Luka and I are screwing around with both of you, or do you think he really suspects you and Bren are fooling around with each other, too?"

Evan shrugged. "Who knows? Either way, I'm in deep shit. And now, officially, a dirty whore."

"Well, that goes without saying," Brennan smirked as he walked by, getting an extra blanket from the linen closet before returning to his room with it.

"Did I ask for commentary? Huh?!" Evan called back. He took one last, large bite. The hand holding the now-empty banana peel fell to his side. Evan's other hand was wrapped around his middle, clasped to the ribs of his bad side, rubbing idly over the spot. Walking a few steps, he tossed the peel overhand into the wastebasket near the door to his and Alek's bedroom. "I've gotta get to bed if I'm going to work tomorrow."

"If you're not up for it, don't go. I make enough to cover the bills anyway," Alek told him.

"It's not about the money. I have to go. And besides, I'd never ask that of you — to pay for me like that."

"That's what people who love each other do. They take care of each other. The last thing I want right now is for you to be crawling under cars and leaning over engines all day when you're still in pain."

"I'll be fine," Evan assured him.

"What if you're not?"

"Then I come home early and reevaluate. Okay?"

Luka was hovering nearby, eavesdropping. Alek, biting back a fresh wave of bitter resentment that Evan noticed anyway, asked Luka, "What's your opinion of this?"

"Evan working?" Luka clarified. "I think we need to let him make the call and support his decision."

"Of course you do," Alek grumbled under his breath. Evan suspected the resentment stemmed from the fact that now they needed to consult Luka about Evan's personal decisions, instead of things staying between the two of them. He could see why that would upset Alek, but it only made Evan feel more loved, and luckier. He hoped eventually Alek could let go of jealousy and appreciate how amazing their situation was, their newly formed commitments to one another.

Alek set his jaw and inhaled deeply.

"Hey," Evan said tenderly to Alek, trying to soothe.

"It's fine. Luka's right. You should be able to decide this for yourself. Where do you want me tonight? If you'd rather sleep with Luka...?" he asked quietly, without looking Evan in the eye.

"I can't sleep without you next to me," Evan mouthed back to him, barely speaking the words, pulling Alek close, his eyes trained on Alek's expression. Planting a hand on the wall behind Evan's head, Alek nuzzled the slightly scruffy skin on the side of Evan's jaw and sighed.

Luka walked over. Alek turned away. Evan glimpsed anguish

in Alek's expression as Luka kissed Evan goodnight, promising, "I'll give you a ride to work in the morning. 'Night, baby. Love you."

"Love you, too," Evan murmured softly, holding Alek. Then Luka went to Brennan's bedroom.

Brennan stood back as Luka walked past and into his room, watching the entangled pair left behind. When Alek didn't move and Evan didn't either, Brennan did for them. He stalked up to them, beckoning to Alek with a sharp, "Hey."

He didn't turn from Evan instantly. First, Alek held his gaze with remorse exuding from every pore, pleading for forgiveness with unvoiced desperation.

"It's okay," Evan told him, releasing him. It was clear, though, Alek didn't believe him.

That didn't stop him from taking Brennan into his arms, kissing the top of his head. Staring at the two of them together, Evan saw them look into each other's eyes in a way they never had before. There was devotion and intimacy in the way Brennan looked up at Alek, who briefly caressed the side of his cheek. Alek seemed on the verge of tears, fighting fervently through some inner battle. Brennan easily drew Alek down for a quick kiss.

Straightening, stepping back, Brennan turned from Alek to Evan. He gave Evan a complicated sort of look. It was dangerous, passionate, devoted, and not brotherly at all. It told Evan a lot of things at once—cementing his suspicion that Brennan, like Evan, held no fault for their indiscretions. It said Brennan viewed Evan as something that was *his*, his blood, his soul mate, his eager, willing lover.

It foreboded a difficult reunion with their father.

"See you tomorrow," Brennan said with love, and with conviction. "Get some sleep."

Then he was gone too, gone to Luka, and it was just Evan and Alek left, with Alek unable to look at him.

"Gimme a few minutes to shower. I kind of rushed through mine earlier and—"

"No," Evan said definitively. "Come on. I'll come with you."

Taking Alek by the hand, Evan led him to the bathroom and shut the door behind them. He turned on the water, waiting for it to run hot. He watched Alek lift off his shirt and strip out of his pants.

"You don't have to," Alek said quietly. "Everything I do just makes things harder for you."

"Get in the shower, Alek. You take care of me constantly. I can take care of you, too."

Evan slowly pulled his own shirt over his head, hissing sharply as a pang cut into him. His hand went to his left side and when he looked up, saw Alek's eyes fixed to the spot and tears sliding down his cheeks.

"Hey."

Alek finally looked up, sniffed, then looked away, rubbing the back of his hand over his eyes.

"I love you, too," Evan said tenderly. "I loved you first." Flattening a hand over his scar, he added, "And this is *not* your fault."

Alek's face crumpled for a heart-wrenching moment and he sucked in a rough breath before composing himself and gazing longingly, urgently at Evan.

They stepped into the shower. Water ran in rivers down Alek's back, washing him clean. Alek caught Evan's mouth in an unhurried, exploratory, sweet and soft kiss that went on and on until the water turned cold, vitality pulsing strongly under Evan's skin to the beat of his heart.

Brennan and Luka sat on the bed, legs folded, postures slumped, a few feet of space keeping them apart. On any other night, they would have already slipped under the covers and pressed close, in search of comfort and sleep. Everything that happened lingered in the air between them, making it impossible to cross the gap. Luka having sex with Evan, Brennan having sex with Alek, the violence between the Popović brothers — they were heavy, inescapable truths.

Eventually, Brennan said, "It just happened. It wasn't intentional to, like, hurt you."

Luka raised an eyebrow at him, picking restlessly at a spot on the fresh bed sheets.

"I know," Brennan admitted, holding both hands up, palm out.

"I'm a hypocrite. On the plus side, I believe you now."

"Gee, thanks."

"You love Evan."

"Bren, don't," Luka started, getting upset.

"No, I'm just stating the facts. I'd be more concerned if you didn't love him. I accept it now. You love him. You want him. And I want Alek, too. Those are things that aren't going to go away."

"Do you love him?" Luka asked quietly, daring Brennan to say it.

"Luka," Brennan fretted, drawing his knees up, looking uncomfortable.

"I just want to know. I have a right to know."

"I agree," Brennan sighed. "But it's not the same with us as it is with you and Ev. I haven't been secretly obsessing over Alek or anything." He held up a hand to stop Luka when he opened his mouth to argue. "Let me finish, please. We've been screwing around since the beginning, right? Me and Alek? You've watched it happen. You allowed it. You've even suggested I fuck both of you at once. It was a continuation of that. Of course I care about him. I'm not ready to call it love."

After taking a few breaths, he added, "It's probably going in that direction, though. What you have with Ev — that's not going away. Me and Alek aren't going away either. I want him. I want you. I want Evan. I want all of you. I'm greedy like that."

Luka nodded, stared down at his fingers picking at a flaw in the sheet. Without anger, but with plenty of defensive sadness, he asked, "Do you love *me*? I mean, honestly."

Brennan became perfectly still. He didn't even breathe. Then he grabbed a pillow and threw it, angrily, at Luka's head.

"Hey," Luka frowned, deflecting the blow.

Brennan was up on his knees, pushing at Luka's shoulders and chest. "*Fuck you!* How dare you ask me that?! Fuck you! *God*, Luka."

His wrists trapped in Luka's powerful grasp, Brennan's fight drained quickly out of him. With his expression blazing with accusation and injury, Brennan's surge of assault quickly turned to defense as Luka pressed him back to the bed and lay atop him.

"I didn't mean to make you cry," Luka apologized, brushing Brennan's cheeks dry. "I guess I just needed to hear you say it. It's been a rough day."

The pads of his fingers skimmed over freckled skin. He fell into the blue of Brennan's wet, shining eyes.

"I love you, Cupcake. I'll love you forever," Luka told him, still soothing away the hurt, stress and recrimination.

"Prove it," Brennan muttered, spreading his legs wider for Luka to settle between them, brushing his fingers through Luka's long hair as some tendrils fell over his eyes, smoothing them back. "Show me."

"Happily," Luka agreed, adding, "I still need you to say it."

"Love you, Luka. You know I'll always love you."

Luka smiled and kissed the last tears away.

Evan slept all night in Alek's arms, first with his head pillowed on Alek's chest, then, when bad dreams woke him, shifted to his good side with Alek spooned up behind him. After that, Evan's rest was peaceful and dreamless. Alek rose at six to get ready for work. Kissing Evan goodbye, he whispered, "Call my office if you need anything, or text me. Don't push yourself too hard."

"'Kay," Evan murmured sleepily. "Love you."

"Love you, too," Alek said, kissing Evan's lips and the center of his forehead.

Brennan was busy meditating once Evan was up and dressed around eight. Luka left Brennan with a kiss to his temple, trying not to disturb him. He slipped on some shorts and a shirt and grabbed his keys, murmuring to Brennan a quick, "Be right back."

Evan met him on the front stoop, his hands in his pockets, drowsily waiting for the cup of coffee he'd had to kick in. With a glance back to the house, Evan said quietly, "You don't have to do this. I can walk. I have a car if I wanted to drive."

"You're not walking. Come on." Luka crossed quickly to the truck parked in front of the house, unlocking the doors with a push of a button. He opened Evan's door for him, getting an eye roll for his trouble.

Once Luka was settled behind the wheel, Evan rubbed a hand over his face and leaned an elbow against the door. "What's wrong with you? Why are you doing this? You don't have to turn everything into a big deal like Alek does, or chauffeur me to prove your stake of ownership."

"Evan," Luka said shortly. "I'm taking you to work. Get over it."

"Yeah, but why? And what's with you and Alek? We already told you, you don't have to fight over Bren and me. You have us. Both of us. You won. So I don't get—"

"Evan!" Luka blurted, interrupting him. He ended the conversation with a pointed, stubborn look, gunned the engine and shifted into drive, rolling down the street.

Realizing Luka was not in a talkative, explanatory mood, Evan sulked in his seat. He tried to let it go, though was quite resentful of Luka's brusque tone.

One block from the garage, Evan's phone rang.

"Shit," Evan groaned, seeing the caller ID. He answered saying, "Hey, Dad."

"Evan, I realize you're probably headed to work—"

"Yeah, I am."

"Okay. I just wanted to tell you myself that I'll be flying in tomorrow night. I'll be able to stay for about a week and a half. I'm sorry it took me so long to be able to come home. There was nothing I could do with the scheduling. I had to finish the job instead of just taking off, but I hope I can make it up to you."

"Dad, you really don't have to."

"But when I get home, you, Brennan and I will be having a little talk."

Evan cringed. Luka had pulled into a parking spot around the side of Mike's Garage and was watching Evan. He saw the reaction. Evan cursed silently, stomping his foot, and frowning heavily with concern. They were attempts to vent some of his building panic while trying to maintain a calm tone of voice.

"What do you mean? What's up?" Evan asked his father.

"I don't want to get into it over the phone. We'll deal with it once I'm there."

"Dad—"

"Take it easy at work. You hear me, boy? I really don't like the fact that you're already back at the garage when you were in the hospital in critical condition just a few weeks ago. If you need money that badly you should have told me."

"It's not about the money!"

"Are you talking back to me?"

"No, sir," Evan sighed. "I'm sorry. I'll take it easy."

"Damn right you will. I'll call you later when I know when my flight is due to arrive."

"Yes, sir."

He hung up and groaned, looking out the side window and away from Luka's pointed stare, but made no move to leave the vehicle.

"What the fuck?" Luka said quietly, anger detectable in his voice.

Fear, huge and fanged, crawled up Evan's stomach, brought by the threat implied by his father's words. Some of the guys he worked with were milling around not too far away. Keeping an eye on them in the truck's mirrors, Evan bit down on his tongue to distract himself with the small pain, fighting panicked dread.

"What the fuck?" Luka repeated, even angrier now that Evan was visibly upset.

"I don't know!" Evan blurted, his voice wavering.

Luka glanced once out the back window and took Evan's hand, stroking the back of it with his thumb. "Baby, talk to me."

"Yeah, *now* you wanna talk," Evan choked out, battling down his emotions.

"What did he say to you?"

"Nothing. He wants to talk to Bren and me. He sounded pissed. Can we not get into it right now?"

"Yeah. No problem," Luka replied softly. "Look, I'm sorry about my mood earlier. There's just a lot going on. You want to go home? Get out of here?"

"No, I'm going to work," Evan said stubbornly, cringing inwardly at how very young he sounded.

"Okay. Is there anything I can do?"

Evan shook his head, tucking the phone away.

"I've got an early shift but Bren will be at home with the car all day if you need anything or a ride."

Evan nodded, one hand on the door handle now.

"Hey, it'll be all right. Don't worry about your dad. He's probably just mad at himself for missing so much."

"Yeah, maybe." Evan pulled on the handle. "Can I ask you something?"

"Name it."

"Did you fuck Brennan last night?"

Luka blinked. "What does it matter? You were with Alek."

"Just tell me. I'm curious. Did you?"

"Yes. Okay? Yes. I did. Did Alek...."

"No. But at least he didn't pull away from me like I'm delicate or disgusting, so it's progress. And I guess when Dad gets here you'll just be Brennan's boyfriend again. It's gonna be hard enough as it is explaining Alek. Maybe it's better that way anyhow."

"Baby," Luka sighed, sounding hurt.

"Don't. Don't call me that," Evan snapped, his eyes damp.

"So, what? You don't need me anymore? You're done with me? Or maybe you're done with Alek, too, since now you've gotta *explain* him."

Too angry to respond or rise to Luka's bait, Evan simply gave Luka a hard stare and said nothing.

Luka rubbed a hand over his face, and bit at the inside of his cheek. "I love you," Luka told him in a small voice.

With an incensed, injured glare at Luka, Evan climbed down to the pavement and slammed the door shut.

Chapter 14
Pressured to Please

Evan was placed on front-desk duty at work until further notice, so he had plenty of time to answer Brennan's texts without drawing the ire of his boss, though he did resent not getting what he considered to be *real* work to do.

Brennan showed up at lunchtime with food, since Evan forgot to bring any and was unable to eat what the other guys were ordering from a local fast food place. Plus, he didn't want to draw too much attention to himself or get more curious questions than he had to about what happened to him all those weeks ago. So, he slipped out the side door and met Brennan at the Chevy, which he drove over. They sat on the trunk with two bowls of pasta. The conversation was very minimal.

They had already acknowledged the fact that their father was coming home the next day. Beyond that, there wasn't much else to say. When Brennan didn't mention Luka on his own, Evan assumed Luka didn't tell him about their fight and chose not to bring it up either.

"Maybe Alek should clear out his stuff. Just... you know," Brennan suggested.

Evan set his jaw and said nothing.

"Where's Charlie going to sleep?"

Evan shrugged. "The couch?"

"But you're not going to have Alek stay over while Charlie's home, are you?"

Staring off into space, Evan imagined what it would be like to have to sleep alone for the first time in months. A cold dread slithered through his veins, reaching outward with icy tendrils. Frustration over having so many people telling him what to do and conversely not being able to be honest about his stressful love life with anyone else was eating at him. He felt crowded in and lonely at the same time. The sense that he would have been better off if he denied all three of the people filling his heart was like a cruel, insistent whisper, infusing him with doubt. There was no denying life would be much simpler, much easier to manage if he didn't have to justify his choices or his relationships with Brennan, Alek and Luka. At the same time, he remembered all too vividly how devoid of basic human interaction and affection his life used to be. Was it even possible that he could make the choice to willingly go back to that pathetic kind of existence? How did you deny true love just because it made your life harder?

Brennan suggested, "We could always share and give Charlie my bed. That was his room, after all."

Evan looked around at the suggestion, astonished. "You're kidding, right?"

"No."

"You really think that's a good idea?"

"Are you doubting my willpower?" Brennan smirked.

"No, I'm doubting *my* willpower," Evan replied seriously.

Brennan smiled wider. Then his expression softened. "How much are you going to tell him?"

Evan stared down into his bowl, hunched over, and mumbled a non-committal response. "I can't believe I don't want him to come home. After everything that's happened…. But now it's just gonna fuck everything up." He popped a noodle into his mouth. "Who knows? Maybe it'll be for the best."

"What do you mean?"

He shrugged.

The rest of his lunch break was spent in silence. Eating beside his brother, Evan met head-on any curious glances they got from the other mechanics and customers. Then it was back to work with a slight nod goodbye to Brennan as he climbed behind the wheel and took off.

Brennan drove over to pick Evan up from work and, after much grumbling, Evan got into the car. Once they were home, Evan busied himself about the house. He cleaned furiously like it could somehow remove the stain of what he'd done with his own twin brother in those rooms while his father had been away. Quiet and withdrawn, Evan let Brennan help him, but didn't indulge in conversation.

At one point, Evan was standing by the sink in the kitchen, staring out into the backyard, wearing a strained expression and waiting for the minutes to tick by, getting him closer and closer to being with Alek again — *and Luka*, his mind whispered. Brennan came up behind him, resting his chin on Evan's right shoulder. Sighing, Evan relaxed, leaning back into the solidity of Brennan's chest. Some of the weight slipped from his shoulders. For a moment, everything was good... until he looked up to see Jimmy through the window, walking up to the back door.

Evan untangled himself from Brennan, cursing bitterly, resenting how Jimmy's appearance was denying Evan greatly needed comfort which Brennan was offering up willingly, unasked. He opened the door before Jimmy could knock. Tired of having people complicate or disrupt the increasingly rare good moments, Evan hugged himself, his expression cold and unwelcoming, and said, "Why are you here, Jimmy?"

Jimmy looked at him with clear hurt and some amazement at Evan's attitude, and Evan instantly regretted lashing out at him. Jimmy's gaze flicked sideways as Brennan moved into view, resting a hand on Evan's shoulder right on the spot where his chin had just been. It was an innocent gesture but there was a hint of possessiveness in its familiarity. Evan felt the connection spark like it was electric. He didn't know what to do.

"Evan," Jimmy sighed. "I'm sorry if I somehow offended you during our talk. It's just that you mean a lot to me and I don't want anything bad to happen to you. I miss getting to see you. The last thing I want is to push you farther away."

"Nothing bad has happened to me," Evan argued lamely. "Besides, you know, the obvious. I miss you too. It's just, there's been a lot going on."

Evan wanted to ask Jimmy what he'd been saying to Charlie. He assumed it was tidbits of information gleaned from Jimmy that had provoked the accusatory tone in Charlie's voice when he spoke to Evan. Conversely, Evan also very much did *not* want to know how much his father was aware of. Ignorance was bliss when the truth could be damning, so he said nothing.

There was a pang of regret too because of how much Evan did miss Jimmy as well—both his friendship and guidance. Without Jimmy there to confide in, all of Evan's secrets had been building up inside, festering. As he became more worried, more uncertain of his choices, the idea of sharing some of that and getting feedback from a friend was something he yearned for. Being with Jimmy had always meant freedom. With Jimmy, Evan could be who he was and say what he wanted, without judgment. All of that had changed now, unfortunately so. Now, Evan couldn't say anything to Jimmy without risking everything.

Seeming smaller and more worn-down than Evan was used to seeing him, Jimmy shifted restlessly just beyond the doorway. Combing his fingers back through his tousled hair, Jimmy said, "I know you have work tomorrow and that the time Charlie's plane gets in is still up in the air, so I don't want you to worry about picking him up from the airport. I'll handle it and keep you posted."

"Thanks."

Jimmy looked up at Evan, then Brennan and took a half-step backward. "I won't keep you, but… can I make one suggestion? You're free to ignore it, but, Evan, I hope you feel like I've given you some good advice over the years. Brennan, we don't know each other as well as I'd like, but you do strike me as a good guy who knows how to make a tough call in a difficult situation. Be honest with him—your dad. That's all. He's not the enemy. He cares about you. Both of you."

"Fine. Yeah. Sure," Evan replied, thinking, *Yeah right. Not likely to happen.*

"And I'll always be here for you if you want to talk, Evan. Whenever you're ready. You too, Brennan. No matter what."

"Yep," Evan muttered.

"Thanks," Brennan nodded.

Jimmy walked away. Evan swung the door shut. Falling back against Brennan, Evan groaned and rubbed his hands over his face.

It was going to be a long couple of weeks.

Alek got home minutes later. After dropping his keys and messenger bag inside his and Evan's bedroom, he made his way into the kitchen where Brennan and Evan were lingering by the back door, following Jimmy's departure. Instantly, Evan turned and went to him, sinking into Alek's arms. Burying his face against Alek's chest, Evan inhaled deeply of the faded scent of his cologne and aftershave, overlaying his natural scent. Alek wrapped a hand loosely around the back of Evan's neck, his thumb brushing through the short hair at the nape. Closeness soothed some of the turmoil.

"How was work?" Alek asked, with an echo of that fearful tone to his voice, probably imagining Evan in pain, putting himself through hell for what Alek saw as no good reason. "How are you feeling? Did you have any trouble?"

"It was fine." With embarrassment, he admitted, "They put me on desk duty."

"Oh, good," Alek said, sounding relieved.

"Yeah, real good," Evan murmured sullenly, hearing the implied, *I told you so*, which went unsaid. "I could have handled the work, you know."

"Ev, it's not a race. You don't have to prove anything to anyone."

"Clearly, I do!"

"Please don't argue," Brennan sighed. "Please?"

The three of them ate a sedate, quiet dinner together. Luka called Brennan to say he was working a double shift to make up for lost hours, so they knew not to expect him. Brennan filled Alek in on what was happening with Charlie and Jimmy, since Evan didn't want to talk about it.

"I tried to convince him maybe you should clear out to avoid an argument," Brennan said.

"No," Evan retorted stubbornly. "Dad knows something. I'd bet money Jimmy told him about you, Alek, so it doesn't matter. But, hell, I'm not gonna hide our relationship from Dad anyway. I'll own up to it."

"He might not be crazy about me sleeping with you under his roof while he's in the next room," Alek said gently.

"It's your room, too!"

"Evan," Alek sighed.

"I've been hiding shit from him my whole life, and now, when I finally want to be honest about all of it, you guys are telling me not to? Do you know how fucking aggravating that is?"

"We're just saying there's a difference between being honest and being... tasteful. It's not a big deal for me to stay at my old place for a little while."

"It is to me!" Evan shouted. "I don't want you to leave!"

Dropping his fork, Alek stood, moving around the table to Evan.

"Damn it, c'mere," Alek said. He sank to his knees beside Evan, reaching out to drag the pad of his thumb over Evan's damp eyelashes. He asked softly, his voice low, "What have I promised you?"

"That you won't leave me," Evan rasped. "But you *are*."

"I'm just going to give your dad some respectful space. I'll still see you every day. I'll make sure of it."

"But I don't want to sleep without you. I haven't been able to sleep without you since the hospital. Why do you think I wake up so early now? You're not here in the mornings so I'm up. I'm always up."

"If it's that bad, you can always come and stay with me."

"Yeah?" Evan asked hopefully.

"Yeah." Meeting Brennan's gaze over Evan's shoulder, Alek said, "Bren will be with you here. He won't let you be alone. Will you, Bren?"

"Promise," Brennan nodded.

"I didn't want to say anything yet, but maybe now's a good time. I've been saving up some money, and looking at apartment listings. I know this is your home, Evan, and I would never make you leave it if you didn't want to. But, if you were interested, maybe we can get a place of our own—all four of us. Someplace open, like a loft, so we didn't have to separate into two bedrooms every night. The three of us could cover the rent while Brennan goes to school.

You wouldn't be answerable to Jimmy or your father anymore. You wouldn't be constantly reminded that we're in your dad's house." Alek watched Evan's face for his reaction. Evan stared hard at Alek, his initial response too big to be conveyed. "What do you think?"

"What do I think? I think you're amazing," Evan breathed. "You would do that? You really want that?"

"Yeah, I want that," Alek smiled. His gaze shifted to Brennan. "What do you say, Bren?"

Brennan laughed and Alek reached out for him. Alek's hand hooked behind Brennan's neck as he was drawn in for a quick, soft kiss.

"Yes. I say yes. God, I love you, Alek. A fresh start for all of us, together? That sounds fantastic," gushed Brennan before pressing another kiss to Alek's mouth.

Seeing the plain affection between them, Brennan's profession of love ringing in his ears, Evan felt something stir inside. Whether it was hope or excitement, lust, trepidation, or jealousy, or perhaps all of those things at once, it was a good feeling — tangible and invigorating.

Alek nipped teasingly at Brennan's lower lip, smiling. He whispered, "No, *you're* fantastic. And I love you, too." Then, he pulled away, his eyes darkened with desire. "What do you say we finish dinner and get this stuff cleaned up? Then maybe move this into the bedroom." He turned at looks at Evan. "It's our last night of freedom. Might as well use it, right?"

Evan's stomach flip-flopped as both his brother and his boyfriend turned their attention on him, their gazes predatory and sharp. At first, Evan didn't know if he even wanted sex from them. It'd been months since Alek had been so blatant about wanting to be with him. Was Alek's newfound openness because Evan had already proved his readiness by sleeping with Luka? Or, was it just because Alek had a chance to be with both twins at once without Luka being there? There was also a lingering worry it had more to do with Brennan than with Evan, and Alek was just including Evan to pacify him. Was Brennan what Alek really wanted? All of these questions rang in Evan's head at once, mixing together until it was all just nonsensical noise.

But, after a few moments, Evan realized they were both looking him over, not each other, and in a way that suggested it was taking *him* they were both interested in. He'd seen that look in their eyes before, just never at the same time, and never quite like this.

It *had* been a long time. Brennan hadn't topped Evan since the attack, and neither had Alek. Now they *both* seemed to want to. Together. Now.

"We'll take it slow, ease you into it," Alek said. "But if you say you're ready for us, maybe it's a good time to see if that's true."

"I, uh. Um." Evan stammered, searching for something to say.

"Interested?" Alek asked, his eyebrow raised in question.

"Am I interested?" Evan echoed. "In—"

"Getting fucked," Alek clarified.

"Jesus," Evan moaned, feeling smaller and defenseless with both of their attention so focused on him in a purely sexual way. He couldn't quite look either of them in the eye. "Yeah, I mean, if *you're* interested. I can handle it."

Hating the quiver in his voice, it seemed to only spur Alek on as he said, "We'll be *very* gentle."

Everything implied by Alek's words was felt in every inch of Evan's skin. His heart beat wildly and he couldn't seem to catch his breath. As Brennan's hand slid up the inside of Evan's thigh, Evan's breath caught on a soft, anxious sound which didn't make it past his tightly sealed lips.

"Oh my god, you're so cute when you're nervous," Brennan grinned.

"I-I'm not nervous."

Alek chuckled wickedly and leaned in close to the shell of Evan's ear, whispering, "With what I want to do to you, Jailbait, maybe you should be."

The threat sent a thrill tickling downward through Evan's body, all the way to his toes.

"What about Luka," Evan managed. "We kind of had a fight today before work. He might be upset if we do stuff without him being here."

"Don't worry, we'll give him a call before doing anything," Alek told him. "And hey, if he gets home in time, he can always take his turn with you too, if he wants, if you can handle it. I'd kind of like to see that."

"*Fuck,*" Evan rasped. He cleared his throat and turned back to his plate, covering his mouth with a hand. "How in the hell am I supposed to eat now?"

Luka was exhausted. Wrapping up a double-shift, he felt the need to get out of the gym and get some fresh air all the way to his bones. He wanted to get back to Brennan and Evan's house and get caught up with everything he'd missed that day, and only heard snippets about via text message.

Jittery restlessness and fatigue set in. He was so close to being done for the day he could taste it. Just a little while longer and he could finally rest. That was when his cell phone started to ring.

He excused himself, stepped away from his client and answered.

"Bren? Hey. I get off in, like, five minutes."

"Yeah, I know. Sorry. I don't want to get you in trouble or anything."

"No, it's okay. The boss isn't watching. What's up? Is something wrong? Are you okay?"

"I'm fine. Christ, now I feel bad about calling. I'm an ass. You're such a sweetheart and...." It trailed off. Brennan sounded like he was kicking himself over something, making Luka instantly worry about what could possibly have happened, on top of everything else. He couldn't take much more, but simple concern for Brennan overrode pessimistic suspicion.

"What's up?"

"No, never mind. I'll just wait 'til you get home."

"Wait for what?"

Brennan sighed, "Alek and Evan are... you know. They wanted me to join them and I kind of volunteered as, like, spokesman of the group to call you and ask permission. They're just fooling around right now, and we were going to try to make it last until you get here, too, so you could join us. But I know things have gotten...

weird. And complicated. So, I'm asking for Evan, for permission to do this with him. You can totally say no."

Luka got perfectly quiet. At first he made no reply.

Standing in a corner of the large work-out space, Luka kept one eye on the woman he'd been training who was currently getting a drink of water, and tried incredibly hard not to say no. He wanted to say no. It was right on the tip of his tongue. The shitty part was he didn't know if he was saying no for Evan or for Brennan. It was blind jealousy and selfishness. Keeping his lips sealed until he knew he'd be able to not just vomit up some childish reflexive reaction, Luka counted to five and tried asking a question instead.

"What are we talking about here, specifically? What are you asking permission for?"

"Taking turns, with Evan bottoming," Brennan muttered guiltily.

Luka had two strong, conflicting reactions at exactly the same time. He was relieved Brennan was not the one giving it up. A large part of him still thought of Brennan as his property, as horrible as that was to admit, even if only to himself. Simultaneously, as images of Evan submitting to the pair of them flooded his brain, Luka came so close to saying no it came out as a swallowed grunt.

Dropping the phone to his side, Luka took a deep breath and tried again.

"You're saying no, aren't you?" Brennan said with both awe and sadness.

Initially the best response he had to that question was to say nothing.

"Gimme a sec, okay?" Luka asked. "It's a little intense to just spring this on me when I've been working all fucking day and... Evan and I, we had a fight. So I'm a little... it's hard to be okay with just... I know I have no right to be so possessive of him. To be honest, if it was *you* they were taking turns with, my answer would be no."

"I don't know if I believe that, but thank you for saying it, anyway."

"Of course you should believe it! It's true! Hell, I'd say no if it was Alek, too!"

"So you want us to wait."

"Jesus...." Luka gripped the phone nearly hard enough to crack the casing. He growled and blew out a breath. "No. I'll be home in fifteen minutes. Twenty at most. I trust you. I trust Aleksy. It's okay. You have my permission."

"Are you sure?"

"Yes."

"You don't sound sure."

"Bren, you're fucking killing me here, Cupcake."

"What are you worried about? Tell me."

"Giving him back to Alek. I'm a selfish prick, I guess. I want both of you for myself. I know what you and I have is strong enough to survive including Alek in it. Maybe I'm just not that sure about me and Evan. I mean we just..." *admitted to ourselves we're in love. I love him so much, Bren. I love him as much as I love you but in this wholly different sort of way and he's got so much emotional baggage with you two. He's not ready for this. It'll screw with his head. I don't think he's even come close to forgiving you for shutting him out, so why would he be okay with you passing him around for the fuck of it? The only reason he'd do it is to attempt to show you he's healthy and able to have sex in some misguided attempt to win you back. He'd do it even if he didn't want to, even if his answer is really, deep down in his heart, a rock-solid no and how can I let you fuck him when I know his answer is no?*

The words lodged in Luka's throat. He couldn't get them out. Closing his hand in a fist, he punched the padded arm of one of the exercise machines and forced himself to trust Evan, too. If he could trust Brennan and Alek, he had to trust Evan just as much.

"But," he continued, eventually. "I don't know. It's just an instinctive thing. I'm working to get past it, okay? I've been sharing with Alek all my life, so I don't know why it's suddenly an issue just because you're people I care about. Look, I've gotta go. My client's waiting. I'll see you soon."

"Okay. We'll be here. Drive safe."

Chapter 15
Three's a Crowd, Four's a Party

Brennan walked into Evan's bedroom, the phone call to Luka ended. The lights were out but a few candles were lit and placed on surfaces around the space, casting a warm, flickering glow. Soft music played from speakers hooked up to Luka's mp3 player. Evan and Alek were both completely naked, their clothes strewn about the floor. Lying on his back on the bed, Evan had his legs drawn up. They were fallen widely open, but when Brennan's footsteps creaked across the floorboards as he approached, Evan tried to close his knees.

It didn't work, since his dick was half-buried in Alek's mouth. With his lips wrapping Evan, Alek used his right hand, working deliberately, unceasingly, with the fingers stuffing Evan's hole.

Evan's thighs gently pressed against the sides of Alek's head. Groaning loudly, Evan shuddered slightly with a wave of self-consciousness. His skin pebbled, tightening, stiffening his nipples. He lifted his hips slightly off the bed with one arm thrown over his eyes. Alek pulled off of Evan with a slurp, leaving him straining, his member flushed dark and fully erect, curving up against his belly. Planting a hand on Evan's left thigh, Alek pushed it back down to the bed.

"Come on over," Alek beckoned to Brennan. "We're just getting to the good part."

Alek pressed Evan's cock flat to his abdomen with the junction of his thumb and index finger, holding it there as he licked a wet stripe up the underside, over a thick, pulsing vein. He flicked the point of his tongue up over the ridge, through the divot and across the head. While licking over the slit, Alek spread the three fingers nestled in Evan's ass and withdrew them slowly.

Evan gasped, his hips tilting up further, chasing the touch of Alek's tongue.

"Lie still," Alek's booming voice commanded Evan. "You'll hurt yourself. Be a good boy and just lay there, or I stop."

"Screw you," Evan growled.

Alek got up on his knees. He leaned over Evan, guiding the arm away from his eyes. Bracing his free hand on the bed instead of touching Evan with it, Alek gave him a wry smile. He pumped his fingers in and out of Evan, prying him open, loosening the muscle. Brennan moved around the bed and sat on the far side of it. Pulling his shirt over his head, he worked his pants and underwear down and off. The whole time, Evan tried to keep staring up at the ceiling. His skin was hot with embarrassment. He lay still as ordered.

As Brennan, naked, shifted closer, Evan's cock jumped, dribbling pre-come. After a nod from Alek to Brennan, directed at Evan's right leg, Brennan pulled it down and open, exposing Evan more.

"Alek, come on," Evan complained. "I'm *so close.*"

Ignoring this, Alek turned to Brennan. "Luka?"

"Fifteen minutes."

Evan glanced between them, his expression questioning as he gnawed on his lower lip. He felt incredibly restless and uncomfortable with both Brennan and Alek's attention on him while he'd been made so submissive and vulnerable. When Brennan stared at Alek's fingers pumping into Evan's ass, Evan couldn't hold in a groan as his skin flushed even hotter with embarrassment.

"What'd he say?"

Brennan gave Alek a telling look. "He knows. It's fine."

"Mm, hear that, Jailbait? Your new boyfriend said it's fine for us to do whatever we want to you," Alek teased.

"Stop it. Don't say that. Don't fucking make a joke about—" Evan tried to move upward, to pull away from Alek and free himself.

Instantly, Alek bore down on him, leaning over him with a hand planted over Evan's shoulder, their faces a breath apart.

"Don't be mean," Evan said softly. "I'm finally getting to be with you. Don't be mean to me. Please."

Alek pulled out, abruptly stopped touching him intimately.

Though he tried to stop them, Evan's lips curled down at the edges in a heartbroken frown. Biting on them instead, he closed his eyes tightly, holding in tears, holding his breath, too, waiting, wanting to disappear.

Alek sighed and caressed the contours of Evan's face, his sadly shaped lips. The tough-guy act vanished right away. He said Evan's name, lovingly.

Opening his eyes, Evan told him, "I don't want to do this if you're going to be like that. I've waited too damn long and it means too much to me for you to shit all over it like that."

Alek's expression twisted with pain. He whispered to Evan between feather-light presses of his lips to Evan's chest, chin, forehead and lips, "I'm sorry. I'm so sorry, baby. I was being a jerk. You're right. You're totally right. I'm sorry. I love you so much. I shouldn't have said that."

Evan realized, then, how as soon as he started to act less confident, less sure of himself and able to handle everything thrown at him, the more it lured Alek in. Maybe it scared Alek to see Evan act like he could take care of himself, without help. It definitely scared him when Evan chose to be with Luka, just as it scared him when Evan started to exercise against Alek's wishes. All of that fear pushed Alek away but being naked, fingered, made hard and wanting, begging for Alek's kindness, showing plainly how Evan had been hurt—it all drew Alek in again. It seemed Evan's vulnerability was one of Alek's greatest turn-ons. It was a thought that caused Evan's skin to prickle with goosebumps, his stomach churning with anxious anticipation for whatever came next.

Brennan lay down beside him, on his side, carefully observing everything in a way that distracted Evan from his worries and bruised feelings. He propped himself up on an elbow.

Evan's hand quested out. His fingers laced through Brennan's when he found them. It shattered Brennan's ability to hold back any longer. He rubbed a hand over Evan's taut abdomen, down to his pelvis. He squeezed once up his brother's dick, getting a wrecked, swallowed cry in response. Evan turned his face away from Alek, toward Brennan. The sad little frown was gone but his anxiousness grew even bigger.

"Is this okay?" Alek asked, tracing the line of Evan's jaw. His other hand quested back down between Evan's legs. Three lube-slick fingers re-entered him.

Brennan reached lower, fondling Evan's balls and the soft skin of his sac. Evan turned his face back to Alek, hiding some of his torment and anguish under the curtain of Alek's hair. Gasping into Alek's mouth, Evan fought to be still as the fingers Alek had buried in him stroked over his inner walls, smearing lube around, feeling him out. Brennan tugged on Evan's scrotum and squeezed lightly. Overwhelmed, Evan shuddered and grunted.

"Y-yeah. Yeah, s'okay," Evan murmured, but when Brennan let him go and instead rubbed down around where Alek's fingers disappeared into Evan's body, around his lube-slicked rim stretched wide around the invading digits, Evan's control started to break. An edge formed in his cries.

Slowly, carefully, Brennan slipped a single finger into Evan along with Alek's three.

Feeling the burn of the added stretch and the way Brennan's finger thrust in when Alek's pulled out a few inches, Evan gasped and trembled. His legs fell open, his knees drawn up. Instinctively, Evan pulled his legs up higher, exposing himself to them, giving them more room to work, and wanting more.

"A-Alek... *Alek*...."

"Does it hurt?"

"No," Evan gasped, breathless.

Alek looked at Brennan, then at Evan. "Add another one."

"I've gotta come." Evan's voice broke and his hands grasped handfuls of the long, dark hair hanging in tendrils around the sides of Alek's face. Brennan added another finger and Evan's mouth fell open around a cry. Alek palmed Evan's shaft, flattening it to Evan's belly. He rubbed back and forth firmly, quickly, with the pad of his thumb, just under the head at the little bundle of nerves there.

"Come on, Jailbait. Come for me," Alek coaxed. "Come for me and let us feel it. Both of us are in you. You feel so good...."

Evan's strangled cry cut off sharply as his whole body quivered, tensing as his seed shot thickly from his cock, painting his body in splatters. Brow furrowing, making soft, desperate noises, Evan pulled Alek closer by yanking on his hair, letting Alek and Brennan finger him to oblivion.

"You know how many fingers you have in you right now?" Evan moaned.

"Are you in pain?"

"Does it look like I'm in pain?" Evan countered, panting, feeling slightly delirious.

Before Evan could anticipate it, Alek pulled his fingers out of him, bringing Brennan's with them, and filled the void with his cock. He drove it into Evan in a smooth, long push that expelled the air from Evan's lungs in a rush. He adjusted the angle of his hips as Alek thrust, rocking in a gentle rhythm deeper into Evan, kissing him, swallowing Evan's fevered, thunderous moans.

Alek kept glancing to Brennan, instructing him with only his eyes on where to touch Evan. Reaching out, Alek grabbed behind Brennan's head and brought him in for a kiss, sucking on his lips, playing with his tongue. Brennan retaliated by fondling the connection of Alek and Evan's bodies, rubbing around the base of Alek's shaft, over his balls. He stroked around Evan's rim and slowly pushed his middle finger in alongside Alek's dick.

"*Fuck*," Evan grunted, his face and body relaxed as aftershocks continued to bombard him. He pushed down onto Alek and Brennan's finger, thrumming from being stuffed fuller than he'd ever been before.

"You feel that, huh?" Brennan smirked. He was watching Evan even more closely than Alek, probably trying to detect if Evan was in pain, even if Evan was trying to disguise pain, which he wasn't. With all of the signs that Evan was enjoying himself, Brennan was only encouraged.

"Yes, I feel it," Evan moaned. Alek grabbed Evan's legs and pushed on them, curling them up so his knees were in his armpits. Pulled so open and violated by two people at once, Evan couldn't really even process it. His thoughts all burned away with the intense stretch and fullness in his ass. Rocking in and out of Evan, Alek kept going. Brennan pushed the finger deeper when Alek drove inward, pulling out when Alek did, too.

"Tell us if it hurts," Brennan instructed.

Then he added another finger. It ached but in a dull way. Evan whimpered.

Brennan instantly began to pull his fingers out, so Evan grabbed Brennan's wrist to keep him inside, murmuring, "S'okay."

"You sure you're okay?" Alek asked, concerned but amazed.

"Yeah," Evan gasped.

"It's just Bren. If you need us to stop, tell us."

"Okay."

Alek thrust in. Brennan's two fingers slid deeper. Evan whimpered more sharply.

"Does it hurt?"

Alek thrust again. Evan pushed down to meet it, clenching up in small pulses.

"...It did for a second, but it's okay now."

"You sure?"

Evan nodded. After a few more pushes, Alek draped himself over Evan and moved in close to his ear to ask, "You wanna try this? Both of us at once? It's up to you."

Evan nodded again.

Alek pulled out. Brennan did too.

"Lie down," Alek said to Brennan. Dark, greedy passion burned behind his eyes. "Evan's gonna straddle you."

The idea of what they were going to attempt was too intense for Evan to be able to look at either of them. After Brennan was on his back, Evan sat up and swung a leg over him, keeping his eyes trained on Brennan's chest, which was rising and falling rapidly. Evan was half-hard again already but more than overwhelmed. He froze, uncertain of what to do. The prospect of being fucked by his brother in front of Alek was daunting enough to paralyze Evan until Alek took hold of Brennan's cock and gave it a few tight squeezes up to the tip.

The move provoked a wanton moan from Brennan, drawing Evan's gaze to Brennan's face like a magnet, allowing him to witness one of the most sweetly anguished expressions Evan had ever seen.

Holding Brennan's member in one hand and guiding Evan down onto it with the other, Alek fed the head of Brennan's dick through

Evan's stretched, wet hole. They both moaned softly. Brennan's eyes fluttered closed while his dick slid inch-by-inch into his brother as Alek pushed Evan down onto it.

Hands planted on Brennan's chest, Evan tried to catch his breath. He leaned slightly forward when Alek pressed a hand at the center of Evan's lower back, guiding him. Evan cried out when Brennan started to snap his hips, fucking Evan with quick, needy movements up into him. Alek held Evan still and hummed in appreciation, "Yeah, good, Bren. Harder. Give it to him. He wants it."

"*God*," Brennan whimpered, planting his feet wider, driving up frantically into Evan's ass. Holding the cradle of Evan's hips, Brennan caressed the shallow grooves just inside of his hipbones with his thumbs.

One of his hands began to slip between their bodies, pushing toward Evan's dick, but Alek warned, "Don't touch him. Not yet."

Alek guided Evan forward even more, until he was almost chest-to-chest with Brennan. They started to kiss breathlessly, gasping against each other's lips as Evan braced a hand on Brennan's chest, feeling his heartbeat race. Brennan's eyes were fixed on Evan's face, searching it avidly, a small frown communicating his worry for Evan, so Evan just tried to kiss it away.

Alek lined up with Evan's opening, above where Brennan was nestled deeply. Pulling Evan's cheeks farther apart, Alek steadied his cock and very slowly but deliberately applied pressure. Then, gradually, Alek began entering him bit by bit. Evan cried out into Brennan's mouth and tried to stay relaxed. It helped when Brennan caressed up Evan's neck, his fingers dancing lightly over the skin.

"You okay?" Brennan asked fearfully.

Evan could only whimper and beg, "Don't stop."

All Evan felt was the burn of the stretch. *There's no way Alek will fit*, he thought.

The harder Alek pressed at Evan's already filled sphincter, the more sharply Evan shouted. But then, once the head of Alek's dick was past Evan's rim, the discomfort eased, shifting to an overwhelming, impossible sort of fullness. Once Alek actually breached him, the head of his cock passed further into Evan, easing the extreme pressure. Alek started to burrow deeper, stuffing Evan to bursting with two swollen cocks.

Evan realized he was still saying it aloud. "Don't stop. Please don't stop," he gasped softly, over and over, while Brennan's lips skimmed over his. Caresses of Brennan's fingers helped soothe away the trembling in Evan's body.

"Breathe, Ev. Just breathe," Brennan urged.

His heartbeat thumped under his skin. Breathing and bearing it were all he was capable of. He couldn't speak but couldn't shut up either, gasping nonsensically. Evan swallowed a sob and shuddered in Brennan's arms, not daring to move a muscle as ache flared and faded.

Brennan let out a gut-deep, wrenching moan as Alek's dick squeezed up besides his own. Dragging open-mouthed kisses over Evan's jaw, Brennan stroked along Evan's sides and lay still.

"Evan…. Oh, sweet Christ. *Evan*," Brennan moaned. "Tell us what you need, okay? Is it too much?"

Alek's breathing was roughened. He was sweating freely, just as they all were, and when his abdomen pressed momentarily against Evan's back, he could feel the slick heat of him.

Only halfway inside, Alek began to rock in shallow movements, in and out. It felt too good. *Way* too good. Evan began to make small, plaintive, primal, wanton sounds of pure need. Brennan was shuddering, thrusting along with Alek, grasping Evan and letting out jagged cries that ripped from between gritted teeth. Alek, huge, hot and determined was against Evan's back and his lithe, sexy brother was flush to Evan's front, trapping him in the middle, filled too full with both of them. Sweat dripped down Evan's temples, down his neck, over his chest and along his spine. He took shaky inhales as his body throbbed and his head spun.

Somehow, any and all hurt vanished for Evan when his lovers began to move. It shifted from torment to pure, exquisite pleasure. Bracing his hands on Brennan's lean muscular frame, Evan just breathed. He gave into them, relaxing, letting them take as much as they wanted.

His lower lip quivered as he gasped for air. His cock was hard enough to hurt but it didn't matter. All that mattered was how good it felt to be taken by both of them, to possess both of them so intimately, and inspire such desperate noises and cries of lust.

The thrusts increased in strength and depth. Alek drove deeper, deeper, and deeper until he was completely buried and Evan's arms were shaking. He was panting, overwhelmed by the impossible, heady feeling of fullness in his ass.

The world fell away and all that existed were the three of them, together. Crying out, Alek climaxed first, unloading into Evan.

Brennan exclaimed brokenly, his fingers denting Evan's skin, his hips snapping, bucking up into him as his orgasm hit next, each thrust made wetter, slicker by Alek's come.

Distantly, there was a soft click, rattle and thump as the front door opened and shut, but only Evan heard it. Footsteps sounded in the hall, approaching.

There was the slightest possibility that Alek didn't lock the door behind him, and someone unexpected, someone who should *not* see what was happening in that bedroom, was coming.

The universe couldn't be that cruel, though, so Evan assumed it to be Luka.

It was.

Even if Evan wanted to move, hide, adjust or do much of anything, he couldn't, filled so obscenely with both Alek and Brennan. Sandwiched between their bodies, impaled on them both, with Alek panting against the side of Evan's neck and Brennan clawing at Evan's thighs, still whimpering, coming inside him, Evan briefly closed his eyes. The room tilted and he realized how lightheaded he was suddenly, that the pain in his ribs was back, throbbing low and constant, getting stronger by the moment.

"Jesus *fuck*," Luka hissed from the doorway, walking to the bed. There was the briefest glare of accusation shot at Alek before Luka touched Evan, his fingers barely brushing Evan's shoulder. Taking in the sight of Brennan beginning to recover from his climax, Luka seemed upset as he frowned down at him. Brennan, who appeared peaceful, blinked his eyes open, staring up at Luka. After a pause, Luka leaned down and tenderly kissed Brennan's dark, kiss-bitten lips.

"We were careful," he whispered in promise.

"I know," Luka sighed. Not once was he able to look Evan in

the eye.

Alek pulled out with effort. Evan made a startled, slightly pained cry, then growled through it as Alek slid completely free. Shifting his legs, adjusting the angle of his hips, Brennan slipped wet from Evan, too. He held tightly to his brother when Evan wavered, until Luka braced Evan for him, rolling him onto his back next to Brennan.

Breathless, Evan winced as he straightened his legs. He was drenched in sweat and still hard, hiding the acute pain in his ribs from everyone, even himself.

Alek crawled up Brennan's body and shifted them both so he was lying underneath Brennan, draping Brennan, who was almost as delirious as Evan, over his chest. Alek cuddled Brennan, tenderly brushing honey-blond, sweat-damp hair from Brennan's face and resting a hand in the dipping curve of Brennan's lower back. This surreal sight was what broke the spell. Luka began to react more instinctively and in a less guarded way toward Evan.

Luka stood beside the bed, hovering. Alek, while holding Brennan so lovingly, said softly in encouragement, "Go ahead."

Nodding once, Luka leaned over Evan, who reached up for him, begging with a glance. After a moment, Luka pulled off his shirt and slipped down his shorts. Lying down between Evan's spread legs, Luka braced an arm beside Evan's head and said quietly to him, "I'm so sorry for earlier."

Evan shook his head and tilted his chin up, wrapping a leg behind Luka's thighs. "It's okay."

"Want me to help you into the shower? You look really tired." Evan shook his head again. Reaching down under Evan's drawn-up leg, Luka lightly touched the slightly swollen tissue of his opening. He scanned Evan's face, searching for any sign of pain, then carefully inserted two fingers, rubbed around and pulled them out, glancing down at them. Thankfully, there was no blood.

Alek and Brennan were watching him, Luka could feel it. Afraid there still might be more accusation behind his eyes than love, he focused only on Evan. Self-conscious with the rapt attention of the two people who loved Evan first, Luka held back.

Utterly lust-drunk, writhing under Luka, rocking slightly up against him, Evan hooked his hands over Luka's shoulders and slung his other leg around him, too.

"Luka," he pleaded.

But Luka didn't want to use Evan like that, or prove his love with sex in front of the others. What he felt for Evan was too precious to allow it. Evan wasn't backing down, though. He was determined.

"Let's do this later," Luka suggested in a whisper over Evan's parted lips. "How's your side?"

"*Please,*" Evan begged.

"Why?" Luka ached.

"I need you. I need you to be a part of this and not stay away this time. You *always* stay away."

The soft sound of kissing made Luka turn. Brennan and Alek were tangled in a passionate embrace. Brennan led the kiss, licking into Alek's mouth one minute, pulling back to tease the tip of his tongue over Alek's top lip the next. He held Alek's face in both of his hands as Alek palmed Brennan's bare ass.

Something loosened in Luka's chest. He could breathe. It was okay.

Evan's eyebrows lifted in a sweetly beseeching expression. With trepidation, he searched Luka's face. Smiling slightly, Luka caressed over Evan's cheek. "I love you so damn much."

The worry lines disappeared. Evan's lips parted for Luka when he began to kiss him. Simultaneously, Luka angled his hips as he drew back, lined up and pushed, breaching Evan's overtaxed body. Groaning into Luka's mouth, Evan arched, pushing down against Luka as he was filled once more. Grabbing a fistful of Luka's soft cascade of hair, Evan exhaled with a sigh as Luka's lips slid down to his neck. Luka's hand folded up around Evan's straining erection, tugging it firmly in a steady rhythm. Groaning quietly against Evan's neck, Luka shuddered and moved in easy, rolling thrusts, unhurriedly riding the clenched, wet heat of Evan hugged around him.

Fingered brushed against Luka's cheek.

He spared one quick glance. It was Brennan — looking on with love shining warmly in his eyes and something else, too; something like gratitude.

Luka's breath came out in a rush and he savored Brennan's touch. Pumping Evan faster, Luka locked up his other arm, braced on the bed, keeping him from crushing Evan under him.

Moments later, Evan was keening, bucking into Luka's hand. Some of his cries sounded familiar to Luka. They reminded him of when Evan was running and he strained his injured side, when the pain would flare. Evan was trying to bear it, to push past it. Luka could see it, and there was nothing he could do.

Luka locked eyes briefly with Alek, biting down on his lip and pumping his fist. Evan's cry choked off and he came all over himself and Luka's hand. Releasing Evan, burying his face in the crook of Evan's neck, Luka thrust hard and fast, chasing release. Evan moaned low and long, his eyes fluttering closed. Luka climaxed with a swallowed whimper, rocking gently into Evan as the aftershocks faded gradually back.

Brennan was lightly caressing Luka's neck and shoulder. Then someone else — Alek — was combing his fingers through Luka's hair, over his scalp, making him shiver. Without even knowing why, Luka sobbed softly. A few tears chased down his cheeks, dampening Evan's skin. Unable to pull his face away and meet their searching gazes, Luka waited, fighting through his swarming emotions.

"Luka," Brennan sighed tenderly, sounding exactly like Evan, a perfect echo.

Luka looked up with red eyes and a bruised heart.

"We'll be okay if we stick together. You don't have to choose."

The words wrung the last of the guilt, regret, and fear from him. He wanted Brennan to be right, but suspected it wouldn't be nearly that easy.

Brennan's head was pillowed on Alek's chest. Alek's hand was cupped around the nape of Brennan's neck holding him, and Brennan's arm was curled around Alek's shoulder. They were so comfortable together, so connected — it was the only thing that allowed Luka to regain control.

Brennan smiled. It was beautiful.

"I love Alek, too."

Luka looked at his brother. Alek curled forward and kissed the top of Brennan's head, embracing him possessively. "He's asleep," Alek said, indicating Evan.

Surprised, Luka gazed down to see Evan's softly opened mouth. He heard his light snore, felt the way all of his muscles had relaxed.

Brennan climbed off the bed. Alek followed. Luka rolled to his side, curling up around Evan.

"I'll go," Luka murmured without looking away from Evan. "Just… can I have a sec?"

"Luka, you can stay with him," Alek said.

"No, you should. He'll be expecting to see you when he wakes up."

The backs of Alek's fingers brushed down Luka's tear-stained cheek. "I'll bring you a couple of washcloths before we use the shower."

"Thanks," Luka said with pure gratitude.

Luka cleaned Evan with the damp cloths as well as he could, then wiped himself down. As the low, steady sound of water beating against the shower walls lulled him, Luka cuddled close to Evan's relaxed form and felt sleep pulling at the edges of his consciousness. He still intended to get up and leave, but when he next opened his eyes, the sun was shining and Evan was smirking shyly up at him from inside the inescapable, miraculous, comforting cocoon of Luka's strong arms.

"Mornin' sleepyhead," Evan smiled.

Chapter 16
Knowing Brennan

Brennan sat cross-legged in front of his meditation altar. The scent of burning sage lingered in the air. Birdsong filtered in through the thin windowpanes. On the surface, everything was incredibly peaceful. Every so often he heard the tap of Evan's razor on the edge of the sink as he shaved off his morning scruff. He could even hear Luka snoring in the other bedroom. Alek was long gone, but had left behind a handful of wildflowers from the yard, picked just for Brennan, because Alek knew exactly how Brennan was feeling that morning, underneath his calm façade.

Staring at the fragile purple and gold blossoms laid on the altar top, Brennan had a nearly overpowering desire to touch them and hold them in his hand, to lift them to his nose to catch the fragrance of their light perfume more clearly. The sage clouded it out. He didn't dare, though. It was better to leave them alone. They might be crushed, or wilt more quickly. They were dying even now, ripped from their roots. There was such little time left.

'Don't just sit in here, thinking about this shit. It's not good for you.'

Brennan tilted his head. A warm breeze tickled his neck. If he concentrated hard enough, he could imagine it to be the silken texture of Alek's dark hair as it whispered against Brennan's skin hours earlier. But no, it was Alek's voice instead — heavy and rich, invisible but full of everything that mattered: air, life, strength, vitality.

'How do you know what's good for me?' Brennan had retorted. Alek's eyes shone golden in the growing amber light of dawn.

'I'm older,' Alek said slowly, adding with the smallest grin, *'and wiser.'*

'*Maybe,*' he had allowed. '*But you don't know me.*' Brennan shivered at the memory of how Alek had touched him then, and where, and with what intent. His lips had parted around a sigh. They'd sealed again with the eager press of Alek's mouth to his.

'*I know you.*'

'*That's not what I meant.*'

Alek had looked at him then, and Brennan felt it even more keenly than he had the actual touch. It was as if Alek had peered inside Brennan's soul and left something behind before pulling back. Sometimes it was easy to forget how they were kindred spirits, Brennan and Alek. With unwanted roles, burdensome responsibilities foisted upon them at such young ages, living forever after with the resentment, struggling with the concept of freedom once those difficult jobs were done. In one look, Alek shared his most personal, most secret sorts of turmoil with him. They were both the worriers, the determined carriers-on. Only when they were together, commiserating, could they find a modicum of peace.

Yes, Alek did know him. Brennan felt it. It was a spark, a warm ember of understanding ignited within him with nothing but love by the strong, incredible man in whose arms he lay.

'*You don't owe him a thing. You don't have to prove anything to that man.*'

Those words actually hurt, because of how badly Brennan needed to hear them, spoken aloud by someone who cared. They sifted through his skin, gathered in Brennan's chest and hardened there, a weight. When Brennan flinched away, Alek drew him immediately back.

'*Hey. Hey….*' His voice was smooth—molasses dripping in strings, sweet as sin. '*He owes* you. *Remember that. He doesn't even get to know you if you don't want to let him. Because that's a gift — the greatest one you have to give.*'

"Alek," Brennan breathed.

Did Alek sense Brennan there, on that precipice, unable to go backward but afraid to take that last leap into the unknown?

It had been the morning after Maggie passed away when Brennan had last been this terrified. Who was this man, their father? What exactly was it about him that made their mother leave and do such a thing as separate her babies? How unbearable must Charlie have been to warrant such action? But if he was really so bad, she wouldn't have left Evan with him. She wouldn't have dared. So, then why did he never come? Why did Charlie never seek out his other son?

The answers might never come either.

The wind shifted and Brennan could smell the flowers. His lips formed a small, fond smile before he bit at the inside of his cheek. If only he could stay in this room and hide. It was his sanctuary, where he discovered the depth of his feelings for both Luka and Alek, and Evan as well. It was where they made love and shared secrets. It was his space. The only one he had left. And, as soon as Charlie arrived, Brennan would most likely be asked to give it up, for a little while at least.

Brennan groaned loudly to expel his stress, curling his knees up to his chest and wrapping his shins with his arms.

'What if he doesn't like me? I'm just a stranger, living in his house, with his real *son.'*

'You're his real son, too. And he loves you. He's loved you since you were just a glimmer of promise in your mother's eye.'

'You don't know that.'

'He's your father, *Brennan. The only one you've got. Of course he loves you. And besides, how could he* not *love you? You're amazing.'*

The jittery feeling that had been with him for hours was becoming more intense and shrill. Shimmying out of his loose cotton pants, Brennan lay down on the purple yoga mat and stretched out with his arms, reaching outward above his head, his toes pointed. Then, he breathed.

"Hey. I'm heading out. Wanted to catch you before you started, so…."

Somehow Brennan wasn't startled, even though he hadn't heard Evan approach. Brennan looked around and saw him there, a few feet away by the foot of the bed. The honest smile in Evan's eyes lifted some of the burden from Brennan's heart.

"Hey," Brennan said. "How're you feeling?"

Sitting up and swinging his legs around, Brennan smirked at Evan's roaming gaze.

"Kind of like I was repeatedly kicked in the ass with a steel-toed boot and simultaneously fucked into unconsciousness. So... good?"

Brennan laughed brightly, and Evan joined him.

"I'll miss you. Wish you didn't have to go."

"Yeah, well," Evan murmured. "If you want to maybe come by for lunch or something that'd be cool."

Brennan was surprised into a smile so wide it made his cheeks hurt. Getting to his feet, he crossed to Evan and wrapped him in a hug, breathing in the scent of his aftershave, shampoo and toothpaste. A hand, slightly callused from hard work, caressed down Brennan's bare back from the nape of his neck to his tailbone.

"You know how much you suck for making me hug you while you're butt-naked and I'm leaving for work, right?"

Still smiling, Brennan asked, "Is it a lot?"

"Such a fucking tease," Evan lamented, reluctantly letting him go.

"Be careful. Take it easy today," Brennan urged. "Oh! And maybe bring a pillow or something to sit on if you're gonna be on front desk duty again."

Evan gave him an incredulous, level stare.

Blinking innocently and with slight raise of his eyebrows, Brennan asked, "What?"

Evan just shook his head and turned to go. Brennan walked him to the door, and when he started to follow Evan out onto the stoop, Evan practically growled with frustration and manhandled Brennan back inside.

"Stay," he ordered, pointing a finger at his brother.

"Prude," Brennan tsked.

Evan began to walk down the path. Pausing, he said, "In case Dad takes your room for now, maybe move some stuff over to mine, or the um...."

"Popo-pad?"

"God, please don't call it that," Evan begged. "Really. It's bad enough when Luka says it."

Brennan chuckled. "Well, it is easier to say than Popović house. Faster. But sure."

"I am really kind of looking forward to, you know, sleeping with you," Evan confessed quietly, scuffing a toe on the cement.

"Okay, seriously, you need to stop being so adorable and go to work before I abduct you for some hardcore cuddling and have to tell Mike you'll be missing work today because you were DP'd for the first time last night and need to rest your pretty ass."

"Shh!" Evan frowned, glancing around to make sure no one, as in Jimmy, was lurking nearby like the boogeyman.

"No, I mean it," Brennan insisted. "It's really annoying how loveable you are. Go to work."

"You've been spending way too much time with Luka. You're being infected with his crazy. I'm afraid for you," Evan said, trying not to laugh and walking backward down the walkway. He nearly got to the sidewalk when Brennan slinked into the doorway, and did a few helicopter twirls with his penis before slamming the door shut on Evan who immediately sprinted back up to the house.

Brennan, laughing happily, peeked out the side window as Evan scowled and sulked down the sidewalk. Floorboards creaked softly in the hallway, farther back in the house, about ten feet away.

"What's goin' on?"

"Torturing Ev," Brennan said matter-of-factly. "But he's gone now, so...."

Luka, also naked, scratched his head and squinted sleepily at Brennan. "No more Evy to play with?"

"Nope."

"Mm. Come snuggle with me."

Brennan thumbed back to the bedroom. "Yoga. I was just starting. Go back to sleep. I won't bother you."

Luka grumbled and shuffled back into Evan's bedroom, reappearing a second later with a pillow and blanket tucked under an arm. "Not gonna get any damn sleep. Friggin' eight o'clock in the goddamned morning...."

Giving Brennan an incredibly put-out look, Luka passed by him and into Brennan's bedroom. Luka flopped down onto the rumpled bed from which he called, "Well, come on, already! If you're going to rob me of my precious beauty rest, you better at least give me a good show. Ooh! Do that one where you hook your feet behind your head!"

"Excuse me, I don't take requests," Brennan scoffed. "You'll take what you get and like it."

"'Kay. As long as I get some nookie afterward."

Walking down the block, Evan pulled a folded piece of paper from his pocket and read it again for the thirtieth time in the past hour.

'Hope you slept well. Really missed you this morning but didn't want to wake you, you looked so peaceful with Luka. Let me know what you want to do as far as your dad goes. I'll be here to back you up if you want, but if I'm just in the way, I'll back off. Your call. Proud of you. Love, Alek.'

Unable to repress the impulse, Evan pulled out his phone and sent a brief text message: 'I missed U 2. Call U @ lunch?'

Without even a hint of apprehension or worry, and only happiness and hope in his heart, Evan continued on his way. Thoughts of his mother flickered through his mind, of what it would be like to be about to meet her. He vowed to himself to check in with Brennan during the day, to make sure he wasn't too anxious.

But mostly, Evan was simply certain it was going to be a very good day, despite how the ominous storm clouds gathering on the horizon might have portended otherwise.

Chapter 17
Different but the Same

The day was a blur. Evan sent text messages back and forth with Brennan while he manned the phones and front desk at work. At lunch he called Alek and told him they'd touch base later that night or in the morning, but he thought it should just be him and Brennan for the initial reunion with Charlie. He simply couldn't get past wanting to be face-to-face with his father before anything else happened in order to better understand where they all stood. There was still lingering tension in the love-triangle formed by Evan, Alek and Luka and, if at all possible, he would have rather put off dealing with it until his father wasn't part of the equation. Evan also wanted to give Brennan a chance to interact with their dad without worrying about the boyfriend issue just yet. One thing at a time, Evan told Alek, and Alek seemed to understand. So Luka packed some of Alek's things in a bag, selecting from what had been moved into Evan's room, and brought the bag with him to the gym so Alek didn't need to stop by the house after work.

Though there was a flutter of anxiousness within Evan at the idea of Alek's things being cleared out, and not seeing him for the next day or so, he knew it was the right thing to do. It had felt like there was a tug-of-war going on between Alek and Luka, with Evan and Brennan acting as the rope. Now, it was as if they'd both let go. It was easier but also worrisome. Alek had been there for Evan since they met, guiding him through the obstacles, giving him someone to lean on when things got rough. Now, for the first time, Evan was acting on his own, without Alek there propping him up.

Mid-morning, Evan had a brief call from Jimmy saying the plane would be arriving around six, and he and Charlie should be back home by seven-thirty at the latest.

Time moved at a strange pace, speeding by, then dragging out more and more the closer it got to the end of the day. Even when the minutes were diligently ticking along, Evan couldn't seem to focus on much. He tried to block out everything happening in his personal life, concentrating only on scheduling appointments, inputting service records into the computer logs, and catching up on paperwork.

After what felt like eons later, seven-thirty finally arrived and found Evan at home, on the couch and seated across from his twin. He was overly aware of the remnants of Alek's things in his bedroom, and of Brennan's things as well. They represented all of the additions made to the household in Charlie's absence, like Brennan's furniture and food, but there were also smaller things. Like Brennan's stash of sex toys tucked away in a bag in the bed of Luka's truck, or the handful of Brennan's kinky underwear, temporarily buried in the bottom of Evan's overflowing mess of a closet. In order to preserve his sanity, Evan had tried not to see what the handful contained, but he'd glimpsed silk and latex before his eyes snapped shut.

When Evan's nervousness began to grow to monstrous levels, the sheer panic in Brennan's expression and posture calmed Evan, like there could only be so much anxiousness at a given time between them, and Brennan was hogging it all.

"Sit with me," Evan said.

"Not a good idea," Brennan argued. "I get really handsy when I'm freaked out. Don't want to meet my dad for the first time while my hand is wedged between your thighs." After a heavy sigh, he asked, and not for the first time, "What if he doesn't like me? What if he thinks I'm this prissy, uptight fruitcake like you did?"

"Hey, I was really impressed by you when we met. You know that. I told you how pitiful I felt in comparison. You're like the fantasy child, perfect in every way. No severe psychological issues to worry about. You're golden."

"What if he doesn't want to know me at all? Maybe that's why he didn't try harder to get home to you. He didn't want to be near *me*."

"Brennan," Evan scolded. "Knock it off. You're fine."

"Then why don't I feel fine?"

"Because it's a big deal and you're just over-thinking shit like I do. You should meditate or something."

"Can't fucking meditate right now," he mumbled, hugging himself and curling forward, effectively bending himself in half so his face was resting atop his folded legs.

"God, you're such a pretzel," Evan marveled. "Why can't I do that if we're essentially the same person?"

"You just haven't tried hard enough. Seemed stretchy enough last night," Brennan smirked.

Evan's stomach flipped at the sudden, vivid memory of having both Brennan and Alek inside him at the same time. Quickly, he forced it away. "Don't remind me. Please."

A car pulled into the driveway — Jimmy's car.

"Oh *god*," Brennan moaned.

They listened, frozen, as two sets of heavy footsteps approached the front door. The knob turned. The door creaked as it swung open. Work boots thudded on the wooden floor, and Evan couldn't move. He stared at a dark, twisted knot in one of the floorboards as, a few feet away, his father said, "Boys. Damn, but it's good to see you."

Brennan stood, fidgeting awkwardly, wide-eyed as Charlie walked up to him. Beyond, in the hall, Jimmy lingered like all of the unspoken secrets and ghosts, filling the room, tainting the air.

"Sir," Brennan muttered, extending a hand as Charlie looked him over with something like awe.

"Brennan," Charlie said softly. Pain etched deeper lines in his weary face, aging him as he reached out with both arms and enveloped his long-lost son in a hug, kissing the side of his face. Evan tried not to watch. The regret in his father's expression was too upsetting to witness.

Vaguely, Evan wondered how Brennan saw Charlie, with his light brown hair and rough-hewn features, if he saw similarity there. Evan never thought he much resembled his father. His finer bone-structure, the shape of his eyes and lips, they seemed too different from Charlie's stark, chiseled masculinity and made Evan feel sorry for Charlie's sake that he didn't have a son painted with the same brush as he was.

"Thank god. Oh, thank *god*. I don't even know where to start," Charlie said. "There's no way I can apologize enough for what's happened. I'm so sorry about your mom passing and that that's what it took to finally get you here, but I'm glad as hell you're here now. I loved Maggie. She was the love of my life. I think that's why she made me so crazy, you know? Thank you for coming and taking care of Evan in my place. I hear you're really good at that, taking care of people."

"Yes, sir," Brennan answered dutifully.

Charlie held him at arm's length. "It's uncanny. Almost exactly the same, but different in really subtle ways."

Pushing his hands into his pockets, Brennan bore the scrutiny, looking a little calmed. "Thanks for inviting me. To live here, I mean. Meeting Evan has been...." He didn't even try to finish. The emotion in his voice told them why.

Charlie's expression changed when he was faced with Brennan's torment. He seemed to get older and less substantial by the moment before their eyes. Clearing his throat and shifting uncomfortably, Brennan seemed glad when Charlie gave his shoulder a brief squeeze and shifted his focus to Evan.

Turning to his seated son, Charlie went to one knee and said sternly but tenderly, "Let me see."

Rolling his eyes, Evan lifted his shirt on one side, exposing his scar.

"God *damn* it," Charlie hissed, touching the wound gingerly.

"Dad," Evan sighed. "It's fine."

"It's not *fine*! What the *hell* were you thinking, involving yourself in something like that?"

"What was I thinking? That some kid was about to get killed!"

"You're a kid, too! You were unarmed! No one knew where you were, what you were doing! You could have died! You almost did! Sometimes it's like you don't even *care*, Evan. Like you just do this shit because it doesn't matter what the outcome is. But it fucking *matters*."

Charlie took hold of his son's face, turning it up to the light. Evan heard him taking a deep breath to soothe his frayed nerves and get his temper under control. "Your nose isn't as bad as I thought it would be. They did a good job setting it. Your teeth still loose?"

"They're getting better," Evan mumbled.

"How about the broken ribs?"

"They're fine."

"Yeah, I bet," Charlie huffed. "I was losing my mind worrying about you. You know that, right? You're gonna put your old man in an early grave if you don't get there first."

Jaw clenched, Evan stared back at his father.

"You're not even sorry you did it, are you?"

Evan didn't blink. He swallowed thickly, his dimples denting his cheeks. "No. I'm not."

"What the hell am I gonna do with you?"

"Does he make you angry because he's a lot like Mom? Because he is. He's just like her," Brennan said, breaking the tension with his crisp, clear voice with its hint of a Southern accent. "Have you told him that? He even looks like her. We both do, but you know that. I mean, it's obvious. Evan does things that might not make sense to you because he believes it's for the greater good. He puts the good of others above his own well-being. He also appreciates things keenly like she does. Or, well… did. Anyway, it's not a bad thing, in my humble opinion."

Complete, perfect silence descended on the room. Jimmy cleared his throat. "I'm, um, going to head home, give you three some space. You know where I'll be if you need anything."

"Yeah. Thanks, Jimmy." Charlie nodded, then rose to his feet, groaning quietly under his breath, "Jesus Christ."

On the short walk to the door where Jimmy was waiting, Charlie took the opportunity to check out some of the changes in décor of the living room and the side bedroom that had been his. The house even felt different, the memories of Evan's childhood buried under layers of foreign new realities of which Charlie was not a part. The bed, the chaise, the plants and paintings, the altar — so many things caught his eye.

"I owe you one," Charlie said in a travel-worn, gravelly voice, low and confidential as Jimmy headed out onto the stoop. "You're a good man. What the hell I'd do without you watching out for them, I'll never know."

"Don't sweat it. Good luck with 'em, though," Jimmy said, looking despondent. "I've just been at a loss."

Charlie nodded, his expression darkening.

"G'night."

"Night."

Pushing his luggage out of the way, Charlie hovered in the hall and said, "Look, the last thing I want is to kick you out of your room after all you've been through, Brennan. I'll take the couch."

"Dad, you don't have to take the couch," Evan sighed.

"We already talked about it," Brennan said. "I'll bunk with Evan. I don't mind. Really, I'd feel worse making you sleep out here."

"Are these just your momma's manners kicking in? Be straight with me, now."

"Maybe a little. Doesn't change anything."

Charlie stared at the son he'd counted as forever lost to him for so very long, seeing some of his own innate stubbornness in him. Brennan stared back, not budging an inch, not backing down. More like his father than he'd ever know.

"Dad, just take the room," Evan said, ever the peacemaker. "There are clean sheets and pillows on the bed already. If you want to grab a shower or anything, I'll help Bren get supper ready."

There was a pause before Charlie relented, saying to Brennan, "All right then. But if you change your mind, tell me."

"Sure."

They had about an hour and a half of peace. Charlie got settled. The food was prepared, with Brennan handling the pasta salad and Evan grilling salmon steaks. Father and sons sat together around the table, eating quietly, with much praise given to Brennan for his healthy contributions. Charlie asked about Brennan's life in Louisiana. Evan let them talk, staying out of it for the most part. The sight of Brennan reacting proudly to Charlie's inquiries made him happy. Evan wanted Charlie to be proud of Brennan, just like he was. Evan also had no idea how to go about bringing Brennan and Charlie closer, so he was glad to see them each making an effort on their own.

It went well enough, but Evan sensed something else, something in his father's glances over to him, darkness behind his eyes. There was mistrust there, and simmering anger. Evan couldn't figure it out.

They finished their meal and the boys cleaned up, side-by-side at the sink, not daring to look at each other too often, or make physical contact except when necessary. They passed plates and silverware, their fingers grazing as Evan washed and Brennan dried.

Evan found himself dreading the moment when the dishes were done, expecting the tension to break and some of the many secrets to begin to be revealed.

The last cup was set in the cupboard. The last pan was stacked in the drying rack. Evan turned and Brennan went to hang up the dishrag on the towel bar on the far wall.

"There's something we need to address before I head in for the night. It's been a long day, but we've got us some air to clear," Charlie said. Cold fear gripped Evan's heart, but he stood his ground, not blinking, not showing any sign of weakness.

He asked, "What is it, Dad?"

"Is there anything you two want to tell me?" Charlie glanced between them.

Oh fuck. Oh fuck, he knows, Evan bemoaned inwardly.

"About what?" Brennan replied innocently, saving Evan from having to respond.

"Well, how about what I hear about people being permitted to live in my damn house without my say so. Having friends is one thing, but letting anyone move in is way over the line and I won't have it."

Evan's eyes fluttered closed, the blood quickly drained from his face. Brennan gave him a look like it was taking every ounce of his will not to go to Evan and hold him, to take his hand and prop him up through the interrogation.

"Luka is my boyfriend, not my friend," Brennan answered

sharply. "Yes, he's been here a lot, helping take care of things while Evan recovers from his injuries. As an adult who pays rent for my room, I didn't think I needed to ask permission for that."

"You're only eighteen years old and this is still *my* house. You *do* need permission! I don't know how Maggie raised you, but there's no way in *hell* you're going to bring men to sleep here with you, taking advantage of you under *my* goddamned roof!"

"Don't you dare speak badly about her," Brennan said with shock. "I'm not your *child*. You don't get to tell me what to do with my personal life."

"*You* are *my child and you will mind me, boy!*"

"Stop!" Evan yelled above both of their voices. "Both of you, *stop*! Dad, Luka isn't the one who's been living here. Alek has. Brennan just said that to protect me. He never asked anyone to move in."

"Who's Alek?"

"He's my boyfriend. Okay? I'll spell it all out for you. Everyone was right about me. Everyone who made fun of me, calling me a faggot like it was the worst thing in the world to be. Ever since I was little I knew. I tried not to be. I tried everything, but I am who I am, whether I like it or not. I couldn't tell you. I couldn't have you hate me, too."

His voice wavered and Brennan was there beside him before Evan even saw him come over, with one hand on Evan's shoulder, looking hard into his eyes like he could transfer courage to him that way, right through the air.

"Keep going," Brennan said. "Tell him about Alek."

Now Charlie looked pale, his elbows planted on the table, his hands folded in front of his mouth, but his gaze was steady and fixed on Evan.

"Alek and I were in a relationship before I was attacked, and he stuck by me during everything. He was at the hospital. Alek took care of me there and when I came home. He never left. Not once. He's been helping pay the bills and taking care of the house when I couldn't move around really well. It's because of him I've been the happiest I've been in my whole fucking life. I'm in love with him, and yeah, I asked him to live here with me. I can't imagine how Bren and I could've gotten through these past few months without his help and support. And I'm not going to let you guilt me into being ashamed of who I am anymore. I don't care who knows."

There was a long, drawn out moment of silence between them, tense and thick, before Evan continued. When he did, his tone was drastically changed from tentative to furious.

"And how *dare* you say those things to Brennan?! Maggie did a *hell of a job* raising him. He's braver than me, stronger than me, smarter than me. He's proud of who he is and you do *not* get to make him feel bad about himself after everything you've put him through, wondering if you would accept him after you gave him away. *You gave him away!* How could you do that?! We should have been together! We should have had each other! We're twins, for Christ's sake! Didn't you ever think we'd miss each other?! That we'd *know* in our hearts what cruelty you forced on us?"

Charlie swallowed thickly, lowering his gaze, eyes shining with unshed tears. He appeared to brace himself for a blow, waiting for the next cutting words to come, and cut they surely did.

"*That's why I did it!*" Evan screamed, his voice breaking apart. "That's why I took all those pills and tried to off myself! You stole that piece of me and I just couldn't be empty anymore. When you took Brennan from me, I always knew, deep down. It left a scar. It never healed. And I didn't want to live that way. For years, fucking YEARS I merely *existed*. I survived. For you. Even though *you* did this to me. To *us*. How could you?! God damn it, HOW COULD YOU?!"

Evan saw his father hide his face in his hands to mask his tears, spilling over now. Taking a shaky step backward, Evan stumbled into Brennan's arms which held him up. It lasted only a second then he was pushing away, toward the back door. Brennan followed. But Evan stopped just inside the threshold.

"If you're not okay with Alek living here with me, then I'll move out. You won't have to worry about me anymore. I'm not a child. You can go wherever you want and forget about me if it's easier. I'm making my own family. It's your choice whether you want to be a part of it or not."

The door slammed behind Brennan as they left. Evan walked

out into the yard, trying to catch his breath.

At the table, Charlie broke into wrenching sobs, the pain of permanently losing Maggie, the guilt of facing Brennan, the terror of almost losing Evan again—it drowned him.

When he managed to pull himself together, he glanced heavenward, and said in a whisper, "He always was your son. His mother's son, through and through. What have I done to them? How do I fix this, Maggie? Tell me, please. Give me a sign. I'll do anything. *Anything*. Just help me help our boys. Help me find a way to make this better instead of worse."

The stillness of the evening did bring one small miracle. There was no sound of the Chevy's engine turning over. There was only the chirping of crickets, the hooting of owls and the murmuring of two low voices, whispering conspiratorially in the dark.

Brennan called Luka to tell him and Alek over speakerphone what had happened, what Evan had done, how he had stood up for himself and Brennan, too. Evan shivered from the night's chill, shocked silent at what he had said to the man who'd been his world since he came into existence.

The call was short. Shocked but supportive as ever, Luka and Alek murmured words of encouragement and love, offering a safe haven if it was needed, but urging Evan to give his father a proper chance to make amends. With professions of love, they ended the call and promised to see Evan and Brennan in the morning, one way or another. The thick, enveloping black blanket of night fell once more as the phone was turned off, its glow extinguished, and slipped back into Brennan's pocket.

The back door opened and a figure appeared silhouetted in light.

"Come in here before the mosquitoes make supper out of you two. Please. I didn't come all this way to scare you out of the damn house."

Evan's feet carried him back inside. He heard Charlie apologizing to Brennan, and waited, standing there like a shell of a person — gutted and hollowed out. When his father's arms wrapped around him, embracing him gently, Evan heard, "I love you. I love you just the way you are. I'm trying to atone for the past. I really am. Please, let me try. I know I can't fix the way things were, the way you both grew up, but I can try to make things better now."

You're still screwed up, a voice whispered insistently in Evan's mind. *Everyone sees it. Charlie looks at you and all he sees is what's wrong with you, just like how it was with Alek and Brennan when you got out of the hospital. You're not a man, like them. You're just a damaged delinquent, a pathetic, sick kid who needs real men to take care of him. You're a burden to everyone who loves you.*

The words still wouldn't come. Only fat tears and embarrassing, aching whimpers and gasps, but the way Evan clung to his daddy like a scared little boy was absolution enough.

Chapter 18
Brutal Honesty

If Evan thought it was bad to find himself screaming at his father, raging with pure anger and shades of hatred in his heart, he was introduced to a whole new spectrum of pain the following morning when Brennan's emotional devastation truly became evident.

That night, the pair of them slept closely, cuddled up to one another, seeking safety and shelter from the world in each other's arms. Dawn shed light on their reality, showing Brennan all of the ways he had lost and everything he would never get back. The light of his life, his mother, had been ripped away from him, and Evan knew that in itself must have been excruciating, but then his faint hope of finding a connection with and receiving affection from his long-lost father was seemingly dashed by Charlie's carelessly tossed out, cold-hearted words accusing Brennan of being the one to cause the problems in Evan's life. More than that, Brennan was left in pieces when Charlie essentially spit on Maggie's memory by attacking her mothering abilities. Dissolving into gut-wrenching sobs, once drained and thoroughly exhausted, Brennan fell unconscious only to wake an hour later to fresh tears and more pain.

The cycle repeated itself again. Brennan cried himself to sleep a second time and Evan stayed with him, not leaving his side for longer than it took to use the bathroom. The first time Evan ventured to the toilet, the other bedroom's door was closed with Charlie inside. The next time, the room was empty. Charlie was in the kitchen and he left the house minutes later, closing the back door behind him, walking in the direction of Jimmy's trailer.

Crawling back into bed and sliding under the covers, Evan's

movement finally roused Brennan for good. Opening his bloodshot, puffy-lidded eyes, Brennan's gaze was like a plea to his brother to pull him from the abyss of sorrow in which he was drowning. The problem was there was no saving Brennan from his circumstances, or altering unchangeable things. Maggie wasn't coming back. Neither of them would get to relive their childhoods with a complete nuclear family. Those years had passed them by and been used up. And there was a very good chance Charlie and Brennan would never get along or bond as a father and son should. Evan couldn't do anything about those things.

But he could help Brennan in other ways. So he tried to, giving it his best shot, as pathetic as it might have been. Because seeing Brennan so forlorn was something Evan simply couldn't bear.

As soon as full awareness hit Brennan, he curled in on himself further and hid his face against the pillow nestled under his head. His breath caught on a violent sob and his hands came up to cover his face when he realized Evan was looking at him.

"Don't watch me cry," he hiccupped. Evan noted Brennan wasn't asking him to leave; he was just ashamed of being so emotionally naked and afraid of seeming ugly for it.

"Why not?"

"I don't know," Brennan whined, exasperated. "It's weird."

"I know you are, but what am I," Evan retorted softly, teasing him.

"Evan," Brennan huffed, sniffling. He rubbed the heel of his hand over his eyes, "It's not funny. I finally meet my dad after dreaming of how it would be to have that moment since I was a little kid, wanting it to be perfect, you know? But it wasn't. He *hates* me and insulted Mom right to my face. It sucks. Everything sucks. *I* suck."

The words made Evan want to cry too. So, he tried to push it the opposite way, out of nothing but self-preservation and unconditional love for his brother.

"Well, it *is* a skill you possess. You're a regular Hoover. It's actually quite impressive, your sucking."

"Stop," Brennan whined, snorting once and trying not to laugh. "Stop being clever and cute."

"I'm sorry, there's nothing I can do about that," Evan said solemnly. "Unfortunately, it's a condition I was born with. You're probably infected with it too."

Brennan rolled onto his back, biting viciously at his quivering lower lip, his cheeks riddled with tear-stains. "He said it was my fault. He accused me like I'm a bad influence. And, I *am*. That's the worst part. I *am* a bad influence. God, if he knew what I've really done to you, he'd do more than hate me. He'd *kill* me."

"Hmm, berating yourself. Now you sound like me," Evan said gently. "I think that counts as progress."

Brennan made a soft, hurt sound and whispered, "I don't want him to hate me. He's the only dad I've got."

Evan dug his fingernails into his palm so deeply he nearly broke the skin and clenched his jaw hard enough to make his teeth ache. He wanted to punch a wall. He wanted to magically vanquish all of the bad, hurtful things in Brennan's world. But he couldn't. Sighing deeply, he chose to keep attacking the horror of it all with humor and said, "Wow, you are really *so* emo in the morning. Maybe we should dye your hair black. You could wear it all pushed forward covering your eyes. And of course there would have to be guyliner."

Brennan snorted with laughter, covering his mouth as soon as the sound was startled out of him. It was tear-choked and heartbreaking, but real—a small miracle. He turned and hugged Evan.

"Stop making me feel better," he murmured. "It's really annoying."

"Fat chance, emo boy. Suck it up. You're good at that."

"*Evan.*"

"I love you, Bren."

Brennan held Evan. He took another breath, trying to break through anguish to some sort of calm, and professed, "I love you, too."

"How did it go?"

"Horrible. Or good. I don't know," Charlie sighed.

In his hands he cradled one of Jimmy's chipped ceramic mugs, filled nearly to the brim with steaming hot coffee. Taking in his surroundings, familiar but sorely missed, Charlie enjoyed the stillness of morning in the rural wilderness of his old hometown. Seated next to Jimmy on a bench outside his trailer, Charlie felt the pull luring him back to his sons, but he needed to do this first, and clear the air. It was his confession, an attempt to lift some of the weight crushing him.

"The kid stood up to me, which is good, not to mention long overdue. But, Christ, the things he said. Not that they aren't true or warranted. I haven't been anywhere near the father he deserves, but I've done my best. And Brennan... Brennan reminds me of myself in a lot of ways. Tough as nails, that boy is. Not willing to take any shit. Keeps his eye on what he wants. Does his duty, even when it ain't fair or easy to stomach. But even just being near him, seeing him — it reminds me of all the moments I should've had with him: his first step; his first words; his first day at school. I should've been there for all of it and I should've been there for Maggie. I should've stopped hiding behind my damn pride and seen her through to the end, no matter what. That was too much to lay on a boy."

Jimmy sipped his own cup of coffee, saying nothing, knowing Charlie wasn't saying these things to get a response.

"Evan told me about Alek. Wasn't sure that he would," Charlie muttered, thoughtfully.

"How about Luka?"

Charlie shook his head, "Nah. Brennan mentioned him, said they were boyfriends, but.... Man, I could beat their asses for what they've gotten themselves into."

"Are you going to meet them? Alek and Luka?"

"Yeah," Charlie grunted unhappily. "Probably this morning." Glancing sideways at Jimmy, he added, "Which is why I'm over here to calm the hell down while I can. Prepare myself."

But Jimmy was giving him a strange, foreboding look.

"What? Why?"

Jimmy shook his head, waved his hand to dismiss the questions. Over the phone, Charlie had gotten an abbreviated account of the complex situation with his sons, and the other set of brothers they'd been dating. He didn't know much about what these other boys were like, specifically. The look on Jimmy's face didn't give Charlie a good feeling about it.

He asked Charlie, "Are you going to try to give them a chance? You should."

"A chance to what? Violate my sons twenty different ways? Swap 'em around between themselves like soulless pieces of meat?"

"So, that's a no?"

"I don't fucking know," Charlie groaned. Slouching back against the bench, he stretched his legs and took a deep breath. "They seemed happy last night, before the argument. They did. Nervous, but happy. I don't get to see Evan happy very much. And Brennan—he deserves all the happy he can get."

"I'm sorry," Jimmy sighed. "I truly am. This must be so hard for you. Does Evan know the extent of what you're aware of? Or how long you've known about his orientation?"

"Nope. He thinks it was some big revelation last night, and I intend to keep it that way. I could be wrong, but I don't think hearing his old man has known his son's queer since before he started sprouting chin hair is gonna sit well with him."

"Unfortunately, I agree with you."

"Besides, I've gotta protect my informant. From what you say, things are strained enough between you and Evan without him knowing how much you ratted him out."

"I wouldn't have said anything if I wasn't honestly concerned about what could happen if I kept it to myself," Jimmy grumbled.

"Yeah, I know."

"Evan used to tell me everything. He would confide in me, and I miss that. I miss his friendship more, though. But if I have to let him push me away in order to keep him from hurting himself, then I'll put my own feelings aside and do whatever I need to do."

They were both quiet for a long while, stewing in their thoughts and drinking their hot, bitter brew.

"You know what the worst thing is?" Charlie asked.

"What?"

"I don't regret keeping them apart for so long. Not if it was gonna turn out like this when they got together. But then maybe this is all happening because they're overcompensating for the shit they went through due to being apart. The loss of affection of one of their parents and their brother. Maybe it's all my fault. What do you say, Jimmy? Am I going to hell for this? For what I've driven my children to do?"

"Hard to say," Jimmy said quietly and solemnly.

Charlie laughed coldly. "Well, at least you're honest."

Presley wandered out of Carter's bedroom clad only in a pair of exercise shorts, his jaw covered with stubble and eyes bleary. Yawning, he wandered into the kitchen. Alek was leaning against the counter by the coffee pot. Carter was sitting at the kitchen table, pushing some runny eggs around his plate with a piece of toast.

Squinting with confusion, Presley said, "Alek. You're home? What's up?" Carter made a slicing motion across his throat, trying to tell him with a pointed look to cut it out with the questions, but it was too late.

Alek stared down into his coffee with a miserable expression. "Charlie's home. Evan and Brennan's father."

"…Oh."

Water burbled noisily through the pipes in the walls. The sound of the shower running in the upstairs bathroom was noticeable by all, just as noticeable as the passionate moans and other sex noises that had been coming from the upper floor not an hour earlier.

"That's a good thing, though, right? He hasn't been back since Evan was in the hospital. It's about damn time he—"

"Evan just came out to him last night," Alek admitted sullenly. "And Charlie accused Brennan of bringing strangers to live in the house and being a bad influence on Evan. Today Luka and I have to go over there and meet the son-of-a-bitch."

"Oh. Damn."

"Yeah."

"Good luck with that."

"Thanks," Alek grumbled.

"You could always lay low," Carter interjected. "Let them sort out their dad and stay out of it. Might just make it worse anyway."

"Mm," Alek grunted, almost in agreement.

When Luka appeared, he was dressed in a light blue polo shirt and khakis, his hair blown dry and brushed out in soft waves, perfectly coiffed, making him look like a model out of a sporty, hip, clothing catalog. Despite his honest efforts to look presentable, though, he was clearly exhausted and as morose as Alek.

Staring down at his phone as he entered the kitchen, Luka sent the message he was typing to Evan then slipped the gadget into a pocket. Shuffling toward Alek without a glance at his other roommates, Luka fell into his brother's arms, letting Alek drag him in by a hand locked up around Luka's shaved-smooth, chiseled jaw for a slow, urgent kiss. He caressed roughly down over Luka's backside. When Luka broke away after an indulgent moment, Alek whispered, "You were amazing."

They had asked Evan and Brennan permission to have sex with each other. Though strange to have to ask for the go-ahead to indulge in something that had always been just theirs to control, they wouldn't have been able to go through with it otherwise. After everything Evan and Brennan had endured and after all of the fighting between the four of them, the last thing they wanted was to cause any more strife. But Evan had given the okay for them both. Brennan had been too inconsolable to reply for himself. It had been even more comforting than usual, for both of them, to have some intimate time together. It was good to remember no matter what might have been going on, or headed their way, they would always have each other. Their bond was a constant, able to weather all sorts of turbulence. Whatever had to happen with Brennan and Evan, they would figure it out. In the meantime, now Alek and Luka had enjoyed a welcome reminder of the strength of their own relationship.

"Evan got him out of bed, but he still won't leave the room," Luka said softly, with a heavy heart. "Aleksy, I have to get over there. I have to see him. I know you weren't sure—"

"Eat something first," Alek replied.

"Not hungry."

Grabbing an apple from the fruit basket on the counter behind him, Alek tossed it to his brother. Luka caught it as his phone buzzed in his pocket. Struggling to get it out as quickly as he could, Luka put the apple on the table and sank into a chair, reading the message with a rapt expression.

Carter continued to pretend to be preoccupied by his breakfast. Presley stared hard at Luka, then went to pour two mugs of coffee, sliding one of them to Luka. With Luka's fingers flying over the tiny keys on his phone, Alek palmed his own phone and quickly dialed a number. He let out a breath of relief when it was answered after two rings.

"You want us to come over?" Alek asked, then paused, listening for the reply. Luka looked up sharply from his seat, then took a sip of coffee.

Alek turned away from them, putting his back to the room, speaking more softly into the phone and hiding his face behind a hand. "Bren, hey, I know it sounded like that, but please give him a chance. Think about what it looks like from his point of view. It doesn't mean — Babydoll, please don't cry anymore."

Shocked, Carter looked up from his food at last, gawking at Alek, then at Luka who hung his head and took another sip.

"We've talked about this, remember? How could he not love you?" Alek said gently, "He's just worried about you. It's what dads do. Listen. Listen to me. You want some backup? You want us to head over? It'd take some of the attention off of you for a while. Yeah? Okay. We'll be there in an hour. Get something to eat. Go for a run. You'll feel better."

Alek sighed heavily, rubbing a hand over his mouth. His posture changed. "You want me to lay him out? Because I will. Just say the word. I've wanted to get my hands on that bastard since the day I found out what Evan went through. I'll play the part of Evan's dutiful boyfriend all day long, but if he hurts you again, I swear to god... Okay. All right. I love you, too. See you in an hour. Hold on."

Alek handed the phone to Luka, ignoring Carter's astonishment at the endearments. Presley caught Luka's eye for a brief moment. Glumly, Luka pressed the phone to his ear.

"Hey Cupcake," Luka started, smiling as he said it, but with sadness in his eyes. For a long moment, he just listened. His face worked, battling to mask the emotions boiling inside him. Taking a deep breath, he asked stiffly, "What can we do?"

Brennan replied and Luka asked, "Is that going to make it better or worse? Okay. I love you. Don't let Evan have too much coffee; he's freaked out enough without adding caffeine jitters. Okay. Bye. Love you too. Bye."

Hanging up the phone, and passing it back to Alek, Luka wiped at his eyes with the back of his hand and grabbed the apple. After taking a big bite, he returned Carter and Presley's disapproving stares with a hard look and asked around a mouthful of fruit, "What? You got a problem with somethin'?"

"...No. No problem," Carter murmured, softening.

"Good," Luka frowned.

"We gonna be gaining a roommate or two?" Presley asked.

"Hopefully not. Not like that, anyway. We'll see. First, we try to smooth things out," Alek said.

"You're gonna smooth *this* out? You two are each screwing both of that man's *barely legal* sons and you think you're gonna 'smooth that out'?" Presley gaped.

Alek shrugged, "Yeah."

"You motherfuckers are crazy," Carter said, shaking his head.

Luka took another bite of his apple and picked his phone back up as it vibrated. He read the message on the screen. "Evan thinks we should try to look nice, but not dress up too much. So, for you, like button down shirt, but no tie?"

Alek quirked an eyebrow at him, "Seriously? You're coordinating our outfits with Evan?"

"Yeah, "Luka nodded. "Oh, and he says to tell you don't you dare show up with your hair slicked back. He says it makes you look threatening. And old."

"Fantastic," Alek groaned wearily. "Is that all?"

"Don't glower too much. And try to look shorter."

"Are you shitting me?"

"What? It's true. You glower."

"He knows I have a phone, too, right?" Alek asked, wandering out of the room, heading to the stairs.

"And don't wear anything that shows off your sexy muscles too much!" Luka called.

Carter snorted into his orange juice, chuckling.

"Okay, that's it. I'm fucking calling him," Alek snapped.

"Sorry, he just got into the shower."

"Of course he did. Fuck me sideways."

Once the door to Alek's room had thumped shut, Presley turned to Luka and observed, "You look like hell, man. What happened to you? You not sleep or somethin'?"

"Don't ask him that!" Carter moaned with dread.

"Oh. That's *totally* Alek's fault. I've gotten used to sleeping next to Brennan, so sleeping with Evan instead is just as good, since they're the same size and cuddle in similar ways, but Aleksy's too big anymore. It's all different, so I finally managed to fall asleep at, like, four a.m. then he got a raging boner around eight and he just kept on fuckin' me 'til about a half-hour ago. The man's got some serious goddamned stamina. Of course the cock ring probably helped. I came three-and-a-half times. It was awesome. But yeah, a nap would really help right about now," Luka said matter-of-factly, chewing more apple.

Presley squinted, "How do you come half-a-time?"

"Stop asking him to explain things! You know what happens when you do that? He *explains things*," Carter scolded. Standing from the table with the pair of them watching him with amusement, he added for good measure, "Don't encourage him!"

"I like when you encourage me," Luka smiled at Presley.

"No, I'm honestly curious. How do you come half-a-time?"

"Presley! For fuck's sake!"

"Well, if you start to, like its crawling right up your balls, you grab really hard right at the base of your nuts and *squeeze* —"

"Do you see? Do you see what you did?" Carter roared, throwing his arms up in defeat as he stormed out of the room. "I'm not gonna be able to get this shit out of my brain for days!"

"He's a mite testy this mornin'," Presley confided under his breath to Luka, winking. "He's kind of *sore*, if you know what I mean."

Luka gasped, "Whoa. Whoa. Wait. Wait a minute. He *bottomed*? First time? It was his first time, right? Oh my god! No wonder. Wow."

From the next room, Carter bellowed, "*What are you telling him,*

Presley?!"

"Nothing, dear!" Presley called back sweetly.

"I've gotta go congratulate him. That's *awesome*," Luka said eagerly, starting to stand. Presley planted his hand on Luka's shoulder and shoved him back down.

"Don't even think about it. I'd like to keep my balls firmly attached to my body, thank you very much, and if you go in there and congratulate him on taking a cock, he'll be wearing 'em as a damn necklace. Keep your ass sat down."

"Eh. Okay," Luka shrugged. "I'll catch him later. Or maybe just install some hidden cameras in your bedrooms. Kidding! I'm kidding. Kind of."

Chapter 19
Defiance

Evan leaned back against the trunk of his car and dialed Jimmy's number. Brennan was out on a run. After asking Charlie if he could bum a few cigarettes, Evan sought out some solitude outside. Without knowing Evan quit the habit months ago after a long, difficult journey toward being nicotine-free, months filled with torment from the effort of maintaining his willpower, Charlie complied with the request and effectively enabled his son's habit once again.

With the lit cigarette dangling from between his lips, Evan figured he had time to smoke two of them and shower the smell away before anyone else found out. There was guilt, but after everything, smoking didn't seem like too horrible a betrayal. It made him feel good, relaxed, as the nicotine entered his system. He savored the taste and liked the instant buzz it gave him. It was like old times, when things were less complicated. He took a deep pull, inhaling and holding the smoke in his lungs, and put the phone to his ear.

The call was picked up right away. "Evan?"

"Yeah," he grunted, blowing out a tendril of smoke from the side of his mouth.

"I was wondering when you would call. *If* you would call. How are you?"

"You just saw me last night."

"Yeah, but now it's just you and me, right? So tell me. How are you?"

"Peachy. Fucking amazing. You?"

"You seem hostile."

"That's because I am hostile. What did you tell him? Hmm?

What does Dad know?"

"I think you should ask him."

"No, I'm asking *you*," Evan snarled.

"Okay. Let's see. You want to know if Charlie is aware of the polyamory or the incest… or both."

Almost dropping the phone, Evan fumbled as he turned it off, ending the call.

"Fuck! Shit! Damn it!" He stared at the phone, his hand trembling and eyes huge with terror. Without thinking, he put the cigarette back in his mouth and inhaled.

He had no idea what to do.

The phone rang. Jimmy.

"*Fuck*," Evan hissed. He glanced at the house with his father inside as he realized he'd been shouting. The phone rang about six times before going to voicemail. Evan started walking. He was fully aware of how this was going to play out. If he didn't take Jimmy's call, Jimmy would come over, so Evan headed in the direction of Jimmy's trailer, knowing he wasn't able to speak about this with him over the cell.

He encountered Jimmy halfway between their homes. Jimmy was clearly surprised to see him.

"Look," Jimmy said calmly holding up his hands like he was surrendering or something, even while there was still a good ten feet between them, "I'm not trying to attack you."

"The hell you're not!" Evan yelled.

"Charlie doesn't know about you and Brennan from me. He might be able to figure it out on his own, though. I mean, you give off a vibe when you're together, you and Brennan, and I wasn't one hundred percent sure about the incest until now, seeing your reaction. I, uh, I guess it's true then, huh?"

"You son of a…."

Jimmy's tone was measured, soothing, like he was talking to a crazy person. "I'm just being honest with you, Evan. And I'm not going to give you any speeches about your decisions or ask why, I *know* why. Yes, I do think it's wrong. That's just my personal opinion. I think you're tainting what could have been a beautiful brotherly bond with sexual intimacy, but it's not my place to judge you.

That's between you and God. My job is to be your friend."

"Yeah, my *friend*," Evan grumbled under his breath.

Shaken, gaze skittering around, Evan sucked hard on the stub of his cigarette. He dropped it, crushing it out with his boot heel, then lit another.

"You're smoking again."

"Fuck you!" Evan shouted; his lips pursed around the butt, gesturing with his lighter, "Really. Fuck you. Wait. Wait a minute. What the fuck does polyamory mean?"

"You're living it. Come on, you're a smart kid. You can figure it out. It's having more than one intimate relationship at a time with the knowledge and consent of everyone involved. Does that pretty much cover it, what's going on with you, and Alek, and Luka, and Brennan?"

Evan whined with horror and stared up at the sky.

"He knows about it," Evan said quietly. "Doesn't he?"

"No. But maybe you should tell him, and be honest."

"Not fucking likely."

"Evan," Jimmy sighed, wearily. "Why? Why wasn't Alek enough for you? Why are you doing this to yourself?"

"I *love* them," Evan told him, his jaw clenched. "I love Luka, as much as I do Alek."

"And Brennan?"

"That's none of your goddamned business."

"Okay," Jimmy nodded, yielding, letting Evan have the last word.

"I need to get back." Turning, Evan stormed away. Though he prayed quietly, Evan overheard Jimmy asking God for temperance and forgiveness for Evan and Brennan's souls. The tall grass rustled softly as Evan moved through it.

Alek and Luka arrived together at the house as Evan finished getting dressed in fresh clothes, the smoke-scented ones already dumped in the washer. Brennan had gone into the shower as soon as Evan had come out of the laundry room and was still there, leaving Evan on his own to handle things when the doorbell rang.

Charlie was sitting in the living room, looking over the medical bills from Evan's stay in the hospital, as well as his copies of the police report. Feeling woozy, blood roaring in his ears, heart pounding in his chest, Evan cleared his throat and answered the door.

"Hey." He nodded to his lovers, whose expressions drooped once they got a good look at him. "Come in. Bren just got back from his run, so...." He waved them inside.

"It's going to be fine," Alek said softly under his breath. Seeming tense and stiff, he leaned in and placed a kiss to Evan's temple. Then he stepped back, waiting for Evan to lead. Luka gave Evan a strained, meaningful look, as if it was taking all of his willpower to not hug Evan breathless.

"Let's get this over with," Evan said, stuffing his hands in his pockets, wishing he had another cigarette. He walked them over to the living room and didn't look up as he said, "Dad. This is Alek and Luka."

He thumbed back at them in that order. Absolute, icy silence filled the room. Evan's gut churned queasily as he braced for the worst.

Charlie was standing. He had gotten to his feet when Evan answered the doorbell, but as he digested the all-too-real sight of his sons' lovers standing before him, hugely muscular and tall, taller than he was, broader too, and much older than he had imagined, something strange began to happen to his expression. His composure slipped and all he could do was imagine this pair of grown men touching his children.

Blistering rage consumed Charlie. Evan, who knew damn well how to detect his father's bad moods, sensed it. They all probably did, but it was Evan's reaction that Charlie could read easiest. It got him to look up with much apprehension at his father. In reflex clearly borne of protectiveness, Alek rested a hand on Evan's shoulder. There was a sort of finality in it that. For Charlie, it felt like losing his son for the last time. His little boy was gone and belonged to someone else now.

"Dad?" Evan squeaked, betraying his age. It only made it worse.

"How old are you? You're twins? Why the hell didn't you tell me they're twins?" Charlie spat before he could bite his tongue to still it.

"We're twenty-five, Mr. Savage," Luka said politely. "I'm sorry I never mentioned it when we spoke. I forget sometimes. Take it for granted, I guess."

"Do you know my sons are only eighteen? They're *teenagers* for Christ's sake. A few months ago this would have been statutory rape and you'd be arrested for assaulting children. Like a pedophile."

"Sir," Luka started.

"Dad!" Evan complained, insulted.

Alek just stood his ground, meeting Charlie's stare, not at all attempting to apologize like his brother appeared to be.

After a glance back at the bathroom where Brennan had been holed away, Evan pulled himself up a little straighter, a determined fire burning behind eyes the color of cool waters. He looked right at Charlie and leaned into Alek, slinging an arm behind Alek's waist.

Alek's lips twitched up in a victorious smile. His thumb stroked once, up and down the side of Evan's neck. It was subtle but very effective at conveying what he likely wanted it to.

"We're very much aware of Evan and Brennan's ages," Alek said. "But they are both quite mature, given the trials they've both been through. I can assure you everything has been completely consensual." It was both a jab at what Charlie had allowed to happen to his sons and acknowledgment of his and Luka's intimate knowledge of them.

Charlie stared at Alek's hand on Evan, and Evan's curled around Alek's waist.

"I see. So, *Alek*, I hear you live in my house now."

"I do. I didn't think it was fair to allow Brennan to take over the duties of nursing another seriously ill person, after so recently losing his mother. And I love Evan very much. I'm committed to him in every way. All I want is for him to be healthy and happy."

"Dad," Evan groaned. "Can you just give them a break? Please?"

"We care very deeply about your sons, Mr. Savage," Luka explained, being the good cop to Alek's bad one. "I realize how this must look to you, but I can assure you we have their best interests at heart. If we intended to take advantage of them, we wouldn't be here in order to get to know you, and let you get to know us. Your opinion is important to Evan and Brennan, and we know that."

Charlie settled slightly, holding Luka's gaze, understanding completely why, of all people, it was Luka who had called him from the hospital, that Luka was the mediator of the bunch. He actually started to like Luka for his efforts and rationality until Brennan finally appeared, emerging from the bathroom with damp, stringy hair and eyes still puffy and bloodshot.

Making a beeline right for Luka, before doing anything else, Brennan pulled Luka toward him, wrapping his arms around Luka's middle and stretching up on his toes to kiss his lips. Luka cupped his hands around Brennan's face, kissing him back and sighing with some anguish, "Baby, look at you."

Brennan let the moment draw out, with everyone's attention on them. When he turned toward Charlie, he leaned against Luka's chest, holding Luka's hand and staring with accusation at his father.

"I guess you all met," he said in a voice hoarse from crying. "Since I heard shouting."

"We weren't shouting," Luka explained, "Your dad was just surprised by a few things."

"You hate them, don't you?"

"Brennan," Charlie sighed, "I don't hate—"

"Just like you hate me for intruding on your perfectly arranged life with your *real* son."

Stricken, Charlie exclaimed, "No! I could never hate you! Why would you say such a thing? You can't really think that. Yes, I regret some of the choices Maggie and I made. I can't ever tell you, Brennan, how much pain it causes me that I missed your entire childhood. You're my *son*. You're precious to me, and it's only because I want you to be safe that I worry about you and the choices you make in your personal life."

"Because it's so terrible to be gay?"

Charlie set his jaw and swallowed back the first retort that came to mind. It wouldn't have been appropriate and it would give away too much of what he wanted to keep to himself for now.

Instead he said, "Do *not* put words in my mouth, boy. That's not what I was referring to. Now, I realize you're not used to the way I tend to speak to Evan, but because you are so very much like him, it is how I've automatically been speaking to you, too. I see now that's inappropriate. I did not intend to hurt your feelings or upset you like I see I did. It's only because I care so much about you that my inclination is to set rules for you. Yes, you are an adult now, technically, but you're still my child, no matter your age, and your mother would never forgive me if I allowed anything to happen to you. I owe her that much, don't you think?"

Dumbstruck and without a comeback, possibly even placated to some extent, Brennan deflated, softening. Some of the tension left the air, allowing everyone to breathe a little easier.

"Now, I think it's about damn time I get to know the two people who have become so invested in your lives. How about we all head over to the steakhouse for lunch on me, and we can talk. Civilly," Charlie suggested.

Brennan rolled his eyes. "I'm pescetarian. I don't eat meat."

"Okay, then you can choose the restaurant, Brennan. Please."

"Whatever," he muttered, but led Luka by the hand to the door.

Chapter 20
Losing Evan

As soon as Charlie asked to be seated at a table in the smoking section of the open-air café, Evan knew his willpower wouldn't hold out. It was a goner.

The five of them took their seats, with Evan next to Charlie and the other three on the opposite side of the table. Charlie pulled out a pack of cigarettes. He lit one up as they looked over their menus. The questions started to come about Alek and Luka's backgrounds: their parents, their family, and their jobs. Evan couldn't really bring himself to pay much attention though. His craving for a cigarette was intensely distracting. It made his skin itch.

He stared at the cigarette pinched between Charlie's fingers and promptly gave up any pretense of pretending like he hadn't taken up his old bad habit that morning. Sure, he figured it would get him in trouble, especially with Alek, but Evan didn't really expect Alek to do much about it whilst under the scrutiny of Charlie.

Charlie stubbed out the butt of his first cigarette. Taking two more from the pack when he saw Evan eyeing it, Charlie lit the ends of both while Luka explained about his job at Sweat Gym as a personal trainer. Luka didn't seem to notice anything amiss, too wrapped up in his story. But Alek noticed, as did Brennan. Their eyes fixed on the glowing embers and followed one of the cigarettes when it moved, as if in slow motion, through the air as Charlie passed it to Evan.

Brennan's mouth fell open like he was about to say something. Alek's reaction was much speedier and more precise. Mid-drag, Evan had the offending cigarette plucked from between his lips, then Alek stubbed it out in the ashtray in the center of the table.

Luka stopped talking abruptly. They all turned to stare at Alek and Evan.

"Hey!" Evan complained.

"What the hell was that?" Alek asked sternly. "After the months of work it took to quit, you just... what? Pick one up like it's no big deal? What's wrong with you?"

"He had some earlier this morning, too," Brennan mumbled, gazing down at his hands.

Evan sputtered, "How do you know that?"

Brennan shrugged.

"I took a shower! I changed my clothes!"

"I could still tell."

"Traitor." Evan made an effort not to notice his father's slightly amused expression as he took in everything, the easy bickering between Evan and Brennan and the protective and concerned tone in Alek's voice.

"You quit? You didn't tell me you quit," Charlie pointed out.

"Well, he did," Alek frowned. "And I'm not about to just sit here and let you start up again, after everything you went through trying to kick those damn things."

"I wasn't going to keep doing it; I just needed a couple today. It's been a hard day, all right?"

That was an understatement if there ever was one. It had all come to a head for Evan, all of the hurt feelings and knee-jerk reactions since the attack, and since Evan and Luka had cheated on their partners with each other; all of the secret-keeping from Jimmy and now Charlie, pretending everything was fine when everything was the furthest from fine it could get. They were sitting at a table together, pretending to be a normal, happy family when they were the polar opposite of normal and above all else, Evan was sick to death of lying, pretending, and constantly bickering with those he loved. All he wanted to get him through was a goddamned cigarette and it wasn't too much to ask in exchange for his sanity.

"No. It's not all right, Evan," Alek countered, holding his ground and just as worked up as Evan, for his own reasons. It wasn't just about the cigarette. Evan could feel it, see it in Alek's face. "This is serious. This is your health. I wish you'd said something earlier about this, like maybe when the first craving hit. You could have called me. Maybe I— we could have helped you resist it if you talked to us first."

Evan rolled his eyes and slumped back in his chair, unwilling to fight or give in.

Luka cleared his throat and attempted to continue what he was saying about being independent at such a young age, without family to rely on, but Alek interrupted after a few seconds.

"It was really important to me to be able to pay my way, you know, rent, insurance, all of that, so—" Luka started.

Still fully engaged in the argument, Alek blurted, hissing across the table to Evan, "How many did you have?"

"*Two.* It's not the end of the world."

Every word cranked the dial up another notch, increasing the tension that much more. There was only so much higher it could go before something snapped.

Clearly angry, Alek said, "Do you really not care about this at all? Because that's what it sounds like."

"Alek, maybe now is not the time to—" Luka tried.

"You seriously aren't upset by this? That he's sucking tar again because of a *bad day* and doesn't even regret it?" Alek countered to his brother.

"Alek," Luka growled quietly, shaking his head tightly once back and forth.

"*I'm* upset by it," Brennan offered.

"Thank you, Brennan," Alek grunted, squinting at Evan.

Oh, that's fantastic, Evan thought. *Now they're both ganging up on me. That's just perfect. Brennan and Alek, making rules for my well-being once again. Telling me what I need to do for my own good.*

"Jesus *Christ*," Evan groaned. Enough was enough. He stood up and walked away, weaving among the tables and heading out through the entrance to the café, away from prying eyes. Alek got to his feet and followed him.

"Lover's quarrel," Luka smiled awkwardly at Charlie.

"They do that a lot?" Charlie asked, stubbing out his own cigarette and tucking the pack away.

"No, Alek's just..." Luka sighed. "Let's just say their history gives him good reason to worry about Evan. It got worse after the attack. Alek gets so afraid of Evan getting hurt or sick, he watches over Evan pretty closely. But he does it because he loves him, and because he feels kind of responsible for what happened at the bar. When he and I were growing up, he always felt it was his job to keep me safe, too, and when things didn't go so great, he always took it to heart like it was all on him. Now with Evan, it's the same thing all over again. Everything bad that happens to Evan is Alek's fault. I mean, it's not, obviously.

"But, Alek and I, being twins, we're built the same way. So, before, when Alek would get upset, he'd vent to me because he knew I'd understand and it'd be done."

He'd push all of that turmoil at me, Luka thought, but didn't say. *Through violence, sex, words, or screaming.*

"And I'd let him," Luka continued. "I'd invite it, because the stress would be effectively dealt with. But he can't do that with Evan. They don't have that twin connection for Alek to use to get his frustrations out. The last thing he'd ever want to do is hurt Evan, so he treats Evan with such care. But then his emotions just build up."

For a quiet moment, he watched the spaces Alek and Evan had filled at the table, afraid for them. Luka realized, suddenly, horribly, how possible it was that it might never work out between his brother and Evan. Left on their own, there was nowhere for the fear to go.

Trying to tell himself he was wrong, wanting to be wrong, Luka at first couldn't speak. Brennan took his hand. Charlie was listening attentively, giving Luka time to finish what he was trying to say.

Slowly, stumbling, Luka concluded with, "He doesn't... you know... want to lose him."

Trying to push his worries away, to focus on what was right in front of him rather than what he was afraid of, Luka let it go as much as he could. Luckily, he was good at that.

"I just don't think Evan's used to the scrutiny, either. No offense, sir."

"Hmm," Charlie grunted thoughtfully.

Luka paused, then said to Charlie, "Can I ask you a question?"

"Shoot."

"How does Evan seem to you? Compared to the last time you saw him?"

"Hmm. I guess he seems stronger. Changed. A lot more confident. But yeah, very much changed. And a hell of a lot more like his mother." Turning to Brennan, he added, "Is that your doing?"

Brennan shrugged. "Hadn't really noticed," he murmured, picking at the edge of his napkin. Lifting his gaze to the café's entrance, Brennan seemed to be reaching out for them, their other halves. Luka knew the feeling. More and more, it just wasn't the same when the four of them were separated.

"I'm sure they'll just be a minute," Luka murmured to Brennan.

"Yeah," Brennan sighed, still watching.

Chapter 21
Hard Truths

Out by the parking lot, Evan walked around the café and the adjoining pharmacy's main building, heading for the shelter of the alley between it and a large, sprawling office complex. With his hands shoved in his pockets, he stepped into the shadows and waited there.

He didn't have to wait long. Alek grabbed him from behind, spinning him and backing him up against the brick wall. Immediately, he started to pat Evan down, feeling his pockets for more cigarettes. When he found none, he planted his hands on either side of Evan's head and bore down on him.

Evan's breath was quickened. His gaze was fixed on Alek's mouth and he wondered if Alek would lash out at him like he did with Luka. Maybe Alek would grab him by the throat, throw a punch or two. Just as he thought these things, though, Evan knew how ridiculous they were. Alek was too wrapped up in protecting him to ever lay hands on him like that.

"What the fuck is this? This little streak of self-destruction?"

"M-maybe I didn't think you'd care," Evan stuttered softly.

"Well, you were wrong."

"I guess I was."

"Do you need a demonstration of how serious I am about this? You need to think about your choices. That's the shit that gets you into trouble. We're going to have a little lesson, you and me," Alek growled.

His mouth hovered above Evan's. Evan's breath caught, his mouth working silently for a second, parting around his soundless

Lynn Kelling

gasp. He knew it was quite apparent how much this was turning him on. Alek reacted in kind, letting Evan bait him. It made Evan feel steadier the more control Alek took of the situation. It was a plea for distraction. Evan needed it to get through the stress of dealing with his father. And Alek seemed more than happy to comply.

"L-like a punishment?"

"Just like that," Alek said in a raspy, low voice, thick with promise. "You want to be hard on your body? You need something to suck on to keep your mind off your troubles? I can help with both of those things, no cigarettes, inevitable emphysema or lung cancer required."

"Wha-what're you…" Evan stammered, then choked off a brittle moan when Alek grabbed a handful of his cock and squeezed it through his jeans. Hips canting forward into Alek, Evan gasped and writhed.

"Jesus. You're fucking hard," Alek marveled, victorious. "You get off on this, huh—the thought of being punished, and some big, strong man putting your ass in line when it needs it? Sure you do… *Jailbait.* You've been acting out for years and no one's ever bothered to spank you for it."

"*Alek,*" Evan moaned. God, it was true. Alek had no idea how true it was.

"Get back inside and if I see you so much as *think* about having a smoke, I'll personally spank your sweet ass raw right in front of Daddy instead of waiting 'til our little meet and greet is over like I intend to do. You got me?"

"I-I…" Evan stammered.

Alek squeezed tighter. Evan twisted helplessly, whimpering, "*Fuck.*"

"You got me, Jailbait?"

"Y-yes. I'm sorry."

"Not as sorry as you're gonna be. What do you want, hmm? The hand or the belt? You ever gotten it good and hard, 'til your ass feels like it's fucking on fire and you can't help but cry out with each smack?"

Evan shuddered, thrusting in a steady rhythm against Alek's open hand, holding on to the front of Alek's shirt, clawing at him.

He was flushed with lust and couldn't meet Alek's eyes directly.

Glancing around them, Alek pulled his hand away and pinned Evan's arms to his sides. "Stop," he growled. "You really think I'm gonna let you get off right now? You think you deserve that? You don't get to come until I let you. Get yourself under control. Now."

Evan gulped. With a deep, unsteady breath, he willed his flesh to soften and his brain to jump-start. After a few long moments he chuckled, asking with a cocky smirk, "What're you gonna do, Aleksy? Bend me over your knee? You're bullshitting me, right? This is some kind of scheme to distract me from smoking."

"Do I look like I'm bullshitting you?" Alek stared, seriously. "Obviously you respond best to a firm hand, so that's what you'll get. Now, we're going back in there, so unless you want Daddy to see your dick tenting your pants…"

"Oh *god*." He groaned. "Stop talking about spanking me then!"

"Stop *asking* about it."

Alek backed up a few steps, folding his arms, prepared to wait.

After a few long, silent, tense minutes, Evan seemed more composed and muttered, "Okay, let's go back. They probably think we're screwing out here or something."

"Where on Earth would they get that idea?" Alek countered sarcastically. "Ready when you are, princess."

Evan rolled his eyes, scoffing, and tried adamantly not to show how a secret part of himself enjoyed that nickname. He started walking and got all the way to the entrance of the café, within sight of Brennan, Luka, and Charlie, but not within earshot. He paused there and said quietly without facing Alek, who he knew was right behind him, "Jimmy knows. That's the real reason why I was smoking. Well, that and Brennan's breakdown which majorly fucked up my willpower. Jimmy knows everything—that I'm fucking you *and* Luka *and* Brennan. He tricked me into admitting it and he threw it in my face before trying to pretend like he didn't hate me for it."

"Shit," Alek groaned.

"I'm not letting him get in my head," Evan said defiantly. Alek moved around to face him, holding Evan's shoulders. "I told him it wasn't his business, and it's not. It… oh, hell." He sighed and braced a hand against Alek's jaw, stretching up. Alek met him halfway. They kissed. Evan's lips parted easily for Alek's tongue when Alek pressed in a little deeper, frowning with concentration and anguish.

They stood there on the sidewalk together, in sight of everyone, and Evan kissed Alek—out of defiance to Jimmy, to Charlie, to the world in general, not caring anymore who saw or what they thought. It scared him to death to do it, but the victory of his boldness outweighed his trepidation by far.

"You're incredible. You know that, right?" Alek said before pulling away.

Taking Evan's hand, Alek led the way back to the table as the three awaiting them watched on.

With the taste and feel of Alek's kiss lingering, reinvigorating him, Evan took his seat and spread his cloth napkin over his lap as their food had already been brought to the table. Clearing his throat, he glanced around the table and said quietly to Brennan, "I'm sorry I upset you. It won't happen again—the smoking. I promise."

Then Evan turned to his father, his jaw clenched and his will renewed. Somewhat startled at the gentle affection in Charlie's eyes, Evan said, "Dad, I should have been honest with you about a lot of things, but I should have told you I quit. I'm sorry."

"You don't have to apologize, son. I don't blame you for being stressed. Especially since a good amount of that stress is because of me, so I'm sorry too, for what it's worth." Evan looked at him with real gratitude. Charlie clapped him on the shoulder, adding, "And I see you two have had your chance to kiss and make up so what do you say we have some food?"

"*Dad*," Evan groaned.

"So, Alek," Charlie started. "Brennan was telling me how he plans to study to be a nurse beginning next semester, and hopes to work at Mercy Gen when he graduates. He mentioned you work for them?"

"Yes, sir. I work in their corporate offices downtown, in the finance department. It's an entry-level position, but a lot of room for growth, which is important to me. Plus, I get full benefits now."

"I thought you worked at the bar? That's where Evan was jumped, right? I'm still trying to piece all of this out from what you've told me over the phone and now finding out the nature of your relationship with Evan."

The questions were like a sucker punch, and Evan winced. All of the good his chat with Alek did melted away. Alek's self-recrimination came right back at the implication of his job being the cause of Evan's attack. Evan saw it in Alek's expression, and the way he pressed his lips together like he was doing so to hold in the things he *really* wanted to say.

Sounding like he was chewing on the words, Alek responded with, "Yes, sir, I did work there, pulling double-duty as security and short-order cook. But I quit months ago after what happened. I would have quit earlier if I knew what the risk to Evan was. The last thing I want is to put your sons in any danger."

"I appreciate your consideration," Charlie told him. "Sounds like you made a good move, career-wise. A desk job has a lot of benefits the HR departments don't list for ya, like not beating your body to hell with manual labor, getting to stay close to home, not coming home at the end of the night covered in engine or cooking grease. That's why I'm so glad Brennan is planning to go to school. Evan, I know you care a hell of a lot about what you do. That's why I never tried to dissuade you from that path, but man... Changing in that blue collar for a white one's usually a good move."

The rest of the meal went relatively smoothly, as each of the four younger men shared select pieces of who they were, what they'd been doing, and their plans for the future with the highly inquisitive elder Savage. But, Evan's preoccupation was with everyone's reactions to one another, to his father's responses to Alek, Luka and Brennan and the contrast between what he knew or suspected, and what was being presented as fact. The game of it all distracted him almost enough to keep his mind off the cigarettes. Whenever he got a whiff of smoke from another table, Evan looked to Alek, who shot him a lightning quick, incredibly sharp look of warning that effectively dulled Evan's craving with fantasies of the promised punishment Evan hoped was coming his way soon.

As everyone finished their lunches and emptied their glasses, Evan's focus shifted to his twin. He tried to gauge how Brennan felt, to read his mind and his heart, sure if he concentrated enough, he could do it. At first, seeing Brennan's expression was untroubled and less guarded, Evan thought he had gotten away with observing Brennan undetected.

He found out he was wrong when, mid-sentence in response to their father asking about Brennan's propensity to cook them all dinner, Brennan caught Evan's gaze and smiled at him with only his eyes. They shone brightly with amusement, a knowing twinkle, deep-seated love and the barest hint of intimate warmth. It made Evan smile helplessly, which he tried to hide behind his cup.

After that, it became quickly clear to Evan Brennan's spirit had been buoyed by Charlie's earnest curiosity regarding their lives and his patience with the limited answers he received. Having control over what Charlie knew about who Brennan was made Brennan feel more powerful and less subjected to helplessness by his fate. Once in a while Brennan would let some small truth go, handing it over to their father. The more tidbits he gave away, the clearer it was knowing aspects of Brennan's identity was in no way a free pass to claim the right to continue to become closer to him. If it was what Brennan wanted or needed, he could put a stop to Charlie's hope to be in his life. So it continued to be a dance between them. Brennan gave a little, Charlie tried for more and Brennan got to decide whether to give it to him.

They all pushed back from the table once Charlie paid the bill, and headed back to the parking lot. At the sidewalk, Charlie patted down his pockets, searching for something he feared he might have dropped. Excusing himself, Charlie went back to the table to look for it while the four younger men continued on.

Their vehicles were parked on the far side of a long aisle filled with cars. Once they got to them, with Charlie safely out of sight, Alek pulled Brennan aside and quickly, tenderly kissed him, saying, "See? There was nothing to worry about. Everything will be fine."

Meanwhile, Luka nearly bowled Evan over in a bear hug, kissing the top of his head and groaning in relief. They'd done it. They survived the dreaded initial encounter. It had gone off without a hitch. Each of them brightened a little, smiling and chuckling, the weight of worry momentarily lessened with the perceived victory.

Inside the café, at quite a distance but with sharpened gaze, Charlie looked on from the shadows, biding his time. He hadn't forgotten anything at the table; he just wanted a chance to see the boys with their guards down.

Alek's lips locked on to Brennan's like it was the most natural thing in the world. Evan smiled bashfully at Luka, sinking deeply into his arms. Charlie wasn't surprised, not by a long-shot, but the finality of the visual evidence still stung. Part of him wanted to murder Alek and Luka where they stood for the gall of what they'd done to his children, luring them into such a twisted kind of arrangement. Part of him wanted to scream at Evan and Brennan, demanding they explain themselves and such behavior. Part of him, though, was simply very disappointed and intensely weary, knowing what this all meant. The lies and charade would either continue on indefinitely, or he would have to confront them and admit to what he knew. There would be the aftermath of that revelation. He'd probably wind up pushing his boys further away. He might even lose both of them forever, or he would be forced to find a way to be okay with this lifestyle they'd found themselves entangled in. Each option was its own hell.

Charlie watched Alek's hand caress down Brennan's lower back to his backside, groping him right out in the open, with no thought for acting with respect and decency. Luka leaned in to Evan's ear, but it wasn't to whisper. He sucked at the side of Evan's neck, right under his jaw. The sight of it paralyzed Charlie, knotting his stomach in a way that seeing Alek kiss Evan outright did not. He wondered how Jimmy had done it for so long, being around the four of them and acting like the deceptive, wanton behavior on display was morally acceptable in his eyes and didn't anger him. Charlie ripped his gaze away and waited for his fists to unclench before attempting to rejoin his family.

The afternoon found Charlie alone with his boys. The three of them sat down by the stream running through the woods not far from their home, trying to fish though the pickings were slim in those shallow waters. Alek and Luka had bid their goodbyes in order to allow Charlie some one-on-one time with his sons.

Since being left to themselves, the air between the three had been slightly strained for a reason Evan couldn't quite figure out. Charlie had been quiet after returning from lunch. Now, sitting on folding chairs by the bank, fishing rods in hand, Evan and Brennan were asked a question which made them both groan loudly, in unison, in protest.

"You boys're bein' safe, aren'tcha? You using condoms?"

"Dad, for Christ's sake," Evan complained.

"That's not an answer, Evan," Charlie frowned.

Brennan spoke up. The look on his face startled Evan. He knew that look.

With a cocky little flip of his hair, Brennan said, "We were tested for STDs months ago at the local clinic. We're in committed relationships. We're being safe. Don't worry."

"So, that's a no," Charlie managed through gritted teeth.

"Dad…" Evan tried, feeling nauseous.

"Condoms aren't foolproof," Brennan retorted. "They break."

"*Trust* ain't foolproof either," Charlie challenged.

"Can we *please* stop talking about this?" Evan whined.

"You're gonna trust your life with them?" Charlie continued, "All it takes is one time, one slip up and you've got herpes or gonorrhea or HIV—"

"It's my body," Brennan interrupted. "I know who I trust with it."

"Dad," Evan shouted. "Lay off. Hell, Bren's gonna be a nurse! He gets it, okay?"

"Yeah," Charlie squinted. "And what about you, boy? You lettin' him screw you without even bothering with a rubber?"

"I-I can't believe you just asked me that." Evan gaped with astonishment, turning crimson. Without looking at his father, he shook his head and tried not to implode from seething embarrassment.

"Look, Charlie," Brennan said severely. "We honestly are doing everything we can to be safe. We may be young, but we're not stupid."

Quiet descended in the woods; the only sounds were the burbling of water over rocks and the twittering of birds in the treetops. Evan refused to meet Charlie's gaze.

"I didn't mean to embarrass you," Charlie said, sighing, after he couldn't stand it anymore. "I just don't want anything bad to happen to you. You've gotta admit you've got damn questionable luck when it comes to your health."

Evan didn't react, just recast his line. Brennan held his tongue, glancing between them.

"I'm trying here, all right?" Charlie said to Evan. "I don't care one way or the other if you're gay. But I do care about you making an effort to watch your ass."

"So to speak," Brennan murmured through a chuckle.

Evan shot him a sharp, disbelieving glare. Charlie laughed with Brennan and Evan scowled, "You're both sick."

On the way back to the house, Evan went on ahead while Charlie and Brennan lagged behind. Pulling Brennan aside, Charlie said to him solemnly, "I've been trying my damnedest to think of all the things I've wanted to say to you, everything that hasn't been said and should've been long ago. There's so much to get past with us, and it kills me, so I'm trying to look ahead, to what's still to come, instead of looking back.

"What I've come up with is this. I think you should concentrate on yourself for a while, your future. It's important and you finally have a chance to be selfish. You don't have anyone to take care of or worry about. I know you're dealing with a lot of change right now, what with being in a new state, a new town, with new people, missin' yer mom and your friends, your old life, but school would be good for ya. Might take your mind off of things and set you on a good path toward having a real career. I want that for you. Dating, relationships, that'll still be there later."

Brennan didn't respond initially as he picked his way over fallen branches and hollow dips in the forest floor. He mulled over what Charlie said and why he thought he might have said it.

It had been nice to not have to be responsible for a change, to laze around and screw around and not have important life-or-death tasks waiting, other than to watch out for his brother. It had been like reclaiming some of his adolescence, being a stupid kid for a little longer before diving headfirst into the process of becoming a man.

Charlie added, "You'd be a great nurse. If you need any help with tuition, I'll take care of that. You don't need to use your savings. I want to contribute."

Nodding, Brennan tried on a smile and warmed to the idea that his father was finally interested in participating in a concrete way in his life.

"It's hard for me to talk about when you and Evan were youngsters, growing up, and all the fighting with your mom. That's part of why I never was able to tell Evan about it. But I don't want you to think I didn't care. She offered, you know, to visit or even just to send me pictures and letters about you. She did send some, once in a while, even when I specifically asked her not to. But...."

Charlie shook his head, his expression clouding over. "God damn, it was hard seeing those. It just reminded me of what I was missing out on. And she would never have come back for good. She flat-out refused. If we tried to do shared custody, we'd have been fighting every time we came near one another and we wanted to spare you boys that. I do have a few pictures of you, though. In one of 'em you're five and at the beach with your shiny blond hair, wearin' these baggy red trunks and a big goofy smile on your face. It's the cutest thing in the world, but it tears me apart inside to see it. You're my *son*, Brennan. I've loved you since before you were even born, and I need you to know you were always in my heart, even if I wasn't able to be in your life."

Charlie sniffed and dragged the back of a hand over his eye when a tear slipped out. Brennan made a small hurt sound and stopped dead in his tracks. After a beat he turned to Charlie and threw his arms around him in a loose hug, the fishing pole clattering to the ground at their feet.

Charlie sighed and held his long lost child tightly, like it would make the wasted years fall away. "I love you," Charlie said again. "And I'm damn proud of you."

Brennan sucked in a rough breath and replied, "I love you, too."

A few feet away, standing up on a hill in a clearing, Evan looked on and smiled.

Chapter 22
Forced and Bound

Typically, it was Luka who would drowsily make his way over to Alek's bed in the dead of night, looking for company. That night, however, with Evan and Brennan busy trying to forge new familial bonds with Charlie, Alek slipped into Luka's room.

"You asleep?" Alek asked softly, lifting the sheets just far enough to slide under them and into bed. Pressing up snugly to Luka's back, he hummed and grinned as Luka drew Alek's arm around his chest.

"Nah," Luka sighed despairingly. "I wish I was. Too much on my mind, I guess. You'd think I was tired enough to manage it."

"Mmm," Alek grunted. Knowing Alek was thinking of Evan and impossible things, quaking with need to purge his pain somehow, Luka felt his twin gently knead his chest, then rub downward over his side, communicating rapidly the reason why he was in bed with his brother. "Maybe I can help."

Luka frowned but stayed quiet. His boxers were pushed down in the back and out of the way, tucked under the curve of his ass as Alek shifted, fumbling quickly free of his pajama pants. It was so familiar, it was all too easy for Luka to fall into the routine of it rather than protest. Surrendering himself to Alek as he had always done and always would do, he curled his legs up slightly and braced himself. Alek spat into a hand. The head of Alek's cock pressed against Luka, unyielding, demanding entry.

This was part of their routine, too. When Alek wanted, he took, just as Luka had been known to take for himself of Alek. But it was the *way* Alek took that always fucked with Luka's head a little.

Bracing an opened hand against Luka's pelvis, Alek drove into him, making Luka spread around him a little at a time. There was no prep and there was rarely any lube besides spit. Alek just entered him like he belonged there, like he was coming home. It took a while to accomplish without doing any damage, but it was the struggle of it that Luka knew Alek got off on. Luka tried not to whimper and grunt, but he did. Impaled and aching, Luka was restless, chest heaving with each breath, toes curling, hands grasping.

It never occurred to Luka to say no. Even if the word was right there, sitting formless on his tongue, it was never uttered. One of Luka's hands shot up and grabbed white-knuckle-tight to the headboard. A guttural, strangled noise sounded in the back of his throat when the burn of the stretch and the force of Alek's grip on his hipbone became too sharp to bear quietly. Alek's mouth latched onto Luka's throat, sucking a mark to it, tasting his cry through the vibrating skin.

Once Alek passed through the first barrier, breaching Luka, Alek's inward thrust got immediately sharper, needier. Luka hissed through gritted teeth, spreading his legs, doing everything he could to ease the discomfort.

"Easy. Easy," Alek whispered.

Luka released a shuddered, sharp exhale into the darkness as the last, pointed drive of his brother's steely flesh saw him fully nestled in Luka's body.

"Easy."

It's your turn, Luka wanted to say.

I just gave you this last night, he would argue. *It should be you made weak and vulnerable, swallowing back pitiful-sounding shouts and marveling at your own innate submissiveness.*

That it *wasn't* Alek giving of himself spoke quite clearly. The dynamics at play might have been the result of a combination of things — one of them being continued vengeance for Luka's display of power in front of Evan and Brennan, strangling him, laughing at him, hinting at the lust provoked in Alek because of the rough treatment. Alek still hadn't really forgiven Luka that, for displaying what his brother was really like when the walls all fell down. Or rather, what they were both like.

They were losing again. They felt it. And this time they were losing so much. They were losing *too* much, so Alek took. He kept Luka close to prevent him from getting lost, too.

They were lying on their sides. Alek pulled Luka's top leg up, farther off the bed, opening him with a hand wrapping under his knee. Alek spread him wide and withdrew, feeling Luka shudder at the friction.

"Shh," Alek hushed.

His head caught on Luka's rim and, with a snarl, Alek drove, hard, right back inside, making Luka's mouth fall open wide with a thick grunt that tried to mask his initial, fragile whimper.

Luka didn't say stop since they did this to each other to hurt themselves. What better way was there? Hurt he who was most like you, most precious to you. Because it was easy. Because they allowed it to happen. Alek, for whatever reason, needed this from Luka, so Luka permitted it. The next night, or maybe the next week, it might have been Alek giving so utterly of himself.

It wasn't about sex or borne out of maliciousness. It came from love, fear, and feelings of being lost, lonely, and confused. Things made more sense after they let this happen.

Luka felt a few hot tears roll down his cheeks, down his neck, collecting in the hollow of his shoulder. Alek took his brother's free hand and weaved their fingers together in a sweetly tender gesture even as he rutted and fucked him.

There was no need to explain, or talk. Luka knew. He understood. It made Alek feel weak and frustrated to have to please such a man as Charlie who would torment his children because of his own inability to maintain a civil relationship with his wife. Alek was angry to see Luka able to do what he couldn't—push past his pride and attempt to reason with Charlie without a single drop of contempt in his voice. Alek was scared because it was all so close to falling apart, everything they'd been trying to build with Evan and Brennan. The tighter they held on, the more it crumbled.

There were other reasons, too. Alek hated Luka as much as he loved him, simply because Luka was his own reflection, constantly present in his life as a reminder of exactly who Alek was and would always be. Or, maybe Alek's actions were due to his failings. If he could have talked about why he needed to hurt Luka, it was possible he wouldn't have had to hurt Luka in the first place. And the anger that was stirred made the cycle turn and turn again.

Finally, beneath it all, Luka knew part of Alek's motivations came from further back in their shared past. Because Alek knew Luka felt like he had somehow brought that initial rape on himself, due to something he did or said or allowed to happen. In recognizing this, furious at Luka for feeling that way, even a little bit, Alek reenacted the crime over and over again, determined to continue until Luka was able to say stop, needing him to say stop so Alek could prove, once and for all, he *could* stop.

But Luka never said stop. He loved Alek too much to push him away like that.

Whimpering softly, Luka hid his face against his arm as Alek climaxed and marked Luka with the proof of their deed. Alek rocked gently into him, coming down, tingling, and slowly relaxing. Then he went still, his breaths evening out, his right hand still laced in Luka's, his flesh still violating his beloved brother.

For a minute or two they lay there, and Luka could have almost convinced himself Alek had fallen asleep, if he hadn't known better, that Alek was wide awake and staring at him, waiting, staving off sleep until Luka finished what Alek started.

Untangling his hand from the headboard, stretching the sore fingers to work out the kinks in them, Luka let his hand fall to his lap, pushing it under the covers. Alek was able to judge exactly how much he had affected Luka by timing how long it took him to jerk off. That night, it took Luka a pretty long time, catching the mess in a dirty shirt.

"Better?" Alek asked him, nuzzling against the soft curls of his brother's hair.

"Mmm. Yeah," Luka hummed, sleepy already. It was better, that was the funny thing. After hours of insomnia, a minute later, he was snoring softly.

And Alek whispered to him, "Love you, Luka. Sweet dreams."

Evan, wearing only a pair of gray boxer briefs, was already in bed and lying down when Brennan wandered in, focused entirely on his phone, typing away on the tiny buttons. Once he was over the threshold, he closed the door to the bedroom, turning the lock into place. Then he drifted over to the stereo, switching it on and letting music from the local classic rock station play at a fairly low volume. Setting his phone on Evan's bureau, Brennan paused, looked up at Evan and smiled.

Clad in one of his trademark pair of thin, clinging yoga pants, Brennan suddenly dashed to the bed, startling Evan. He rolled from his side onto his back just in time as Brennan landed astride his legs, perched over him with hands planted above Evan's shoulders.

Leaning down close to Evan, Brennan closed his lips around Evan's earlobe, biting it gently. Brennan's fingers skittered over Evan's bare chest to his left nipple, pinching the silky flesh between his thumb and the side of his index finger.

"Ahh," Evan gasped, pressing bodily up into Brennan's fingers, turning his head to the side to give Brennan more access to his ear even as he groaned quietly, "Knock it off."

"That was Alek," Brennan rasped with amusement, tweaking Evan's nipple harder. "He and Luka just gave me permission to have you. Isn't that great?"

"Yeah, that's *fantastic*," Evan said with dripping sarcasm. "Dad's in the next room, ya psycho. He's one insanely thin wall away."

"*Asleep*. Asleep in the next room," Brennan clarified. "I just checked. He's got ESPN on and snoring away in the armchair. No worries." He licked with the tip of his tongue up the side of Evan's neck and nipped sharply at Evan's earlobe. It made him moan softly before Evan abruptly choked off the sound.

Pushing Brennan away with force, holding him at arm's length, Evan said sternly, "Hi. Have we met? Have you not lived here since August? *He will hear everything!* No. No way. Stop it. Bren. Fuck. Brennan. *Bren*."

Brennan stopped grinding rhythmically against Evan's crotch, rolling his hips forward and around, and instead reached quickly under the bed after lunging to one side. He came up with a thick roll of tape, ripped off a small piece and slapped it down over Evan's mouth. Then he guided Evan's arms up above his head. What Evan didn't know was when he was out of the room, Brennan had tied a length of cord to one of the bars of the headboard and tucked it down near the mattress, out of sight. Now he used this cord to bind Evan's wrists tightly in place.

Evan's eyes shot open wide. He was bucking in an as-yet-unsuccessful attempt to throw Brennan off of where he was perched on Evan's narrow hips.

"Not gonna work, baby," Brennan drawled. "You'll never be able to throw a Louisiana boy. I've been riding since I was in diapers. I'm pretty fuckin' good at tying a knot, too, so there ain't no gettin' away from me now. But we've gotta be nice and quiet so Daddy doesn't hear, so *shhh*." Brennan smirked, pressing a single finger to his lips.

Evan groaned and shivered when Brennan slowly slid Evan's briefs down and off. His dick was already starting to get hard. Brennan stared at it, mouth watering, thinking distantly of all of the ways Evan had tried to hurt himself in small or large ways, and Alek's whispered suggestion earlier that maybe all Evan needed to be able to stop was to have someone else put in charge now and then. Out of everyone, Brennan wanted Evan to trust him most of all, so his plan was to show Evan he could trust his twin absolutely, in even the most dangerous circumstances.

Sure, there was an added benefit in getting back at Charlie for all of the ways he'd failed Brennan by fucking Charlie's chosen son right under his nose. And maybe, though he shied away from the thought as soon as it formed in his brain, part of Brennan wanted to hurt Evan for his own sake, for making Brennan love someone else so much only to threaten to die and leave Brennan alone again.

Brennan's reasons were complicated and tangled, but all that mattered, the thing driving him on most of all, was the stiffness of Evan's cock.

Slinking back up Evan's body, in a long, deliberate movement, Brennan thrust against that proof of Evan's desire. Brennan's erection dragged along Evan's, squeezed between their bodies. The thick line of Evan's dick twitched against his brother's pelvis, begging for more, and Brennan loved it. He sucked a kiss to Evan's throat and said darkly, "Have I mentioned I'm *really* determined to fuck you senseless now that I've got you all to myself? Gonna do such dirty things to you, Ev... all while Daddy's only a few feet away. You just think about that a while — all the ways I'm gonna penetrate you tonight with Charlie so close by but so very unable to come to your rescue. Better be quiet and obedient for me, now."

The pads of Brennan's fingers tapped the tape down tightly over Evan's lips. Evan's nostrils flared as his breathing quickened and he tested the cord wound around his wrists, tugging on it a little. It was the only attempt at protest or struggle he made, and it only lasted a moment before he gave it up. Brennan's teeth scraped over Evan's throat and Evan's only response was to throw his head back, exposing the full length of his neck for Brennan's pleasure.

Evan couldn't even try to pretend he didn't think Brennan dominating him was sexy as fuck.

His head came up off the pillow as he peered apprehensively down his body when Brennan slid lower. The tip of Brennan's tongue curled, flicking up over the stiff nub of Evan's nipple, then began drawing little circles around the areola before Brennan simply sealed his lips around it and sucked. That was bad enough as it was — in a good way — but then Brennan pushed Evan's thighs apart and proceeded to make a loose fist around Evan's stiffened cock, not trying to give Evan any sort of relief, just to make him crazy with arousal.

It worked. Evan whined in feeble complaint and tried to shut up but then Brennan started to rub in tiny swoops over the tip of Evan's weeping cock, playing with his slit, tracing around the head. Evan was able to bear it silently for the first couple of minutes. Brennan nearly sucked his nipple raw before nipping at it with his teeth, tugging on it and increasing the delicious, small pain which rocketed down to Evan's dick. It twitched against Brennan's hand. Brennan chuckled almost soundlessly and shifted to Evan's other, neglected nipple. Evan attempted a gentle but desperate little thrust against Brennan's hand but it only caused Brennan to loosen his grip even more, pulling his palm away from Evan's skin when he moved to rub and get some friction. He played only with the head, stimulating the nerves.

After a solid fifteen minutes of that, with Brennan alternating nipples, he left them bruised with marks from suckling and biting them for so long and so intensely. Evan's cock was dripping wet with pre-come and swollen enough to hurt. Every gentle graze of Brennan's fingertips was like fire licking his shaft, and his balls felt so heavy and full it was like they were about to explode.

That was why, initially, Evan was nothing but grateful when Brennan changed tactics, altering his method of attack. Brennan shifted down between Evan's legs, getting comfortable on the bed.

He took one long, pointed lick from root to tip up Evan's cock, licking away a trail of pre-come and humming quietly with pleasure at the taste only to pull away and sink lower, leaving Evan's aching erection untended.

"Mmm!" Evan grunted sharply in complaint, surging up as far as his tightly bound arms would let him in his quest to rub his over-hard cock against something and get off. He scowled in frustration at Brennan who just smiled wider and palmed Evan's butt cheeks. Brennan pulled them apart and tilted Evan's hips slightly as his pink tongue slipped out, his darkened eyes closing. With evident plea-sure, Brennan licked deliberately over Evan's hole, circling around and around it before teasing the end of his tongue at the clenched knot in the center.

The air rushed from Evan's lungs. His eyes rolled up in his head as delirious, forbidden, heady lust lit him up. Brennan pointed the thick muscle of his tongue and breached Evan with it, moving in and out of his rim, shallowly, getting it wet with saliva.

Evan had showered for almost a half-hour after the fishing ex-cursion, both to get clean and also to avoid further 'quality family time' that night if at all possible. He had cleaned everywhere, doing everything he could think of to occupy his time in the stall, putting off the inevitable return to the living quarters to have dinner with Charlie and Brennan. Now he was glad for it as Brennan stretched him gently but with determination, pressing obscene, wet kisses to his opening as he licked over Evan's inner walls, tongue-fucked his rim with pulsing little penetrations, pulling out completely only to thrust back in, letting Evan really feel it every time he was breached.

Legs fallen open wide, Evan curled his knees back of his own accord, without prompting or guidance from Brennan, presenting his ass like a wanton whore for servicing, because yeah, it really did feel that good and who cared if Charlie heard anyway. In fact, he was so far gone he decided it'd totally be worth bearing the horror of being discovered for just a few more moments of Brennan's tongue stuffed up his hole, his soft, silky lips kissed up around the rim.

Brennan curled and twisted the muscle of his tongue, licking everywhere he could reach. When he still wanted more, he buried a finger in Evan as well to pull him open wider and tried to lick farther.

It went on for longer than Evan would have thought possible, his thighs trembling, his reddened cock dripping pre-come in a puddle on his belly.

By the time Brennan got up and reached for the lube, Evan was so desperate to get fucked, he was actually crying silent tears. They leaked from the corners of his eyes, his whole body throbbing and flushed with the pulsing of blood through his veins. Every single inch of him was oversensitive and highly reactive to each touch Brennan gave him. Sweating, straining, growling near-silent curses behind his gag, his short hair plastered to his forehead in dark, dripping spikes, Evan watched avidly as Brennan coated his dick with the shiny lubricant.

Brennan leaned back down. He favored Evan with a few swipes of his flattened tongue over his drawn-up testicles, taking rolling, wide licks over them. Then he twisted two fingers up Evan's asshole, smearing lube, making Evan shudder and buck, fucking himself down on Brennan's fingers like a slut, his face contorted with glorious anguish. Brennan watched this, how hot for it Evan was, eating it up.

Planting a hand beside Evan's head, Brennan aligned himself with his brother's slick, puckered entrance as Evan wrapped his legs up around Brennan's back, ready for it, willing to do absolutely anything in order to get Brennan's cock in him.

So slowly it was torture, Brennan pressed the head of his dick into his brother, being overly careful as he entered him, spreading the ring of muscle. It hugged the bulbous crown, opening for him more the harder he pushed. Needing to come, to move and hump Brennan's cock, Evan whimpered and tried to press himself down farther onto Brennan but he didn't have enough leverage or slack to do it. Brennan's lips parted in a soundless groan, his eyes rolling back as his eyelashes fluttered closed. The head of his cock slid past Evan's rim, nestling there as the muscle closed up, hugging behind the ridge, locking their bodies together.

Shuddering subtly with the intense, taboo pleasure, Evan waited for Brennan to thrust, needed it desperately. When he didn't thrust — when he just started to make one of those maddeningly serene, focused-but-calm faces like he did when he was doing yoga, controlling his breathing — Evan grew worried.

Brennan didn't move, he stayed right there, barely inside Evan. Tied to the bed, his dick hard as iron, a cockhead lodged just inside his ass, Evan was frantic but trapped. Growling back in his throat, Evan tried to stay still and not freak out. His body thrummed and Brennan was a statue, not moving a muscle, his back bowed, his arms both planted on the bed beside Evan. Evan's legs were wound around him but Brennan's legs extended down the bed. Knowing it was futile, Evan murmured and whined, pleading wordlessly with his brother to fuck him but the lustful, greedy nature of the begging, keening sounds only made Brennan moan, inspiring him to hold out longer, to see how long he could last, mastering his own need to push deeper. Evan suspected if he sounded like he was in pain or truly scared, Brennan would end it in a heartbeat, but Evan wasn't either of those things. He was just horny and impatient.

Finally, Brennan relented and moved, driving into Evan in a very gradual, measured push, going so easy on him more sobbing tears slip from Evan's eyes. Brennan made love to him gently, in long, deep strokes, kissing over Evan's jaw and neck, even kissing his lips through the tape. It was the hottest thing Evan had ever experienced. A few times, Evan managed to grind down onto Brennan hard enough for his cock to bob up and skitter over Brennan's body in a slow drag before slapping back down against his own. It was as much as he could get, but the denial was just an added spice heating up the sex that much more.

Brennan came silently, with an expression of wrenched bliss.

Purged, he pulled out and lay beside Evan on the bed, catching his breath. Meanwhile, Evan mewled behind the tape and writhed on the bed, strung up by his arms which were still pulled over his head. His dick was so erect and swollen dark it became painful.

As soon as Evan crossed over that line, as if Brennan felt him go over the edge the second it happened, he acted. Feather-light, gentle as could be, Brennan stroked Evan's shaft, root to tip. He did it again and again. Everything in him focused on the touch, the tug, Evan snapped his hips. He erupted, shooting in a wide arc. Hot come splattered up to Evan's chin, down his sweat-streaked neck, over his chest. Brennan pumped him through it as Evan trembled, all sound choked off completely in his throat.

Brennan pulled off the tape.

Evan moaned oh-so-softly, "God, Bren. *Brennan.*" He thrust within the loose grip of Brennan's fist, riding it out, looking blissfully delirious. Evan kept spurting come in little pulses. Brennan lowered his head to lick Evan's belly clean, eliciting a thunderous moan from Evan that broke off for fear of Charlie.

An hour later, Brennan and Evan had cleaned up with wipes from a canister typically kept hidden under the bed. Evan was lying boneless on the bed on his stomach, looking sated and supremely happy. Brennan was propped up on his side beside Evan, drawing patterns over the curve of Evan's bare ass with his fingertips.

On a whim, Brennan rolled so he was on top of Evan's back.

Evan moaned softly, smiling and spreading his legs to make room. Brennan pressed a kiss to the back of Evan's neck.

It made Evan arch his spine in a gentle curve, his ass pushing up off the bed. Brennan's dick perked up at the clench of Evan's butt cheeks around it, twitching, thickening fast, so Brennan drew his hips back a few inches, altered his angle and, without warning, with a single hard thrust, entered Evan again.

Evan grunted, startled, before he clapped his lips shut. His hips tilted, his back bowing even more to meet Brennan's next push, taking his whole length easily. Brennan bottomed out with a light slap of his pelvis against the bottom of Evan's ass.

"*Evan*," Brennan moaned, biting his lip and pounding into him, driving his cock hard and fast. Strangled, broken sounds emitted from Evan as he fought to be quiet, so full of Brennan so fast. When Evan rocked down against the mattress, seeking friction, Brennan held him down to prevent it. He drove in with force and forbade Evan's release. It just made it even better. Evan's rectum was come-slick and slippery, hot and tight. Brennan fucked it until he was climaxing a second time that night, emptying another load into his brother. Seeing stars, tingling everywhere, he swayed as he recovered. Without pulling out, he collapsed on top of Evan, still holding him down, breathing hot against his neck as Evan whimpered.

"Bren, please. Please let me. You make me so hard."

"No," Brennan growled. "You just fucking lay here and take it."

Evan moaned, pulling him in for another kiss.

Chapter 23
Hit and Run

When Brennan began to stir, rising slowly out of heavy sleep and unsettled dreams, he was too groggy to be able to pinpoint the sound he was hearing. They'd been up half the night having sex and were still nude, tangled in each other and a sheet which didn't hide much at all. Brennan was spooned up behind Evan with his hips tucked snugly against the tight curve of Evan's backside. They were both in dire need of a shower and still sticky with come. Brennan's morning wood was perfectly cradled in the crease of his brother's ass and his left arm was looped around Evan's body, his hand palming Evan's lower abdomen. Evan was using Brennan's bent right arm as a pillow, holding it tenderly with both hands.

They both were on their sides, facing the door, and Brennan wondered at first if he was dreaming. A muffled, gruff voice he didn't initially recognize was cursing and there was a strange rattling sound. By the time he managed to blink his eyes and squint in the direction of the noises, it was too late.

The turning of the doorknob was accompanied by a terrible metallic popping as the lock was released from the other side of the door. The low cursing was Charlie, and he was about to come into the bedroom.

"I don't want you damn kids locking this!" Charlie was complaining. The knob had turned, the door opened up. "It's almost lunchtime and neither of you have showed your faces and it's damn time you wake...."

"Shit. Evan! *Evan!*" Brennan shook his brother with one hand and made a useless attempt at grabbing for the sheet. But, there was no hiding. Charlie had stepped into the room. Staring at his sons, his eyes had grown frighteningly wide. His teeth were bared in a ferocious, wild expression.

"NO!" Charlie bellowed, lunging forward, grabbing at the bed's sheet, and at Evan. "NO! NO!"

Yanking roughly at Evan's arm, Charlie pulled him half out of the bed, away from Brennan, before Evan was even really awake.

The violent tug freed Brennan's arm, which had been stuck under Evan's head. Evan woke, panting and whimpering in fright. His free arm came up to protect his head and ward off blows he seemed to anticipate. The instinct came from the nightmares about the attack, Brennan realized. But it wasn't just a dream this time. It was real. Evan just barely managed to prevent himself from taking a hard fall on his bad side as Charlie continued to try to manhandle him. Ripping his arm from Charlie's grip, Evan scrambled to his feet and backed up a few steps as he tried to understand.

"*You!* You did this! You did this to him! My... *My god!*" Charlie screamed, sounding crazed. "Get your sick, goddamned hands off of my son!"

Brennan had rolled off the far side of the bed and grabbed the first pair of pants he saw. He got them on as fast as he could.

"GET OUT!" Brennan yelled back. "Leave him alone! Get the hell out of our room!"

Evan was looking everywhere, at Brennan pulling on a pair of Evan's pants; his horrified father; himself, covered with dried come, scratches, and love bites; the bottle of lube on the nightstand; the roll of tape Brennan had used to cover his mouth; the length of cord draped over the mattress which had bound Evan's wrists; and the stained, soiled sheets. It was all there. There was no disguising anything.

"*God no,*" Charlie moaned, hands going to his head, clawing at it. "Not this, please.... YOU! You've been touching my boy?!"

"I AM YOUR SON, YOU STUPID SON OF A BITCH!" Brennan roared right back, even angrier than Charlie. Shock was slowing Charlie down, but Brennan had the benefit of a clear conscience to keep him somewhat level-headed.

"Evan, my god!" Charlie sobbed, covering his mouth with his

hand, looking like he might be sick.

Evan had grown pale — too pale — and fast, which worried Brennan more than Charlie at that point. Brennan scrambled over the bed as quickly as he could.

When Charlie began to advance upon Evan again, Brennan put himself between them, arm outstretched at chest height to keep Charlie away. He could hear Evan's labored breathing. It sent a chill down Brennan's spine, because he could *feel* how scared his twin was, and there was no one else to help them. It was all on Brennan.

"Get *away* from him!" Charlie snarled. He knocked Brennan's arm away and hit Brennan across the face with the back of an opened hand. Pain flared in Brennan's lip and jaw as the knuckles connected.

"You're brothers! He's your twin! How could you?!" Charlie ranted, looking between them. Behind Brennan, Evan was finally moving, grabbing things. Brennan figured he was getting pants on as well, but didn't know for sure, he couldn't take his eyes off of Charlie. "It wasn't bad enough you two were letting grown men swap you around between themselves, but *this*?!"

"Shut up! Shut up and get out!" Brennan yelled in Charlie's face. "Just leave us alone! *Leave!* That's what you're good at, so GO!"

While Brennan was shouting, Evan slipped past him, a pair of unfastened jeans pulled up around his hips, holding shoes and a shirt.

"Evan?" Brennan called fearfully, his voice wavering. "Ev?!"

But Evan dashed from the room, bolting down the hall. The farther he got, the faster he ran. The front screen door slapped shut. Brennan took off after him, but Evan was already climbing into his car when Brennan got outside. The engine started and the Chevy reversed at dangerous speed out of the driveway, spinning slightly once it hit asphalt. Then, it sped down the road.

Heart racing, panting, and confused, Brennan spun on a heel. Charlie was still there, glaring and seething. Brennan was alone, and he was in danger. Barefoot, shirtless and with the taste of blood on his lips, Brennan started to run.

Feet flying, arms pumping, he took off in the only direction he could, drawing from instinct and knowledge of how Evan survived on his own for so long. The air was cold and he shivered, his teeth clacking together. Too slowly, the trailer came into view and grew steadily nearer. The pain in his feet from stones hidden in the grass, cutting into his soles, the ache in his heart, and the chill in his skin was all he knew. The echoes of Charlie's screams reverberated in Brennan's mind, and he knew he'd never be able to forget those words, and the way Charlie so quickly discarded Brennan as *other* while Evan was "my son," "my boy."

When Brennan reached the patch of earth where Evan had died, he felt like dying as well. Collapsing against the trailer's door, knocking weakly, he struggled to catch his breath and calm down. Shaking, wheezing, vision blurred with tears, he saw the door open. He prayed, hard, it would open to something better, that he wouldn't be turned away.

Jimmy stood there and looked almost as shocked as Charlie had, which made Brennan whine in fear. For a second or two, Jimmy was too busy staring at the sight of Brennan, barely dressed, bleeding and crying, to speak.

"Please," Brennan begged, his voice giving out just as his body threatened to as well. "Charlie saw us. He hit me. I have nowhere else to go."

"Evan?" Jimmy asked.

"Took off. Got in his car."

"Shit. Come in. You're freezing… Here, I'll get you a blanket," Jimmy said, bypassing his initial shock and taking action. He opened the door wider and helped Brennan up the stairs, guiding him to a chair and dashing off to get the blanket, which he returned with immediately. Wrapping it around Brennan's shoulders, Jimmy took Brennan's chin in hand and examined his bleeding lip.

"Are you okay?"

"No," Brennan sobbed, shaking his head.

"God, I never figured him for the type to strike his child," Jimmy said sourly. He went to the sink in the tiny kitchenette and wet a paper towel, then came back to carefully clean the wound.

"What if he follows me?" Brennan cried, staring at the closed door. "What if—"

"You're safe here, Brennan. I promise. I won't let him near you.

Not if it's come to this."

"Thank you," Brennan sighed. Relief flooded him, carrying away most of the adrenaline that had kept him buoyed. "I wasn't sure you would help me, after what I'd done."

Their eyes met, and Jimmy bowed his head after a moment, looking pained. "I will always be here for you, Brennan. Know that. It's not my place to judge another's sin. We all sin, in our ways." After a heavy exhale, he added, "I already knew about you and Evan. But I never thought.... We need to find Evan. When Charlie found you, you were...."

"Sleeping," Brennan murmured, drawing the blanket more closely around him. "He was yelling things, like it was my fault, like I *forced* Evan to do it. I didn't. *I swear*." Some of the defiant anger came out beneath the words as tears coursed down his cheeks. Jimmy, looking deflated by Brennan's words, handed him an ice cube wrapped in another paper towel for his lip.

"Here. This should help with the swelling. Did he hit you anywhere else? Are you hurt?"

"No. No, it was just.... He was *so angry*."

A heavy, rapid knock fell on the trailer's door.

Brennan shrank back into the chair, terrified, grasping the blanket tightly.

Jimmy laid a hand on Brennan's shoulder and swore with a steady, calm gaze, "I'll handle it. Stay here. He doesn't get to hurt you anymore, okay?"

"Thank you."

"Jimmy!" Charlie yelled from outside.

"Yeah!" Jimmy called back, going to the door.

He opened it a few inches as Charlie started saying, "You're never going to believe—"

"You shouldn't have hit him, Charlie," Jimmy interrupted. "He's a *child*—*your* child. I know this is a shock, but all you're doing right now is making it worse."

"He's here," Charlie said, dumbstruck. "Is Evan?"

"No. But you better pray he doesn't wrap his car around a tree, or worse," Jimmy said sharply, his own anger coming to the surface. It helped Brennan feel steadier, to hear it, especially since it was directed at Charlie. He couldn't see Charlie from where he was sitting, and didn't want to. Drawing the blanket higher, burrowing down into it, Brennan felt trapped.

"I need to speak with Brennan."

"No. You need to calm down."

"I am calm!" Charlie yelled. "They were naked! Wrapped around each other! They're *brothers*, for Christ's sake! *Why would they do this?!*"

"I don't know, but if Brennan's crime is loving Evan the wrong way, yours is beating the son you abandoned, in a fit of rage. *You* did this, Charlie. You drove them both off! Where did you think they'd go, if not to each other?! Thank God I was here to help Brennan but Evan is still out there, thinking God knows what and he needs to be found, fast. Have you tried calling him?"

There was a pause, then Jimmy cursed, "Shit."

"What? What happened?!" Brennan demanded, standing.

Jimmy turned back toward him and held up something in his hand.

It was a phone—Evan's phone.

Jimmy called Luka while Brennan showered. After Brennan emerged from the bathroom, dressed in a sweatshirt borrowed from Jimmy, there was food and coffee set out on the table for him. Taking a seat, drawing the plate and mug closer, Brennan kept his head down but dug in, feeling starved. He knew he needed fuel to keep him going because he couldn't stay. He needed to go again, and find Evan.

"They're on their way. They're going to stop at the house and get some of your things together. I don't think anyone expects you to return to Charlie's place. Not today, at least. You're welcome to stay with me, of course, but Luka assumed you'd be going to stay with them."

"Yeah. Thanks for the offer, though. Um, where do you think Evan is? Where would he have gone? He was...." In his mind's eye, Brennan saw Evan bolting from the house, then flying down the road like his worst nightmare was right at his heels. "He wasn't thinking. He was just *running*. One night, when Luka and Alek were fighting, I ran, too, but I just, like, picked a direction and took off just to get clear of all of the yelling and drama. If Evan's doing the same thing...."

Jimmy sat down across from Brennan and sagged a little, rubbing his forehead with a hand. "There's no way to tell. It's worse that he got in the car. He could have gone anywhere, really. Just the fact that Luka and Alek haven't heard from him either worries me. They're his support system now, but if Evan feels he can't turn to them, either, it's not a good sign. He doesn't have a phone, probably doesn't have money. If Evan is panicking and closing down.... He has no other close friends, no family. Usually he'd go for a walk in the woods, but if he's driving.... We'll have to just drive around, check coffee shops, places he's gone before. He could have just pulled over somewhere to think, regroup. Charlie is already out there looking, but I think if Evan saw Charlie coming, he'd just take off the other way as fast as he could, or hide. I told Charlie to give it up, let us handle it, but he's stubborn. Evan is... precious to him."

"Yeah, I've figured that out," Brennan murmured.

Before long, Alek and Luka arrived in Alek's truck. A bag was slung over Luka's shoulder.

Jimmy and Brennan came outside to meet them. Alek and Luka both gave Brennan a hug, looking furious once they saw his split lip, the bruise on his jaw and how shaken he was. Brennan knew they'd already gotten the whole story from Jimmy.

"This is your stuff," Luka said. "Toothbrush, phone, wallet, clothes, shoes—anything you'll need."

"Thanks," Brennan said, not leaving the safety of Luka's encircling arms. "We have to go. We have to look for him. Maybe we should split up, go in different directions, and cover more ground. He must be so scared."

"We'll find him, okay?" Alek told him, looking determined and ready for a fight, which made Brennan hope they didn't run into Charlie again. The last thing they needed was to make things worse.

Alek's truck was parked beside the trailer. They opened the door so Brennan could climb in. After helping him up, Luka followed, sliding in as Alek jogged around to the driver's side. They waved to Jimmy, saying, "We'll call if we see or hear anything! Let us know if you hear from him!"

"Will do," Jimmy said solemnly. "Good luck."

They turned the truck around and headed back down the long driveway. Sitting tensely between the Popovićs, Brennan said, "We've gotta keep our phones on and the lines open, in case he calls. He's gotta call one of us sooner or later, right? He'll find a pay phone or something."

Luka drew Brennan into a hug and kissed the top of his head. "He'll be okay. He's just scared. Freaked out. He's always liked his space when he's felt overwhelmed, right? He'll go off somewhere to think and get himself together. That's all this is."

"How can you be sure?"

"Because I know him, just like you know him," Luka said confidently, taking Brennan's hand while Alek drove on. "We have to trust him."

"Before, he would have done something terrible," Brennan argued fearfully. "He might have tried to hurt himself. But... he's changed. He has changed, right? He wouldn't really...."

"He wouldn't," Luka told him, looking certain. He stared at Brennan's lip and jaw, frowning, and hugged him again. "He wouldn't."

Chapter 24

Lost

It was past midnight, but Jimmy's phone was still going off regularly like it was the middle of the day. Alek was frantic, since many hours had passed with no sign of Evan; Luka was preoccupied with reassuring an increasingly pessimistic Brennan. Charlie was at a bar, drinking it off despite Jimmy's disapproval.

But, maybe more than anyone, Jimmy understood Evan, and if he didn't want to be found, he wouldn't be. It was as simple as that. He'd learned from that day when he was fourteen if you really intended to get lost, you had to go farther than your own backyard. Jimmy knew Evan still wished, now and then, he hadn't been found, that he'd been allowed to die in peace. If Evan, who had just experienced the worst shock of his life, wanted to vanish, he would. He would find a way. The only thing they could do was wait, hope, and pray.

Alek and Luka had driven around all day, in every direction, looking for Evan's car. One of the first places Jimmy had checked was the shelter where he and Evan volunteered, but Evan wasn't there and hadn't been seen.

At ten minutes to one in the morning, Jimmy's phone began to ring again.

He answered, recognizing the number, and said, "Yeah. Hey Pedro."

"Evan's here. He was asking if we had a bed available. Could barely keep his eyes open when he walked in, poor kid."

Everything that had been wound tight with dread in Jimmy for hours upon hours finally loosened. Slumping in his seat, letting out a profound sigh of relief, he groaned, "Oh, thank God. *Thank God.*"

"Made me promise not to tell anyone he was here, though, so you didn't hear from me."

"No problem. Thank you for calling. I thought... well, it doesn't matter now."

"Yeah, I know how it goes."

"I'll be there soon."

Of all things, it was the shower that decided him. For over twelve hours, Evan had been driving his way through two full tanks of gas, not staying anywhere long. And for every minute of that time, all he could feel was the dried come on his thighs and in the crease of his ass. All he could see was Charlie backhanding Brennan across the mouth and raving like a lunatic.

Evan knew he was a terrible person. He'd been damned to hell since he was fourteen for trying to take his own life, so adding the sin of incest onto that wasn't going to do any more damage than had already been done. But Evan thought the worst thing he'd ever done was what he did that day in running out of the house without taking Brennan with him.

There was no excuse. Faced with Charlie, with no way to defend himself, Evan simply had fled. It was primal, instinctive. Before he'd even gotten a block away, he knew he'd made an awful, unforgivable mistake in not waiting for Brennan. His brain hadn't let his body slow down to turn around and go back, though. He'd been crying most of the day about that particular failure.

The horror of being faced with Charlie's actual reaction to seeing his twin sons post-coitus caused Evan to make a mistake. It was a hell of a mistake, but there was no reasoning through it, no way to process what had been happening after Charlie pulled Evan off the bed, half-asleep. It all seemed to happen automatically, like he wasn't there at all but was only watching, like a spectator. He'd heard the screams, with Brennan yelling right back, saw the look on his father's face and had gotten behind the wheel of his Chevy before he'd even been able to stop, breathe, and think.

But he should have waited for Brennan. It was a lesson in patience Evan never intended to have to learn again. He knew he needed to think things through and speak up rather than heeding his gut reactions. He *knew it*. It was what drove him to suicide when a single conversation with Charlie might have resolved most of Evan's confusion and heartache. It caused him to chase a stranger from a bar, without stopping to alert anyone else of perceived imminent danger, and almost got Evan killed a second time. And that very day, it had driven him to betray the person who meant more to him than his own life.

Unable to face anyone, even himself, he'd turned the rearview mirror away so as to not accidentally catch sight of his reflection, and he drove. Calling Alek or Luka, let alone showing up at their house, alone, was out of the question. The passing scenery and simple act of making progress, putting distance behind him, had been the only thing that had made any sense and gave any relief. But he felt disgusting and knew he must have smelled awful. After avoiding human contact as long as he could, despite hunger pains, the constant drooping of his heavy eyelids warned him to pull over and get rest before he hurt anyone else. So, he'd gone the only place he knew would let him in without a single question or expectation.

The added guilt of taking a bed from someone else who might need it more than him was just another layer on the heap. He'd barely made it through the shower without passing out and was asleep before his head hit the pillow on the last cot in the long line of them at the shelter where he'd been volunteering for years.

The blackness of unconsciousness took him.

Then, hands were moving him.

"Lemme sleep," he complained, letting go of consciousness with effort and drifting away again. Not even the hand on his face, the lips on his cheek, and the lifting of his body from the bed could wake him.

For a while, he knew nothing. It was blessed, dreamless rest. He stirred again when he was once more grabbed and lifted, but the comforting scent of Alek's skin only had Evan burrowing deeper into the strong arms carrying him. He lifted a hand to wrap the side of Alek's neck and dozed off once more.

Time passed.

Fingers tenderly brushed the hair back from his forehead. Someone was holding his hand, stroking the skin gently. A body the same size as his own was nestled snugly against him with a hand laid on his waist.

"I'm so damned sorry," he whispered urgently to Brennan, crying already with profound regret, before even opening his eyes. "*Oh god....*"

"You're okay," Brennan murmured, not angry at all somehow. "That's all that matters."

"But, *I left you.*" He opened his eyes and saw his own face, and his own blue eyes staring back at him. The only notable difference was the wound on the lip, surrounded by an ugly bruise that stretched downward, over Brennan's jaw. "I left you alone with him, when you had to be at least as scared as I was. I was such a coward, and you were *so brave.* Are you okay?"

"Now I am," Brennan told him, holding onto Evan's waist more tightly. "Worrying about you all day was so much worse than him walking in on us. But now you're home. You're here. Safe. So, screw Charlie. So what if he knows? I won't give you up. Not for anyone. He can't make this choice for us, Ev. He can scream or smack me around—"

"No, he *can't,*" Alek said severely.

"But it won't change the fact that I love you," Brennan finished.

"What if Mom was still alive? What if she'd found out like that?"

"She already knows," Brennan whispered. A pair of tears slipped down his cheeks and he angrily wiped them away. "She's in a better place, somewhere she can watch over both of us. She knows, trust me. That's something I've been living with for months."

Evan finally glanced around, opening up his perception beyond the range of Brennan. Alek was lying on the bed with them in his old bedroom, behind Brennan. It was his fingers that were brushing lightly over Evan's forehead and temple. Luka was sitting on the edge of the bed, holding Evan's right hand.

"Jimmy…" Evan murmured, piecing it together, or trying to.

"He found you," Luka said. "Then called us. Alek and I went

with him to get you from the shelter and carried you home while Bren stayed here with Carter and Presley, where we knew he'd be safe. You were worn right out, baby. Jimmy was there today for Brennan. Brennan ran to his place, afterward. Jimmy let him in, gave him something to wear, let him get cleaned up and took care of his lip."

"I understand why you've always felt safe with him," Brennan admitted. "He knew about us, but he didn't judge me for it. He still took me in and treated me with respect. He's a good guy."

Evan felt the love of the three of them washing over him. The combined focus of their care, their worry and attention was intense, and unlike anything he'd experienced before. It was different than when he was in the hospital, before he'd fallen completely in love with Luka. They were all in it together now. They belonged to each other and, in a lot of ways, it was the four of them against the world. He felt then, how his cowardice had hurt and scared all of them.

"He should have hit *me*. I deserve it," he heard himself say.

"Hey," Luka scolded. "Don't say things like that. No child deserves to have their parent raise a hand to them, *ever*."

"After what he saw, I can't blame him. I just wish it had been me, instead."

"No," Brennan said sharply. "You're done putting yourself in harm's way. I couldn't be there to save you at that bar, none of us could. But I'm glad I was there to keep Charlie away from you. All of us are here now, to protect and defend you any way that's needed."

Evan struggled to get up, shifting to a seated position, drawing fractionally away from the other three.

"I don't blame him for being upset," Evan murmured, the guilt overwhelming. "He's not a bad person. Anyone would be upset, seeing their kids like that. It wasn't fair to him."

"Fair?! He picked the lock! He barged in without knocking!" Brennan argued, sitting up as well.

"Bren, he's only ever had to deal with me, and look at what I've put him through. I was in a fucking mental ward for months! Of course he's gonna pick a lock if he suspects something's going on! We were careless. It doesn't matter. It's done."

"What do you want to do?" Alek asked. "Where do we go from here?"

Evan sat back against the headboard and thought about it.

"I meant what I said about getting our own place," Alek added. "You can both stay here until we find something. There's no reason for either of you to go back to that house."

"He's been trying to call," Luka said, looking right at Evan. "Charlie. He's desperate to speak to you. Alek and Bren won't answer, but I can't help it. He's your *dad*, Ev. He doesn't want to lose you. Maybe you should talk to him. He's remorseful about what he said to Bren, and for lashing out. Spent most of the night at the bar where you were attacked, from the sound of it, getting wasted. He's at Jimmy's now, trying to beat a nasty hangover."

"I don't know," Evan sighed. "I need coffee. Food. Something. I need to think about it. It's just... a lot."

"No problem," Alek replied, trying on a smile. "Whatever you need, okay?"

They brought up a tray laden with food and coffee, and gave Evan some space to eat and wake up. He took another shower once his stomach was pleasantly full, and was surprised to find a bag packed for him when he got out, stocked with essentials and some clothes. It amazed him how the other three had managed to be so thoughtful and practical while he'd been reduced to blind, selfish impulses. He tried to imagine Alek or Luka packing it for him, possibly braving an encounter with Charlie to do it. Alek, Luka, and Brennan had all been so brave. It just made Evan feel like that much more of a screw-up.

When he was finally dressed, Evan retrieved his cell phone, left for him on Alek's nightstand.

He dialed and brought the phone to his ear.

"Evan, thank you for calling. How are you?" Jimmy said as soon as he picked up.

"Fine. Weird, but fine. I kind of feel like the biggest jerk in the world. Is he there?"

"Yes."

"Can you let me know when he's gone? I'd like to come over, but I can't see him yet."

"Yeah, I'll give you a call. Shouldn't be long. You're more than welcome to stay here as long as you need to. You know that."

Evan took a moment to ask himself if he did want that or not, to stay with Jimmy. One thing was certain; Evan couldn't go back home, even if Charlie left. He could never stay in his old bedroom again without reliving those awful seconds where everything he never thought could happen, had. It didn't feel safe anymore. But if not there, where could he go? Alek and Luka's house was already packed with people. There was nowhere to get away to, no privacy or respite from the endless pit of guilt making him nauseous. And though he felt secure and at ease with Alek and Luka, Evan wasn't sure he was ready to defend his relationship with Brennan, even to people like Carter or Presley. He didn't have the will to lie or pretend, either.

At least, if Evan stayed with Jimmy just until he'd gotten over the shock of Charlie finding out, he could let down his guard for a little while. Jimmy already knew everything. It was a huge step to commit to living with Alek, Luka, and Brennan indefinitely. A few days in a familiar place to make up his mind about it, and the repercussions, seemed to be the best course of action when so much was in turmoil.

"You mean it?"

"I do."

"I just... I can't go back to that house. I'll just keep seeing...." *Screaming, violence, fear, shame.* "Bad shit. And being here.... I love them so much, but it's like jumping out of one fire and into another. I don't know if I'm ready to commit to this yet, but it feels like my only option. I mean, I have no space of my own here, no privacy, and even before Charlie arrived, there'd been tension, arguments, and.... Two days ago, I had a house, a bedroom, and now...."

"It's not your only option. Come. Stay here for a few days if it'll help. It's not a big deal and it might help you get some perspective."

"Okay. Thanks. Can I ask you one thing, before I go?"

"Of course."

"Bren and Dad... is it hopeless? I can't stand the thought of them hating each other forever because of me."

"They made these choices on their own, Evan. I know I keep thinking of you and Brennan as kids, but you're not, really. You're adults. Both Brennan and Charlie are adults. You're not responsible for the behavior of other people. If they each make the effort to resolve this, it can happen. It's not hopeless."

"Good. Thanks," Evan smiled.

"I'll call you in a few."

"Thanks Jimmy."

Evan found Luka, Alek and Brennan downstairs, speaking in hushed voices but all of them looking worried. They stopped speaking and turned his way as he made his way down the stairs and into the living room. Did they already know? Sense it somehow? Was his pattern of selfishness really that apparent? They'd spent a whole day searching for him when he took off, and here he was, doing it again the next day.

The amount of self-hatred he felt in that moment was crippling.

"Hey, how's it going?" Luka smiled.

"Good. Um," Evan glanced around. "I guess Bren is going to be staying here then."

"Yeah," Brennan nodded. "Since Luka's the one who's started a dialogue with Charlie, he's going to work out a time for me to go move out my things. I don't want to go back there alone when I could possibly run into him, not if he's still upset. I'll put most of my stuff in storage until we get a lease on a place."

Anxiety crawled under Evan's skin, creeping up his chest to squeeze his throat. It was all happening too fast. It all felt so final. He couldn't help remembering how distraught Brennan had been after his first failed attempt to connect with their father. Maybe he was just jumping to conclusions to avoid more drama, but if Brennan and Charlie stopped communicating entirely, he knew they might never find a way to start again. It was possible their already fractured family was shattered permanently. "But it's not... it's not hopeless. Yeah, Charlie was upset, but it doesn't mean you two can't ever —"

"It kind of does, Ev," Brennan argued. "He can't un-see what he saw, and I won't deny my relationship with you to him, now that he knows about it. It's out. I've made my choice. The things he said to me, the way he practically disowned me for touching you... that was worse than being hit. He's still trying to make all of this my fault, like I'm maliciously trying to hurt you. I'm not ready to give him another chance, or know if I ever will."

"But," Evan said, stumbling over the words, glancing at each of them. "There has to be something I can do to fix this. I don't want to lose him completely. I barely have him now and we already lost Mom. Maybe if we try, if *he* tries... it won't have to be forever?"

They said nothing. Alek bowed his head, averted his eyes. Luka did too, after a moment. Brennan never looked away but was just as stubborn as their father. If his mind was made up, and Charlie's as well, maybe it really was done, their relationship ended before it ever really had a chance to begin. But where did that leave Evan? His survival and stability had always depended on Charlie. Would Brennan even want Evan to attempt to salvage things with their father, or would Evan be forced to choose between them? Was there even really a choice at all?

"Okay. I guess there's nothing else to say then. Um, I'm leaving."

"What?" Alek said, sounding alarmed, his gaze locking onto Evan. "No, we only just found you a few hours ago!"

"No, that's not what I meant. I'm not running. Not anymore. I'm just... confused, and scared, I guess. I appreciate the offer to let me stay here for a while, but I can't. I need to let some of the dust settle and try to figure things out. I don't think choosing to live together indefinitely is a decision we should make when we're all upset for different reasons. Things have been... rocky... with us. All of us. The fighting between you and Luka; Luka and I had a fight the day before Dad got here, too; me with just trying to get back to functioning normally and working again now that I'm healing; and now betraying my father who did everything he could for me, all by himself... It's too much. I can't even separate things in my head anymore, or figure out how I feel about specific things. I'm just *upset*.

"I need to stay with Jimmy for a few days, and get my head

straight. I love all of you so much… Aleksy, Luka, Bren… but this is my *whole life*. I need to make sure whatever I decide to do from here on out is the best choice. I made a really bad decision once. I gave up, stopped trying, and I know now what I stand to lose. I don't want to lose anyone anymore, not if I can help it. Can you just give me a few days? Please?"

Brennan was crying again, softly. He hugged himself and Luka went to sit beside him on the couch, slinging an arm around his shoulders. Alek stood, still staring at Evan, pleading for impossible things without any words at all.

"We need you," Alek told him quietly.

"It's just a few days."

Alek nodded, looking defeated.

Evan retrieved his bag from upstairs. As he slung the strap over his shoulder, his phone rang. Jimmy told him the coast was clear. Evan let him know he was on his way.

When he came back downstairs, Brennan was waiting at the foot of the stairs. His gaze was trained on his bare feet. Alek and Luka stood just behind him, protective as ever. Evan kissed Brennan's forehead, promising, "I'll call soon. No more running. Cross my heart. I'm here whenever you need me."

He briefly embraced Alek and Luka in turn. Each of them whispered, "Love you."

"Love you too," he told them.

"Evan?" Brennan called in a weak voice, tears streaming down his face, his nose red from crying. Evan felt his heart break a little, to see him like that. "I love you, too."

His voice broke on the words and Evan went to him, kissing his lips, drying his eyes. "Keep an eye on these two for me," Evan told his brother. "You know right where I'll be, anytime you need anything. Okay?"

Brennan nodded, looking miserable. Evan walked out to his car, which was parked in front of the house, going before he lost his resolve and ability to leave at all.

Chapter 25

Incomplete

"Can I ask one thing?" Jimmy said, breaking the silence that had lasted most of the day since Evan had temporarily moved into the trailer. Evan was sitting at the table, holding a glass of tap water and staring blankly into space.

"Mm," he hummed in answer, not even blinking.

"Can I just ask why?"

The question hung there, between them. The silence swallowed it up. In his mind's eye, Evan was tied to the bed, lust drunk, and Brennan was atop him, thrusting. Time skipped forward and Charlie was just beyond the bed, revolted and furious. The back of Charlie's hand knocked against Brennan's mouth all over again and the memory of his sweet brother's expression of heartbroken betrayal cut Evan deeply.

It was too much to sift through, too many layers.

He had no good answer for Jimmy.

"Just because," Jimmy started, still trying, always trying. "Charlie said, from your... positions... it looked like Brennan was doing the... touching, and there were marks on your body. I'm doing my best to be understanding here, Evan. I truly am."

"Okay, first off, it wasn't Brennan *doing* anything. It was *us*. Asleep. Me and him, together. Anything else that may or may not have happened isn't anyone else's business. We're independent, self-sufficient adults. Brennan didn't *start* anything or lure me into *anything*." Evan sighed, blowing out the anger, and shook his head. In a meeker, calmer voice, he said, "I don't know what else to say... He's the rest of me, Jimmy. He's everything I never had and always needed. Can't you see that? I'm *nothing* without him. I'm a dead boy in the grass. *I'm* the lost one. When I'm loving him, I feel whole in ways I never thought possible. He makes me glad to be *alive*."

Jimmy lifted his hand to brush his eyes with his fingertips and Evan looked up to find him crying. Jimmy, who was always so strong, would always be back there, years in the past, trying to save him, just as part of Evan would always be back there, too, giving up all over again. Once a choice that big had been made, there was no taking it back. It would always be, and it would always hurt.

It was terrible to see Jimmy cry.

"It's just flesh, Jimmy. It's trying to feel not so alone and needing to be wanted. I gave my body to anyone who was interested in it, for a long time. You know all about that. The kids my age… they alienated me, harassed me. I was too scared to try to make any sort of connection with them. The first person to touch me in a sexual way was a twenty-eight year old man named Drew who was a friend of my father's. He'd stopped by the house one day when Charlie happened to be out, because Charlie was *always* out. Drew was the first person to make me feel like maybe I wasn't doomed to be totally alone, and maybe there were other guys out there who wanted the same things I did, but… *I was thirteen!* Every time Drew came to see me, I was *so glad.* But looking back on it now?" Evan's expression twisted as disgust and shame swelled like sickness inside his gut. "Is loving Brennan really worse than *that*? I let predatory older men stick their hands in my pants in dirty bathrooms and alleyways, long before I was legal. They'd play with my dick or suck me off. *That's* what loneliness drove me to. *That's* the awful part. Brennan isn't the worst of it. He's the best. There are no boundaries between us. We're the same person, pulled in two. Letting him love me is… completion. His love makes me *glad* you brought me back. It's one of the few things that does."

Jimmy sat down on the other side of the table. He reached out and took Evan's hand, holding it. His eyes overflowed with tears and hurt, but the simple act of linking their hands felt like forgiveness.

"When you're that lonely," Evan continued, needing to say all of it, to be rid of it, finally. "You'll do *anything* to make it go away.

There's a lot I shouldn't have done, so much to regret. I regret that night, you know."

"Don't," Jimmy pleaded, closing his eyes. It said a lot, Evan thought, that Jimmy knew what he meant so quickly.

"I regret putting you in that position. It wasn't fair."

Jimmy's gaze shifted to the door of the trailer's only bedroom, and Evan knew he was there again, too, when Evan's last hope of finding something normal and good had slipped away. It had been the final straw, though he would never say so to Jimmy. Maybe he didn't need to.

"I just wanted you to love me, you know? I was a stupid kid. You're a good man, Jimmy."

Evan's gaze fell from Jimmy's downcast eyes to their linked hands. It had only been a smile, an attempt to kiss, to touch. So innocent, but not. Evan had been fourteen. There was no way Jimmy could have understood how much the rejection hurt, coming from the one man who'd never let him down before.

"Have you told them about that?" Jimmy asked in a pale imitation of his normal, robust voice.

"No. There's no reason to. It's the past. It's gone."

Jimmy nodded subtly. "With Brennan, was it as bad as Charlie assumed?"

"Probably," Evan said defensively. "So what? It wasn't one night, or one time. It's a feeling, not an act."

Reading into Jimmy's expression, Evan laughed, but it was a cold sound. "You two think this is his fault. It's not. What do I need to say so Brennan stops being the scapegoat? This isn't something he made me do! *I* did this. *I* wanted it. *I* begged for it. Charlie fucking punched Brennan in the mouth for touching me when I needed *so badly* for him to touch me! And you, the look on your face right now... I'm *not* the victim. I'm *in this*."

"Who started it?"

"Me," Evan said simply. "I got hard. Bren noticed. He thought I'd try to off myself out of guilt. He was terrified of that, so he countered my boner with a kiss. *Hell* of a kiss. Kind of a slippery slope after that."

Evan sipped his water. There was more air to clear, though.

"You told Charlie about the twins, how Bren and I were having sex with both of them. Dad knew. It was one of the things that came out of his mouth when he found me and Bren in bed."

"I was *concerned*," Jimmy argued.

"Mmm," Evan hummed skeptically. "You know, if you're ever jealous of the people I choose to trust instead of you, you can just say so. Our relationship's all about honesty, right, Jimmy?"

"You done?" It sounded tired, beaten down.

"Maybe," Evan replied, feeling equally exhausted by it all.

"If you do this, and move in with them, you know how difficult and complicated that will be, right? That's a lot for someone your age to sign up for."

"Maybe I can handle it. Maybe all I've been missing is a family who won't abandon me and need me as much as I need them."

Jimmy just stared at him with an unreadable expression, so Evan drank his water and went back to enjoying the silence. Sometimes words did more harm than good.

Three nights had passed since Evan had gone to stay with Jimmy. For each of them, Brennan had slept with Luka in his room while Alek was left on his own. If Brennan happened to wake during the night, he usually saw Alek's bedroom light on, across the hall. Come morning, it was clear the sleepless night had taken its toll on Alek. Each subsequent sleepless night only made things worse. Soon, he had bags under his eyes. His attention lapsed often, enough that Brennan began to worry about him driving to work, so Brennan insisted on driving him there and picking him up. His temper was short and he was never in the mood to talk.

It was close to eleven p.m. when Brennan went up to brush his teeth and get ready for bed. Luka appeared in the bathroom doorway, leaning against it while Alek shuffled past with a laptop in hand. He never seemed to cease his search for the right apartment for them. It was like he'd resolved not to rest until the task was complete.

"So look, he's been in rough shape, right?" Luka said under his breath to Brennan, nodding in Alek's direction. "Maybe just for to-night, I'll sleep next to him and see if it helps, but only if it's okay with you. I know you don't have insomnia issues, so if you think you could get by just for one night, so Alek can get sleep...."

He sounded so hopeful, Brennan knew he couldn't say no, as much as he didn't like the idea of sleeping alone, either.

Nothing had been the same since Evan had left. Their foursome had been revolving around him since he was attacked at the bar, so now that they were missing him, their little group was noticeably disjointed. Alek was snapping. Luka was increasingly worried about his brother and drawing into himself. There was no lightheartedness or joy. It was just getting through the day, wasting time until Evan's return, and it was awful. Part of Brennan had been angry since Evan left, and it was the part of him that felt he and Luka should have been able to be self-sufficient as a couple, like he once thought they were. Now, they'd become too dependent upon their brothers to feel normal alone.

"Yeah. Fine."

"You don't sound like it's fine. Should we all cram into one bed?"

"No," Brennan sighed. "You're right. He needs you. Go on. It's just one night."

Luka smiled. He came up and held the side of Brennan's face in his hand, brushing the skin gently with the pad of his thumb. Leaning in closer, Luka closed his eyes. Brennan frowned. He watched as Luka tilted Brennan's chin up and kissed him lingeringly.

"I know what you're doing."

Luka straightened, letting go and looking confused. "What am I doing?"

"You're pretending I'm him."

"No, I'm not."

"Why are you denying it? Just admit that you miss him!"

"You're being paranoid."

"Paranoid. Remember last night? I was on my hands and knees with your dick up my ass and you moaned his name."

That stopped him. Luka flushed with embarrassment and Bren-nan could see the wheels turning in his head, trying to remember.

"What's going on?" Alek demanded, looking disappointed in

225

them for disturbing his diligent scanning of the rental listings. "Stop arguing."

"You're not the boss of us," Brennan snapped.

"What's wrong with you? What's your problem with Luka?"

"He keeps pretending I'm Evan."

"You're crazy," Luka said, trying to laugh it off.

"He called me Evan while he was fucking me."

"When were you fucking him?" Alek asked Luka.

"Last night," Brennan said.

"I didn't go to bed until four in the morning. I was right across the hall, by myself, and here the two of you are, nice and cozy. Just because it's the three of us instead of four doesn't mean I cease to exist, you know."

Brennan could see how hurt Alek was. It was in the shape of his eyes, the softness of his voice, and it made Brennan feel like the biggest asshole on the planet, so he pushed the bad feelings the other way, getting angry instead of going anywhere near his suffocating, intense remorse.

"Say his name. Say Evan," Brennan dared Alek. "You haven't even said it in, like, *days*."

"You *are* crazy," Alek replied, not giving in to the bait.

"It's bad enough I see him doing it," Brennan ranted, letting out some of the frustration that had been building inside him. "You really think I want both of you double teaming me while I'm just your stand-in for the guy you really want? I *know* you can't fuck me without thinking about him, Aleksy." .

"He's not dead, he's just *not here*," Alek growled. "Just because we miss him doesn't mean we don't care about you, you know."

"Say his name!"

"No!"

"What if he *had* died? You'd become a total psycho wouldn't you? You'd probably ask me to dress up like him and everything."

"He's not dead!"

"STOP!" Luka yelled, holding his head in his hands. "Jesus H. You," he pointed at Brennan. "Cool off. And you," he took Alek by the shoulders and led him to bed. "Need some fucking sleep."

A half hour later, Brennan was lying in Luka's bed, alone. He didn't even know why he'd said those things to Alek and Luka. He was as bad as Charlie, vomiting up shitty verbal barbs to make other people feel bad, just so he wasn't the only one in pain.

A Popović-shaped figure crept to the bedside over the creaky floorboards, and it took Brennan an embarrassingly long time to decide it was, in fact, Luka. He knew if the tables were turned, and one of the Popović twins was away, he'd be tempted to fantasize once in a while to fill the huge gap left behind. He couldn't blame them for doing the same thing.

Luka sat on the bed and leaned down to give Brennan a kiss. One of his hands cradled the side of Brennan's head. "He's out like a light," Luka whispered. "Are you okay? I'm sorry about the Evan stuff."

"No, I'm sorry. I'm fine. Go back to Alek. It's obviously helping him to have you there."

Luka sighed and looked longingly back at the doorway. "But you need me, too. I really am sorry if I called you the wrong name last night. It was late, and I must have just been really tired —"

Brennan groaned, blushing. "Don't. I lied."

"What?"

"I lied, okay? I admit it. You didn't call me Evan, but you *have* been acting weird and —"

But Luka was already standing up and was clearly pissed off. "You *lied*? Why would you lie about that?!" he hissed, trying to keep his voice down, despite his heightened emotions.

"I just wanted you to admit you do it! That you pretend I'm him!"

"Do you pretend I'm Alek?" Luka countered.

"No!"

"Then why do you think *I'd* do it?! I don't pretend you're Evan!"

"At least you can say his name. That makes one of you."

Luka closed his eyes and held up his hands. "I quit. I'm done. We'll talk in the morning, but for now, just go to sleep. I love you, but you're still being crazy. Good night."

"'Night," Brennan grumbled.

Luka left the room. Brennan continued to stare at the ceiling.

A few hours passed. Still, Brennan couldn't fall asleep.

It was stupid, really. There was no reason for him to keep lying there like that, so he got up and slipped on one of Luka's sweatshirts. He scrawled a note and left it on the empty bed, took a set of Luka's keys and tiptoed out of the room, down the hall and right out the door.

Evan's phone buzzed. He had it on silent mode, since sometimes Brennan or Alek would text him in the middle of the night about stupid shit and after it woke Jimmy the first time it happened, Evan learned to at least turn his phone's volume all the way down.

It was Brennan. The message was strange enough to cause Evan to sit bolt-upright in bed, instantly.

'I'm outside.'

"What the fuck?"

He climbed out of the trailer's fold-out bed. The door was only a handful of feet away. He opened it to find Brennan, standing there in a sweatshirt that was at least fifteen sizes too big for him, in the pitch black, in the middle of the night.

"I couldn't sleep," was all he said, shivering.

"Get your crazy ass in here," Evan said, waving him in before the cold blew all the way through the trailer and woke Jimmy.

"Stop calling me crazy!" Brennan hissed.

"That's the first time I have!"

Brennan wound his arms around Evan's neck, leaning into him, and moaned softly. "God, I've missed you. It's been awful. Nothing works the way it should without you."

"Come on. If you're tired, then sleep," Evan said, pulling Brennan's arms off of him and guiding him to the bed.

Brennan kicked off his sneakers and lay down. Evan lay next to him and wrapped an arm around Brennan. It soothed an ache in Evan's heart. Comfortable and peaceful at last, he was quickly asleep with Brennan snoring gently in his arms.

Jimmy emerged from his bedroom to a surprise. He had no way of telling when Brennan had arrived during the night, but there he was, sleeping fully clothed next to Evan, who was dressed in a t-shirt and pajama pants. They actually looked sort of sweet together, with Brennan held snugly inside Evan's embrace like a beloved teddy bear. There was nothing obscene about it. They just looked like two young men who loved each other very much.

For long minutes, Jimmy stood there, taking in the sight of them like that. He tried to imagine how, in different circumstances, with less clothing, for instance, such a sight could make someone angry enough to scream and become violent with the boys in that bed, but he couldn't make the leap. As much as he might have privately disapproved of their relationship, he couldn't deny what was right in front of his eyes.

But he had to leave in order to get to the shelter before breakfast was ready to be served, so he wrote a note explaining where he'd gone and left it on the table for them, then silently slipped out.

"He's gone."

Luka held up the note for Alek, who was still lying in bed.

"What do you mean, gone?"

"I mean, he's not in there."

"When did he leave?" Alek asked, sounding worried and scowling at the paper like it was the cause of Brennan's disappearance rather than the explanation for it.

'Went to Ev' was all it said.

"Don't know. The truck's gone."

"Jesus," Alek groaned. "You think he was there all night?"

"Maybe."

"Jimmy would really let them sleep together like that?"

"Guess so."

"You know what this means, right?"

"Yeah," Luka said, nodding, feeling his heart start to beat harder as dread set in. "If we're not careful, we'll lose both of them."

Chapter 26
Time to Choose

It was Jimmy who arranged the meeting. Brennan had been the hardest to convince, but Evan knew he had powerful sway over his brother's emotions and played them to his advantage, since it was an emergency. Jimmy made the calls, figuring out how to get Evan, Brennan, and Charlie to sit down together at his trailer for a supervised talk while he lingered nearby, just in case.

Alek and Luka were there, too, at a distance, waiting by Alek's truck.

Evan sat next to Brennan, across the picnic table from Charlie. Things were tense and awkward, to say the least. There was a cigarette in Evan's hand, and that seemed the focus of most of their collective attention. Evan didn't care. The nicotine was helping him stay level and kept his anxiety manageable. He tapped ashes into the glass dish he'd brought out for that purpose and asked, "Well?"

"I'm sorry for what I said, and for hitting you, Brennan," Charlie said. It sounded pulled from him against his will and sincere at the same time. Evan puzzled over this as he set the filter of the cigarette between his lips and inhaled.

"Do you have to?" Brennan said to Evan without looking his way.

"Today? Yes," Evan answered.

"Fine." Redirecting his attention to their father, he said, "You're not going to get an apology from us, if you're waiting for one. You're not getting an explanation either. You can either accept us as we are or say goodbye. Your call."

"You mind?" Charlie said to Evan, indicating the cigarette. Evan passed it over and let Charlie take a drag. Then he passed it back. "Thanks."

"Yep."

"I, uh," Charlie started. "I found some videos in a box in the house, Brennan, of you and Maggie. There were some swim meets in there. A few holidays. There was even one of your prom. That was, uh..." he sniffled, blinked bloodshot eyes clear as they watered. "That was hard to watch, far gone as she was then. But it was important for me to see those. I'm sorry I didn't ask permission from you first, and I'm sorry I didn't knock, but none of this is easy for me either. I love you boys. You're all I have. And I wish I could *save you from this*. I wanted better for you. So much better."

"We've both wanted better our whole lives," Brennan shot back. Evan just smoked his cigarette and watched a hawk circle overhead.

"The four of you are together in this?"

"Yes."

"Well." He sighed. "I can't lose you. Either of you. I hate this, but I don't have a choice here. I'm just going to say... if you'd consider talking to someone, like a therapist, in confidence, it would make me feel a lot better. I'll happily cover the cost. Life won't be easy for any of you if this is the way you're going with it. Secrets don't keep forever, trust me. But I'm your father and I will always be here for you, no matter what."

He gave it a moment to sink in.

Then, he asked, looking mostly at Brennan, "Okay?"

"Okay," Brennan agreed, still sounding defensive.

"Brennan, you're still planning on going to school?"

Reluctantly providing the information, Brennan said, "Yes. I'm working on applying for next term."

"Good. I'd be willing to help you compare schools, or cover the cost. Just keep me posted. Keep me, you know — in the loop."

Brennan nodded, picking at his nails and looking unsure of himself. Time slowed down. Evan could feel Charlie watching them both, sitting there, side by side. It made him want to cry. It was awful.

Suddenly, it all became too overwhelming. A choked sob was

overloud in the stillness.

"Oh, my boys," Charlie cried, covering his mouth, losing his grip on the pain and letting it all spill over. "*My beautiful boys. I'm so sorry.*"

He came around the table and desperately gathered Brennan up in his arms, gripping him tightly to his chest like he could pull him that way out of his life, out of circumstances and into a safer place. Trembling, vision blurring with tears, Evan had to look away.

"I'm so sorry!" Charlie moaned. It was a heartbroken sound pulled from the core of his being, beyond all of the tragic mistakes which could never be undone.

Then Evan was up and stumbling away from the table. Alek caught him first, holding him as he broke down in powerful, hitching tears.

"It's okay. You're okay, baby. You're okay," Alek murmured lovingly as Evan wrung out the hurt.

He was pulled away from Alek. Charlie had gathered him up instead and again made that terrible, terrified, tear-choked plea, "I'm sorry, Evan."

"Me too," Evan whispered. He saw Luka holding Brennan, whose eyes were dry but skin pale as death. The cigarette had fallen to the grass and lay there, smoldering.

The meeting with Charlie had rattled them as much as it had helped. But, life went on and still Evan stayed away. Alek had work. Luka did too. Left behind at the house, Brennan spent some time with Carter and Presley.

The next evening, Alek got home from work before his brother. He had a text message on his phone from Evan, promising to call once he was done his shift at the garage.

Dropping his coat by the door, Alek followed the sound of music to Carter's bedroom.

Inside, sat Brennan and Carter, huddled around a guitar perched on Brennan's lap. Carter helped Brennan align his fingers on the strings as he played one chord, then another. While Carter sang a lyric from one of his songs, Brennan joined in, harmonizing with him. Carter's voice was stronger, and fuller. Brennan's voice was raspier, softer and low, but good.

Alek smiled to himself in the doorway, listening in, hoping not to be noticed. Too quickly, Carter looked up, seeing Alek there. Brennan stopped singing abruptly, embarrassed.

"Your twang comes out when you sing," Alek grinned.

"My *twang*? Oh, fantastic," Brennan said, handing the guitar back to Carter, murmuring, "Thanks."

Brennan stood and raked his fingers through his blond hair.

"You don't have to stop," Alek told him. "I've gotta go get changed anyway. For the record, I love your twang."

Alek chuckled when Brennan rolled his eyes and hunched his shoulders with even more embarrassment.

"You're good, Bren," Carter said. "With some practice you could be great."

"Yeah, we'll see. It was fun though," he smiled at Carter. "Can we pick this up again later?"

"Absolutely. Everything okay with Evan?" Like everyone else, Carter was helplessly noticing who'd been missing, an absence which had been causing tension in the house for days on end.

Alek opened his mouth to speak, but no sound came out. No words fit the great helplessness he felt. "I'd rather not talk about it. I hope so."

"If there's anything I can do..." Carter offered.

"Thanks, man." He stood back and let Brennan through the door. "Maybe give him a call sometime, talk about normal, stupid shit. Might be good for him to be reminded he's got people wondering about him."

"No problem."

Giving Carter a grateful, tired smile, Alek began walking to the stairs. Brennan was waiting at the bottom for him. Taking Brennan's hand, Alek brought him along. Once they were in Alek's room, immediately Alek started unbuttoning his dress shirt and searched for a clean t-shirt to wear instead. Brennan sat cross-legged on the bed, watching.

"So, darlin', how was your day? What'd ya do?"

Brennan warmed at that and said, "I did more research on the best nursing programs in the area. Actually, Charlie helped a little bit. I guess he's been spending his free time driving and calling around, collecting brochures and applications and stuff. He dropped them all off, gave them to Carter. It gave me a great place to start, at least. It was the most normal father/son-y thing that's happened lately."

Brennan smirked, biting at a thumb. "I also got some of those videos back from him that he was talking about. I wound up watching a couple. There was one of a talent show at my high school. A couple of friends and I had a band for a while and we played. It got me reminiscing. When I told Carter about it, he said we should play. Anyhow, um, what else...."

Alek slipped out of his trousers and stepped into some jeans.

"Oh, the prom video. Tommy, my ex, was my date, technically, I guess. We didn't really make a spectacle of ourselves, we just went together. But before the prom, when I was waiting for Tommy to pick me up, I set up the camera on a tripod and put on some music and danced with Mom. Like Charlie said, she wasn't doing too well at that point. She was really weak, so I had to kind of hold her up, but she was so happy, just dancing with me. I couldn't watch the video. I just kind of held the disc, as weird as that sounds, and thought about that day. It was nice to remember her being so happy."

Brennan stared at his lap, his fingers twisting together.

After a long moment of watching him, just a sad young man desperately missing his mother, overwhelmed by his tumultuous relationship with a father he barely knew, Alek flicked on the stereo. Holding out a hand, he said to Brennan, "C'mere."

Blinking up at Alek, Brennan paused before putting his hand in Alek's and letting him pull him off the bed. "What are you doing?"

Alek didn't answer. He wrapped a hand around Brennan's waist and kept the other linked with Brennan's hand, pulling him closer until they were chest-to-chest. They eased into movement, just a slight swaying back and forth.

"You don't have to."

"I know," Alek said. "I want to."

They continued dancing long after the song ended, with Brennan's lips pressed against the front of Alek's shoulder. Alek's nose was buried in the silky strands of Brennan's hair, breathing in the scent of him.

"You're not even going to *try* to take advantage of me?" Brennan teased, some of the words being muffled against Alek's shirt.

"Not today," Alek told him, tightening his grasp on Brennan's hand, caressing the side of it with his thumb.

Alek heard footsteps ascending the stairs, approaching his room. The door was open but, at first, he paid it no mind. After Alek had become aware of his brother's form in the hall, leaned against the doorframe, he glanced Luka's way without interrupting the dance.

Luka smiled with love, tenderness, and sadness in his eyes. He pushed his hand into a front pants' pocket and rested his head against the trim of the door, seemingly mesmerized by the easy affection between Brennan and Alek. Alek smiled back.

"You wanna join us?" Alek asked.

"Nah, I wouldn't wanna butt in."

Brennan turned, seeing Luka for the first time. "Hey."

"Hey, baby."

"Dance with us," Brennan coaxed, beckoning Luka with a meaningful glance.

Luka gave in, and walked over to them. Coming up behind Brennan, Luka pressed against him, wrapping his arm around Brennan's smaller form to Alek's waist and closing up Alek and Brennan's clasped hands in his own. Sandwiched between them, Brennan chuckled and grinned hugely, letting his head lean back against Luka's chest as he tilted his chin up for a chaste kiss from Alek. Then Alek gave Luka a small kiss as well, though there was a bit more urgency in it.

"This is nice," Brennan sighed, moving with them, wrapped in love and the forms of his lovers.

"Yeah," Alek agreed. "Yeah, it is."

Luka was the one to break away. He didn't have to say why. Alek could see from the look on his brother's face how upset he was. Luka turned and quickly left the room. Brennan started to turn as well, concern for Luka reflected in his expression.

"Give him a minute or two, okay?" Alek asked. "Please."

The dance over, Brennan went back to sit on the edge of the bed. It was too quiet in the house. Though Luka's bedroom door had been shut, they could still hear him crying, so Alek closed his door as well. Luka deserved the privacy.

"I wouldn't take any of it back, you know," Brennan said while staring down at his hands, folded neatly in his lap. "I wouldn't undo what I have with Evan... or you, Aleksy. Even if we don't make it. I just wanted to tell you that, before."

"Don't talk like that," Alek sighed.

"I'm not a fool, you know. I know what this is. We don't work without him. It's all or nothing." His voice softened even more as he added, "I don't even know if Evan and I work without you two, and that's the scariest part of all."

Alek walked to the bed and crouched by Brennan's feet, gazing at him and folding his hands over Brennan's.

"We're here," Alek said, smiling with more bravery than he felt. "We're not giving up."

"Good," Brennan smiled back. "Thanks for that."

That night, a small miracle happened. Evan came over for dinner with Alek, Luka, Brennan, Carter, and Presley. Carter had invited him. They didn't talk about Charlie or the future. They just shared some of Brennan's amazing macaroni and cheese and watched a football game on television. All of them looked a little worse for wear, with bags under their eyes and tension in the way they sat, moved and even spoke to one another, but it was a start.

After a little while, Carter and Presley left to give the foursome time to be together without complications or added pressure, which was good, because Alek could see how close Luka was to losing his composure the entire time. Luka held Evan in his gaze almost constantly, as if expecting him to run off yet again, at any moment, deciding it was all too difficult to bother working for. That cemented it for Alek, more than anything else. He'd never seen Luka so desperate to make something work. They had no choice anymore. Egos needed to be put aside, along with everything else. The only way the four of them would be happy, was together, them against the world.

When the clock ran out and the game was over, Luka glanced at Alek with almost stark fear, which was only intensified when Evan sat forward on the couch and said, "Well, it's getting late."

"So what?" Brennan said, glancing quickly around at Alek and Luka for support. "Jimmy didn't give you a curfew, did he?"

"No, but we all have work in the morning," Evan explained. "'Cept you. Not a dig or anything, just saying."

"You can stay if you'd like," Alek interjected. Gratitude seemed to flow from Luka at that. Fear of Evan leaving them seemed to have left Luka unable to speak. "No complications. I just miss sleeping next to you. We all miss you."

Looking hesitant, Evan didn't respond right away. He glanced at Alek, then Brennan, then his own hands.

"Please."

The plea came from Luka. He was biting hard at his lip to keep from crying again. Glancing away, Alek closed his eyes and waited for Evan's decision. It felt like a pivotal moment. This would either be the first step toward the end, or the first, blessed sign of possibility.

"Okay," Evan answered, finally.

When Alek finally managed to drag his gaze upward, breathing a little easier, his heart warming slowly, he saw Evan get to his feet and walk to where Luka was sitting beside Brennan. Luka bowed his head, averting his eyes as emotion got the best of him, and was embarrassed by it. But Evan took Luka's face in his hands, got down on his knees in front of him and kissed him for a long time.

That was the beginning—their beginning. Brennan smiled at Alek with pure joy, and he knew. They still had a chance, they just had to work for it.

Chapter 27
Ending, Beginning

Charlie had visited with Evan almost daily, as much as he was able to, given Evan's schedule and stress levels. Usually, Jimmy was there, too. They only talked about safe things, like the weather, work, and sports. It was an attempt to move on, and Evan appreciated his father's efforts, awkward as they were.

Evan was glad he'd chosen to remain apart from Brennan, Alek, and Luka for a little while, not only for appearances sake, but also to assert his independence.

It was Evan's choice to wait for peace to settle on the group and his own inner strength to grow before moving forward. Through with relying on others to care for him, guide him, or prop him up, Evan was standing on his own two feet for the first time in his life. He had asserted and exposed his true self to everyone that mattered. It was the most he could do. He couldn't change anyone's opinion of him or his choices, he could only live with them and try to progress from there.

Charlie had let Evan down in a big way by not finding a way to come home when he was needed. Logically if not emotionally, Evan understood the reasons why it had to be that way. It was, however, one of the reasons why Evan felt no need to be there to see his father off when it was time for him to leave. They said their goodbyes in private, beforehand, just the two of them, outside Jimmy's trailer.

Evan's reliance on Charlie had diminished greatly, in a healthy way. As the weight of guilt and secrecy was lifted, likewise eased was Evan's feeling of responsibility to make his father happy with him. It was Charlie's task to learn to accept Evan, as well as Brennan.

All Evan could do was to be steadfast and patient in the meantime.

Comfortable with who he was, or at least honestly trying to be, Evan's first way of expressing that was to let Charlie have his time with Brennan, and to step back in a respectful way when Charlie went to catch his plane.

Charlie gave Evan a brief hug, saying, "Keep in touch with me, ya hear? Any more medical bills that come in, just send my way. And if any of you ever want to come out for a visit, give a call. I'll set it up."

"Yeah, Dad," Evan murmured, straightening, standing his ground.

"Look," Charlie started. "About Brennan.... I'm not gonna get into it. Promise. Just... try to be careful? Use your head. Please. You two mean too much to me to see things get any harder for you than they need to be."

"Okay," Evan replied, accepting the advice without argument.

"How are you feeling these days? Better? How's your side?"

"Stronger," Evan admitted.

"Good. I'm glad. You know I love you, boy."

"Yeah, Dad. I know. I love you, too."

That evening, Brennan, Alek, Luka, and Jimmy drove with Charlie to the airport. Alek and Luka didn't need to be asked to come along, they simply continued to offer their support in hopes of, possibly, cementing Brennan's tenuous bond with his only living parent, something they never got to have. They said their farewells in the cavernous, bustling airport, filled with people pulling suitcases, loaded down with bags and packages.

Jimmy helped Charlie tag and organize his carry-on and his checked bag. Luka and Alek stood beside Brennan.

There had been no further discussion between Charlie and Brennan regarding the nature of Brennan and Evan's relationship. Brennan would not apologize, nor would he beg forgiveness or give excuses. He simply was incapable of caring about the nature of Charlie's opinion of it all. Each time Charlie seemed about to broach the subject with his son, he was met with the look in Brennan's eyes telling him in no uncertain terms if Charlie dared to threaten, accuse, or condemn Brennan for what he'd done, Charlie would only be met with a list of his own crimes against his family, thrown back in his face.

At a standoff with each other, Charlie and Brennan recognized their failings and, despite them, chose to try to make an effort to get along.

Brennan, the day before, had received a congratulatory gift from his father in anticipation of a letter of acceptance regarding his application to nursing school. On his last evening in Whippoorwill, Charlie pulled up to Alek and Luka's house with a shining, white Chevy.

It was beautiful, a perfect counterpart to Evan's black version. Brennan was overjoyed, literally dancing around the lawn while Alek and Luka chuckled with amusement. Then, Brennan dove behind the wheel and took off down the road, testing out his new ride, which was meant to ease the commute back and forth from school.

Originally, it had been Evan's job to facilitate Brennan's search for a car, but it was something Charlie had wanted to do for Brennan himself. And Brennan was thrilled he had, as much as the gift was a blatant attempt to buy his affections, because every time he drove it, every day he went to school, Brennan would be able to lay hands on the proof of his father's commitment to his future. It was the best gift he'd ever been given, apart from the gift of Evan, himself.

"I want a weekly report on your schooling, and how you're doing," Charlie told him, his carry-on bag slung over a shoulder.

"Absolutely."

"Alek. Luka." Charlie shook each of their hands in turn. "I have your solemn word you both will do everything in your power to take care of my boys?"

"Yes, sir," they replied in unison.

"I don't need to tell you how much they mean to me. They're all I have."

"We feel the same way," Alek said.

"Good."

"It was good to meet you," Luka told him, solemnly. "Hopefully, you can visit again soon. We know how much Brennan and Evan need you to be part of their lives."

"Indeed. I'll surely be visiting again before you know it. I love the hell out of my boys, even when I'm not here with 'em. You know how to reach me in the meantime."

Charlie backed up a step, another, then another. He stopped. Sighed. "Brennan...."

Brennan walked forward, leaving Alek and Luka behind, letting his father hug him and kiss the side of his head. "I love you, son. With all my heart."

"Thanks, Dad," Brennan whispered back.

"You promise to call me as often as you can, and to not dodge me *all* the time," Charlie said in a strained, emotional voice.

"I promise," Brennan smiled.

It was easier for everyone once Charlie left. Evan stopped by his old house once in a while to get clean clothes, but didn't stay there long. Brennan had already moved out, so the house was strangely empty. The plan was to rent it out once Evan had figured out where he wanted to live. It seemed unavoidable that they would all move in together, though they were somewhat caught in a holding pattern. Evan wasn't comfortable invading the house Alek, Luka, and now Brennan shared with Carter and Presley. Visiting was okay. Living there wasn't.

Three days after Charlie flew out of state, Alek took them out to dinner. It was a cozy, modern place. They sat in a booth, which gave them more than enough privacy, though Evan was hyperconscious of the stares they always seemed to get when the two sets of twins were in public together. The four of them were an oddity, and attention was unavoidable.

With Evan seated next to Luka and Brennan next to Alek, they ordered their meal and got comfortable. Luka kept taking Evan's hand. Alek had his arm around Brennan. It was nice.

"So, what's the occasion?" Evan asked. "There's an occasion isn't there? I can feel it."

"Yeah, okay. There is," Alek confessed. Brennan nudged him and smiled.

"Do you know?" Evan asked his brother.

"No, I'm just happy," Brennan beamed. "I love you guys."

"Oh my god, he's so fucking adorable, I literally feel like I need to eat him," Luka said.

"Wow," was the only response Evan could come up with to that. Laughing, he turned back to Alek and said, "You were saying?"

"I found a place. I went by during lunch today and I think it could work. I mean, it's not perfect, but it doesn't have to be a permanent solution. It's cheap enough without being a total pit and the landlord already promised to agree to any renovations we'd require. He even said we could take down the wall between the two bedrooms if we wanted. But that would be for down the road. I'm too eager to get in there to wait for any construction delays. So, what do you think? I've got the floor plan on my phone, if you want to check it out. It's downtown, above some shops. Two bedrooms, two bathrooms. Plenty of parking."

Brennan bounced a little in his seat. Luka was smiling behind his hand, like he was trying not to let on how happy he was. Alek looked so hopeful, vulnerable, and eager to please; it took Evan's breath away. Glancing around at all of them, Evan said, "I love you guys."

Suddenly, Luka came at him sideways and bit Evan's ear. Laughing, Evan exclaimed, "Help! He's gone cannibal!" loud enough to draw stares from nearby patrons. Brennan snorted with laughter while simultaneously trying to act dignified in order to counterbalance the spectacle of Evan's wrestling with Luka.

An elderly couple *tsk*ed at them. Evan and Luka made a greater effort to compose themselves, straightening the cloth napkins on their laps, smoothing their hair and clothing.

"I love you guys, too," Alek grinned.

"Oh, that's not fair!" Luka complained earnestly. "Now I'm the last to say it and it doesn't mean as much."

Ignoring his brother's comment, Alek asked Evan directly, "So, you'll join us? You'll move in?"

"Of course I will," Evan answered, feeling more bashful by the moment with the amount of heat in the way Alek was looking at him.

"We can move in tomorrow if we want, or start to, at least. The keys will be available in the morning. We'll need to rent a truck to haul all our stuff over, but this is it. It's really happening. It's ours."

"I'm so excited!" Brennan gushed. Alek leaned in and kissed his cheek.

"I still haven't said it!" Luka said, bursting with frustration, his hands splayed in the air on either side of his head. "I'm a terrible boyfriend." This was immediately followed by an oddly strangled noise and a strained expression, complete with bitten lower lip.

With his hand hidden underneath Luka's napkin, Evan gave Luka's groin a second rolling squeeze, just like the one that had just gotten him to nearly swallow his tongue, from the sound of it. He was careful not to let anyone else see the movement of his arm.

"Oh, I'm sorry," Evan frowned. "I didn't quite catch that."

"What're you doing?" Brennan asked, then turned to Alek, "What's he doing?"

Luka curled forward slightly, bracing his arms on the table and slowly turned his head sideways to glare at Evan, who kept kneading Luka's rapidly stiffening cock.

"Nothing," Evan smiled innocently, playing dumb.

"There will be consequences," Luka warned in a slightly breathless voice through gritted teeth.

"Like what? Alek threatened spanking and there was zero follow through," Evan whispered.

"I'm not Alek. I don't threaten, I promise. And I promise my hand will connect repeatedly with your bare ass, tonight, before I fuck it into the bed."

"Maybe I don't believe you."

"Maybe we need to get the check."

"We haven't even eaten yet!" Brennan pointed out.

Luka grabbed Evan's hand to still it, then drew it out from under the napkin, wove their fingers together and held him in a vise-like grip.

Evan could only smile. In fact, he couldn't stop, especially given the expression on Luka's face.

"You still haven't said it, you know," Evan pointed out, stifling laughter.

"I love you guys, too," Luka growled.

"Damn," Brennan murmured, "it sounds a lot dirtier the way you say it."

"Evan," Alek said in a supremely calm tone. "Please keep your hands off of Luka's dick while we're in public. That's something else we need to discuss, for the future. The rules."

"We're talking sex rules, aren't we?" Brennan asked. "Awesome. Oh, look! Here comes our food."

While the waitress set out their plates, Luka continued to give Evan a sidelong, heated glare filled with plenty of dark intentions. It only served to make Evan's dick as hard as he'd made Luka's, which was only fair, considering. Soon, Evan was hunched forward over his plate, just to hide his tented pants, but Luka noticed and managed to get his hand in a similar arrangement as Evan had.

With the first squeeze, Evan only grew still and made an effort not to drop his fork. When the second squeeze lingered, constricting the head of his cock, Evan couldn't hold in a soft grunt, his face growing red, fast.

"Luka, seriously?" Alek scolded. "Save it for home. Official rule number one: All hands above the table when we go out to dinner so we don't get blacklisted at restaurants. Lemme see 'em. Come on."

"Can I uh, just go use the restroom for a second?" Evan murmured.

"No," the other three answered in unison.

"I could have had to pee, you know. It's entirely possible."

Chapter 28
Letting Go

Back at the house, Evan wanted to stop outside for one last cigarette before going inside with the others.

"Nope. Hand 'em over," Alek said, hand held out and waiting. Evan begrudgingly set his pack of cigarettes on it and let Alek confiscate them.

"It was going to be my last one."

"Mm-hmm."

"I've been under a lot of stress."

"Mm-hmm."

"I'm quitting, as of now. And this isn't stalling."

Alek's left eyebrow rose and he just stood there, waiting. Luka and Brennan were already inside.

"I don't suppose I could request a private spanking? Somehow, it's a lot worse knowing there's going to be an audience."

"Keep stalling, I dare you."

"Goddammit."

The first thing Evan had looked for when they pulled up was the presence of other vehicles at the house, but Carter and Presley were out. Hopefully that was just happy coincidence and not because they were told *why* they needed to clear out. Evan crossed the threshold and the hall, then began to ascend the stairs with Alek at his back. His stomach was a riot of apprehension, though it wasn't like he hadn't done worse before. It was just a spanking, not that he'd ever really had one of those. He'd been spanked during sex, but not on its own, separate and distinct, with people watching.

As he reached Alek's bedroom, he saw Luka sitting there on the edge of the bed. Brennan was in the chair across from the bed, like he wanted a front-row seat. Then, Evan noticed the leather belt by Luka's side, curled up and waiting.

"Fuck," Evan groaned, hesitating. But Alek's hand flattened itself on his back, guiding him forward and into the room. The door was closed and locked behind them.

"Open your pants," Luka directed, with all seriousness. It was always a heady experience when Luka's constant levity was suddenly replaced with dark intent.

"You're making me nervous." Evan fumbled at his fly and pulled down the zipper.

"Lie down, ass up, over my lap."

Evan's heart beat faster, and it was difficult to breathe normally. All of their eyes were on him. Part of him was still waiting for the punch line, but Luka looked like he meant business, and Evan was getting off, hard, having Luka's dark side unleashed, just for him.

Unsteadily, embarrassed, keenly feeling Alek and Brennan's gazes, Evan bent himself over Luka's lap. It was an awkward position and it was hard to brace himself until Luka guided him to lie with his torso over the bed. That was probably out of concern for Evan's injured side, and he welcomed the ability to get more comfortable. Luka shifted his legs slightly to get Evan's ass tipped at just the right angle. Then he hooked two fingers in the back of Evan's pants and yanked them down, a few inches below the curve of his ass. His briefs were next, tugged down so his whole ass — and nothing else — was exposed. Evan couldn't help but imagine how he must look to them, and his pale backside in the dimly lit room. It was mortifying in a way he wasn't used to during sex. It made him feel very young and guilty. Many of his mistakes came back to him then — the cheating, the lying, the running off, the hiding, the smoking… all of the ways he'd hurt people he cared about — and he couldn't deny the punishment felt justified, for more reasons than some public hand stimulation in a nice restaurant.

Luka arranged Evan's shirt, getting it out of the way, and gave his pants another yank, his legs pinned together with the fabric bunched around them like that. Then, Luka's warm hand came to rest on Evan's buttocks, which clenched slightly in response.

"I want you to tell us why you think you're getting this spanking."

"'Cause I uh… smoked a bunch of times and tried to hide it, and grabbed your crotch in the restaurant."

"Anything else?"

"I didn't tell you when things started to bother me, and when I started to get stressed out."

"Are you sorry for what you've done?" Luka asked quietly.

"Yes," Evan answered honestly.

"Do you know you deserve this?"

It was like his face was on fire, the blood was so hot under the skin. Partly, it was the position of being bent ass-up over Luka's lap like an impudent child, with blood rushing to his head, but mostly it was just profound embarrassment.

"Yes," he replied again, his voice even rougher. Why had he wanted this to happen again? He couldn't recall.

"It's going to hurt, I won't lie about that. It's supposed to, but I'm only doing this because I love you. Once this punishment is done, it means you can let go of everything you feel guilty for. You'll be forgiven by all of us, completely. It's total absolution. Do you understand?"

And he did, so he answered, "Yes."

It was about so much more than the smoking, the public indecency, and the lies. It was about all of it, everything Evan had been carrying around inside, causing him to doubt or feel bad about himself. Luka was giving him a way to be free, to let it all go and start fresh.

God, he couldn't remember the last time he'd been so apprehensive. To have them all staring at him, at his pale ass, and Luka's hand poised to slap….

The first smack startled him, and he gasped at the sting. The sound of Luka's palm connecting with soft flesh was jarringly loud, making the shame worse. The second strike followed immediately. Three. Four. Five. Evan stopped counting at ten and it seemed each successive hit got sharper, harder, his butt clenching tight just after every sting, just as the pain spread into the muscle. He realized he was crying out softly and tried to seal his lips shut. Somehow, this only made Luka's opened hand fall with more force, each smack loud and clear. The pace slowed, the pause between strikes growing longer, and that made the pain grow. Time allowed the ache to radiate outward and inward, heating the skin and tenderizing the muscle. The wait seemed to magnify the intensity of the smacks when they did fall.

He was grunting in surprise and complaint. It seemed it would never be over, blood beating hot in his face and his ass. Soon, it began to hurt more than he could stand. His hands wanted to go back there and cover himself, to ward off more pain.

Suddenly, Luka stopped. His hand lay gently on Evan's sore, throbbing buttocks, caressing the skin.

Evan moaned.

"Give him the belt," Brennan said.

"Maybe he's had enough," Alek countered.

"He was smoking just minutes ago. He'll do it again if you don't give him a reason to think twice about it. Trust me, I know, because I'd do the same thing in his place. But it's more than that. Evan has to feel like the punishment fits the crime, so it can be done. We need it to be *done*. The *belt*, Luka," Brennan insisted.

He was talking about Charlie, Evan realized, and being caught. But maybe that wasn't all. Maybe Brennan understood Evan had been hoarding guilt and self-hatred in places within his heart that should have held love and hope. Remembering how he'd run off and left Brennan behind, scared and trapped, then Evan wanted the belt, too. He needed it. "Do it, Luka," Evan rasped. "He's right."

Luka's hand lifted away and didn't come back, which meant only one thing.

It took a few seconds for Luka to arrange the belt in his hand in just the right way. Evan wasn't watching, though. He couldn't look. He could only brace himself.

The bed shifted slightly. He felt Brennan's hand slip inside his, and Brennan simultaneously began to caress the back of Evan's head, his fingertips carding through the short hair to soothe.

The first crack of the belt over the meat of Evan's ass hurt so much worse than the hand, the air rushed from his lungs all at once. He squeezed Brennan's hand. The second lash made him shout.

There was a pause, and he groaned, "Oh, god...."

It was making him hard, the combination of Luka's ferocity, Brennan's devotion, and Alek's caution pushing all of Evan's buttons at once.

Three times more in succession the leather bit his skin. There was a too-brief pause, before the belt began to strike him again. Growling through the pain, Evan accepted all of it as long overdue penance for a lifetime's worth of bad decisions.

Then it was over, just like that. Evan was sweating, holding his breath, whimpering in pain.

"It's done, baby," Luka said tenderly. "Breathe. Love you...."

Luka's hand ran over his skin, a caress that gave Evan goosebumps.

"Love you too," he replied.

Then more than two hands caressed him, more than four. It did feel like forgiveness, and Evan was grateful to have loved ones caring for him who weren't afraid to tell him when he'd done wrong, before the guilt took him too far.

He lost himself in their touch for a while, not wanting to move or break the spell tying them all together. Groaning, still holding onto Brennan for comfort, Evan felt one of his lovers spread his cheeks. Two wet fingers sheathed themselves in him. That was Alek, Evan sensed without having to open his eyes to look. Evan could feel him there, at his side, needing to shift things in a way that would give Evan release and relief.

Crying out hoarsely with nothing but pleasure, Evan felt the digits slide deeper. The position made him helpless, made him want to squirm or fuck himself back onto Alek's hand and he couldn't shut up. The fingers twisted, stroking his inner walls, seeking, searching. They found his gland, triggered it, and he convulsed, grunting hard and thrusting reflexively against Luka's thigh.

"That's it. Right there. Know you love it, Jailbait."

Evan grasped Brennan's thigh, yelling through the bombardment of sensation. Luka's fingers shifted closer to Evan's rim, keeping him held as open as they could get him, while Alek kept tapping that sweet spot. Sweating more, panting, he couldn't stop humping Luka's thigh as the fingering drove him wild.

"Easy, Ev. Easy now."

They still didn't want him to hurt himself, and pull something in his side. His ass was fair game but not that, which almost made him laugh aloud. Brennan was still caressing the back of his head, holding his hand. A third finger slid up into him, and it was different, the wrong angle. It pulled at the muscle, rubbing gently, and he knew it was Luka.

Evan climaxed with a small sob, thrusting hard against Luka's leg. They worked his ass loose, coaxed him through it, and still Evan came and came and *came*, soaking his pants. A fourth finger pressed in beside the others and Evan's rough exclamation filled the room. Luka's two fingers hooked in, pulling the muscle open from inside while Alek stroked plenty of lube along Evan's passage.

"Need your ass wet," Alek said.

"Wanna fuck you, Ev," Luka confessed. "Have to feel you."

"*God yes....* Please. Don't stop...."

Lower lip quivering, ass filled and cheeks on fire, he knew they hadn't even started with him yet, and he couldn't wait. Anything they wanted to give him, he would gladly, greedily take.

They had Brennan lie down on the bed, on his back, with most of his legs hanging off the edge. Then, they arranged a slightly, pleasantly delirious Evan atop him. There was a pillow under Brennan's head to lift it and they moved Evan into place so his balls were right above Brennan's mouth. Right away, Brennan gathered them up in a hand and began taking long licks over them, once in a while sucking on the skin, or letting one half of Evan's sac sink into his hot mouth to be sucked for minutes at a time.

That was hard enough to deal with, but then Luka moved up behind Evan, kneeling between his legs, by Brennan's head.

"Nice and relaxed for me now, baby," Luka warned, just before he fit his fat cockhead at Evan's slicked hole and pressed against it for entry. His hands pulled Evan back by the hips, making him take it even as Evan grimaced and his ass burned with the stretch. The head popped through, lodging just past Evan's rim and Evan panted roughly. Brennan sucked on his balls, humming, and likely staring at the sight of Luka's lube-slick cock impaling Evan's asshole, as he had an upfront view.

"Open up. Breathe through your nose, Jailbait," Alek instructed. He was shirtless and had his cock out, too. He pressed it down to align with Evan's mouth. Parting his lips, Evan moaned as that thick, heavy cock slid back over his tongue. Evan closed his lips around it and sucked, but already Alek was thrusting back farther, into Evan's throat.

"No, that's it, baby. Stay open for me. Just relax. We'll take care of you."

They began moving in tandem, both pressing inward at the same time, stuffing him at both ends at once, then pulling back only to repeat the process. Each inward thrust stuffed his ass so full it made him want to shout or grab onto something for purchase. He couldn't shout, though, because each thrust down his throat caused embarrassing grunts and wet sounds. There was no controlling it. He just had to let it happen. His cock struggled to stiffen again, so Brennan gave up licking his balls and instead fed Evan's member into his mouth, mouthing at the head as the twins pounded him from both ends. Brennan, Luka, and Alek were caressing him everywhere as he gave his body over to them. To be worshipped with that amount of touch and attention was an indescribable experience. Both twins were moaning, crying out in chorus and it was impossible to distinguish one identical voice from the other.

"Good, Ev."

"So fucking hot."

"Oh god.... Love you so much, baby...."

When Evan's breathing became too uneven and heavy, Alek pulled out and changed tactics. He took hold of Brennan's legs, folded them back past Evan's shoulders and pushed his saliva-soaked cock downward to line up with Brennan's ass. Evan watched it go in, pressing very slowly to compensate for the lack of prep. Brennan whimpered around his mouthful of Evan's cock, but took it. As soon as the head was through, he trembled and panted, easing into it. Alek slid deeply at the same time that Luka re-entered Evan, and both Evan and Brennan moaned, the same sound, echoed.

Luka pulled out completely, thrusting up through Evan's crack, kneading his sore, well-spanked ass. It made Evan hiss with ache. Four fingers twisted slowly up into him, and he cried out, grabbing hold of Alek's waist and bowing his head.

"Love the way your hole looks taking Luka's hand, Jailbait," Alek panted. "Pink and wet and fucked...."

"Suck him, Ev," Luka instructed. "Suck Bren's cock and I'll give you mine. Wanna see it. Want you to taste him. Make him shoot down your throat."

Evan did as instructed, using his tongue to catch Brennan's erection, taking it all the way in. Brennan cried out and Evan's cock slipped from his mouth. Luka grabbed Evan by the balls, tugging sharply on them, drawing desperate sounds from him. The fingers slid out of him, replaced a moment later by Luka's massive dick. It slid in to the hilt on the first push. Evan kept sucking while Luka took him, going fast and harder. His hips slapped in a steady, quick rhythm against Evan's tender bottom.

With a heavy groan, Luka came, giving Evan the whole load, holding there until he was spent.

It soon became apparent there wasn't enough energy left in Evan to get Brennan to come, so Luka eased him back until Brennan fell, wet from Evan's lips. Their bodies still joined, Luka brought Evan back to sit on his lap behind where Brennan laid, legs in the air in a wide V, ankles in Alek's grip. Alek grimaced with intense concentration and took Brennan's ass for a ride with long, slow strokes.

"Hands behind your back," Luka whispered in Evan's ear. Evan moved them there, felt Luka hold them with one hand. The cock up his ass felt enormous, made him frantic and restless, like he couldn't breathe. But, he needed to come. His dick was a red, rigid line, jutting up between his legs. Luka began toying with it, brushing the head with the lightest grazes of his fingers, while intermittently slapping the underside lightly with an opened hand.

Evan begged, squirmed, and couldn't tear his eyes away from the sight of Alek fucking Brennan. When Alek took rough hold of Brennan's erection, jacking it for a few seconds, then pressing it back to his stomach, rubbing the underside as he pinned it there, Evan came. His seed shot in an arc over Brennan's face. Drops sprayed his lips, eyelashes, freckled cheeks, and chin. Luka stroked him through it while Evan trembled through the aftershocks. Brennan sucked the come from his lower lip, arching his back as Alek rubbed his cockhead and gave his ass the full length of him. Leaning down, Alek licked Brennan's chin clean, then pushed his tongue into Brennan's willing mouth. They moved together and came in unison, clutching each other and coming down slowly.

The house was dark and quiet; the only noise came from crickets chirping outside and the gentle creaking of floorboards by the foot of Alek's bed. On the bed, two gorgeous, young, freckled twins lay naked and entwined in sleep. Brennan's leg hooked around Evan's as they faced each other, with the top of Evan's head tucked just under Brennan's chin. Evan's arm was wrapped around Brennan's waist while Brennan's hand lay against the side of Evan's neck.

Luka could only stare. Slowly, he raised his phone and snapped a picture. The flash was bright, but it didn't rouse them. They were too tired to be bothered by such insignificant things.

"What are you doing?" Alek scolded in the lowest whisper, sounding fiercely protective. The display of devotion only made Luka smile. He didn't blame Alek. There was a lot on that bed to want to protect.

"Memories," Luka said simply. "I want to always be able to remember them like this."

That shut his brother up.

"Send it to me," Alek muttered softly.

"No doubt. Fuck, they're beautiful, aren't they?"

"*This* is how lucky we are, Luka. *This* is our responsibility now. You ready?"

Their gazes locked. Looking into his brother's eyes, Luke knew there was no part of him that wouldn't give anything, do *anything* for the two people on that bed.

"Absolutely," Luka smiled.

Chapter 29
Home

The drive across town was surreal, to say the least. It would be the first time for Luka, Brennan and Evan to see what was to be their new home. Alek drove Evan's car, since it fit them all nicely and he knew the way. Evan was in the passenger seat. Luka and Brennan were in the back. Even just to be in the car together, as one group, going to see the place that would be theirs and only theirs, was one of those moments where Evan could truly feel he was living his life. He wasn't watching it pass him by, or wishing it was something better than it was. He was fully engaged, grateful, and so happy. The past couldn't hurt him. The future wasn't his concern. The present was a gift.

He loved Alek, Luka, and Brennan so much, he couldn't believe his luck. As unlikely a unit as they were, they worked. They filled gaps for each other, and every one of them was essential for creating just the right balance. Sure, it was scary, but what good was the day-to-day without a thrill to get the blood pumping? He knew they were bound to make more mistakes, but Evan was willing to do the hard work. If he screwed up, he would try to make it right again, and would try to remain patient with his lovers, should he be the one slighted.

The time he'd asked for in order to make up his own mind was, in retrospect, very much needed after all. The decision to take a small break from the challenging romantic and practical dynamics of existing in a foursome was the first of what Evan hoped were a series of good choices. He was much more confident in his own skin having survived one of his worst nightmares. It had left him stronger.

He'd been able to process his biggest sources of trouble and reorder his priorities. Brennan came first for him, just as Luka and Alek did. Those three were the core of Evan's life, his new family. It was time to leave the old, familiar safety of his childhood home. He wasn't Charlie's little boy anymore.

Looking around the car, Evan saw Alek, still professional and composed despite his casual attire, his hands wrapping the wheel at precisely ten and two, his gaze focused on the road ahead. Behind him, to his left was Luka, wearing a grin that only hinted at the excitement and joy Evan knew bubbled up within. Their eyes locked briefly, and warmth infused Luka's face. Evan couldn't help but remember Luka's confession, not so long ago, of loving Evan the whole time without realizing it. Their love crossed lines, but once the lines were gone, anything was possible. And Brennan, glimpsed in the side mirror, a reflection of Evan's reflection. Brennan didn't see him looking, he was too busy gazing out the window at the world flying by. He was a survivor, just like Evan, whose fierce care and loyalty was one of Evan's greatest blessings.

The car rolled to a stop in front of the new building. It was attractive enough, located on the second floor above some tidy, well-kept shops. The whole street was quaint and welcoming, bustling with shoppers, people walking their dogs, out enjoying the cool but pleasant weather. The street was lined with trees and pots overflowing with flowers.

Alek cut the engine and they all got out. Evan smiled at the wonderment he saw in Brennan's eyes, taking in the sight of a place that wasn't just new to him, but to all of them. They could make it home together. There would be no more need for Brennan to feel like the outsider in a new place.

Luka wandered over to the shop directly in front of them, cupping his hands against the glass to peer nosily inside. Alek, shaking his head at his brother, dug the door key out of his pocket. Taking Evan's hand like it belonged to him, Alek led the way up to the street-level door. Once he'd unlocked, it opened up to a flight of stairs leading to the second floor.

"We'll have to get copies of the key made," Alek said. "A couple of them for each of us."

"In case we lose one," Luka added. "And we can probably move over most of our furniture from the two houses and Bren's storage locker—"

"Next weekend, renting a truck," Alek added.

"But it'll be pretty big so we could just swing by to get everything in one day."

"As long as we get most of it packed this week."

"Since we already asked Presley and Carter to help out."

Evan climbed step after step, right behind Alek, with Luka and Brennan bringing up the rear. Near the top, someone goosed Evan, making him yelp. Laughing, Brennan gave Evan an innocent look, as did Luka, when he glanced back to see who did it.

At the landing, Evan turned to his brother and asked, "We're not gonna start speaking in tandem like that, are we? It's a little scary."

Before Brennan could answer, someone goosed Evan again, squeezing quickly between his legs from behind. He made an equally embarrassing noise, crying out, "*Fucking....* Quit it!"

He glanced behind him to Alek and Luka, neither of them giving away who did it.

"That's hilarious," he said. "Please keep doing that."

Alek said, "We only grab your ass because we love you."

Then Luka asked, "You remember that day we played touch football?"

"Sure," Evan murmured distractedly. "Why?"

"Look," Luka grinned, doing something on his phone. He held it up for them to see. On the screen was a picture taken of the four of them, just after the game. They were all laughing, arms slung around each other as they posed for the shot, taken by Presley.

"We should get it printed out really big and hang it right here, at the top of the steps, so we can see it every time we come home."

Brennan gave the center of Luka's chest a hard shove, knocking him back against the wall. Twisting a fist in Luka's shirtfront, Brennan kissed him firmly on the lips. Luka moaned softly. Pulling back, Brennan said heatedly, "You're so fucking romantic."

"Oh Cupcake, you have no idea," Luka smirked, with a look that implied he was planning god-knew-what-else for their new home. Brennan made a giddy, impatient sound, snagged Evan's hand and pulled him into the apartment with him. Alek and Luka followed them in, wandering further into the space.

"It's not huge, because, you know, we're not rich. Yet. But see?" Alek gestured around. "This is the living room. The dining table would go over there, next to the kitchen. There's enough space on that wall for Luka's exercise equipment and the bedrooms are through there." He gestured to a short hallway to their right.

Evan took a long look around. To the left were some tall windows overlooking the street and the majority of the living area. To the right was the kitchen, with counters that wrapped around in a U shape, along with new-looking appliances, the hallway and a door.

"That door leads to a walk-in closet," Alek said, going over to open it and let them look inside. "The closets are all huge. Great storage. It makes up for the limited space out here. At least all our stuff will be hidden away."

"And two bathrooms!" Brennan exclaimed, smiling hugely, more happy than Evan had ever seen him before. Evan wanted to tackle him to the floor and kiss his breath away. They could christen the space, mark it as theirs—and no threat of anyone unwanted walking in, unannounced. "One off of each bedroom. Isn't it great? We won't have to share anymore."

Luka cleared his throat, loudly, on purpose.

"What?" When both of Luka's eyebrows shot up, Brennan— oblivious—demanded, "What'd I say?"

Then, Luka gave Alek a look, which Evan understood perfectly. Brennan was still playing catch-up, though.

"For now," Alek said, seeming to speak for both of the Popovićs, "we'll be split up into two bedrooms. It doesn't mean anything though, if we don't want it to. We can ease into the living arrangements before deciding how things are going to work between the four of us."

Evan wondered when they'd discussed things between them, suspecting it was while he and Brennan had been allowed to sleep in Alek's bed as long as they wanted to, the night before.

"Ev," Luka said, "you and Alek wake up early for work, so it makes sense anyway that you're together. Bren and I have weirder schedules with his classes and my flex hours at the gym. We're more likely to all get our sleep with the wall between the bedrooms in place. Other than sleeping though...."

The Popović twins again shared a look of agreement which Evan wasn't privy to.

Alek picked up where Luka left off. "We share everything. Food, sex—"

"Sex *with* food," Luka added.

Brennan elbowed him in the side, saying, "And clothes. You would look really hot in my yoga pants, Ev."

"You would, actually," Alek agreed with a dreamy expression as he seemed to mentally play dress-up with Evan's body. After a moment he blinked his eyes clear and said, "Where was I? Oh. Yeah, and most importantly, we share whatever is on our minds. That's a rule."

"He threatened to make a sign for the wall and everything," Luka told Evan behind a hand.

"I heard that," Alek warned. "This is only going to work if we talk about anything that's bothering us before it becomes a problem. Agreed?"

He looked at each of them in turn. Luka nodded, humming, "Mm-hmm."

Evan muttered, "Yeah, okay."

"No problem," Brennan echoed.

"I mean it."

"Okay," Evan insisted. "So, wait, can I sleep with Luka or Brennan once in a while if I want to?"

"You have to ask Alek for permission first," Luka answered, quite seriously, without a hint of a smile.

"You're kidding, right?" Evan asked, laughing a little.

"No, I'm not kidding."

Evan looked over at Alek, who had trouble holding his gaze without glancing away. He was embarrassed, Evan realized.

"What if I fall asleep on the couch next to them?"

"I'll carry you to bed," Alek said. "Sleeping is mine. It's my time with you. We've agreed."

"You and Luka agreed?"

"We all did," Brennan said softly, biting at the edge of his lip.

"While you were staying at Jimmy's. We talked about ways to make sure everyone's needs were met. You can add anything you need to, but so far these are what seemed to be the best solutions for the three of us."

"Wow." A hot tickle wriggled its way downward from Evan's gut. Astonishingly, he started to get hard, thinking of Alek arguing to stake his claim in Evan during the nights. Evan shoved his hands into his pockets to hide his arousal and tried to fight a rising blush. "Yeah, okay. The sleeping thing is kind of hot. But you're seriously okay with me having sex with them whenever I feel like it?"

"You have to let the rest of us know when it happens, if not before it happens, then soon afterward," Luka said. "That only applies with me and Bren for you. You don't need to tell the two of us when you're with Alek. Alek will tell you if he's with me or Bren. It works the other way around, too. Brennan has to tell me if he's with you or Alek. Does that sound fair?"

"Yeah," Evan nodded after thinking about it for a few seconds. "So... what? I call or text Alek and say, hey, we fucked?"

"You have to give some details," Brennan said, answering for Alek who still seemed oddly quiet. "Oral, anal, handjob, whatever. I mean, *you'd* want to know, right?"

"Yeah, I guess I would. Wait. You guys all talked about *all* of this already?"

"It wasn't the same while you were away, Ev. We argued about stuff, more than usual. We were trying to figure out the fairest way to set this all up. We all want it to work. It means a lot to each of us. It's kind of a big deal."

"There's one more rule," Alek said, speaking up again, finally. "No bondage without everyone's permission first."

"Huh." Evan glanced at Brennan, who looked a little guilty. "So if you wanted to tie me up, Aleksy?"

"I have to ask Luka and Bren first. If one of them says no, it means no."

"Spanking?"

"Spanking is fine if it's just part of sex. If it's punishment, that's different. We all need to be there."

"This all seems a little complicated. What if I forget something and break a rule?"

"Anyone breaks a rule, the other three collectively decide on re-percussions."

"You okay with all of this?" Luka asked Evan. "We know it's a lot to take in at once."

Surrounded by the promise of the empty apartment, his head full of new rules and responsibilities, visions of what his life would now be like, Evan considered his answer.

"Works for me," he said, after some thought. "But, one question: Alek, does this mean you and Luka are gonna lay off each other? No more taking shit out on each other?"

"No means no," Luka said, looking right at Alek, whose expression contorted with apology and regret. "From now on, Alek and I are going to ask for permission first, too. No assuming. No forcing. Aren't we, Aleksy?"

"I'm sorry. *I've said how sorry —* "

Luka quieted him with a soft kiss. Alek's hand came up, tangling it Luka's hair, drawing it out.

Luka touched their foreheads together and said, "Me too. I'm sorry, too. We go forward, remember? No more looking back."

"Love you, Luka," Alek murmured, getting himself together. Evan watched attentively, trying to understand, and only began to glimpse the truth. His and Brennan's hands folded together in silent promise to never need to apologize to one another like that, ever.

Chapter 30
Knowing You

"Look, I can't talk right now," Evan said. "Can I call you later?"

"Who are you talking to?"

"Nobody."

"Nobody," Alek echoed. "I see. Give me that. Give it."

He snatched the phone from Evan's hand and demanded in a very jealous-boyfriend-like way, "Who is this?"

Evan rolled his eyes, then watched the torch fires dance. They were citronella, to keep the bugs away, and ringed the blanket Alek had laid out on the grass in the same secluded meadow which had been the site of their first date. The afterimage of the golden light stayed with him as he tried to let his eyed adjust to the pitch blackness beyond their cozy circle. The woods in the distance were a dark smudge. Anything could be out there, especially at night.

"What if there are bears?" Evan wondered aloud. "I've heard of bears being seen in this area. Not often, but…."

"Carter, why are you calling my boyfriend when we're on a date? Do you know how rare it is to have him all to myself? No, he's not naked. Neither of us are naked!" Alek said loudly, looking grouchy. "It's a *date*. Is this about fantasy football again? Oh my god, the two of you. He'll call you back."

He hung up the phone and tossed it away, into the grass.

"I'm never gonna find that now, you know," Evan sighed. "But about the bears…."

"If a bear shows up, I'll protect you. But there are no bears."

"How do you know? I felt better when we were in a truck bed. I don't think it was this dark before either. And last time we rolled around in the dirt like this, I was so banged up, Bren wanted to kick your ass around the block." The memory made him grin, especially in retrospect.

"What happened to the Evan who didn't care if he got hurt and was so fond of wandering off into the fields and forests to escape it all?"

"Guess I don't want to hurt anymore, or need to escape," he admitted. "Except from bears."

"Doesn't mean you can't live a little," Alek passed him a plastic goblet filled with a sour-smelling burgundy liquid. "Here. Drink."

Alek was dressed in one of his work outfits, complete with loafers and tie, which made Evan, in his jeans, sneakers, and light blue sweater, feel like he was out with his babysitter instead of his boyfriend. There were some moments when the seven year age difference between them could really be felt. He'd always had a thing for older men, though, so it was a distinctly pleasant feature of their relationship in Evan's eyes.

The stars were out and the sky clear. The Milky Way was a smudge of light streaking above their heads, from one end of the vastness of space to the other, with the trees in the distance catching a few falling stars. He couldn't help but admit, to himself at least, that it was romantic. Bears weren't even really a concern; the real issue for Evan would always be the ravenous beast that was the powerful sexual chemistry between them. Evan was the sole focus of Alek's lustful attentions for a little while and no matter how much time passed, it still made Evan feel exquisitely, intoxicatingly vulnerable.

"Are you trying to poison me?" Sniffing the contents of the glass, Evan scrunched his nose mistrustfully.

"I'm *trying* to expose you to more cultured indulgences. This is wine. Merlot, specifically. Give it a try. Gulp it if you have to. Or is the innocent, virginal child act meant to turn me on?"

"Oh, I would never do something like that," Evan managed to say with a straight face. "Though you are dressed to intimidate right now. If you look at the two of us, you're the professor, I'm the schoolboy. And now you're clearly trying to get me drunk, which… okay, yes, is hot." He raised the glass to his lips and tipped it back.

Once, Evan would have thought of Alek's current demeanor as that of "new Alek," but not now. Alek was just Alek. He had the advantage of being more mature than Evan, in many different ways. It wasn't such a bad thing to have someone so beloved at his side, willing and able to set a good example and help show the way to begin to be an adult.

The schoolboy talk was putting some serious heat behind Alek's hazel eyes. As Evan's anxious anticipation skyrocketed, he tried to talk his way through the nerves and said, "You think Bren and Luka really went to the hockey game? Maybe it was just a ploy to get the apartment to themselves? Or maybe it was a cover for something bizarre like pole-dancing lessons," Evan asked, just before downing half the glass of merlot. The taste was worse than expected. "Ugh, oh god. Awful." He downed the rest, just to be done with it and handed the glass back to Alek. "Fuck, dude."

"Refill?" Alek asked, smirking.

"Pass."

"Tonight's about us. Just us," Alek reminded him. "Don't worry about them."

"What if Bren gets way too wrapped up in the game like he always does and starts arguing with some crazed fan? And you know how cuddly Luka gets. What if some homophobe sees them holding hands and follows them out to the parking lot and — "

"Babe," Alek said tenderly at Evan's worry. "They'll be okay. Promise."

He set down his plastic goblet, too, inside the little picnic basket they'd brought along. Then he slowly crawled over to Evan on his hands and knees, causing Evan to instinctively sit back, his hands braced on the ground behind him. Evan wrapped a hand in the tie and let Alek guide him down flat onto his back atop the blanket. His body was pressed into the soft grass below with the weight of Alex lying flush upon him from chest to ankles. Curls of brown hair hung between them, tickling the sides of Evan's face. "Thank you for not taking me to a hockey game, Mr. Popović."

Alek laughed despite himself, then mastered his expression, doing his best to look the stern elder. Leaning in, he nipped at Evan's lower lip and slid a hand up Evan's sweater. It made Evan moan and thrust reflexively against all of that hard muscle pinning him down.

"You're welcome," Alek murmured. "I do know you, you know, *Savage*." A knee drew up between Evan's thighs, parting them, nudging his balls. "This is Brennan's sweater, isn't it?"

"Yeah," Evan breathed, letting his head fall back as Alek sucked at his throat. "He wanted to put me in a pair of his khakis, too, but I told him we were going outside, not to a fancy restaurant."

Quick, rough, and efficient, Alek reached down between them and yanked open Evan's fly, then slipped his hand swiftly under the fabric. Fingers greedily wrapped Evan's fully hardened shaft, tugging it free. A few more pulls at the fabric left him exposed to the night and the fireflies.

"Fuck," Evan groaned, hiding his face in Alek's neck, or trying to. "Why the hell am I this nervous?"

"Because you know me, too," Alek grinned wickedly.

Holding the tie felt good, like he was somewhat in control, but Alek seemed to sense this, intent on unraveling Evan's composure completely.

"Hands off," Alek instructed. After waiting for him to let go of the necktie, he guided both of Evan's arms upward, above his head, holding them there with one hand while the pad of the index finger of the other drew small circles around the tip of Evan's dick. That meant he could feel exactly how wet Evan was already, and that he really was trying to drive him crazy.

A self-conscious, breathless little laugh broke free. Biting his lip, trying to shut up, Evan became quickly overwhelmed with how much power little things held over him. The inability to touch, but only be touched, the light tickling which only reminded him of how well Alek knew where Evan's most sensitive spots were, the power dynamics at play... it made him want to beg, spread, and surrender. Alek really did know him well.

"No underwear," Alek murmured. "It's almost as if you *knew* how badly I needed to get inside your hot ass tonight."

"Yeah, just a feeling I had," Evan replied, his voice breaking softly, in ways he didn't want it to. It was just a little nakedness, a ghost of a touch, but it felt like a lot. With Alek, it always would.

"*Fuck*... God, how do you do this to me?"

"Love to make you wet, Jailbait," Alek whispered against Evan's mouth, right before angling his head more sharply to kiss him deeper. Evan opened readily and made a low, plaintive noise, tasting wine on Alek's lips, yielding to his tongue and teeth. Alek nipped Evan's lip, hard enough to hurt while, simultaneously, let his fingertip ride through the divot in Evan's crown. It made him quiver and thrust. Then Alek's tongue was in his mouth again. The hand on his wrists renewed its grip as he undulated, riding the finger, unable to stop.

"Let's see if you can follow orders. Keep your hands above your head, right where they are."

"'Kay," Evan grunted, then swallowed an embarrassing whimper as Alek nipped kisses down Evan's chin and throat. The borrowed sweater was pushed up. Alek's mouth sealed around his nipple, sucking it stiff, then tugging with his teeth, which released him reluctantly only to scrape down his abdomen. Alek paused before getting to the scar. Kissing it tenderly, lightly, here, there, and everywhere, Alek then moved lower to lick at the ridge of Evan's hipbone. Alek's hands pulled the jeans down while his lips sought Evan's tip, mouthing at it. Evan lifted his ass to help Alek get the pants down farther. His cock was sucked down to the root and he felt Alek swallow around it before pulling off.

Evan was waiting for Alek to remove the jeans entirely, strip him naked, but it didn't happen. Instead, he gripped Evan's thighs, pinning them to the blanket and took a long lick over Evan's sac and up the underside of his cock only do it again, and again. Evan rocked slightly into the touch, shuddering, wanting so much more.

"Ple-please..." he begged, stuttering, mouth falling open around a moan as Alek lingered, flicking under the ridge with the very tip of his tongue, teasing right there.

Crouched above him, Alek let go, got off of Evan's legs and growled, "Flip over."

Breathing hard, heart racing, Evan rolled onto his stomach, folding his arms above his head.

"Pull your knees up."

The jeans were tangled around them, holding his legs together, but Evan slid them upward, until they were almost under his hips. The position put his ass in the air. Moaning, he felt two licked-wet fingers press through his hole then pull it open. When the wet muscle of Alek's tongue slid in between them, filling him up, Evan quivered and cried out. The tongue moved in and out of him, licking hard over his rim on the way out, curling to trace along his passage when it was in deep. Alek sucked his rim, pulled off.

"Who was it?" He asked in a rough voice.

"Does it matter?" Evan countered, gasping.

"Maybe."

"Luka," Evan cried, letting the sound carry, not holding anything back as Alek's fingers lodged themselves deeper, and pried him open farther. Then Evan was filled again and *licked*.

"Cherry." Alek breathed out a little laugh and scraped his teeth over Evan's right cheek. "Details. Come on."

"It was just... *fuck, please...* fingers. He fingered the flavored lube into me after my shower, watched me get hard. Wanted me to masturbate, while he..." the rest was lost in a hard moan.

"Did he tongue you?"

"Alek...."

"Did he?"

"*Don't stop....* No, okay? It was for you."

"Remind me to thank him." Three fingers entered him, pushing in to the last knuckle, twisting on the way back out. Evan felt Alek shift, then braced himself as fingers were replaced with something else, something much broader, and he was held still as it drove into him.

The positioning made him yell. Evan clawed at his head as he was entered, body throbbing around the massive cock sheathing itself in him. Alek held still there once he was fully seated, caressing the backs of Evan's thighs. Rough sounds were coming from Evan, uncontrollable.

"Gonna be dirty with me, Jailbait?" Alek whispered, tugging back, pushing in. Goosebumps spread over Evan's skin.

"Alek... wanna feel you. Please...."

Alek shifted their positions again, folding his larger body to Evan's back and easing him forward without pulling out. Once they were lying down flat on the cotton blanket laid atop cool grass, Alek's body covering his, Evan could reach back and weave his fingers through the silken strands of Alek's long hair. The rich scent of the burning candles, overlaying that of crisp night air, earth, and trees, was shot through with sex and sweat. Grasping the blanket's soft edge, his fingers tickled with damp blades of grass, Evan gasped softly as they rocked together. Folded up in Alek's strong arms, Evan found himself grinding down against the blanket counter to his thrusts. The maddening effects of Alek's talented fingers and tongue had left Evan fully hard, his blood running hot, and every inch of him oversensitive. But, he was held down, able only to try to press back then roll his hips forward, seeking relief. Alek's long, inward strokes had his cock dragging against Evan's gland only intermittently, making him quiver, beg and moan more sharply each time his body lit up with the contact. He was lost in it all, coming undone. The heat of their skin, the roughness of their breath, coming harder, overtook his senses. Each thrust drove in a little harder than the last, chasing a release which was so close, just out of reach, falling back every time Alek did.

Alek kissed the back of Evan's neck, then below his ear, and Evan writhed in pleasure, tipping his hips up just a little more, pulling Alek in just a little closer.

It all fell away, everything but them, together. Alek was heat gripping and filling Evan, moving him in small pulses as he was driven into with ever-growing force and quickness. All he knew was the scent, the touch, the need, the sighs, and low growls as they clung to one another and rode it out as slowly as they possibly could.

Wrapped in Alek and possessing him utterly, Evan found peace, coming with a tremble and gasp. Fingertips caressed him along his arm, down his side, across his hip as he clenched in flutters around Alek's thickened flesh, still rocking, taking him through it. Teeth scraped along the shell of Evan's ear, sending a pleasant shiver shooting down his spine. Alek whispered, "Love you, Ev. Always."

"Always," Evan echoed, promising from the bottom of his heart. He found Alek's hand, which folded up around his, holding on.

So much had changed, so fast, since the bar, since their worlds shifted forever. Alek had found Evan in so many ways. He'd been brave enough to try, to care, to grow, and adjust. They'd both made mistakes and gotten hurt, but all that mattered was how grateful Evan was in that moment for all of it, even the pain.

Alek's low moan and his last, desperate push, told Evan it was done, for now. But Alek stayed within him, his hands gripping Evan tightly, covering him like shelter, home, safety, and hope in the dark. It was the best place to be – held and possessed so completely.

"I'll love you forever, Alek," Evan swore, kissing their linked hands, completely surrendering to the embrace.

He knew the night wouldn't last. Eventually, they'd return home, ready to share important pieces of themselves, their hearts, and bodies with Brennan and Luka. They were Evan and Alek's cherished other halves, and they would always be needed, as they were needed in return. But Evan knew he and Alek would always drift back together, at the end of every journey, and every day, pulled by common devotion. They were the first to fall, and were still falling, tumbling into love that only grew.

"I'm glad I'm here with you, that I have this. I was so close to gone, it scares me now. I almost never knew…." Alek nudged Evan's cheek with his nose, found his lips and kissed them. "You make me so happy."

"That's all I ever wanted."

About the Author

Lynn Kelling began writing in order to tell stories that weren't afraid of the dark, didn't hold anything back and always strived to be memorable, forging lasting attachments between character and reader. Her inspiration comes from taking a closer look at behaviors and ideas lurking at the fringes of life—basically anything that people may hesitate to speak of in mixed company, but everyone wonders about anyway. Her work is driven by the taboo in order to expose the humanity within it. Lynn is an artist, designer and lover of any form of creative self-expression that comes from a place of honesty and emotion, whether it's body art or opera. She has had multiple novels published, has written over fifty works of erotic fiction of varying lengths, and always has several novels in progress.

ForbiddenFiction Works by Lynn Kelling:

Deliver Us Series:
Deliver Us
From Temptation
Forgive Us

Twin Ties Series:
My Brother's Lover
Dual Affairs
Double Heat

Manse Series:
Learning from the Master
Bound by Lies

Other Works:
Whatever the Cost
Arctic Absolution
Song of the Lonesome Cowboy
Threshold (Anthology)
Cursed Blessings (short story)

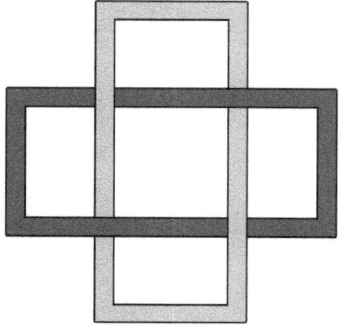

Twin Ties Series

Four men—two pairs of twins—search their lives for love, comfort, and belonging. Evan and Brennan were separated early, and struggle to find a way to be brothers. Alek and Luka, who grew up together without much parental support, provide experience and advice when the two sets of brothers begin dating each other. As the brothers find places for one another in each others' lives, they find themselves confronting—and crossing—all manner of boundaries and limits. With no one but each other to rely on, they must deal with threats from rest of the world, from curious strangers and hostile ex-lovers to judgmental families.

You can find out more at the Twin Ties page
at http://forbiddenfiction.com/collection/twin-ties.

About the Publisher

 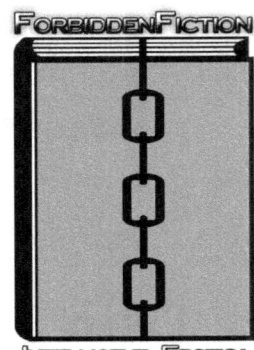

ForbiddenFiction.com is a publisher devoted to writing that breaks the boundaries of original erotic fiction. Our stories combine intense sexuality with quality writing. Stories at Forbidden Fiction.com not only arouse readers through sensations, but also engage them emotionally and mentally through storytelling as well-crafted as the sex is hot.

ForbiddenFiction.com is also designed to be a social reading environment. You'll have fun even if just reading the latest post each day, yet you will have the chance for so much more. Readers and authors can be part of ongoing discussions of specific works and individual authors as well as more general topics.

Sign up for a FREE Membership today at ForbiddenFiction.com.